The Marvel Universe is an argument with the spiritual consequences of our popular culture, an unawareness fogged by the conflation of addiction and transcendence: escapism and art, comic book and myth, Instagram and reality, narcissism and grief, Chadwick Boseman and Bobby Seale. It's also a novel by Bruce Wagner, which is to say, it's funny as hell (even when it *is* hell) and only about Hollywood per se. I don't want to speak for Wagner, but I think he'd agree that Hollywood, in addition to being a necessary subject itself, is a necessary subject as a mirror and a metaphor. *The Marvel Universe: Origin Stories* is culturally necessary. This is not a matter of opinion."

—Sam Wasson

THE MARVEL UNIVERSE

Arcade Publishing books may be purchased in bulk at special
discounts for sales promotion, corporate gifts, fund-raising, or
educational purposes. Special editions can also be created to
specifications. For details, contact the Special Sales Department,
Arcade Publishing, 307 West 36th Street, 11th Floor, New York, NY
10018 or arcade@skyhorsepublishing.com.

Arcade Publishing® is a registered trademark of Skyhorse
Publishing, Inc.®, a Delaware corporation.

Visit our website at www.arcadepub.com.
Please follow our publisher Tony Lyons on Instagram
@tonylyonsisuncertain

10 9 8 7 6 5 4 3 2 1

Library of Congress Cataloging-in-Publication Data is available on file.

Jacket design by David Ter-Avanesyan
Cover painting *The Garden of Earthly Delights* by Hieronymus
Bosch

Print ISBN: 978-1-64821-051-8
Ebook ISBN: 978-1-64821-052-5

Printed in the United States of America

THE MARVEL UNIVERSE

origin stories

A NOVEL BY

BRUCE WAGNER

Arcade Publishing • New York

CONTENTS

Also by Bruce Wagner

Force Majeure
Wild Palms (graphic novel)
I'm Losing You
I'll Let You Go
Still Holding
The Chrysanthemum Palace
Memorial
Dead Stars
The Empty Chair: Two Novellas
I Met Someone
A Guide For Murdered Children
*ROAR: American Master, The Oral
Biography of Roger Orr*
The Met Gala & Tales of Saints and Seekers

PUBLISHER'S NOTE

The poet's, the writer's, duty is to write about these things. It is his privilege to help man endure by lifting his heart, by reminding him of the courage and honor and hope and pride and compassion and pity and sacrifice which have been the glory of his past.
—William Faulkner

Bruce Wagner's novel, *The Marvel Universe: Origin Stories* was due to be published by Counterpoint Press in 2020. After turning in the manuscript, Wagner was told that the language of his new novel was "problematic"—cancelspeak for content that might be perceived as offensive. In an awkward phone call, the editor told Wagner that only a handful of pages could be published "in their current form." Implicit in the editor's remarks was that the author must tread carefully when writing about outsiders. Outsiders—the *other*—are the dominant theme of Wagner's many novels. He is well-known, critically and popularly, for the compassion and lacerating spirituality with which he imbues his characters.

With his novel suddenly orphaned, Wagner did something unusual—he released *The Marvel Universe: Origin Stories* for free on the internet. In an unprecedented move, he told readers that they could alter, translate, or shape the text into any medium, royalty free. His only caveat was that *The Marvel Universe: Origin Stories* live on in its intended, unexpurgated form on brucewagner.la.

Since then, different versions of *Marvel* have been released, including a deluxe limited edition priced at a thousand dollars.

A year later, I was introduced to Wagner through his agent, Andrew Wylie. I immediately signed a contract with him to write what became his next novel, *ROAR: American Master – The Oral Biography of Roger Orr*. *ROAR* was a deep exploration of a biracial artist who became transfeminine late in life. It's fitting to say here that Wagner told me he had written twenty or so pages of the book as a précis and shown it to one of the big East Coast houses before ending up at my door. His contact there was thrilled by *ROAR*'s premise (and the writing as well). Then came the inevitable call from the embarrassed editor-executive who'd been championing him—it seemed the powers-that-be ultimately found *ROAR* too . . ."problematic."

I believe in art and those who create it. Great art *is* problematic—as spectacularly problematic and dangerously unpredictable as our dreams, our fears, our desires. As problematic as life itself (and death). Wagner's novels are essential, scabrous, poetic reflections not only of the times in which we live but of the messy, magnificent triumphs and disastrous failures of being human. *The Marvel Universe: Origin Stories* has grown in stature since its stealth release and we are proud to publish it at Arcade, Wagner's new home.

Bruce Wagner is a major artist. When *Marvel* came my way, I did what any serious publisher would do—made it into a book that both provokes and gives solace, a living thing that reminds us of the mysteries of the world and can be passed from hand to hand, heart to heart.

Nothing problematic about it.

Tony Lyons
Publisher of Skyhorse/Arcade

for Jamie Rose

BOOK ONE

THE NEW MUTANTS

be careless what you wish for

Now must we sing and sing the best we can,
But first you must be told our character:
Convicted cowards all, by kindred slain

"Or driven from home and left to die in fear."
They sang, but had nor human tunes nor words,
Though all was done in common as before;

They had changed their throats
and had the throats
of birds.

—*WB Yeats*

SOME YEARS AGO

METAMORPHOSIS

ALI NELL

Oh, Diary! My Insta followers jumped 23,000 the morning
I posted an Avedon-inspired black-and-white selfie/mugshot
with the caption:

> Okay, lovebugs, here's the thing – I have ALS, but it doesn't
> have *me* (not just yet).

As #iamlenaheadey once so aptly put it (*where* she put it is up
for grabs!):

> FECKING otherworldly amaze-balls.

Oh, and I changed my bio to:

> **Ali (oops!) Nell**
> Actress. PK (Preacher's Kid). Body, Mind, Spirit activ-
> ist. "And Betty when you call me, you can call me #ALS."
> #pilgrimsprogress #✝natenALS #ALSnellThatEndsNell
> #ALSinWonderland #whynottakeALSofme
> **675k Followers 1,803 Following**

Of course, that wasn't *all* I wrote 'cause I was super-mindful about not doing a big blab. There'll be plenty of time for that! For my coming out, best keep it simple, stupid. My boy-gal pal Ripley wholeheartedly agreed. But I was really glad I added an amaze-balls funny-wise Mark Twain quote to the amaze-balls heartbreakingly tender-wise Rumi one, 'cause I didn't want it to be too heavy. It's already wayyyyy heavier than anyone expected (especially me). Humor's definitely what will get me through this, if I get through it at all – 10% of us ALSheimers live more than 10 years, and you know what? I'll frickin take it. Stephen Hawking powered thru, right? With wit and grace to spare.

He's so fire.

I'm ashamed to admit I secretly worried (OK maybe not so secretly) that no one would even care! That all the haters would say I was a sympathy whore. Like, Trump would tweet "Ali Nell is a washed-up, psycho-sympathy whore. *Not* a good person!" But guess what? Of the thousands of comments, not a one of em was shitty or even borderline harsh. Tho *mayyyyyybeeeeee* Ripley was doing a little redacting as he read, you know, skipping the cruel&creepy stuff, but it sure *seemed* he was just dizzily hopping from flower to flower and pollinating without pause to clean anything up. Ripley said he never saw such blanket Internet goodwill, he was ranting how even that Danish billionaire got trolled when those scummy terrorists blew his three kids up in Sri Lanka and also informed (wish he hadn't) of all the snarky (the adjective gives too much dignity) comments online after a baby got carved from its mama's belly by that freaky "womb-raider" in Chicago last year... and the baby lived! Can you imagine one day having to enlighten it as to the circumstances of its birth? Sheesh. Guess Sharon Tate lived in kinder, gentler times, huh? Anyway, Ripley kept saying I was the unicorn that broke the Internet by bringing out the best of it – take that, vile World Wide Web! Kill em with tweets 'n' kisses, I always said… how my fans and supporters were all saying how beauuuuutiful I am, how sexy (?!), how BRAVE, & group-hug emoji-crying and that many had written "we ♥ you 3000!!!!!!!" in 20 different languages – plus all kinds of lovely imaginative GIFs, a popular fave was Dany Targaryen clinging to her baby's neck and mouthing "Dracarys" as Drogon vomited fire onto King's Landing, now captioned in melty, blood-red letters spelling out **A L S**. To put it succinctly, the Universe blow-darted big-time sunshine, rainbows, and lollipops up my soon-to-be-paralyzed ass.

And oh! Emilia Clarke HERSELF DM'd me, saying take courage (in the Queen's English, not Dothraki), something, she added, she needed in abundance whilst in the throes of clandestine aneurysms she famously suffered during the first seasons of GOT.

She invited me to the San Vicente Bungalows next time she's in L.A.

Oh, Dany Girl! *The pipes, the pipes are calling…*

The most touching posts came from ALSers (ALSettes?) whose cases are far more advanced than mine – & from those who've lost loved ones to "our" godforsaken disease. I actually got a weird shiver of pride as a new member of the family… talk about being humbled, Diary. But I guess "that's what ALS does," as Geico would say – makes you buy kneepads 'cause you're pretty much living in prayer. Guess I could have taken humility lessons somewhere else, but hey, yup, I'll take it. "I'll take it" is my new mantra. Like the song says, "Why not take all of me?" Beggars and pilgrims can't be choosers and all roads lead to Humbletown AKA the City of God AKA the Celestial City (from Grandma's favorite book, *Pilgrim's Progress*, fyi).

Been crying two hours nonstop 'cause I'm so blessed...
even peeked at myself for the first time in three days – had been
avoiding the mirror 'cause I've been depressed. Get over yourself, girl. Ripley says I look 5 years younger but maybe that's
just ALS working its early magic. (Sniff.) Yuck, those puffy
ugly-cry eyes! Used and posted ROC RETINOL CORREXION
ANTI-AGING EYE CREAM TREATMENT ($18). Also, G. DAY
GINGER + ASHWAGANDHA ENERGY BODY WASH ($32)
and the amazing crystals of THE GOOP MEDICINE BAG
($85) – smoky quartz, red jasper, carnelian, citrine, unakite
jasper, sodalite, amethyst and clear quartz: for clarity, serenity,
courage and emotional strength. Just call me a rock star. (But
Betty? You can call me ALS.) I'll need all those and more...

Speaking of which, BILLIE EILISH just DM'd, she's a
serious fan of *Arrested Development*, which she said she only
watched because she was in love with Sasha! (That's who I
played on the show, Diary, *need* I remind you. Sometimes
I need to remind *myself*.) She was SO sweet & funny and
OMG as it turns out, Billie lives with her parents, like, TWO
MILES from me. What, Di, are the odds of that? She said
she's hardly home anymore but the next time she is, we'd
have a playdate. I went on YouTube and she talked about her
Tourette's and being made fun of about the condition before
anyone really knew... so she's had her brushes with adversity, and at an age way younger than me when I got tasered
by ALS. She asked if I wanted to attend a private little show
at the Troubadour and I said fuck YEAH! but need to see how
I feel "on the day." For a sec I thought oh I better go or she'll
be insulted and I'll lose a new friend but then I realized that
was just my standard low self-esteem SHITE was kicking
in (as Emilia would say. Oops, really dropping names here,

huh, Di? Will stop forthwith.) Because of course Billie would understand...

One must always come from love, *not* fear.

Been feeling a little foggy. As the Scarecrow said, "If I only had a brain" – but *apparently* a brain's the one thing ALS isn't really interested in takin', 'cause it's the last thing to go. (Sniff. Sigh.) ALS is such a typical guy that way – he's only interested in my body!

Ripley said that as my Insta grows, I'll be rolling in it. As of today I get $800 for tags/sponsored posts (Kim K gets a million+!!!!!) and am poised to collect *fifteen-hundred* when (if?) I reach a million followers. I'm all about ALS Awareness but won't turn my nose up at cash money – tho one day (not *too* soon, please, Mr. ALS?), I won't have the proper motor neurons to "turn my nose up" at all! Tee-hee!

* * *

Sunswept Easter Sunday: lolling on a pine-strung sling in the midst of an eccentric, curated garden surrounded by black tulips, black calla lilies and hundreds of *Schwarzkopf* – laughing to herself because the "black roses" made her think of a thousand anuses.

Butthole, don't fail me now.

An impish phrase bubbled up: rectal betrayal.

lol! –

In the weeks since going public, hella largesse came her way. Friends, acquaintances and strangers opened hearts and homes, sending random, waggish, zanily creative gifts. Useful ones too: the Apatows got her a beribboned Alinker walking bike, hand-delivered by their daughter Maude. Ali used to babysit Maude and her younger sister, Iris.

She had a perfectly lovely bungalow in Highland Park – bought with Marvel TV show money – but it was *so* much fun to "couch-surf," as a sober friend put it (an A.A. *thang*, apparently), to glamp in far-flungish abodes. So here she was, courtesy of Sharon Osbourne, hanging with a few friends – and her still user-friendly bowel – rocking in a hammock that looked out on a private beach. "Dearest, you *must* stay in one of our empty properties. It's in Point Dume above Pirate's Cove." She loved Sharon! "You're gonna get through this," said Sharon, like the Mother of All Boot Camp shtarker-Moms she was (and *is*), "and we're gonna get through it *with* you." Can someone please send that woman an Iron Throne? Scratch that, she's prolly already got three. They knew each other from *The Talk,* when Ali was doing press for *Stan Lee's Te Deum* and *Arrested Development.* Still hadn't met Ozzie though. Their son Jack was diagnosed with MS a few years back, so Ali's surprise Instannouncement touched a nerve. Ali's pride usually sabotaged offerings of love and generosity; now, everything that happened just seemed part of what she called "my whytewitch wedding shower." Ali had just invited tens of thousands of followers to watch her exchange vows with the Dark Prince ALS, vows that slowly-quickly would take everything away, everything she had, everything she deserved, everything she dreamed of.

But – as Grammie used to say – it was *all* a dream. And what, she asked herself, could be more gorgeous, adventurous and true?

Barely into ALS courtship, she hadn't changed much physically. Her famous eyes were still green, flecked with silver and onyx like the *Vogue*-featured terrazzo of a long-dead couturier's Ischian bolt-hole. Her smile was puckish, still half-fuck you/half-welcoming – an Aubrey Plaza-Audrey Hepburn meld. Atop the head was a torch of burnt sienna. The flatchested, sinuously boyish body (Ripley said, "Where were you when Jeffrey Epstein needed you?") was still aroused by human touch. For a few months after the diagnosis, she orgied with famous and unfamous exes, coming harder than she ever had in her youngish life. Fooled around with drunk bffs too, and groupie gals, and a FedEx driver (ground), and had crazy Raya hookups… *OMG, Spike Jonze, my obsession! God Bless you, Raya!* It became a bit of an underground thing for a moment to fuck Ali Nell – post-ALS, post-Insta-post-Ali Nell – a thing for *her* too, because she wanted rude adolescent company in the crash car as it rocketed toward God's demolition derby speedway. There was mad religion to it and a reckless beauty that stabilized; all that stink-grind got her out of her head. She was determined to cuckold her heavenly matchmaker, if only for a while. *I can do a little demolition myself, so fuck y'all.* She could blow good and bad motor neurons to Kingdom Cum with the best of them. *Tha's right.* For a little while, like a holy whore – Time's Up! *for real*, ha! – she ritualistically washed and tenderized her body in anticipation of rolling off the ghat into the ancient, smoky, corpse-strewn River Gehrig. Her lovers seemed wilder too. The girls – paleskinned tattooed ladybugs – sure cried more than usual during the act, and the boys-to-men, whose vanilla sex stylings she was familiar with got guiltily pervy, inventive, athletically incandescent, their blown-out comfort zones rendering them prodigies of flesh. Her last-legs *ch'i* was contagious: all the scared sacred mortality clits, cocks, and clocks of her hookups were ticking. Sleeping with Ali was *hot* and hotly anecdotal, electric, electrically shaming, criminally *interesting*: half-mercy fuck, half-rape, half-horned-out, hallowed chore and consecrated exploitative sisterfuck… half-*historic*.

Something they could tell the grandkids one day.

She got em all high on the FireFly vapes she got for free, having bartered product for IG endorsements.

There, in the soft wind, rocking in the hammock, Ali suddenly got the stomach-jitters of a child before its first cruise on the open sea. She shut her eyes. As her meditation guru suggested, she became a lava lamp, its gelatinous gobs moving in slothlike syncopation to the waves. The contrapuntal melody of ocean – the Point Dume ocean, rich people's ocean, ocean of the neurological normies, whose lungs, limbs and rectums remained fiercely loyal to commands – the abandoning ocean that ebbed and flowed not for her but the lucky ones who were cordially scheduled to end in old age – *that* ocean's emerald, algaeic waters rose and fell with magnificent insipidity, a watered-down insult opera, fifty yards out.

Two torturous years of misdiagnoses – Guillain-Barré, then Lyme, then sciatica – finally coalesced to a death sentence. Her career had faltered years before and the absurdist, fatal revelation scrambled her brain. At night, she had dreams of winning, she dreamed she'd won, that something good and amazing had happened. But then she got locked in her dented Prius and couldn't get out because the door handles were gone (that *Forensic Files* she saw about an abductor removing the inside door handles from the van he used, to steal women)… and worst of all, she was late for a party at her old friend Tom Ford's. She started digging around in the rat's nest of backseat junk food litter looking for the handles. During a sweaty noon-time nap, Gavin Newsom called to say she'd been selected to be the First Woman on Mars, and that her ALS "is a plus, because we need someone who won't move in the capsule" –

What if all along she'd been poised for mythic glory?

What if the inconsequential victories and humiliations of a vain, clownish, go-nowhere showbiz career were in fact part of a superlunary mandala?

Meghan had moved from *Suits* to Sussex; why wouldn't the exodus of Ali Nell entail a royal entourage as well?

Yes: like Meghan holding a scepter, or Dany Targaryen clutching the long, scaly neck of her beloved, Ali Nell would gallop to the Celestial City in a cavalcade of ruined neurons and rogue microbes, numinous carriage wheels sparking, her ineffably useless body attended by followers and alit by a nimbus of Infinite Love.

JOAN GAMMA

"The Fat Joan" (she sometimes called herself that, in playful homage to The Fat Jew) added another supergrrrl to her Insta carousel: @alinell.

But her yearlong IG troika fixation still burned bright: Billie, Millie and Greta (Billie Eilish, Millie Bobby Brown and Greta Thunberg), her O.G. spirit animal road dogs. Watching those babyfat bodies (Greta's being the least babyish) slowwww-wwwly witch into womanhood gave her erotic transport. Billie legendarily shielded herself in crazy *LV*/Gucci tents, blaming her parents for "this body and these chubby fingers" but Millie was starting to dig playing dress-up, morphing from nerdy Comic-Con queen to 35-year-old haute hooker. And Greta…

well, Greta looked middle-aged. Girl needed a *makeover.*
Though she was by far the butchiest, with an adorable troll-
scowl that made her the hottest of Joan's three virtual concu-
bines. She related most to the Swede (whom she sometimes
called Thin Joan, as in *of Arc*) because of Greta's erstwhile
depression, anorexia and *selective mutism.* How hot was *that?*

Oh, Greta!

One day the pigtailed warrioress would be hers...

The only *other* enchantress (until Ali) Joan deemed worthy to follow was Anya Taylor-Joy – who was a little older,
like Ali – *not* because of those shitty, try-hardy M. Night
Shyamalan movies, no, but out of Joan's obsessive love of
Anya's debut in *The Witch.* That ending! She'd masturbated to
it a thousand times. In the film's last few minutes, Anya's frosh
class coven levitated past dark treetops in ecstatic slo-mo, a
menstrual-ruptured fangirl rapture of ascent to hellish heavens that gave Joan hormonal seizures of FOMO and satanic
Sapphic envy. *The Witch* was released in the same week of the
same year Joan's parents were killed; her shrink would've had
a field day with *that.* Plus, the *small* detail of Anya marrying
the Devil, their union sanctified by the murder of her mom
and dad (!). But Joan never talked to the therapist about her
Anya crush or anything related. She had to keep *something* to
herself... and she wasn't in the mood for her shrink to insinu-
ate she was a pedo.

Anyway, she'd already shared so much.

Just *now,* Joan "The Fat Joan" Gamma was all about Ali
Nell, who happened to be even older than Anya. The 25-year-
old was famous for three things: a brilliantly mordant guest
arc as Sasha Meriwether on *Arrested Development* (a role that
Joan, like Billie E., had *so* seriously identified with back in

the day); playing a sorceress in the short-lived Marvel show
Te Deum; print ads for ASOS, Breitling watches, and more
lately, The Row. Ali didn't seem to be acting much anymore
but Joan occasionally saw things on social media, like when
the paparazzi snapped the star and her wienerdog having coffee in Highland Park or when Ali posted decade-old #tbt pics
of hangs with big-and smallscreen costars, now legends she
once outshone.

Ali Nell had classical sass and soft, timeless beauty, with
that combo of black humor and heart-on-sleeve that always
got Joan's wet.

But A the fuck LS!

How, how, how?

Whatever – it flipped a miracle switch and Joan stopped
being hungry.

Background:

In 2015, right after her family was slaughtered in the house
in Holmby Hills, Joan started gaining. She really stepped up
her game in the last two years – when she turned 16 – inhaling 8,000 calories a day and hardly moving from her bed. She
remembered the random day she locked in on the TV show
My 600-lb. Life, astonished by the longing it aroused. She fell
in love with the marooned draperies of flesh and the angsty,
lachrymose, babyfaced divas as they perched – daintily, coyly,
sadly, codependently, apologetically – upon the smear-stained,
sheetless lily pads of mattresses thrown haphazardly into living rooms, bedrooms, U-Haul vans. Mattresses were the indis-
pensable accoutrement of the colossal-sized life. Nearly 400
pounds herself now, Joan was transfixed by the slim, careful enablers, usually family members – their own children! –
as they administered sponge baths, patiently exploring the

blurry, viewer-censored folds guarding undiscovered decubiti and skin-stamped filth.

One boy (always boys and girls to Joan, no matter their age) was almost half a ton. His legs, as if drawn from an illustrated fairy tale book, had grown fungus-lichen; he looked like a pasty, demolished centaur and was breathtakingly beautiful to her.

She religiously aspired to such transformations. Joan hadn't weighed herself in over a year, not since her birthday in December (she and Billie Eilish both turned eighteen on the 18th), when one-point-seven billion of the Gamma Family Trust irrevocably became hers. Now she *felt* the threshold of 500 pounds coming, ¼ *ton*, like a rolling orgasm: floating above a high hill on her magick carpet mattress, catching labored breath, she finally caught sight of the distant, welcoming kitchen lights and chimney smoke of home.

She knew she would arrive by summer.

Yet, what were the origins of this morphology?

Too easy to say she was recreating the immobility forced upon her by the homicidal event… that was the therapist's line. She escaped being murdered by hiding beneath a more prosaic, still magic mattress, on the day their home was invaded by a deranged former "associate" of her parents. She heard them being killed – first her mother Vi then her father Raphie then her older brother Tabula – and stayed frozen, paralyzed by sounds (and smells) of carnage, followed by the unearthly morbid silence. The staff had been given four days off and it was *five* before the police found her. At 14, when the trial began, during long stretches of psychotherapy and estate executor drama, she began festishizing confinement and close spaces, fantasies drifting and solidifying into bondage. Her lodestar was a documentary she stumbled on about the hitch-hiker Colleen Stan, kidnapped by a married couple. Colleen was kept beneath their waterbed in a lightless, soundless box – for years. Years! She used a bedpan, like all the big captive babies on *My 600-lb. Life*. How could anyone survive such a thing without going mad? Where did that kind of mental fortitude come from? Such was the Joan-koan she turned over in her head, wavering between the certainty of knowing she'd have lost her mind beneath the waterbed and the certainty she would have kept it – circling the conundrum like an animal excited by the smell of its own shitblood. Her radical eroticism was inflamed by news events, like the parent-killing abduction of Jayme Closs. (The under-the-bed dungeoning of *that* one totally reignited her bewitched B&D bewilderment.) Even reading about a socialite stuck in an Upper East Side elevator set her off. Any sort of luckless, terminal entrapment would do.

At 16, a wealthy friend of Joan's parents told her about a cult that branded women like animals and she got so excited by the idea, she got wet as she listened. The shrink said the bondage kink was born of trauma but Joan wondered if it wasn't in the DNA – after all, weren't Mom and Dad close with the outlier Cyan Banister, genderqueer angel investor of Uber, PayPal, Postmates, et alia? There was so much she didn't know (nor ever would) about her parents.

Apart from whatever else, Joan inherited their smarts. When Vi's estranged father Bud Wiggins filed a lawsuit contesting his absence from the will, Joan made sure that regardless of how fat or wild or crazy-seeming she got, no shadow of a lunatic relative or rogue executor could ever darken her day. She paid the most expensively aggressive legal minds in the land to forge an airtight guarantee that she could never be vulnerable to a fickle conservatorship.

No one's ever gonna Britney me.

In the wake of those victorious days, she dreamt of becoming an anonymous, paid pinup on supersizedbombshell.com. She wanted to be cared for, wanted to date men who craved what she was and where she was heading. She sought out the community of gainers and encouragers, the community of feeders, fooders and feedees. She went to their musty houses and bonded with the ones who sought utter immobility. She followed the "fat wars" – two ladies vying to be the heaviest on Earth – with the same addictive vigor of a *Bachelorette* fan.

> Susanne Eman currently weighs in at a staggering 728 pounds and is hoping to beat the current record for Heaviest Woman Ever by reaching 1200 pounds by the time she reaches 41.

The competitor, Donna Simpson, clapped back online:

> Susanne says she's the world's fattest mom but doesn't understand that Guinness gave me the record because I was 532 pounds when I gave birth.
>
> Susanne wasn't that large when she gave birth.

The boyfriend said, "Fatness is a journey. We know 1000 lbs. is not going to happen tomorrow but it's a journey." It was a privilege, he said, to wash her each day.

That's what Joan wanted: to be washed like the feet of a master, to expand until rooms no longer contained her, and floors were so weakened she dropped down to the gates of

Heaven-Hell itself – the opposite of Anya's levitating journey but an ecstatic, wicked journey nonetheless, and one all her own.

When the money came, she earmarked $25 million for a still-projectless production company called Fat City Filmworx. Her biggest splurge was the acquisition of a Lucian Freud "Fat Sue" painting for sixty-five million; but when Ali Nell and her unfathomable, magnificent disaster flipped Joan's switch, *fat* was *out*: she wanted to trade it in for an attenuated, ramrod Giacometti or tiny Degas dancer or shimmering mystical El Greco anorexic. *A the fuck LS!* Now *that* was confinement! Eerie, elegant and inevitable, *that* was ascension, to take up residence for eternity under the waterbed of the cosmos! Like beggar and pilgrim, it forced you to your knees. The little *Arrested Development* actress who gave Joan succor in a darkly comic role that hued so eerily close to the heiress's fractured, rarefied life, a role that echoed Joan's prayed-for scenarios of catastrophe (though she never could she have imagined the nightmare in Holmby Hills that was to come), *that* girl, Ali Nell, became her guru-mother and scapegoat saint *in a seismic instant.*

And Joan Gamma became a devotee in the only way that counted: she would starve herself, sans gastric sleeve, till only the after-banquet tablecloths of skin were left.

BUD WIGGINS

Dear Manny,

"*Hello, it's me*" –

– said Lionel Richie, to anyone who'd still listen...

All right now put your dentures back in and say how-die to your ol friend and erstwhile running (stumbling?) partner, the enfant terrible manqué/one-hit wunderkind formerly known as (drum roll) the critically-esteemed lit'ry man Buddy Wiggins! He of the low-sales/critically-praised blast-from-the-past! He of early bloom and early frost!

I'm hoping this lands in your lap. (I give it a 30-70 shot.) Grailroad shuttered, I know, I know – the little imprint that could was good to you (and me too) – and I'm hoping Random Louse forwards this to wherever the hellfuck you may be. Oh, and please do not be dead, pal. I forbid it…

So: if this sad little arrow finds its mark, I pray it finds my favorite (my only!) editor – and his Clarice – in fine fettle. Dear Clarice! She was always exorbitantly, inordinately kind to me, long after your patience expired. Give her my love and heart, Manny. I mean it.

I don't have access to a computer (they took my library card away, too) so forgive the shockingly anachronistic method of correspondence. Hence my lack of googlesucking to Sherlock your last known whereabouts, mugshots, net worth, bla bla. I know, I know, such a bore, but my laptop kept getting spilled on, puked on/spermed (when it wasn't being pawned.) Just keepin it real, old friend.

But enough about you!

Manny, I have a serious ASK (that's right. I'm still an askhole).

10 months ago, I made a deal to write a memoir. I know, I know – breaking news! Bud Wiggins to write second book after 40-year hiatus! Stop the small independent presses! It's about the death of my daughter Vi and her family (of course it is. So lay offa me), a story I'm sure you and most of Amerika

already overdosed on, tho maybe it's time for a revisit... my pub thinks so anyway. (Yes I have a publisher, shocking I know, & more on that in a moment.) There's actually a few TV/film projects in the works on said topic, one of em pursued by my old school chum and current bestie Garry Gabe Vicker (he might actually hire me to consult), otherwise known as Gigi (my middle school nickname for him), the reluctant King of 70s three-camera sitcoms, who, in a supreme act of reinvention, mutated into the current big macher-showrunner behind Netflix's dramumentary "Golden State" (soon-to-be-streaming-near-you) about the eponymous killer ... so's I got three COUNT EM book offers right after the murders happened and said NO to em all. Wanted to stay away from any kind of notoriety or bad faith/ill gain-ish things till it all worked out (or not!) in the courts. I honestly thought I'd legit be taken care of by my daughter's estate, but NOOOOOOO as Steve Martin once said. Vi and I had our differences and difficulties but I was led to believe that the executor, along with the input of my granddaughter Joan (the sole heir), was empowered to amend the will with a codicil allowing yours truly a small stipend, and that they were conducive. From the pecuniary goodness of their hearts, blah... As you may already be well aware, through the good orifices of a thousand high- and low-brow magazines, newspapers and websites, I decided to fight the good fight for what I felt I deserved, which, <u>BELIEVE</u> me, was less than a sliver, more like a <u>hair's-breadth</u> of the money pile, ahem, that was shall we say "available." (Naturally it was never reported that I pledged a percentage of whatever that gift might have been to the very reputable Victims of Violence org.) While things were being resolved, I chose to remain completely respectful, turning down a rain of $$$ from tabloids and fancypant media outlets both. Needless to say, my careful considerations came to naught. I should add that throughout the whole sordid affair, the only one my heart cried out to was and still <u>is</u> my granddaughter Joan, with whom I was barred contact, under threat of ye old restraining order. Alas, I never knew her well, but was hoping to fill the vacuum of family left by the horrible tragedy. Her mind was very sadly and effectively poisoned against me, first by her mother then by executor/estate attorneys. I'm about to reach out to Joanie to inform her of the book deal – Katy, bar the door! – which I believe is the morally correct move. I stress here that my intentions regarding that project are, as ever, honorable and pure, and <u>très litteraire et pas une exposé</u>.

The book is with a house called PSP – Press Send Press (do you know them? ever heard?). They're in the "classy exploitational" niche and just garnered some rather good critical attention from NYRB for a quasi-poetic novella/essay written by an almost-victim of Ted Bundy (it aktually ain't half-bad)... they seem to specialize in "reimaginings" – you know, observations/monologues from the <u>victims'</u> POV. Anyhoo, my deal was for <u>10 TIMES LESS</u> what I'd originally been offered.

Old novelists and beggars can't be choosers...

So here's my ask, old friend: are you still in the editing game? Cause I sure could use Manny Rosen's legendary gimlet eye on the pages scrawled so far. PSP wants the book like friggin YESTERDAY but you know I don't work like that, always was a scofflaw with deadlines, plus I don't trust em (PSP) for shit, PLUS they're hitting the <u>reimagine</u> thing too hard, wanting me to write it from my grandkid's point of view – which I'm not even sure I can do LEGALLY, their lawyers are supposedly looking into it (I've had enough

courtrooms to last me sixteen more lifetimes) – they're gunning for a stream-of-consciousness dramatization as Joanie
hides under her bed as an "ear-witness," I fucking <u>HATE</u>
that idea but agreed cause I was desperate for the advance.
(Which I've already blown. sigh). Initially, I said, "Oh, you
mean like 'Executioner's Song'?" and <u>of</u> <u>COURSE</u> no one
knew what the eff I was talking about. So's – ! Any help
that you, O genius editor of yore, can provide this here hack
would be manna and Manny from Heaven. C'mon now – for
old times? (Just reminded myself of *The Godfather.* When
Tessio says, "Can you get me off the hook, Tom? For old
times' sake?") I promise you shall be richly rewarded in the
afterlife, Mister Manfred Mann, or at least in the hot hot
afterparty, if the Devil still budgets for that. Times are tuff.

As a 10-fingered exercise, I've been warming up with
memories of Mom (Dolly) and Dad, growing up in Beverly
Hills and all that jazz… avoiding/dancing around the murders
and dreaded <u>imaginodramatization</u> thus far – but sorely need
some of your BRILLIANT FUCKING FEEDBACK.

Anyhowzer...

DO write back pretty please to the P.O. Box provided
(mail keeps getting broken into where I live) and say "I do."
And <u>SOON</u>, brotherman, if you're so inclined, cause I ain't
gettin any younger keemo-sahbee. In the meanwhile, will try
to get you a phone number to call as well –

this Bud's for you,
xxxxx

* * *

He always depended on the kindness of rich, estranged boy-hood friends.

At least, one of them.

Garry Gabe Vicker was his alter ego and fellow Beverly Hills High alumnus. The thing that cemented their bond was running away together and taking a Greyhound to Palm Springs when they were 12. Growing older, they shared a first-fuck girlfriend; watched a cleft-chinned surfer buddy get pulverized by a VW van as the three dashed across PCH to body-surf; were arrested for public drunkenness and whatnot. In the years during which they lost touch, "Gigi" managed to get himself hired by Norman Lear, writing sitcoms. He graduated to directing them and created hit shows of his own. By the time he was in his mid-fifties, he practically had his own wing at the Museum of Television & Radio.

Bud took the Via Rodeo less traveled. He dropped out of high school and drove limousines at the Beverly Hills Hotel, acquiring an addiction to opiates and speed. Still, Garry envied his friend – in the early days – because in his late-ish twenties, Bud managed to write a dark Hollywood novel called *Wild Psalms* that critics announced was Important in the way television could never be. It was notable that the author avoided the "sophomore curse" by never writing a second book.

The men rekindled their friendship and saw a lot of each other in their 30s and 40s. Garry bought dinners at Musso's and Spago's, the Grill and the Palm, never asking his guest how he managed to survive. (Better for both to avoid the topic.) He had a hunch that Bud was being supported by his mother Dolly, living on and off at her condo.

When they were fiftysomething, Bud did his usual thing: he vanished. Then, five years ago, at 60, he reached out. The murder of his daughter, son-in-law and grandson sent shock-waves through L.A. (Dolly died before all that) and he asked for Garry's help. Bud's delusion was he'd be sliced off a wafer-thin piece of the estate, the way he used to ask for roast beef at the deli. He came to believe that through a creative, genera-tion-jumping sense of empathy and forgiveness, the only sur-vivor – his granddaughter Joan – would be a deus ex machina, a generous avatar of mercy. At the very least, he cynically hoped she might have the exasperated impulse to rid herself of the "Bad Grandpa" who'd become a pesky ghost and litigious nuisance – and find the backbone to order counsel to just *pay the old piece of shit off*. But that was the voice of his daughter Vi; Joan would never have spoken so harshly. Joan didn't have the history or meanness in her to hate him like that – *no one* could have hated him the way Vi did, even from the grave.

Was it asking too much?

Was it really so unlikely that his grandchild, bored by the inherited bloodfeud bile and bullshit, might dare question its origin?

Was it so ludicrous to believe it was possible for Joan to find it in her heart to make a real Christmas for ol' exiled, long-suffering Grandpa Bud? They were family, they were survivors (in their fashion), they were artists and half-mad – couldn't Joan draw solace from that? She must have read her grandfather's threadbare Wikipedia entry, out of curiosity. Would it mean nothing to her that he was a once-celebrated writer?

If Joan *did* come around, if she flew in the face of advisors and decided to close the final chapter with a lump sum pay-ment, what would such backhanded largesse look like? He'd thought about that a *lot*. The inheritance was vast enough to be obscene; the numbers were incomprehensible. Bud was certain she'd be counseled against providing him an extralegal windfall because the will was ironclad and ruthlessly clear about his exclusion. It would be argued as well that he never spent much time with his granddaughter, and never even tried (a lie). Their last encounter was when Bud crashed the funeral in Mill Valley. Joan had the sense – and grace – to have security usher him past the media gauntlet to a secret entrance. It was likely she'd been told to do so in order to avoid a scene... but still. She gave him a nervous, smelly hug at ceremony's end before they hustled him away.

Whenever Bud got high, he "reimagined" that hug, fantasizing it as the magical moment a waxy seal was melted onto the envelope containing the ten-figure settlement to come.

After the burial, it took nearly five years to sort things out. A few months before the triple murder, Vi and Raphie signed Warren Buffett's The Giving Pledge, joining fellow billionaires in writing a lucid, elegantly heartfelt letter to the world in which they proclaimed the intent to give away their entire fortune by the time of their deaths. The pledge wasn't legally binding, of course, but a balance between the Gamma's charitable wishes and the lifetime needs of the troubled, then 13-year-old sole survivor needed to be struck with Solomonic consideration.

Bud had been estranged from his daughter Vi for over thirty years and he wasn't even sure why. Because he drunkenly tried to kiss her on the mouth on her Sweet Sixteen? Because when she was 20, he slept with her best friend? Because when she was 11, she found one of his speed pills in the carpet and had to be taken to the ER?

Media attention naturally focused on Joan but because she was underage they were forced to stay at arm's length. There were rumors that the Holmby Horror had left the heiress permanently scarred and unhinged. When she turned 17, a blurry telephoto image of Joan's giant, half-nude body being mechanically swiveled into the back of a custom van sent waves of derision and compassion through the Internet. Some closure came when police finally cornered the killer at a Holiday Inn Express in Seattle. He turned out to be an employee of a Gamma start-up who claimed the couple cheated him out of a $100 million. (Bud could relate.) They threw a stun grenade into his room; he'd already blown his head off.

The first thing Garry Gabe said when Bud called was, *If there's the slightest chance you'll be compensated, you sure as hell need to try.* The Koreatown pharmacist who sold Bud Adderall and oxy shared the same opinion. The lawyer Gigi recommended opened a friendly dialogue with the estate on Bud's behalf. Initially, Team Gamma was persnickety, but began to play ball. "It is in your client's best interest not speak to the press." Bud was thrilled that his best interests were being considered at all! The implication being that the executor might be of a mind to consider a settlement... On the strenuous advice of his attorney, he respectfully laid low. He further ingratiated himself by punctiliously informing – through his attorney, of course – of every interview he turned down: *48 Hours*, *Sixty Minutes*, the BBC; the *New York Times,* WSJ, the *Washington Post*, *Vanity Fair*; sundry true crime reenactment shows; books on the affair being written by journalists high and low. The more he cozied up to Team Gamma and followed orders, the more convinced he became he'd be rewarded for his valor. Still, Bud never mentioned the requests to write a memoir. The offers ranged from a quarter- to half-million dollars – chump change, but still tantalizing. At least now he had a Plan B, should all else fail. He was starting to get a hard-on for writing prose again.

In his twenties, Bud made his debut (and finale, as it turned out) with a novel that deployed a dirty, mordant scalpel in its autopsy of what was still called Tinseltown. The *succès d'estime* didn't pay the bills and he worked as a chauffeur to support himself while writing. Drugs and creative paralysis blacked out the years; even Scott Fitzgerald, patron saint of showbiz losers, would have looked askance. Through his fifties, he lived off Dolly's meager inheritance, and eternally futzed with a memoir about growing up poor in Beverly Hills. At 65, the money long gone, Bud gigged for Lyft and Uber. When he ran short of making his monthly nut, Garry Gabe advanced him on his $940 social security check. The showrunner offered a bulk sum "to get you on your feet" but the novelist was too proud.

He hid his drug addiction from Garry – and his scratcher habit too.

A year ago, he started buying the colorful $5 tickets at 7-Eleven but, like all of his habits, he soon lost control. Scratcher money was less than what you could win in the numbers lottery but your chances were far better and the results immediate. You could scratch a $200,000 win on a five-dollar ticket, $750,000 on a ten, five million on a twenty, and ten million on a thirty. The most he ever won was $500 but at least a half-dozen times he collected $100 on five- and ten-dollar tickets. He'd also won $200, $250 and $400. Bud was convinced all he needed was a nice first score to get a leg-up. You had to pay federal taxes on scratcher jackpots over $599 but didn't have to pay state. If he could just win a $100,000 ticket,

he knew bigger wins were soon to follow; that's how the algorithm of chance worked – the faucet was hard to turn but once
you did, the water just flowed. He never considered himself to
be a gambling addict because the way he looked at it, it was a
veritable certainty he would one day win.

And win big.

It occurred to him that any reparations from Team
Gamma, whether wholeheartedly generous or reluctantly pragmatic, would most likely be in the ballpark of a big scratcher
win. Anything in the "two comma" category, for example
$10,000,000, would of course be optimal. Five million was
more than agreeable; a million or two, though disappointing,
would definitely be in the "leg-up" category. After the settlement
was signed, sealed and delivered, the icing on the cake was that
he'd now be free to line his pockets with memoir money – a
few hundred thousand, if Bud's instincts were correct – unless
an agreement with the estate forbade him. When the yuletide
ruling finally came down without his name mentioned, Bud's
attorney refused to appeal. Adding insult to injury, the court
warned that if he ever tried to contact Joan Everhart Gamma
again (*My granddaughter! The gall! The arrogance! The injustice!*),
he would be slapped with a restraining order. Bud fell into a
steep depression that he never quite climbed out of.

It was time for Plan B.

When he approached the publisher he had given the cold
"memoir" shoulder to, they all declined. Too much time had
passed, they said, and so many books had already been written or were *being* written about the case. He wound up signing
with a small house, Press Send Press. In six weeks, he spent
the $25,000 advance on drugs and scratchers.

* * *

Wildman Bud,

I'm in shock (a nice shock) – mostly, because your letter found me in Maine, where it was forwarded. The oddest thing is that I wasn't supposed to be here – in Maine – so no one knew where I was, not even my son, let alone the incompetent, traitorous fuckers at Random Acts of Unkindness House. That's one for <u>Believe It or Not</u>. And yes, miracles do happen, my telepathic old friend. The universe always (sort of) looked out for us, no?

I need to make some amends that are a long time coming. I feel terrible on a few counts. Firstly, of <u>course</u> I followed the trial and was in shock over the death of Vi and her husband – and your grandson. As Wittgenstein said, "Whereof one cannot speak…" That poor little boy… and of course little girl Joan. I know that you and Vi weren't close (which may be an understatement) but I've spent more nights and mornings feeling like a jackass for never having reached out. I can't defend myself, save to tell you that I was triggered –my own abandonment and grieving issues, which I'm learning about late in life through therapy. Too late in life, alas…

Secondly, I always felt that I failed you on the career-side, Bud. "Wild Psalms" was a fucking hard act to follow – its sheer hard-crystal brilliance – and I was honored to be the doula during its difficult birth. Books like that seem to come along once in a lifetime, my friend. But I think I was a bit too laissez-faire – I could have been a lot more proactive in pulling that second book out of you. Could have been tougher on you, no doubt, more of an <u>editor</u>, less an enabling friend. It's no excuse but you know I had that cancer scare around that time and it did a number on my head and body. And Clarice & I were going through a rough patch too.

I sent Clarice that hug you wanted to give her, and she no doubt received it – but I lost her last summer to lymphoma. It still doesn't seem real... aren't we tragic, funny creatures, Wildman? The Maine house has been on the market – bought a century ago with the raise I got as a reward for publishing you! – and the reason I'm here is to give it a look-see because a neighbor wrote to say he thought I had a squatter. (Turned out to be a bear. Ah, rural life.) I've been retired for 10 years now so that "gimlet" eye's more than myopic, it's blind. But of <u>course</u>, Wildman, DO send anything you wish, I'd be thrilled. (& make me feel useful for a change.) We made magic once – <u>you</u> made magic – and I'd love nothing more than to watch you do it again. Publishing, and the world (as you know) has changed since then, certainly not for the better. Can't seem to get excited about any of the flavor-of-the-month novels that old rag NYTRB is in a hoopla about.

I suppose that just makes me out of touch, old, or both.

Guess they're the same.

All my love,

Manny

PS. Am damn glad you sent a long-handed letter. I'm more tired of fucking emails than you could know (not that my inbox is exactly full). But DO send a phone number. Hey, buy yourself a burner if you have to, like the ones I see on all those cop shows I'm bingeing.

PSS "Oh, and please do not be dead." I promise not to be, friend, for a while – if you promise same.

A L I

[a photo of her on the beach at dusk]

14, 383 likes

alinell This. This life. I know. We are all diamonds. This wild and tender world. I know. I think it gets better. This life. Smile when you may not feel like it. Set small goals. The grin may stick. This girl: broken and unbreakable. I'm reading Grammie's favorite book 'The Pilgrim's Progress' (with its beautiful subtitle 'From This World To That Which Is To Come'). John Bunyan's a ROCKSTAR. (ask Louisa May Alcott.) If I tell you we're on our way to the Celestial City, all you're expected to say is, 'I know, right?' And BLESS @courteneycoxofficial and @renezellweger for fotobombing me with love. They've been AMAZEBALLS soldiers in Nanci Ryder's fight against ALS. (Nan is our very own homegrown Dany Targaryen) and bless @katyperry, another PK (Preacher's Kid!), who took the time to bring me to the amazing Kanye West's Sunday Service, I'm still crying. So blessed. And blessed to be in conversation with the parents of the amazing Jaci Hermstad whose identical twin was taken at age 16 by ALS on Valentine's Day 2011 and now has a rare form of the disease called FUS p525L mutation. 'Cowgirl Jaci' is 25 and has been in NYC for treatment with an experimental drug called ASO. It's crazy expensive and that needs to CHANGE, NOW! I am learning *so* MUCH about Tregs (T-regulatory cells) and leukapheresis… meanwhile, making friends with the enemy, learning to love the Dark Prince ALS. "My hope is that this research changes ALS from a death sentence to a life sentence." (DR. Stanley H. Appel) HELL TO THE HELL TO THE YEAH!!!!!
ALSismyteacher #loveisALSyouneed #mohammedALI vs #mohammedALS = serious ROPE-A-DOPE for ALS!

View all 771 comments

bellahadid ✦✦✦✦✦✦ love you the most bravegirl

> **alinell** @bellahadid love you too my love you are beautiful outside and within

chrissyteigen bebe you killin it every day in every way. see me soon?

> **alinell** @chrissyteigen mi wheelchair ramp es su wheelchair ramp, chiquita

courteneycoxofficial so so blessed to know you. this girl. this woman. this warrior. what a gift you are and what joy and courage you bring to the world #mynewsoulsista #alswarrior #teamnanci #teamali #teambraveheart

> **alinell** @courteneycoxofficial You. You. You! I am the one who is blessed.

entertainmenttonight you are a shining example of courage and we salute you @alinell!

bodeesahtva we share the same birthday, would love to interview you for my podcast on rights for the differently abled , when you … more

saviour9617 pilgrim's progress lives like a beggar in the shadow cast by the great thomas a kempis, author of ""the immitation of the Christ," if you … more

candacecupcake ALS took my daddy on Father's Day. PLEASE LOOK INTO NurOwn. Made by Jews, it has the potential to be the first ALS therapy to improve patient functioning as a regenerative medicine. Like CAR-T therapies, it uses your own cells to excrete and promote neuronal survivability. It still needs to pass the federal RIGHT-TO-TRY legislation. Phase II trials showed NurOwn slowed progression of the disease following multiple dosings. Phase III trial is … more

* * *

She cried nonstop at Kim and Kanye's. It was so tribal, so inclusive, she felt like a gooey, boho-human again. It was a coming out, as well; Ali hadn't been around so many people since the ALS/Insta post that rocked the world. Or small showbiz parts of it anyway.

A chauffeured Mercedes van picked her up at the cottage in Highland Park. (Katy Perry sat alone in the back, the bestest surprise.) Ali could still walk but tired easily and it was more practical, on longish outings, to use a wheelchair. She couldn't believe the singer had reached out. Ali had never been a huge fan of her music but always loved Katy's look: those perfect, outsized features – an airbrushed, WW2 pinup kind of beauty. In her head, she always pictured Katy as her Grammie's favorite, Rosie the Riveter, but when she saw her in costume on a Disney-themed *American Idol*, she forever became Snow White. And she loved when Katy told a churchy contestant "I'm a PK too" – Preacher's Kid – the same as Alice Cooper and Denzel and so many others Ali hadn't known about. She knew there'd been bad blood between Katy and her evangelical parents and was so happy to see the air had cleared when Mom and Dad showed up in the *Idol* audience. Things might not be perfect between them but at least they seemed to have reached a place of loving grace and acceptance.

Ripley, her right arm and confidante, was away on a shoot but arranged for a hair and makeup gal to come by early Sunday morning. Ali said she could do her own face but Ripley strenuously wouldn't allow. "This is your *debutante moment*, girl, and you best take it *seriously*. You're going to be the belle of the ball – and you better look the part!" She was so glad because the woman he sent was an angel, covering up her new outbreaks – weird, tiny carapaces that sprung up overnight (she hadn't yet sent the images to her doctors), itchy and hard-patched and tortoiseshell shiny. Ali was so nervous about her excursion to Calabasas that she hadn't slept. Her plan was to tell Katy *everything* – they'd been emailing but when the singer picked her up, it was such a genuine surprise – all the shit about Ali's dad having an affair with a married (male) parishioner in Tulsa, how the scandal blew a hole in their world, how things got so ugly that at the age of thirteen, Grammie scooped her up and moved them to *The Virginia Starr* motel (written on the building in cursive, like the title card of a classic old Western), a shabby but clean little lodge in Toluca Lake. They waited for Mom to come but she never did. Her father did though, crashing into their room like a runaway preacherman from a flea market Flannery O'Connor paperback. He got soused for two weeks before relocating three hours northeast, changing his name and starting a congregation in Baker with money stolen from the old church.

Grammie read to her from *The Pilgrim's Progress* at night. ("If anyone's nosy enough to ask," she said, "tell em you're being motelschooled.") When Ali's attention wavered, her grandma confided that the book was the basis of *Little Women,* which Ali subsequently devoured and adored. She hired cabs to take Ali to auditions. The charismatic young girl was a quick study and booked jobs right away: Doritos, Cottonelle, Starburst. Soon they made enough to move to an apartment in Valley Village. A casting agent liked the "Sassy Teen" she played in a Febreze spot and asked her to read for *Arrested Development.* An hour later, they called to tell her she'd won the part of Sasha Meriweather, who became the cult favorite's cult favorite. When Grammie died in 2016, Ali buried her at Hollywood

Forever. She missed her every day of her life but was grateful her grandmother hadn't been around to see her ace the audition for ALS.

A year later, Ali returned to Oklahoma City to bury Mom, who died drunk, in a wrong-way wreck. She knew that Grammie wouldn't have shed a tear. She never forgave her for abandoning Ali.

There was so much Ali wanted to share but hadn't expected Katy to show up at the house and got so nervous that KP did most of the talking. She even asked Ali her shoe size! The singer talked a bit about her own adversity, and bouts with depression – which Ali thought terribly sweet – adding that Kanye's new thing was "healing with light." She said the Wests invited her and fiancée Orlando to Arizona for an amazing tour of a gigantic underground "earthwork" created by the artist James Turrell called the Roden Crater. Ali actually knew of Turrell, which made her feel less of a lummox. She fell in love with his work a few years back when she saw an exhibition at LACMA; the experience of light-filled rooms stayed with her for weeks. As Katy chattered away, Ali put the crater on her bucket list – she needed to check it off and soon, before the logistics of the ALS Traveling Medicine Show became too daunting.

When the van arrived at the compound, she was assaulted by a blur of cornflower sky and sunflower sun, of teeth and touch, as white-robed strongmen lifted her onto the wheelchair. Sights, smells and cartoon smiles hit her like buckshot: like being in a hothouse heaven.

And suddenly, she was in a meadow, enraptured by a choir on a hillock singing "Father Stretch My Hands." She choked on her tears, wrung out by the glorious, godspelled spiritualism and fatal sentimentality of – as her IG liked to put it – *this life*. The light and air held a pungent, mystical, SoCal crispness; she closed her eyes as flocks of voice dipped, dived and lifted, their hawks' hearts on scrubby currents of windsward.

> Father, I stretch my hands to thee
> Stretch my hands to be free
> No other help I know
> No other help I know of
> My Lord!

She thought of a favorite passage from *Little Women* (lifted from *The Pilgrim's Progress*) where the girls

> play pilgrims, as we used to do years ago. We call this hill the Delectable Mountain, for we can look far away and see the country where we hope to live some time. The sun was low, and the heavens glowed with the splendor of an autumn sunset. Gold and purple clouds lay on the hilltops, and rising high into the ruddy light were silvery white peaks that shone like the airy spires of some Celestial City.

Holding court from her chic black-matte chrome-and-leather wheelchair – gifted by Chrissy Teigen – with the whimsical *YSL* logo Ripley painted on it, Ali felt like Meghan Markle on one of her secret L.A. jaunts. A few hundred folks gathered, most of them strangers to her, though unexpected friends soon materialized then evanesced, dreamlike, to say their effusive hellos – Zoë and Shailene, Shia and Rumer, Hailee and Emma. Someone said Rick Rubin was there with Tyler the Creator. (Two of her major heroes.) Chris Pratt introduced himself.

"Katherine's obsessed with your Instagram." He was with his pastor, Chad, who invited her to his congregation at the old El Rey, in mid-Wilshire.

During a lull in visitors, Ali closed her eyes, meditating on the perfect moment. *This. This life.* She felt alive and at peace.

A hand touched her shoulder.

"Hey there you!"

She blinked at the woman. It was Patricia Arquette.

"Patty!"

"I am *so happy* to see you."

"*Thank you* for all your beautiful DMs!" said Ali. "And *please* tell me I wrote back – "

"You so did! And oh my God, thank *you* – for everything. It's so funny because I was just going to write to ask if you wanted to come to the house for a dinner I'm having for Ronan."

"I would *love* to! This is actually the first time I've been out since" – her eyes squinted for comic, melodramatic effect – "since *the reveal.*"

"Ha!"

"I came with Katy," she said, knowing it was a little show-offy, but feeling the name-drop's warm, all-rightness.

"I love her *so much*," Patty said.

"I didn't think I'd know anyone but it's *crazy* who's here."

"Yeezy pulls *such* an amazing group of people. His new gospel album's about to drop. He kinda owns the God space, right?"

"He's, like, *everything*," said Ali. "And it's so crazy beautiful here! I want it to be like this *forever*! Can't it stay like this forever?"

"Now *is* forever."

"Will you keep saying that, Patty? Would you? Can you be my own personal Marianne Williamson? Because I'm not ready to go yet, I am *so* not ready to go!" Ali looked at the sky, imploring, "Lord, don't take me!"

Patricia laughed out loud.

"You're not going *anywhere* – the Lord has plans for you, girl. I mean, clearly!" She knelt and put her hand in Ali's, who, in her side vision, became aware that people were watching their little moment as if it were historic, causing another wave of love-warmth to surge through her faltering bones like a sound wave. "Thank you," said Patty, in hushed, holy earnestness. "*For everything you do.* For everything you're *doing.*"

Ali, the half-famously self-aware gamine, flashed that sardonic, half-famous smile. "Just bein' *me*, Patsy-Pat – while there's still a me to be. And what about *you,* girlfriend, thanks for all *you* do. Your work's been so *amazing.* It's such a golden time for you, Patty, such a *renaissance* – "

Her eyes fell on her friend's enormous chest, taking in the slogan on Patricia's t-shirt: MAY THE BRIDGES I BURN LIGHT THE WAY.

"Aw!" said Patty. "*Thank* you. But you have no *idea* – though maybe you do! – of how many people you've touched. How many you've *helped.* How much *love* there is for you, and how much you *give.* The Beatles were fucking right! The love you make is equal to the love you take."

"That makes my heart sing," said Ali, tears in her eyes. "The *support.* The *love.* I *feel* it. There are no words." Eyes shut in communion, their fingers interlocked. "Soon there *will* be no words – I guess that's one of the weird gifts of ALS. And I'm not being morbid – "

"I know you're not," said Patricia, eyes welling up.

" – just truthful! You know that movie *The Red Balloon*?"

"Oh my God, I can't believe you said that. It's totally my favorite."

"That's how I think of myself now – a red balloon. One day I'll float up, up and away, to the place without words."

"'The place without words.' So beautiful...but *until then*, we're gonna hang onto your legs a while and keep you close, 'kay? Cause we need you *here*. The world needs the fucking *healing* you bring. You're doing what *Kanye's* doing, only on a *cosmic scale* – just don't tell *him* I said that! He's very competitive!"

"Hahaha!"

"Naw, Kanye'd actually *love* that I said that, he would totally agree. Have you met him?"

"Not yet."

"Oh no! *Kim* knows you're here, has she come over?" Ali shook her head. "We'll fix all that in a minute. And you *have* to meet Pastor Rich! He married Kim and Kanye, he's here from Miami..." She looked off and said, "Is that him? With Kourtney? I'm not sure Justin's here but *Ryan* is, he's so much fun! He co-created Drew, Justin's clothing line. But I *really* want you to meet someone, she's, this, this *amazing* girl – "

"Oh yes! Please!"

"My company has a new deal with Netflix and she's the first thing I'm bringing. Or *hope* to, if she *lets* me. Be right back!"

Patricia kissed her cheek and walked off, in search.

Moments later, Kanye appeared, looking like a sweet, handsome, electrified child. The preternatural grin scared her but his eyes and spirit were contagiously inviting. His scalp was dyed in soft reds and yellows and she liked how he probably did that for *himself*, not for the amusement of his kids. And she *loved* that they'd named their latest baby "Psalm."

Grammy would have approved.

"God bless you for coming," he said. "My wife follows you – she's the one who told me all about you. I wanted to give you these." A smiley-face assistant held out a soft suede sack. Kanye opened its cinched mouth, pulling out pink sneakers. "They're fire – about a thousand dollars on the aftermarket. We'll bring them up to the house and see you later."

He was called away.

Patricia reappeared, trailed by a woman in a golf cart that looked exactly like a Tesla and was later revealed to be a gift from Elon Musk.

"Ali Nell?" said Patricia, breathless. "Meet the *amazing* Joan Gamma."

"I love you!" said the girl, extending Ali a giant paw for a shake.

"I love *you*," Ali riposted, punch-drunk with good will.

"My friends call me The Fat Joan."

She roared with laughter. Ali never met anyone so operatic. It was impossible to know how large she was. ("I'm 40 stones," she said, "and fucking *stoned*.") Her face, widened and bloat-stretched as if by the tricks of an app, was still beautiful – a rubbery shock-aria of sorrow and joy, of pain and braggadocio, of bottomless tenderness and sorrow.

"I am *such* a balls-out fan of yours," she said. "Not just *Arrested Development* – Sasha Meriwether saved my life when I was little! – but your IG. It's *genius*. I am *totally obsessed* with you."

"Oh my God, that is so sweet," said Ali. "At least, I *think* it is!"

A shy girl stood just behind the cart. At first, Ali thought it was Scarlett Johanssen.

"This," said Fat Joan – she told Ali to leave off the *The*, but Ali wasn't having any of it – "is my *other* brand new friend, Billie Eilish."

Ali stuttered the phrase du jour, *"Oh my God,"* adding, "I *love* what you do!"

"I DM'd you," said bashful Billie.

"I know! I know! And I wrote back! The Troubadour! That was so *sweet* of you to invite me! I feel so bad I couldn't come but I wasn't – "

"No worries. Come to *any* of my shows, any time! Backstage pass for life."

"It's so *crazy* who's here!" said Ali.

"Fuckin amazing," said Billie. "Did you see Lennie James? From *The Walking Dead*? He's so fire."

"My favorite meet was the rapper Fat Joe," said Joan.

"He's fire," said Billie. "I just saw him in *Scary Movie 3*. He's so fire."

"'Fat Joe?' I says I says. 'Meet Fat Joan.'"

"Hahaha!"

"I'm gonna throw a dinner," Joan said to Ali conspiratorially. "Squads are so *over* – but we're gonna bring em *back*! The Bod Squad – the *fat* bod squad – starring me, Piggy Lipton."

"Hahahahahaha!"

(That was Patricia.)

"Joan Gamma is *crazy* fire," said Billie, like an official endorsement.

"Kanye gave me pink Yeezys!" blurted Ali, and was immediately embarrassed. She was on celeb overload.

"Aw, don't tell me *that*," said Billie. "I'm bout to get jealous."

Ali's cheeks reddened. The amplified sacred chorus broke through to save her.

> We on an ultralight beam
>
> We on an ultralight beam
> This is a God dream
> This is a God dream
> This is everything
> Everything

Billie and Joan turned toward the voices, instinctively – maternally – resting a hand on each of Ali's arms.

Her heart knew that if the Dark Prince of Amyotrophic Lateral Sclerosis took her – raped her right now in this celestial Calabasas castle – she would have no regrets.

JOAN
[*FaceTime*]

PIETRA Hi, Joan!

JOAN Oh hi.

PIETRA Hello? Joan? Wait. You just froze –

JOAN I'm here.

PIETRA – oops, you're frozen. But I can still hear you, can you hear me?

Ah! There you are!

JOAN I took it off wifi. Sometimes it's

PIETRA – said "poor connection" –

JOAN better with, like, just the 5G.

PIETRA I seem to have more luck with Skype.

JOAN I like FaceTiming.

PIETRA Well let's try. How are you?

JOAN Fine! I'm fine.

PIETRA How's the diet going?

JOAN Great – *really* good. A tooth broke in my mouth when I was sleeping.

PIETRA What?

JOAN The dentist said it's from my Dr Pepper addiction. Because of all those Dr Peppers –

PIETRA But that's terrible!

JOAN My staff did a kitchen intervention – my idea, actually. The house is now soda-free. Plus we did a total sugar exorcism.

PIETRA Oh that's *wonderful*.

JOAN I've already lost a stone. 15 pounds.

PIETRA Joan, that's amazing! So you don't think you're going to need the stomach surgery? The gastric –

JOAN No staples or sleeves for *me*, no thank you, ma'am. I'm a twelve-hundred calorie-a-day girl – on a bad day. I'm trying to keep it around 800.

PIETRA You're being supervised? Medically?

JOAN Yup. As they say in O.A., the obsession has been lifted. And it's so funny about my tooth because I used to have dreams about my teeth breaking. *All the time.* Just like crumbling or falling out like mahjong tiles. Vi used to – my mother used to play that with her kinky friends… I remember having those dreams from like when I was *eight*. Then after my brother and parents died, all my dreams were of being buried alive.

PIETRA Can you tell me more about that?

JOAN I think they had more to do with me hiding under the bed, during, uhm… the days I spent under the bed before they like found me – I remember thinking if I so much as *breathed*, that he/they/who*ever* would *hear* me and come *git* me. Like drag me out. And remember thinking I didn't want to become part of all those stinky smells... that's *totally* what I believed. So for a few years I dreamed I was in a coffin hearing the dirt shoveled over the lid – like Uma in *Kill Bill*. I think *Kill Bill 1* not *Kill Bill 2* – but oh my God, there was something so *sexual* about that scene for me! Uma buried alive... then one day I wasn't under the *bed* anymore – I mean, in my dreams. I was out of the box or the coffin or the mattress or whatever and dreaming I was a princess in a castle, like a prisoner-princess. And I'd step off the turret into the air and started *flying*. I had *so* many dreams of flying. I don't really have them anymore, they're like pretty rare now. Flying dreams are supposed to be about personal freedom, huh.

PIETRA They can be. Or of escape.

JOAN Isn't that the same? [*pause*] Lately, all I dream of is Ali Nell!

PIETRA The girl with ALS that you talked about. Tell me more?

JOAN I dreamed we were under the bed together. I was crying but she held my hand and made it all better.

PIETRA That's lovely.

JOAN She's so fucking *inspiring*. Did I tell you that we actually met?

PIETRA No. But you mentioned giving her a foundation grant. You were talking about your plans to give grants to Greta and – was it Millie?

JOAN And Billie – Eilish. I'm so *stoked*! We haven't heard back from Greta and I haven't made the offer to Billie yet – but Millie's *so excited*. She's gonna use hers to save the tortoises, I

love her. On Insta, she calls herself "the Mother of Tortoises." But I have something special in mind for Ali... and May is ALS Awareness Month! Isn't that like too perfect?
PIETRA So, Ali is a wonderful new friend.
JOAN Much more than that. It's like we're totally on the same journey. But together.

* * *

How else to explain their encounter at the Kardashian-West's?

After meeting Ali, she ruminated over the kismet of her impulsive decision to attend. It'd been ten months since Joan left the house for anything social. For a dwindling circle of friends, she was just Joanie, Fat Joan, the traumatized Old Soul murder-martyr; for the world, she was a curiosity, a bonafide chimera and pop-cult myth, the poor little (very) fat (very) rich girl who hid under the bed during the family bloodbath. She'd been invited to the chicly exclusive Sunday Service by Patricia Arquette, who was putting on the full-court press for Joan to sign off on a limited series about the heiress's young, eventful life. She was both flattered and insulted to be the latest train wreck on Patty's fetishized Emmy-bait wish list of fat, hideous-looking women. And besides, Patricia was *way* too old to portray her, a minor detail that seemingly left the actress unfazed. Patty's big idea was for Young Joan to be played by a tween, before the actress appeared in a fat suit, stuffed with all those awards she'd become famous for – Joan called them Golden Uglies – limning the present-day heroine (487 pounds and counting) in a state-of-the-art, digitally enhanced, all-enveloping body prosthetic. *Could be worse,* thought Joan. *She could've pitched me Beanie Feldstein.* Patty explained how CGI would erase 30 years from her face and "anyway, the time-jumping script is *nonlinear*, which helps us a lot." Joan audited enough meetings with Megan Ellison (once her babysitter) to know *nonlinear* was code for *bullshit*. If she'd said that Guillermo del Toro was interested in directing, at least it would have gotten Joan's attention. Instead, on the way home from Kanye's, Patty revealed her Dream Team shortlist of helmers: Olivia Wilde, Greta Gerwig, and some lady who directed every single episode of *Homeland*.

Uhm, really?

Still, she had an amazing time in Calabasas. Joan did a little research before she went, watching *KUWTK*, believe it or not, for the very first time. She laughed out loud when Kanye said that he only agreed to do his wife's show because he could talk right into the camera, a break-the-fourth-wall move that reminded him of *The Incredibles*. "I see our life becoming more and more like *The Incredibles*, until we can finally fly." Joan *loved* that. To her surprise, the more she learned about Kanye, the more complex and layered he got, the more poetic and endearing. But she also saw the potential to provoke; the genius-with-bipolar-superpowers shtick got old. She found herself with mixed feelings about la whole fucked up famiglia but he was so kind to her on Sunday that she felt remorseful for being so judgey. Maybe his sweetness came from the extra effort of civility required whenever he went off his meds – or maybe it was artificially induced by his meds – or maybe he was so genteel because he knew how rich she was. Kanye creamed his coffee for anyone in the billionaire club. She had to give it to him, even if sometimes he rubbed her the wrong way. Joan read somewhere that when he was hospitalized for losing his mind, he scrawled on a piece of paper *Start a church in Calabasas*. Now here they were, on a windblown, Christ-like day. Maybe he *was* Mr. Incredible. That would make the missus "Elastigirl," which sounded about right.

Kim didn't get off so easy. Joan sniffed at her latest incarnation – becoming an attorney to free all the murderers. She watched something on television about her taking up the cause of a "wrongly convicted" man accused of killing a dozen homeless people on L.A.'s Skid Row. *Wrongly convicted* was trending – almost overnight, Truth had become a general problem. All you had to do was shout, *This did not happen!* – even while it was happening – and you were good to go. There she was, in Kyliner and Elastigirl SKIMS, telling an obsequious oh-so-serious interviewer that evidence had been tampered with, adding that when she and her client finally met, she found him "thoughtful and honest." Thoughtful and honest! A single meeting! Joan wished there could be a second press conference, asking the ghosts of the dead to add their encomiums.

Her anger was of course tied to the murder of her own parents and brother. The other side of that rage was deep shame, and Joan winced at her self-righteousness. *How dare you judge that woman, who at least is trying to do good works, when you sit there playing sick* Beautiful Dark Twisted Fantasy *mindgames of fuck, marry, kill: fuck Billie (had to see what was under those nutty LV tent-clothes), kill Millie (cause she was too kind, funny, talented, perfect) and marry Greta*.

Forgive me, Kim!

But all *had* to be forgiven.

Mrs. Kardashian-West was family now – the family of sacred handmaidens who had fatefully conspired to bring her the sainted Ali Nell.

* * *

Ali brought her to Hollywood Forever to show her Grammie's grave.

Joan picked her up in a customized truck. (Bodyguards followed in a convoy of Escalades.) Entranced, delighted cemetery visitors took pics of them riding amongst the tombs in Joan's bespoke Tesla buggy, uploading images to the Internet. The odd couple enjoyed the attention.

"Guess *we're* a pair to draw to, huh?" said Ali.

Joan guffawed. "I love that your grandma's buried here. I have a grandpa I *wish* I could bury here!"

"After we met," Ali finally confessed, "I read everything about you. I'm like an *expert* now. Oh my *God*! Joan! Your *story* – "

"Crazy, right?"

"It's – *beyond*. Is Patty going to... are you going to let Patty – "

"What is *wrong* with that bitch? Does she think she's Charles Laughton? No *way* I'm going to be her next fat white sacrificial lamb."

Ali started laughing and couldn't stop.

Joan looked around, inhaling the air outside the Judy Garland Pavilion. "Have you come here to see movies?"

"Yeah," said Ali. "*Totally* great. I saw *Beetlejuice*."

"*Love* that movie. I came when they showed *The Incredible Shrinking Man*."

"Is that – is that the one where he's caught in a spider web at the end and cries, 'Help me! Help me!'?"

"That's *The Fly*."

"Oh!"

"It's funny that you thought it was *The Fly* though, 'cause at the end of *The Incredible Shrinking Man* he's fighting a spider

for food. And he says in a voiceover, 'I recognized that my illness was rooted in hunger.' I can frickin *relate*. Then suddenly
he feels like his body's just… gone. No more hunger, no more
fear. And he's not afraid of shrinking anymore."

"It sounds *amazing*."

"Supposedly, the ending was like really *unpopular* with the
audience. People wanted him to return to normal size – but he
keeps shrinking! I love that. That they made that choice. And
he has this *epiphany* that's he's going to become a *microbe*."

"Oh my God, I want to see it!"

"We can totally screen it tonight. I want to remake it with
Del Taco. He loves it."

"Who?"

"Guillermo. Del Toro. I call him Del Taco."

"He's so amazing. I loved *The Shape of Water*."

"I worry about him though, the boy's getting *thick* – he's
almost fatter than I am! But he *loves* him a kitschy old horror flick, long as it's smart, with a soul. He keeps talking
about remaking *Nightmare Alley,* another totally amazing film.
Anyway, at the end of *The Incredible Shrinking Man*, when he
like loses his fear, the dude says – I know it by heart, I'm
obsessed! – 'Suddenly, I knew the infinitesimal and the infinite
were just *two ends of the same thing.* The unbelievably *small* and
the unbelievably *vast* eventually meet, like the closing of a
gigantic circle…'"

"Oh my God! Joan! I'm totally getting goosebumps!"

She tilted her head, peering into the blue vault of sky as
she continued the soliloquy. "'I felt my body dwindling, melt-
ing, becoming nothing. My fears melted away, and in their
place, came acceptance. The vast majesty of creation had to

mean something – then *I* meant something too. To God, there is no zero... *I still exist.*"

"'To God, there is no zero,'" echoed Ali. "I *love* that. That is *so beautiful.* I'm putting it on my Instagram."

Joan turned to her, emotional.

"That's what *you* did for me, Ali."

"What do you mean?"

"When you told the world what was happening to you, my bullshit fears just... all went away. See, my whole thing, my whole *nightmare* is – *was* – about being wedged. Getting stuck in tiny, tiny places and being unable to move. Just stuck, and no one rescues you, no one can hear you cry or scream, you just lay there hallucinating and panic-weeping for weeks or however long it takes you to die. That's why I got so fat, in my mind it was the only way I could *live,* you know, to already *be* trapped, like, *be* wedged, in my own body, like as a way of inoculating myself against that fear. To *get myself first,* before 'they' came. My shrink calls it 'making friends with your fear,' right? I tried to do that, but not in a *good* way... I wanted to make a coffin out of my body so I could be at some sort of peace. It totally doesn't make sense, not that it has to. And when I read what happened to you – what was *happening* – I just... felt I didn't – need to do that anymore. Because of you."

At last, she saw Ali softly crying, and was touched.

"There's something," she went on, "called The Giving Pledge. Started by Bill Gates and Warren Buffett. Warren's, like, my godfather or god uncle, whatever. He's amazing. People with too much money sign a pledge to give everything away before they die. Vi and Raphie – my folks – signed but didn't live long enough to disperse anything. I mean, in the proper way. So I'm going do it *for* them. I'm gonna leave this world the same way I came in, Ali – with nothing. I'm gonna be a microbe again! The unbelievably *poor* and the unbelievably *rich* eventually meet, like the closing of a gigantic circle. It's so fucking true!"

"I think you're the most amazing girl I've ever met – "

"Gonna give it *all* away. Gonna give *you* some – all the money you'll ever need. Not just for medical stuff, but for anything you *want* or *need* on your journey. *This* journey, *our* journey. I'll be right by your side. (If you'll have me.) See, I'm disappearing too."

Ali was moved but taken aback. "Joanie... I don't – I just want to be your friend."

"And I think we should make a movie together!" she shouted, ebullient, ignoring Ali's entreaty. "Would you like that, Ali Oops? Wanna make a movie with me?"

Ali started to laugh-cry then Joan did too. There was nothing to do but joyously play along. "Like, with Guillermo?" said Ali. "Like, make the *Shrinking Man*?"

"No way! We're going to make something else."

"Let's make *The Fly*!" said Ali, half-joking.

"Nope." She squinted her eyes like a forest witch. "I researched *you* too, friend – your Instagram archive, anyway. And what I've decided," she pronounced resolutely, "is that we're gonna make a movie of *The Pilgrim's Progress*. And guess who we're gonna dedicate it to: your Grammie. How does *that* sound? How does that sound, Ali Oops?"

B U D

Manfred Manny,
<u>Oh, oh, oh</u>... Such sorrow over dearest Clarice. A yahrzeit candle for her is burning in the kitchen sink (one of those tall, Bodega Jesus ones, I think Clarice is laughing); the light it casts in the dark is the shadowplay kaleidoscope of this absurd human dramedy. I embrace you, old soldier.

More later. ("Whereof one cannot speak...")

Bud Schulberger né (Hamburger) Hamlet

* * *

For years, standing in line at convenience stores, Bud barely noticed the drunks and minimum wage schmucks making their scratcher selections. The game meant nothing to him; then, as if overnight, it meant everything.

He got his feet wet with two-dollar tickets but after a month of losing or winning $10 or so a day, Bud won $100 on a $5 scratcher and couldn't shake the thrill. He liked using "lucky" coins to do his scratching: special pennies found on the street or in dishes the unknowing clerks kept by the register. He even took to using A.A. "30-Day" sobriety chips he'd collected over the years.

Bud loved reading about people who hit it big. The most you could win on a scratcher, in California anyway, was ten million – peanuts compared to the nine-figure jackpots dangled by Powerball, Mega Millions and Fantasy Five. The instant gratification was what grabbed him. You bought a ticket and

BAM, ten seconds later you were rich. If he heard about a woman winning five million on a scratcher she bought from a vending machine, Bud played vending machines for a few weeks; if he read about a guy winning a million on a Monopoly scratcher, Bud got strung out on the same. There was a show called *My Lottery Dream Home* on HGTV hosted by a flaming, tatted queen who dropped in on recent scratcher winners looking to upgrade their current craphouse living arrangements. After reaping millions at the local liquor locker or gas station, the cretins invariably said they were looking to spend "in the two-hundred-fifty to $300,000 range." Maybe that was an unexpected side effect of winning: the heavens opened and slapped common sense into poor white trash. One time, the show deviated from scratchers, featuring a man who won $180 million on a California Mega Millions ticket that he bought at a 7-Eleven. He wound up buying an entire mountain range.

Bud became a disciple of the Church of Probability, engaging in the predictable, age-old catechism – questions, not answers – of any zealous novitiate. Did the man who played consistently have a better chance at winning than he who played just once in a while? If Bud bought the same $20 scratcher and lost four times in a row, did chances increase of the fifth ticket holding a silent, mocking fortune? Should he ignore the intoxicated, invincible feeling after a big win – say, $400 on a $30 scratcher – and stop playing for the day? (Whether it was even possible for him to do so was another question entirely.) Or should he double-down in hopes of riding that elusive, *conquistador* energy and hyper-spacing to a massive win? There was much mythology out there, like the tale of the man who won a thousand dollars on a ten-dollar scratcher then bought another a few minutes later that yielded five million. And how to explain the phenomena of what the lottery offices deemed "lucky retailers"? It was like the Good Housekeeping Seal: banners with the phrase were strung across violent, seedy liquor stores, pricey fuel emporia and hypermarkets alike. Was it a matter of foot traffic? Or *were* some vendors luckier than others? Peeling the onion further, could it be that there was such a thing as a scratcher *genius loci* – not generally, but lucky *for Bud himself*? There were a few retailers he masochistically frequented that never failed to empty his pockets. The puzzlement extended to the tickets themselves: he "never" won certain scratchers, but "often" won certain others. He became haunted, taunted, consumed, confounded and enthralled by the celestial riddle of randomness that at its core seemed anything *but* random. He even strove to see a trending correlation between merchants who were sour- or stone-faced, sometimes hostile, versus giddy ones who ritualistically called out, "Best of luck!" – a gentleman at Lucky Liquor actually kissed the Big Win scratcher before handing it off – but there seemed to be none.

He was at a 76 in Toluca Lake. The customer ahead was buying scratchers. When he left, Bud stepped up to get some of his own.

The Indian clerk whispered, "See him?" Both looked out the window to watch the man heading to his truck. "Last week, he won $750,000 – *here*."

He was excited to be in such close proximity to a big winner. "Wow. What did he play?"

"The $10 Mystery Crossword. The man still comes in – he got a brand new SUV. He's buying more now than he ever did."

Bud avoided the crossword puzzle scratchers because they were confusing. It was too difficult to figure out if you'd won.

A few days later, he found himself in an unfamiliar part of town. He dipped into a grungy mini-mart on Pico. Bud was trying to lay off playing the more expensive tickets for a few days and spent a pleasant half-hour buying five- and ten-dollar scratchers. He was about $100 in the hole and decided to splurge before leaving. Recalling the conversation in Toluca Lake, he asked for a $20 Mystery Crossword. Bud was certain it was a loser and quickly rubbed off the bar code, expecting to see the dreaded "NON-WINNER."

When he held it under the scan, the machine said

File Claim Form
$5,000.00

In shock, he showed it to the counterman, who said, "Nice win!"

The clerk told him he better sign the ticket in case it was lost and someone tried to cash. Bud's hand shook as he wrote his name.

On the way to the Lottery District Office in Van Nuys, Bud was convinced he'd been sanctified and was now blessed. He pulled over and looked up his ticket on the website. It said the odds of a $5,000 win on that ticket were seventy-five hundred to one.

7,500 to 1!

He celebrated by snorting up a crushed Adderall, certain that a "hyper-space" win was coming his way.

Five thousand was just the beginning.

Pulling back onto the highway, he began to fantasize. One of his favorite scratchers had a winner-take-all bonus box at the top. On the bottom, it said, UNCOVER A "BIG WIN" SYMBOL, **WIN ALL 25 PRIZES AUTOMATICALLY**! He was convinced that was his fate, if not in the next week or month, then by year's end.

He imagined the lottery office would look like a building designed by Disney Imagineers but it was a storefront in a drab business park. He sat in a plastic chair, waiting. There was only one other customer and he wondered how much she won. On the walls were photos of men and women holding six-foot long cardboard checks. One was for half-a-billion dollars. Bud superimposed his face on the smiling winner.

When it came his turn, he was greeted by the happiest bureaucrat on Earth. It wasn't like the DMV, where people came to throw shit. Those who entered here thought he was Saint Peter.

"How much did she win?" Bud asked of the woman who just left.

"The usual," said St. Peter. "A thousand." The novelist immediately felt more special. "In this office," the jolly man added, "zeroes are heroes."

He handed over his ticket and driver's license and the man excused himself. Bud glanced at the list on the clipboard where the day's winners were tallied in longhand. It was late afternoon and there were about fifteen names. All had $1,000 written next to them except for one near the top that read $100,000.

Bud felt less special.

When the fellow returned, he handed over paperwork to fill out.

"How long before I get the money?"

"Ten, maybe twelve weeks. Sometimes much sooner."

"Are taxes taken out?"

"Nope! The full amount. But next year, you'll get a W2."

* * *

Dearest Granddaughter…

I'm writing to you now (though my "inner circle" rather overdramatically warned against it) because, well, at this point, I have nothing to lose. There's far too much to say, so I'll keep it simple.

I'm begging you, Joan, to find it in your heart to drop me a line, personally; a cease and desist letter from the estate would be so boring. (As would a literal siccing of the hounds.) And out-of-character too, from everything I've gleaned of your heart, and actions. I shall never forget your kindness to me on that terrible dark day of the memorial.

I've been thinking of my mother – your great grandma Dolly, whom you never knew – thinking of her quite a lot lately because I'm working on a book about her life. Invariably, a book about <u>my</u> life as well, but I refuse to employ the m-word: memoir. Dolly and Vi were much alike: vivacious, iron-willed, hardheaded. (!) The latter attribute can be a wonderful thing, but also wall people – and Love – off. I know this through experience, having spent much time on the other side of that wall, peering over…

But I've said too much too soon, and probably all the <u>wrong</u> things. I suppose that's what happens when there's such a surplus of words and feelings held back through the years. Forgive a sentimental old man…

One thing the executors – and Vi – can never take away from me is my Love and genuine concern for <u>your well-being</u>. It may be hard to believe, Joanie, but I want nothing from you! I don't know how long I'm going to be around and only wish to do something of which I was remiss during the time your mother was alive:

To get to know you.
– and you, me.

Very truly yours, and with great affection,

Your grandfather,

Bud Wiggins

THE HUNGER ARTIST

ALI

Oh, Diary! I hope the July 4th fireworks at Joan's didn't freak you out or keep you awake; I know how you like your beauty rest. Probably gave you a little PTSD, huh – Post-Traumatic Stress Diary. Tee-hee.

I'm *soooooooo* sorry I haven't written more. I've been traveling traveling traveling, mostly with my Joanie. Even when she can't come along, I'm sent on my way in a private jet with a nursing team and too many Hermès blankets folded over my legs to count. I am so blessed. It sounds so buji but it wouldn't be humanly possible to do this any other way. Par example: last week I had a consult at the Mayo Clinic (Minnesota) (and how crazy is that), THEN to the Healey Center for ALS @ Mass General to meet its director, the AMAZEBALLS NEUROLOGIST Merit Ester Cudkowicz... then OFF to nyc to do *Watch What Happens* with the sweet and almost-as-amaze-balls-as-Dr. Merit Andy Cohen. Ohhhhh! Di, I was soooooooo nervous!!! 'Cause he can be kinda nasty but his peeps said he's the biggest pussycat since becoming a dad and prolly's even gonna cry while interviewing me... WHICH HE DID!!!!! OMG. And THEN I had a super-special visit with Jaci Hermstad, the braveheart redheaded cowgirl whose twin, Alex, tragically died from ALS in 2011. They'd been thinking Jaci was wayyyy in the clear but ALS is pitiless and Jaci "got" it too. She's at New York Pres getting infusions of an experimental drug (the docs call it "Jacifusen"!!!) that my team's looking into. (And when I say "team," I mean JOAN!!! Hahaha tee-hee.) Jaci's parents are amazing and spiritual, and *love* that I'm a PK. We spent the morning throwing scripture at each other like Frisbees but they won with Phillippians 4:13 – "I can do all things through Christ who strengthens me." Jaci's become quite the celeb herself, having been visited by a golden retriever puppy named Walt (who *happens* to have 5,000 followers on Insta) and Caroline Rhea (Hilda from *Sabrina the Teenage Witch*) – and… yours truly! Jaci was on *The Today Show* too but had to leave early cause she wasn't feeling well but no one told me. ☹ So when I arrived to tape I got mightily bummed (so selfish!) because we were gonna do a whole segment together, that'd have been SO cool.

Then I wanted to go to Florida to meet the amazing man who started the Ice Bucket Challenge (Pete was a superstar baseball player in college, diagnosed with ALS at 27) but Joan put the kibosh on that. She said it was just too too much. She's my guardian ANGEL but pleeeeeease don't get jealous, Di, 'cause you're my true and first love. (Just don't tell Joan.)

So I flew back to LA for the *Walk to Defeat ALS* and was verrrrrrry very tired but insisted on giving Nanci Ryder the "Walk Hero Award." Suit up and show up, as they say. Poor Nance! Always so beautiful and healthy but then she got breast cancer and after that, ALS. God has special plans for us all – "I can do all things through Christ who strengthens me" – but when I saw her claw-y hands, bloat-face and perfectly done hair, I got scared. She can't talk or move. It was like looking into a crystal ball; *teach us to number our days*. The brilliantly talented director Stacy Title was there too (tracheotomized, in a cyborg friggin wheelchair that put mine to shame) – another bride of FrankenALS. Guess we're all just bachelorettes gathered for black rose ceremony... Courtney Cox was cheerleading with her *sweetest* daughter Coco (Arquette), and (former) sister-in-law Patty, too – and Chris Pratt! Small world, huh, Di? Everyone kept asking where Joanie was and I kept telling 'em she's a rambling gal, not my sister's keeper, blah. I wonder how Nanci and Stacy pay for their ginormous medical/caregiver bills, and what I would do without Angel Joan. SO frickin grateful; I'd be shit and shinola outta luck. I was so nervous before my speech that I was glad I made Ripley run to CVS for Depends (forgot to put em on that morning) 'cause my stomach's gone totally crazy – Joanie's been all over the Mayo folks to find out what the eff is UP. If I have the energy, I still want to meet with Rabbi Yitzi Hurwitz (sp?), who was diagnosed in 2013. He writes a blog about the Torah by using his eyes and talks through a PC like Mr. Hawking used to do. He even gives marital advice! I guess he'll never be giving ME any nuptial counseling... sigh. (Unless he counsels the Dark Bachelorettes on how to please their man.) Tho maybe I should just ask, How am I gonna DO this, Mister Rabbi? 'Cause right now it's fun (*sort* of – you know what I mean, Di, I know you do) – flying here and flying there and being fussed over by Joan and sundry. But what happens when I lose all control? When my Team has to wipe my butt and even the tears from my eyes? What happens when I'm trapped, Diary, when I'm WEDGED, like the stuff of Joanie's nightmares? What happens when I can't move a muscle and don't want to write a blog with my eyes or even cast a gaze toward my beloved Saint Joan? What happens then?

When I just want to die –

Sorry for getting all morbid on you. Please forgive.

And oh! This *awful* thing happened…

I added some Goop jewelry to my cart but only as a wish list. I was dreaming that maybe I could barter for it by letting them advertise on my IG down the road (when/if I garner more followers) – but Joanie (she's so crafty!) got into my account on a ruse and bought me those amazing emerald earrings!!! I don't even want to tell you what they cost… but that's not the awful thing. No. The awful, terrible thing is that one of them *disappeared*. I don't want to tell her about it yet because she'll think it was the housekeeper, whom I know had nothing to do with it – who'd steal *just one earring*, anyway? And I know it's selfish but I don't have space for drama of ANY kind. I had Ripley look everywhere under the bed and in all the crevices… nada. I'm hoping it'll turn up.

So say a little prayer, Diary, will ya? Before I get diaryr-rhea. ☺

It's crazy how important J-Gamm's become in my life. She fusses over me but it's her health I'm worried about… tho she's doing beautifully and already lost 75 pounds!!! She's my incredible shrinking womanchild but I wag my finger at her not to go and become a microbe on me & disappear. (We finally watched the movie together and it was fecking ama-zeballs.) That would just be too cruel. She wants to give me "everything" but I need to be careful careful careful, Di… I don't want to lead her on because I think she loves me, well, o-'course she does, I *know* she does, but I think she might just want it "all" – y'know, the full romantic monty. Is there a difference between loving someone to death – tho really, it should be "loving someone to life" – and being "in love"? Isn't it all one and the same? I'm not attracted to her that way, but with Love, size don't really matta… it's all Infinite, right, Di? We put words and phrases on things but how far would I be willing to go, to show my love and gratitude to my Angel Joanie? If I went "that way," would it make me some kind of whore? Oh, that horrible word, invented by men! Did you know, Di, there's a religion in India (Ripley told me, so it must be true) where prostitutes are considered sacred? Apparently, they sleep with noblemen, and lepers too. Because they're the ones who – in their purest forms – truly love, uncondition-ally, in the name of that which created us all. I hate that word "whore," hate that women use it to shame each other in the same way men do. Grammie used to call my mother that but I knew it was in anger. But she could never bring herself to say anything bad about Daddy, who did so much to destroy us…

Interesting, huh?

But what if I loved Joan back – in the way I think she wants me to – without boundaries? I ask because I know you won't judge. Would that be so wrong? I don't have the luxury of time for "right" or "wrong"! Without the luxury of time, there *is* no right or wrong, there *cannot* be… I just can't sepa-rate out love. Maybe never could. How do we do that, anyway, Diary, without being small and petty? How do we not give "all" to a being who gives us EVERYTHING, every second of every minute of every hour of every day? Joanie gives me real <u>and</u> metaphorical jewels, makes me laugh till I pee and makes sure I see the best doctors on Earth and one night last week even flew us to a private isle in Vancouver for a candlelight dinner!!! And OMG, Di… she wants to buy me a HOUSE – did

I forget to tell you? – in Point Dume. And when I tell her NO, and promise I'll move in with her when I can no longer manage, she says, "I'll be the one to move in with YOU. 'Cause I'm the one who can't manage without you." Oh oh oh! Then she holds me in her arms like my mother never did and maybe not even Grammie. She teaches me so much and makes me wonder if I'll ever be able to accept love or know how to give it, "properly."

Joan loves that word, "properly" –

Diary, DO help me find my way…

I put on a brave face and exhaust myself staying busy like a whirligig but deep down I'm so frightened, not even deep down but right-on-the-surface. I see my body in the mirror and my head's starting to loll to the side. My eyes look bulgy and my hair's starting to fall out and what's left is getting snowy-white streaks. I can't stand up too well by myself anymore. I smell – AND smell things that aren't there, too – otherworldly scents that I'm certain no one's ever smelled before. And YUCK – Joanie's noticing cheese string coming out of "little tar pits" on the back of my thighs and is bizzy emailing pics of them to the Mayo (barf). Dr. Joan - she actually would make quite a brilliant doctor, I tell her she's young enough to make that dream happen – said she thinks it looks like Morgellon's, the syndrome Joni Mitchell had or still has – and wants them to rule out Myasthenia Gravis, and Progressive Bulbar Palsy too, which she says are ALS mimickers –

Oh, Diary…

What's a soon-to-be-dead girl to do?

* * *

Her life was full.

MS, Lupus, and Lyme already had their day in the sun; it was ALS' time to shine. Tim Green, the former NFL player, just gave a kickass, cry-happy interview on *60 Minutes*; thanks to Joan, Tim's doctor, Merit Cudkowicz, was on Ali's team. Jimmy Kimmel started an ALS charity because "one of our long-time, most beloved co-workers" had been diagnosed. If Rabbi Yitzi Hurwitz, Nanci Ryder, Stacy Title and Tim Green were the disease's workhorse standbys, Ali Nell was its newly anointed gamine and favored courtesan, the reigning People's Choice.

In this moment, she was white-hot famous, not just for her courage and humor in the face of the unthinkable, but via her sensationally improbable alliance with Joan Gamma. The folkloric union of an actress whose luminous beauty was becoming encased and deformed in front of the voyeuristic eyes of the world with a tragically orphaned, elephantine baby-billionairess was a reality show the public couldn't resist. People yearned for, *demanded*, a reversal of fortune, which could best be effected by them becoming a romantic, car-crash couple. Why couldn't they just gamely face the music and dance? While most Internet opinions smugly gave them their space, trolls leveled accusations of hypocrisy. "If we *were* dating, I would *definitely* say so. But Joan is truly the sister – sometimes the mother! – I never had. Who happens to be an angel IRL." Sometimes, though, Joan and Ali couldn't resist having their fun, like when they went to Craig's for dinner with another "odd couple," Sarah Paulson and her 77-year-old girlfriend, Holland Taylor.

There was great sorrow too. *Te Deum* was being rebooted as a feature and Marvel asked her to be the mom of Melissa

Eerie, the young sorceress Ali played on the old television show. She had to say no, even when the studio said the part had been rewritten for Melissa's mother to be paralyzed as the result of an epic inter-dimensional battle. Ali was heartbroken but there was just no way she could physically do it. To make matters worse, she would have had three scenes with Anya Taylor-Joy, who'd already been cast as the Soulsword-wielding Magik in *The New Mutants*. Ali loved Anya – they met when the actress came to the Fat City production offices for a general meeting about *The Pilgrim's Progress*. On a good day, she saw everything as a spiritual challenge; on a bad one, she begged Joan to fly her to one of those clinics in Switzerland to die.

The numbness was unpredictable. She took to wearing dozens of rings because the weight made her remember her hands. The rippling muscles of her thighs in spasm mesmerized, looking like digital sandstorms. Without warning, in the middle of a song, her lovely voice juddered and became cartoonishly nasal, making her friends benevolently laugh out loud. But the skin eruptions were the worst, reminding Ali of the weird armor on Magik's skin that metastasized on her body each time the warrior swung the Soulsword. Doctors abandoned their initial, glib diagnoses – psoriasis, eczema – conjuring fabulist theories to account for the fleeting spurts of green and black sweat oozing from her glands ("We believe it's a form of *chromhydrosis*"); the soft, Saharan blistering of her buttocks ("*Erythropoietic Protoporphyria* is the only thing that makes sense"); the fishy scales of *Ichthyosis vulgaris* and blue-gray agyrian taint of silvery tissue; the sensuous, velvety underarm patches ("*Acanthosis Nigricans*"); the flaps of loose skin ("*Elastoderma*") mirroring Joan's now fat-deprived arms and belly; and the inexplicable three-day appearance of *Lichen amyloidosis* that made Joan nostalgic for the fungal Sequoian fat-boy who once was her favorite on *My 600-lb. Life*.

In the dead of day, Ali wondered, *Am I mutating?*

Into what?

Am I becoming...

...Joanie?

JOAN

Down to 330 pounds and no one could believe it.

Ali joked that she should change her name:

Thin Joan.

Slim Pickins.

Tiny Bubbles.

The rapid weight loss couldn't be explained by the Metforim prescribed by Dr. Regis to offset gains caused by the spectrum of neuroleptics that stabilized her mania and recent peekaboo psychosis – grey market hallucinations that Joan called "counterfeit Birkins," real enough to fool Victoria Beckham herself.

She was focused on a single episode of *My 600-lb. Life*, watching it over and over. Milla, a gorgeous Black, shrunk from 750 to 150 – the most dramatic loss of anyone on the show ever. Flashbacks from the beginning of her journey showed her brood of preteen children giving sponge baths in bed; like careful, Lilliputian archeologists, they daintily lifted the heavy folds, wiping and scrubbing, polishing and toweling down. Joan freeze-framed the fleeting glimpse of the foul, charbroiled 40-lb. lymphedema that colonized Milla's crotch, resembling a Death Cap mushroom. (Many episodes later, the surgeon Dr. Now would slice it away.) Way back when, Joan remembered willing herself to surpass Miss Milla – *I have a dream* – to reach the half-ton mark and beyond.

But that was before Ali Nell.

Now, she measured her life in B.A./A.A. time: Before Ali, After Ali.

* * *

The new offices of Fat City Filmworx once belonged to Howard Hughes.

Ali kept saying that she didn't like the production company's name, that it was "too mean," so Joan cheekily changed it to Not So Little Women Projex, as both goof and homage to the novel built on the bones of *The Pilgrim's Progress*. Instead of making a script their first priority, they had fun wasting time looking for a director to attach him- or herself. Joan thought *big* – Scorsese-big (Marty was expensive, but for hire) – though it seemed whenever the maestro went religious, his movies tanked. She wanted something epic that still had a light touch. When Anya Taylor-Joy dropped by, she raved about Josh Boone, director of *The New Mutants,* the film she just wrapped. He also directed *The Fault In Our Stars* and Joan liked that because she wanted *TPP* to have heart. While she wasn't so sure about "Marvelizing" John Bunyan's book, she had to admit the notion of needing superpowers in order to reach the Celestial City was intriguing. Ali fought for a woman to be at the helm, "like Patty Jenkins or Sofia or even Olivia." Predictably, all were enthusiastic but said they preferred not to attach themselves without seeing a script. When Joan spitballed directors with Jodie Foster, the actress said, "Why don't you reach out to Mel?" *So* genius. Mel Gibson made total intrinsic sense, because after that Sunday at Kanye's, Joan found herself on a providential chapel run, attending services at Hillsong, Zoe, Agape and First AME. She asked Jodie to wrangle a hard-to-get invitation to Mel's Church of the Holy Family in Malibu. Apparently, Malibu and Calabasas were the New Jerusalems.

Who'd o' thunk?

The search for a screenwriter began. After slogging through the usual Academy Award-winning mugshots, Joan had a wild notion – why not write it herself? Or better yet, with Ali? *Hell the fuck yeah!* They'd do their thing then pay an Oscar gunslinger to doctor it with the agreement Joan and Ali would get sole screen credit, even if only a handful of their original pages survived. (Joan made her bones as a negotiator during the estate struggles.) *No problem.* For $200,000-a-day, you could probably get Steve Zaillian to suck off an active shooter at a synagogue.

She was just starting to get comfortable with the idea, when propinquity met serendipity.

Joan and Ali were attending a Zoe Church event at a cool, defunct art deco palace on the Miracle Mile. Chris Pratt came over to say hello. They'd met him twice before – at Ye's in Calabasas and at the ALS Walk when Ali gave Nanci Ryder the Hero Award. Joan was amazed at how great Chris was. He was young but had suffered lots of adversity. His dad died of MS and his son, a preemie, still suffered medical issues. What captivated her was how *funny* he was, and how he wore his profound spirituality so loosely. He was so wondrously comfortable in his own skin. (He and Ali really clicked, ping-ponging scripture quotes the first time they met.) After the run-in at Zoe, Joan and Ali threw a few dinners for the actor and Katherine, his new wife.

They *loved* his origin story. He'd been kicking around Maui when he was young, drugging and sexing, when a stranger approached; two days later, Chris found Jesus. When Joan said that he needed to change his name to Jesus *Chris, Chris* the Lord, he laughed – he was the furthest thing from being stuffy. Ali was shocked when Joan told her she'd never seen *Guardians of the Galaxy.* "How is that even possible!" said Ali. "He's friggin' 'Star Lord'! Star Lord! How perfect is that?" The universe agreed, with the star part anyway, and gave him one on Hollywood Boulevard. They watched the ceremony on YouTube. Chris stood before family, friends and fans with those thirst trap, God-next-door looks, humbly informing the crowd that "the Lord has done great things for us and we are filled with joy."

He reciprocated their love, overwhelmed by the couple's biblical sufferings: Ali's lionhearted grace as slow-fast havoc was wreaked on her body and Joan's buoyancy in the wake of unspeakable, ghoulish tragedy. When he asked if she had any surviving family, Joan dismissively mentioned her grandfather. She acidly, comically referenced the old man's venality, making light of the lawsuit he waged against the estate – and his recent personal note, a sanctimonious effort at détente. The actor listened with his usual close, respectful attention, then spoke of his father, who died in an assisted living facility "defiant and depressed by the betrayal of his body." He looked at Ali when he said that, drawing her in. "He just sat there and watched TV for ten years."

Impromptu, Chris recounted the story a friend told him about the legendary tennis player Arthur Ashe.

"Arthur Ashe got AIDS from a blood transfusion – they didn't screen for it back then. He gave an interview before he died. He was asked, 'Do you think it's unfair? Do you ever think that? That it's unfair you got AIDS?' Arthur said, 'It's God's will.' The interviewer said, 'Do you pray to be healed? Do you pray for God's healing?' 'No,' said Arthur. 'I pray for God's Will.'" Chris sat back, his face clear as a cloudless blue sky. "I thought that was pretty amazing. Because he didn't want anything for *himself* – he knew that what is, is. There was no reason to wish or pray it otherwise." He peered at Joan, right into her secret places. "I had a tough time forgiving my dad for giving up. Not just giving up on himself, but on us. On *me*. Romans 7:15-20 says, 'For I have the desire to do what is right, but not the ability to carry it out. For I do not do the good I want, but the evil I do not want is what I keep on doing. Now if I do what I do not want, it is no longer I who do it, but sin that dwells within me.'"

It seemed to Joan that the homily was meant to show her the way, a far different way than she (and her mother) had taken with Bud Wiggins. Suddenly, a feeling came over her – the same feeling triggered by Ali's inaugural ALS Instagram share – of letting go. But this time, it felt sacred, as if she was calling on God's will and His healing, all at once.

Chris looked at her as if he *knew*.

He smiled and said, "Forgiveness is the best revenge."

* * *

Chris couldn't believe that he never read *The Pilgrim's Progress*. He gulped it down in one sitting.

When they FaceTimed, Joan didn't dare tell him he'd be perfect playing the lead (named *Christian*, which she felt was another omen).

If that came to pass, it would be God's Will.

To her surprise, she *did* find herself asking if he'd ever written anything. Chris said he'd always wanted to but lacked the focus.

"*I'll* give you focus," she blurted out. "Write our fuckin movie for us!" She felt the wind knocked out of her by unseen forces. "God just told me to say that, Chris – I am dead serious. I'll give you all the time and help and resources you need. Jesus will too, 'cause as you know, He loves ya."

She knew by his smile that he would do it.

A L I

[*a vintage photo of the Smoke House*]
119,188 likes
alinell #tbt That night. That woman. This dream. Grammie (who looked more like Cloris Leachman than Cloris Leachman) took us to the Smoke House, in Burbank. Right across from the studio. Amazing 40s watering hole. Musso's in the Valley. Red booths and old waitresses. If you squint you'll see Glenn Ford. Orson and Rita. Abbot and Costello. We were celebrating because I'd just been cast as Sasha in *Arrested Development.* Grammie said, "Order anything, Miss *Sashay.*" So anything it was: fried onion rings, pork chops and a banana split. Like one of those last meal request prisoners give on Death Row – except I'd just gotten life. That

role handed me my life. (Such as it is.) (Back on Death Row
🙁.) (Oh well.) I remembered wishing my mother was there.
The next time I'd see her was in the mortuary in Oklahoma
City. This life. That woman. This dream. On that Smoke House
night, L.A. was burning. My 15-year-old self loved that it was
on fire. We had an old convertible. On the way back to our
Valley Village apartment – we'd moved from a motel called
The Virginia Starr – Grammie and I sang to the ashy wind.
Mom's favorite Peggy Lee. "What a lovely way to burn." And
all I could think was, Life will never get better than this. But
guess what it did. And does. And will. No matter what. (It
will because it's God's will.) Right NOW is the best there is.
"Right here, right now, there is no other place I want to be" –
thank you, Jesus! (And Jesus Jones.) RIGHT HERE RIGHT
NOW keeps getting better. This. Yes. This, right here. Right
now. So pass it forward, please, on this #tft (Throw Forward
Thursday). Because right now rightnow is all we have. All
we ever did. Or will. Or want. Or need. Ain't it grand?
G'night. #thepowerofnow #nowvoyager #smokehousenights
#feverdream #whatalovelywaytoburn #righthererightnow
#nootherplaceiwanttobe

View all 2,771 comments

anyataylorjoy you are my unicorn omg #throwfor-
wardthursday i LOVE
    alinell @anyataylorjoy love you, Magik. Through Time and
    Limbo. Crying because I couldn't do Te Deum with you...
patriciaarquette soooo beautiful. I want you to write a
book please. I have so many memories of the smokehouse, I
went there with my dad. I love you and thank you thank you
thank you for the gift of YOU.

alinell @patriciaarquette love YOU baby. want to read YOUR book too please

katherineschwarzenegger you are amazing. My heart breaks and breaks open. Thank you for teaching grace and giving us all God lessons.

alinell @katherineschwarzenegger such a lovely thing to say! smile-crying

adybarkan Rachael and I would love to buy you and Joan lunch if you're ever passing through Santa Barbara!

alinell @adybarkan omg SO honored. We will DEFINITELY take you up on that invitation! And THANK YOU for EVERYTHING you do re healthcare activism. I am halfway through audiobook of "Eyes to the Wind," SO amazing, you're a true warrior, I am learning so much from you, Ady!

ALSyoumetyourmatch yr hair in IG beach post? Wasn't sure but looked like dreads. if so, please STOP, (said with Love) ✦✦✦ yr courage shedding light on this terrible disease but Ali PLS stay in your cultural lane!!!

mamaoohmaomao @gwynethpaltrow Our #GOOPGLOW family just got a sibling, our incredible @ goop body luminizer it is AMAZING, it just gives your body a beautiful candle lit glow all day long and as always it's non-toxic and packed with beautiful ingredients so get those legs out. #goodcleangoop

saviour9617 {LEVITICUS} The Lord said to Moses, "Say to Aaron: 'For the generations to come none of your descendants who has a defect may come near to offer the food of his God. No man who has any defect may come near: no man who is blind or lame, disfigured or deformed; no man with a crippled... more

BUD

More than five years after the murders, and around the time the court definitively excluded him as a beneficiary of the Gamma Family estate trust, Bud stopped paying rent. It had been frozen at $1,300 a month for almost 30 years but the current outlay on drugs and scratchers made payment impossible. When he first moved in, the son of his Korean landlord was a shy, 15-year-old kid. The boy with the novelty name "Keith Moon" was in his forties now. He inherited the building when his mother died in 2011.

While Joan Gamma was duly ordained as the youngest, fattest pinup ever to grace the pages of Forbes' "The World's Billionaires," in a national sidebar of comic relief, Bud Wiggins, alternately the father, father-in-law and grandfather to the victims, got spoofed for his venal, thwarted efforts, and became fodder for talk shows. (Bill Maher called him "the Fifth Beatle, the Gamma family's own Pete Best.") The lapsed tenant hoped Keith Moon wasn't a news junkie, because for months he used clippings of the pending ruling to encourage his landlord to believe "big money" was on its way. To the casual reader, the articles implied that Mr. Wiggins was seriously in the running to reap tens of millions from the estate. The novelist made Keith a winking offer. "When I get the monies" – he always used the plural – "I'll take the whole building off your hands for three times the asking price, as a thanks for your kindness and patience. Only if you're interested, of course."

In March, three months of rent and goodwill to the wind, Moon pulled the rug out from under him. He stood at Bud's door and said, *The court denied you*, forcing the stoned scratcher-adept to do a song and dance.

"My team totally expecting that," said Bud. "That's the *game.* You get much more if you win on *appeal.* We wanted – *needed* this to go to appeal."

"I know you want to buy the apartment house," said Moon, with a sardonic smile. "Maybe I'll let you, Bud – *maybe.* We'll talk! If I *do* decide to sell, you'll just pay fair price. But until then… *try paying your rent!*"

Moon liked the old man as much as his mother had, but by July the unkempt tenant owed $9,100. This time when he knocked on the door, there was coldness in his eyes.

"*Man, you gotta move.*"

(He was *Man* now, and no longer had a name.)

Bud smiled and nodded, as if he'd been asked to bake a cake.

"I'm *serious,* man. You gotta fucking go!"

* * *

Dearest Manné,

Here's the promised excerpt from my "virtual memoir" (publisher's phrase) for Press Send Press. It's a dirty job but someone had to do it. (Apparently, lil ol' winemaker ME.) My working title: "Angel Investor" – which the pub HATES btw…

Under the mattress now, I can hear them being killed. My jeans are soaked in pee & just got my period. I was always so scared of monsters under the bed & now it's me: I'm my own monster now. I lie here thinking of the Auden poem, "Night Mail": "Thousands are still asleep,/Dreaming of terrifying monsters/They continue their dreams/But shall wake soon & hope for letters/And none will hear the postman's knock/Without a quickening of heart/For who can bear to feel himself forgotten?" Well, Mr. Auden, I'm not sure I'll "wake soon" – if only I <u>was</u> dreaming – the screams of my mother and father & brother only seem to make me fall deeper into sleep. If police <u>or</u> postman finally knock (please let it be the police) I hope I can stay here, forgotten – yes, Sir Auden, <u>for-gotten</u> – until I vanish into the molecules of the floor like "The Incredible Shrinking Man-Girl"* [there's MORE, Manny – SEE ATTACHED PAGES]

*I'm doing my research – read a recent interview where Joan said "The Incredible Shrinking Man" was one of her favorite flicks.

* * *

Buddy-Boy,

I read the long excerpt, with interest.

Putting on my Editor Hat, I'd say it's a tad phoned in. And I wondered as I read, <u>Whose voice is this</u>? How old was your granddaughter when this happened? 13? The pee&period stuff (& are you <u>really</u> going to use ampersands?) seems cutesy-precocious-crude? Her family's being slaughtered close by, and it's reminding her of... Auden? Really? Somehow I don't think so, Bud. I was expecting/hoping for you to set the scene – would like to see Joan and the others <u>before</u> the terrible Main Event. Are you rushing through because the content is too personal/painful?

Please enlighten, if you can...

Putting on the <u>FRIEND</u> hat – I know things have been dodgy financially, but there <u>must</u> be another way. There's something <u>unsavory</u> – please forgive, Bud, but my heart's in the right place, it always has been when it comes to Things Wigginsian – there's something bad-faithy about this particular archaeological dig. It seems to me that even in my ripe old age and obsolescence I could make a few calls, and maybe, just *maybe* – with a submitted 50 pages of your best – secure a decent advance on the Bev Hills/Dolly memoir – weren't you calling it *Confessions?* Seem to also remember an alt-title too, *The Sorrows of Old Wiggins* (?) – that I know you've been working on for a hundred years. Now, <u>those</u> are the pages I'd like to see. You DID send me some chapters long ago and they absolutely blew me away (don't have access up here to my archives): if memory serves, they were lyrical, and astonished. It seemed to me then (and most likely now, if I could get another gander) that they went beyond <u>anything</u> in "Wild Psalms" – which is saying a <u>lot</u>, my beloved, talented friend...

But I hate to rain on your parade, as cash was already advanced and I know you're sorely in need, and in need of guidance.

I sympathize, believe me, with your pecuniary plight. Been there done that, oh boy have I, and it's only recently that I've managed to see myself clear. (Clarice's incurred medical debt almost put the final nail in my coffin as well.) The task at hand, as I see it, is to get your sun out of eclipse. I want it to shine in the sky and on all the waters (and Kindles and iPads) of Amerika and Earth. Because <u>that's</u> the real you: the old-young Master who wrote with marvelous outrage and towering elegance about that tough old broad we knew by the name of Dolly Wiggins.

May I paraphrase Clarice Starling? (Just watched "Silence of the Lambs" for the ten-thousandth time.) "You see a lot, don't you, Bud? Why don't you turn that high-powered perception at yourself and tell us what you see – or maybe you're afraid to."

So... wouldst thou give my modest proposal some thought?

Do refresh my memory if you're able, and send the pages re Dolly, or <u>anything else</u> from the mem. It'd give this editor – this <u>friend</u> – great pleasure to revisit.

With all respect, THAT is where your genius shines.
Manny

* * *

Bud went looking in his computer to retrieve what Manny asked for.

Of course, he was right.

The poetic, brutally candid "confessions" were what he *should* be working on – not some petty, *phoned in*, blood money bullshit. He found the old file and began to go through it. He read the forgotten chapters with a serene detachment and pleasure. And was moved, because it felt as if he were reading the work of an author whose voice he extolled.

One of the sections was particularly evocative. After Dolly passed away, he began to have a recurring dream that she was back, tucked away in her shabby south of Wilshire apartment, waiting for him. He bridled, in panicky impotence. *But how can it be she's still here? And why haven't I gone to see her?* The dream was suffused with a strange, poignant melancholy. It was so real that each time, Bud resolved to rush over.

Yet never arrived.

In the middle of his meditations, as in the Auden poem, the postman *did* knock, in a sense – a neighbor appeared at the front door with a misdelivered letter. Bud thanked her. He sat on the couch and stared at the envelope, trying to decipher its meaning.

The letter was from the State Controller.

Bad news – the government was dunning him for money.

He took the bill by the horns and tore it open:

A check for $5,000.

He'd completely forgotten about the scratcher win.

To celebrate, he snorted a Ritalin pill he found under the stove a few days ago.

Bud was elated. He'd give the money to the landlord – it wouldn't make him current but would definitely stall his threatened eviction from the Fountain Capri. He concocted a story for Moon that the estate decided not to fight the appeal. Opposing counsel had reached a settlement – millions were forthcoming. In good faith, the executor sent *monies* to make Bud "whole," partial reimbursement for the cash he spent on food, gas and miscellany during the prolonged deliberations. Then he had a better idea: give Moon *half* and try his luck with scratchers. When he got another big win, he'd pay the balance of the rent *and* fill the larder with a month-long stash of Adderall, Vicodin and coke. (It'd been months since he treated himself to coke.) He would get to work finishing the *Confessions*. In the meanwhile, Manny would make a deal with Random House, maybe even Knopf, based on pages already written.

He'd put the whole shitty, schlocky debacle of the book about his granddaughter aside, and pay back PSP with his new advance.

In his daily "research" on Joan, he came across an online *Vanity Fair* piece that described the offices of her new production company.

"7000 Romaine" was the storied building once owned by Howard Hughes. The check from the Controller was a sign for him to act on an impulse he'd been mulling. It was time now and felt right.

What did he have to lose?

He showered and took a Lyft ride over.

JOAN

She was manic and should FaceTime Pietra before things got out of hand.

It probably didn't help that the 15-foot high commissioned painting by Kehinde Wiley of Greta Thunberg holding a SKOLSTREJK FÖR KLIMATET placard glared down at her as Joan sat at a Rick Owens petrified black wood desk. The zealot's virtuous, incorruptible stare seemed particularly unforgiving, like a Grimms' Fairy Tale goblin – "my Gammagoblin" – admonishing the heiress's aberrant desires. A smaller portrait of Chris Pratt as Star-Lord (a Shepard Fairey) beamed temperately from another wall, providing balance if not pardon.

Lately, her fantasies around Greta, Millie and Billie were in overdrive. She told herself the sexual frenzy was a result of repressed dividends paid on the principal – Ali Nell. Joan showered the hobbled actress with money, not kisses, because having her advances rejected would be emotionally unendurable. *That's* what made her libido go wonky... still, the excuse was (mostly) a lie. The heart wants what it wants and what Joan's heart wanted was white-wedding-witch virgins.

She'd already reached out to Greta's mom, a stunning-looking opera singer who looked like she stepped out of a Bergman film and was famous in her own right. Joan offered to fund a nonprofit of Greta's choice with an initial $20 million contribution. She hadn't yet heard back – Team Greta was notoriously protective, predictably in the midst of giving Joan a deep vetting. Apart from the magnanimous, no-strings gift, she couldn't help believe that being orphaned by her family's murder was a real plus; research would reveal that Joan was endlessly dragged through the mud of the Internet, just as Greta had been for her idiosyncratic, spectrum-y passions. (She hoped the pigtailed prodigy of the North would relate.) Joan watched a show where Amy Schumer talked about her husband being on the autism spectrum and how his disorder made him incapable of lying. In a flight of fancy, Joan imagined marrying Greta then double-dating – two wild women and their tell-no-lie idiot savant spouses.

She stopped daydreaming long enough to book a FaceTime session with her shrink. She made a few more calls, arranging for a specialist to do a deep dive into Ali's strange new dermatological symptoms. It was hard to focus, so she went back to reading an article about Kanye.

He was always talking about how being bipolar was his superpower. When Greta said in an interview that Asperger's was *her* superpower, Joan wondered, *Hmmm. Then what the fuck is mine?* Gaining 400 pounds then losing it? Check. *Family being murdered?* Check. *Coveting bodies of underage white girls?* Checkmate. Kanye was saying in the interview that his wife was addicted to true crime shows – which made total sense, because Joan had a feeling that Kimmy was stanning her from the day they first met. KK'd probably watched the 4,000 dramatizations that sprung up in the wake of the Holmby Hills Massacre.

Back to her reading: Kanye was #3 on the Forbes "Richest Entertainers" list, right behind Kylie and Taylor Swift. When it was announced, the TV anchor said, "Congratulations to all!" – like someone just had a baby. She clicked a link in the article and watched a video of him crouching at the center of a mandala made from all the sneakers he ever designed, a thousand husks in varying stages of evolution arranged in a circle. Standing in the midst of what he called his "miniature vehicles," he actually compared himself to Picasso. He said each prototype had a spirit, as if they were sentient beings. An emperor clown – *so* fuckin' silly. Of the gazillion other things he was doing, Kanye was developing shelters for the *unhoused*, weird, beehivey structures with sky-domes for healing light to pour in. "Everyone needs to live in a James Turrell!" he shouted. The man who designed his own home as a monastery, an alabaster altar of wabi sabi porn, was busy creating auteur shit-closets for rough sleepers to park their stinky, schizoid asses.

She laughed to herself and said out loud, "Guess I must have a thing for Kanye. Maybe *that's* the one I should marry."

* * *

Chris Pratt was hard at work on the screenplay and loving it.

Joan reread the "Palace Beautiful" section of *The Pilgrim's Progress,* where the four virgins – Discretion, Prudence, Piety and Charity – weaponize Christian for his journey through the

Delectable Mountains to the Celestial City. She decided that Discretion was Greta ("Stoic" was more accurate); Prudence was Billie (because she kept her body hidden away); Piety was Millie (whose euphoric purity always prevailed, sometimes annoyingly) – and Charity was... Joan.

She would give them everything, to make herself worthy and atone for her sins. Her love would be unconditional, unpolluted, free of the filth of physical desire. But was that really possible?

Maybe she needed to join a Topanga Ayahuasca group, something that Ali talked about wanting to do before she "left the planet." Or get shot up with Ketamine until her licentious brain got broken...

During these jangled reflections, an assistant called. There was a man in the lobby who claimed to be "a relation." He gave his name as Bud Wiggins. Joan peered at the painting of Greta, for counsel; the Scandinavian scold dared her to do the right thing – the *Christian* thing.

The painting of *Chris the Lord* did the same, though with tenderness.

"It's fine," said Joan. "Let him come up."

* * *

Her grandfather looked haggard and grotty.

Joan hadn't seen him since he trespassed the memorial; his janky looks startled. The black-and-white image she still carried with her was the author photo of *Wild Psalms*, when Grandpa was thirty years younger – at least. After Vi's death, she was surprised to find a copy of the novel in her mother's private library, hiding in plain sight.

He made pro forma apologies "for the ambush, which wasn't my intent," and then his face collapsed in snorting tears. Joan's lip began to quiver as her own scaffolding unexpectedly tumbled. A picture of the two could have been plucked from any daytime television show's saccharine reunion episode. Joan's outburst was more restrained yet still impressive. A tandem summer storm thunderclapped the room, surprising them both.

"Oh Jesus! Jesus! Jesus!" he shouted, in-between tremors that shook his whole body. "Joanie, you have made this old man very, very happy! You can throw me out of your office now – "

"I'm not gonna throw you out. *Yet*."

He guffawed. "Thank you, thank you, *thank you*, Joanie! Thank you, *Joan*... God oh God, I feel like 10,000 pounds was lifted off my chest! Hoo hoo! Am I dreaming? This is *everything* – I ever wanted. It's *all* I wanted..."

She handed him a box of Kleenex. He blew his nose, dabbed his eyes, and looked around as if he'd just landed on the moon.

"You know, I'm pretty sure... I think I actually used to have an *office* in this place – back when someone thought *Wild Psalms* would make a good movie. We know how *that* turned out! But, *yes* – I *remember* – this used to be a real, old-fashioned *writers* building..."

He began a long coughing jag.

Wincing concern, she finally said, "Gramps, you okay?"

He smiled at the endearment. "I'm just getting over a bronchial thing – seem to get clobbered twice a year. It's *stubborn*, takes a few rounds of antibiotics to get over. Augmentin – 875 milligrams, twice a day for two weeks. And steroids! Which do a number on your tummy, not to mention kidneys and liver. My creatinine's been through the roof." She handed him Evian and urged him to drink. "Listen, Joan, I wanted – I need to make amends. About all the legal... *nonsense.*"

"There's no need – "

"No no no, there *is,* indulge me, let's clear the air and *talk about it,* so we *never have to again.* I got – I was a little bit *crazy.* I never – *cared* about the goddam money, you need to know that, Joan! You need to *believe* it. I *never* cared – and oh God, I don't know what Vi told you through the years. I don't know if I *want* to know! That's what's so hard – to – just – I guess all that folderol was a sadly misplaced, *destructive* way of getting your attention. And for that, I'm so sorry. Forgive me! Oh God, you had enough terrible things to deal with, and I was just... adding myself to that godforsaken list. I was out of my mind! You know, the *simple* and *awful* and *tragic* thing was, all I wanted was to say, 'Look at me! Over here! I'm your grandpa! I *exist.*' Which is to say it was a perverse and *unforgiveable* way of reaching out – to *you*... because your mother shut me out of her world so completely, and I – "

"It's okay! It's okay, Bud. And by the way I had nothing to do with all that – the fucking 'estate.' I was just struggling to keep my head above water. It was a *monolith*, a *machine*, and they pretty much kept me shielded from everything, that was their *job*, or at least they thought it was – to 'protect' me. Ha! Not just from you... I do think now it was probably kind of necessary – *then*. I fired them all! But I've been thinking – that's why it's kind of amazing that you showed up – I've been thinking I really want to undo some of that... damage. That it's time."

He hung his head like an exhausted crusader, humbled by the long, nearly fatal journey to his Maker. He dared not imagine what she would propose, for if it was what he hoped for, he might die on the spot.

"Are you writing? Are you writing, Bud?"

"Thank you for asking! Yes – yes, I'm writing. It's the only thing that keeps me sane. I've been working on a memoir."

"That's right, you mentioned that in your note."

" – mostly about my mother, Dolly. Your great-grandma*ma*."

"I was so sorry we never met."

"You have the exact same eyes and mouth."

As Bud spoke, a bothersome, alternate truth simmered below the surface. He knew that Joan's eventual awareness of the exploitation book – should the news come from anyone but him – would erase all good will and potential windfalls. His only way out was to throw himself at her feet and make full penance. He must confess that the contract was signed in a fit of poverty and rage. He'd explain how he spent the paltry advance on food and rent, and ask for a loan to pay the publisher back so that he could extricate himself from bondage and feel human again.

Like a *grandfather* again…

Instead, he dissociated, listening to the faraway babble of his own voice riffing on the book he was writing about his mother. Which led to Bud to speak of his first wife – Joan's grandmother, Cora, whom she knew nothing about. Bud and Cora met when he was 26. He was driving a limo and took the 17-year-old and some of her girlfriends to their prom.

"That night, your mother was conceived in the backseat."

"Oh my God, that's amazing."

"She was from Pacoima and I was a Westside boy. We got married. Vi was ten-years-old when her mother died."

"How?"

"Aneurysm."

"It's crazy that Mom never told me any of that."

Bud shook his head and shrugged.

"Vi stayed with me until she was, oh, about 15. Then *bam* one day she was gone. Lived in a commune up north, I think. Didn't hear from her till she was 20, when she called to say she was marrying your dad."

He started coughing again, but quietly, as if it were a cover for having run out of things to share.

"Do you need anything, Bud? Do you need money?"

"No! No – I'm fine. *That's not why I'm here!* I'm totally fine." Again, he dissociated, eavesdropping on his voice as if it he was in an adjacent room. "The folks publishing my memoir gave me a healthy advance – not as healthy as my advances *used* to be! But more than adequate. They're very excited about the pages. They even hired my old editor from Random House! He came out of retirement to work with me on the book."

"That's wonderful." She sat beside him. "Can I be frank about something?"

"Of course," he said, too eagerly, trying not to look paranoid.

"Whatever happened between you and Mom... *personally,* I don't want to live with that kind of energy. I'm really glad you came. The timing's kinda spooky. And look, I don't know what kind of health insurance you have – is it Writer's Guild? Medicare? – but if you need a check-up, if you need to go away for a while to a... *wellness* place – like the Golden Door – or *rehab*, wherever, I'm totally happy to help. Okay?"

He was trembling; it was too much. She put an arm around him.

"Thank you," he stammered.

"You're my freaking *grandfather,* okay? Right? I wouldn't *be* here without you. So, let's try and put all this bullshit behind us. Cause that's what it is, just bullshit. I think we can. Right? Don't you?"

ALI

Even during the siege of alarming changes to her body – daily, hourly, sometimes minute-to-minute – she was grateful. Truly, the universe had lifted her up to the skies. It had given her Joan – precious Joan! – whose job it was to breathe life into her, to cajole and resuscitate, to tug on the string of the red balloon, keeping Ali closer to Earth, if just for awhile.

One windblown Sunday at the end of a long, blindfolded drive, Joan wheeled her from the van, and when the Mardi Gras masque lifted, there it was:

Sharon Osbourne's Point Dume house, with its lullaby hammock, "black roses" and foamy, roaring sea. She'd wrapped a ginormous black satin ribbon around that healing house.

"It's your forever home," said Joan, presenting her with the deed. It was in Ali's name. "No one can take it away from you."

The red balloon wept for three days.

So many blessings!

Two million followers on Instagram now, triple the number she had before announcing her disease. *And* co-producing a movie that would honor Grammie's memory!

How was any of it possible without God's will and His grace?

She resolved anew to take the good with the bad, because both were manifestations of His will.

* * *

A glittery carapace covered her lower back and a small crater on her right buttock refused to heal. One of the doctors called it a "decubiti," typical of overused injection sites. "There's probably a Cracker Jack prize at the bottom," said Joan. (*What would I do without this woman to make me laugh?*)

Yet the most astonishing revelation came from a new man on the medical totem pole. The delightfully named Dr. Pirouette was beginning to believe Ali had been misdiagnosed. He was pursuing a hunch that she was in the throes of a "nasty little chameleon" that mimicked ALS.

Translation (at least, to Joan and Ali): *not a death sentence.*

The perspicacious Dr. P, a fellow at the Harvard Department of Stem Cell and Regenerative Biology in Cambridge, had already made breakthroughs in the study of the protein TDP-43 and how it binds to RNA. In just a week's time, he mixed a "cocktail" that allowed Ali to walk a half-hour each day without wheeled assistance. Part-corticosteroid, part-synthetic amphetamine, it improved her mood, boosting Joan's as well.

* * *

[*Ali managed a charming, herky-jerky dance when Ellen introduced her, not even needing to use her cane until the very end. The Ellen Show audience was on its feet, caterwauling in delight, emotional, clapping and shrieking their approval*]

ELLEN: Well, *you've* had an amazing few months.

ALI: Oh my God, yes!

ELLEN: And things continue to get more... amazing. I think most of us know what happened – what's *been* happening – but for those who don't, can you tell us what's been going on?

ALI: Yes! Okay. It's a long and winding road!

ELLEN: Take your time. But be brief. [*laughter*] I'm kidding.

ALI: I haven't – I hadn't been *feeling* well, for... about two years.

ELLEN: Two years, wow. And you'd been having symptoms –

ALI: Yes.

ELLEN: Because most of us would have gone to the doctor. Did you? Did you go to the doctor?

ALI: Not for a while – I waited much longer than I should have. And – a lot of the symptoms were – confusing. You know, I'd get so *tired*... but I thought, "Oh, that's just because I've been working so much." So, I pushed away any – I just think I was in denial. And really scared! Because I knew something was seriously wrong.

ELLEN: What kind of symptoms did you have?

ALI:	Fatigue. I mean, *extreme*. And numbness, what they call neuropathy.
ELLEN:	So when you finally got the diagnosis – of ALS – when did –
ALI:	In January. And part of me was, *Oh no.* Because "ALS" – those letters strung together – that's just something you never want to hear. Because, you know, I'd been thinking it was Lyme or Parkinson's or maybe even MS. And I'd also been having these weird *outbreaks* –
ELLEN:	Oh wow.
ALI:	– on my skin and the doctors thought it was a kind of psoriasis. So for a while they were thinking it was psoriatic arthritis, which is the worst kind. You can die from it.
ELLEN:	Wow.
ALI:	…but I was actually – when they said it was ALS, a part of me was actually *relieved.*
ELLEN:	Because they finally had a name for what you had.
ALI:	*Yes.* And I thought, "Okay. I'll deal." Whatever's coming, I'll deal.
ELLEN:	So you decided to share your journey with the world… and did an amazingly courageous thing. You announced it on Instagram.
ALI:	Yes.
ELLEN:	Which I think is amazing. Because by making a very private, personal issue *public,* you've helped so many people face their own fears, whatever those fears may be. But the Internet can be a scary place. The trolls and the bullies –

ALI: It *can*, and I've had my share. But I've always
       tried to have compassion for those people.
       They must be suffering, they must have terri-
       ble wounds to lash out that way. [*applause*] But
       I think, just, that most of me thought, "Girl,
       you *already* have ALS." How much worse could
       it be?" So when a troll says, "Hey, rich celeb-
       rity, just die already," I just clap back and say,
       "That's the plan! It's God's plan for *all* of us, so
       why don't you just *chill* and be *nice*?'" [*laughter,
       ovation*]

ELLEN: You're amazing. How many followers do you
       have?

ALI: I just crossed two million this morning.
       [*whoops, applause*] It's *crazy*.

ELLEN: And you brought some people with you today.
       Your posse.

ALI: They're amazing. Ripley's here – he's my BFF.
       And Joan – Joan Gamma, who's been so much
       in my corner. [*applause*] She saved my life –
       what's left of it! [*groans, laughter*] Joan's help
       funding my medical journey. She's giving so
       much now, not just to ALS research, but to a
       whole panoply – did I say that word right? – a
       whole ****load of research into what they call
       "orphan" diseases. [*laughter at the bleeped word*]

ELLEN: I think I liked panoply better, even if you said
       it wrong. [*laughter*] Actually, the proper pro-
       nunciation of panoply *is* ****load. [*audience
       laughs, whoops*] Now, a little birdie told me you

	have a very special new friend hiding out in the Green Room.
ALI:	Chris Pratt... [*whoops, applause*] – and his amazing, beautiful wife Katherine. I've been to church with Chris and that's been *amazing* for me. He just signed up with us – with me and Joan – on a secret project we're doing...
ELLEN:	For Marvel? [*audience whoops*] Because I heard they're rebooting my favorite show *Te Deum* [*whoops, applause*], and –
ALI:	No, not *Te Deum*. But I can't... really... *talk* about it. Joan said I'll get in trouble if I do!
ELLEN:	Well, we wouldn't want that. I wouldn't want to get you in trouble with Joan. [*looks at note-card*] Before the show, you told me you had something you wanted to share...
ALI:	Yes. It's kind of amazing – and scary, too. Through the research of amazing doctors and scientists at Johns Hopkins and the Mayo, I've just learned that I may not have ALS. [*audience gasps*]
ELLEN:	Wait – what? –
ALI:	They think I *may* have some as-yet unclassified disease process that sort of... *mimics* ALS, but with a – a totally different trajectory... it's too early to tell, but –
ELLEN:	Is that *good*? It sounds like *good* news.
ALI:	It *may* be...
ELLEN:	I mean, if there's a chance this won't end where you've been thinking it would – because in one of your Instagram posts, you wrote beautifully

about Stephen Hawking, and how you feared that –

ALI: It's too soon. The doctors just don't yet know. But they're amazing. They said we're in deep waters, that's actually how they put it. So, there's uncertainty for me again – which I've kind of been living with. But I'm trying to have hope. In some ways, I'm right back to where I was before the diagnosis – of ALS – and I'm always trying to lower my expectations...

[Suddenly, a collective gasp from the audience is followed by shocked screams and applause. The camera follows Ali and Ellen's swiveling heads to reveal Billie Eilish, sheepishly entering stage left. In her excitement, Ali wobbles as she struggles to stand as Ellen and Billie rush to steady her. Billie and Ali embrace. Ovation and applause continue.

Moments later, the audience roars as Chris Pratt enters, stage right.]

B U D

He phoned Manny for the first time since they'd been back in touch, not only to share the shocking "family news" – his rapprochement with Joan – but to formally announce his determination to abandon the pulpy "reimagination" book and jump headlong into finishing *My Confessions*.

His editor didn't pick up.

Bud lay in bed, feeling like he was on an ecstatic holiday. The hallucinatory outcome – his granddaughter's improbable peace offering – erased the trauma of the last five years. Replaying their meeting in his head, he was embarrassed by her mention of rehab. Bud pledged to get clean, or cleaner anyway, and hatched a game plan. He would draft a proposal to Joan for an advance (not a handout) in the amount of, say, $250,000 – maybe three-fifty, he needed to think about it – *whatever* the amount, it had to be a number that seemed plausible in regards to allowing him to comfortably finish his memoir.

He looked in the mirror. His skin was wan; the platysmal bands of his neck made him look like a cartoon buzzard. The years of snorting pills had left his nose in the early stages of collapse.

Fuck that – with a little bone from the rib, a little bone from the ear, the docs on Botched *could fix that in about three seconds.*

He sat on the toilet, dumbstruck by a Lightbulb Moment: he would send Joan excerpts of the *Confessions*, so she could feel "a part of" – and begin to comprehend the scope and beauty of his remembrances. She might even see a lot of herself in him, learning much about her great-grandmother Dolly and grandma Cora along the way. Joan wanted to make movies, didn't she? Which meant she wanted to be *artist*. Of sorts… she was still so young, still finding her way. By reading his work, she'd gain respect for her lineage. For he, Bud Wiggins, her grandfather, *was* an artist, the real deal, and it was only fitting she would be his Medici. Time for Bud to widen the vista.

Keep your critics close, and your family closer.

Emboldened by Manny's enthusiasm, he'd already sent excerpts to two old friends – Wylann Partland and Digby Colt.

He met Digby, heir to a parking garage dynasty, in his late twenties. Bud had been mailing around his grim, type-written short stories of Hollywood to a small tribe of friends when Digby suggested they publish them on desktop. The end result was the elegant chapbook, *Wild Psalms,* that put Bud "on the map." (The collection was the kernel that later became the novel.) It was decades since they'd spoken. Bud did some googling – remarkably, Digby was still knocking around the Business, haunting its fringe like a loser emeritus. He was born rich and didn't profit from his hobbies: mentoring film students (prickly, washed-out millennials of bespoke, TBD gender) and guesting on expired or broken-linked podcasts. Old Digby was still in the game! Spreading sterile seeds of wisdom, hard-won by a "producer" now approaching his 40th anniversary of tilting at pretentious, eclectic, dead-in-the-water windmills.

Bud had a second brainstorm.

Why not have Digby publish the *Confessions,* as he had the original fables? It'd be a marvelous, come-full-circle hook for press interviews.

He reached out to the contact provided on IMDB. When they finally spoke, Digby was a little guarded, but that was just his Waspy way – the bland default of entitled condescension. He blathered about how the world had changed and he knew nothing about the "marketplace," let alone book distribution (not that he ever did). Back then, the luck and bravura of youth was on their side. Still, it was lovely to be in touch again, to feel the warmth of those days of wine and roses. At last, Digby mustered some excitement and said, "Send me those pages!"

Then there was Wylann Partland.

Before she was a bestselling author and critics' darling, Wylann was a wealthy sitcom writer – and great champion of *Wild Psalms*. Her insecurities and ditsy personality masked a fierce ambition and rigorous, willful intellect. When Bud's novel came out, she threw a lavish party for him at her Bel-Air home, and a *second* party celebrating John Updike's review of *Psalms* in *The New Yorker*. Years later, when the release of her own fiction was regularly featured on the cover of *The New York Times Book Review*, Wylann gave interviews where she generously acknowledged that she "owed my career to Bud Wiggins." *He* was the one who first encouraged her, she said – an assertion whose proof Bud couldn't recall.

After Manny's paean to the lost pages of *Confessions*, Bud got in touch with Wylann to see if she'd be open to throwing a blurb his way. It was premature, of course, but the promise of an endorsement from Wylann Partland would not only be an ego-boost, adding fuel to the creative fire, but certainly help Manny in his cause to rouse a six-figure book deal back East.

She was delighted to hear from him ("*Oh my God*, I'm in the middle of a tour and not talking to *anyone*. But when my assistant told me *Bud Wiggins* was calling, I…") and genuinely thrilled he was working on something new. "It's been way too long," she said. "I *love* it."

She told him to email the excerpts forthwith.

"I will devour them!"

He felt like the old maestro again.

* * *

Because he had no money in the bank, he endorsed the $5,000 State Controller check to Garry Gabe, who cashed him out.

Garry was enchanted by the story of Bud's reconciliation with his granddaughter. Whenever they were face to face, though, he worried about his dilapidated-looking old friend. He found himself engaged in a constant internal negotiation as to whether he should offer Bud A) a job; B) money; C) permanent residency in the garage apartment of a rarely visited home on North Bedford (Garry preferred the beach house and the ranch in Ojai); or, D) all the above. After all, they were brothers. As Bud related details of the reunion with Joan – and the renewed vow to complete his long-abandoned "memory book" – Garry's worry lines crinkled into a smile. He *wanted* to say something about Bud's health, *wanted* to Jewish mother him and shout, *Please take care! And stop doing whatever it is that I think you may be doing!* but decided it could wait. The man came bearing good news and Garry didn't want to rain on his parade.

* * *

On the way home, Bud stopped at his dealer – a Koreatown pharmacy that dispensed in bulk, off the books.

He drove to a cavernous liquor store on Sunset, a kind of lottery clearinghouse; the city was dotted with places like that. Aside from the stacks of tickets displayed behind the counter, it housed a dozen industrial-sized vending machines. Throngs of poor people clustered at the myriad grimy counters, scratching away.

After buying the pills and treating himself to a hundred-dollar lunch at the downtown Pacific Dining Car, he still had forty-five hundred in twenties left from the wad Garry advanced him. He immediately bought three $20 Monopoly scratchers, two of which were losers. When he scratched the last, instead of a number it said GO – an instant $200 payback. He took it as an omen to play his favorite, a $20 game called Big Win. On the left of the ticket were eight "lucky numbers" – and 25 on the right that were their potential matches. All 25 numbers had a different "win" amount. (The lottery geniuses only printed *four* Big Win tickets – each returned $5 million – but the odds scratching a big boy were three-million-to-one.) Above the two groups of "lucky" and potential "matching" numbers was a little WIN ALL BONUS window – if you scratched it and the words BIG WIN were underneath, you won every single prize that was listed beneath each of the 25 numbers on the right side of the ticket. He'd played the game hundreds of times and never scratched off a BIG WIN, and never expected to. The probability was so unlikely that Bud never focused on it, often retrieving a losing ticket from the trash because he'd forgotten to give the BIG WIN window a cursory, futile scratch.

Bud bought two tickets and lost.

Then another two and lost.

Then another two and lost.

In his experience, it was unusual to lose six times in a row.

Usually with six bets you'd at least win even money on *one*; the odds were in your favor, "Gambler's Fallacy" be damned. In a rare fit of prudence, Bud decided to fold his cards and leave. But on the way out, he put $40 in a vending machine and bought a $30 ticket called $10,000,000 Bankroll – plus a ten-dollar called Precious Diamonds.

In another fit of prudence, he didn't bother scratching the tickets on the hood of his car but drove off instead.

A few blocks later, he pulled over.

Precious Diamonds was a loser – but Bankroll returned $500.

Oh, that was *very* good.

The State Lottery website said the odds of a $500 win on that particular scratcher were 300-to-1.

He had an ironclad rule: whenever he won $100 or more on a single scratcher, he'd stop playing for the day. He was already in violation yet had profited by $500.

Sometimes it paid to go outside of the law.

He decided to cash the ticket then see how he felt. Usually, only the bigger grocery stores had enough cash on hand to pay out a $500 win. He went to a Pavilions in West Hollywood. They were used to big winners and didn't bat an eye. It was like visiting the cashier of a Vegas casino.

Now he had close to 5K in his pocket – after the pills and the Dining Car, scratchers had made him whole.

He decided he'd buy a few more Big Wins and call it a day.

But not at Pavilions – the vibe didn't feel right. He'd find an obscure gas station. Maybe even fill up the tank while he was at it. Two birds. He always seemed to have better luck when he filled up the tank.

He found a shitty Sinclair station way down on Olympic and bought two Big Wins and scratched the window on both. He was stunned. Underneath one of the little portals, it said...

BIG WIN

He couldn't believe what his eyes were telling him, but there it was:

He had won all 25 "matching" numbers.

Bud's heart began to hammer.

He was shaking so much that he didn't scratch off any of the twenty-five individual dollar-amounts to see what he had won. Instead, he scratched the bar code at the bottom and walked over to scan the ticket at the machine. He knew a "Big Win" didn't necessarily mean you'd won five million. It could be *one* million – or *two*.

Whatever it was, it had to be BIG.

He stood at the scanner, in a stinksweat – how much was he looking at? Bud downscaled expectations, thinking, *At the very least, it's a hundred thou.* In lightning speed, he saw himself at the Lottery Office, smiling for the camera like a cretin, holding one of those six-foot-long checks. He rehearsed what he'd do with five million... after taxes, say, it's four-and-a-half, maybe just four. He'd buy a house in Palm Springs – for a million dollars, you could get a Modernist palace. A few hundred thousand more, and you bought yourself a joint with Rat Pack provenance. He would finish *My Confessions*, writing in the evening as the desert winds gusted the palms and rippled the pool. He'd hire a doctor to monitor amphetamine and painkiller intake, to keep it copacetic. Invite his granddaughter for a weekend of bonding, without telling her how he got the money – only that he'd held onto his book earnings and invested them through the years...

He took a deep breath and prepared to slide the bar code under the scanner. Bud realized that he hadn't written his name on the back, which you were supposed to do if you won more than $500. He hoped he wouldn't pass out when he saw the amount confirmed onscreen. Whoever came to his aid might steal the ticket; if that happened, he hoped the security cameras were working.

The machine beeped, then read

You're a Winner!
$100

There was some mistake.

How could the "wins" of 25 numbers add up to $100?

He ran it under the scanner again... then scratched off one of 25 numbers. The prize was *three dollars*. He scratched another – $3 – and another – $3 – and another – *$10* – and another – *$10* – and another – $2...

It never occurred to him that a "win all" could be anything less a massive amount. But the Scratcher Gods were crafty; their algorithms, brilliantly maddening. For the average sap, the mischievous Ticket Imps thought a $100 return on a $20 ticket *was* a big win.

Disheartened, Bud tried looking on the bright side.

A win was still a win.

When he got home, a note was on the door.

It was from Moon.

Bud *planned* to give him twenty-five hundred in good faith – half the amount of the Controller check – but after the Big Win fiasco, he leapfrogged around the city, playing more scratchers. They got the better of him. By the end of the day, he only had $800 left.

He crushed some pills, gathering the powder with the folded scrap of paper that read

How can your furnishings/personal items still not be placed in storage? The sheriff comes tomorrow and you are OUT my friend. I am regretting to say

JOAN
[FaceTime]

JOAN – and he looked so – so thin and so sad, so, like – ruined. I mean, I swear I thought he was literally going to die! Right there on my couch!

PIETRA Because he hasn't taken care of himself...

JOAN Oh my God! Life has not been fucking kind! He was, like, full-on shaking. I think he probably couldn't believe I asked him up – you know, agreed to see him. Because – I guess there was still the threat of that stupid restraining order hanging over him or *whatever* Gestapo bullshit, and he probably thought I was gonna have him arrested!

PIETRA You felt compassion.

JOAN Plus – oh my God, Pietra, he's like a total, full-on drug addict!

PIETRA And how did it feel, to suddenly see him?

JOAN It was actually *weird* because I'd been *fantasizing* – I mean, since Chris kind of *shamed* me – haha! – by telling me that story of his dad... so I'd been thinking of reaching out to him. So when my assistant said he was suddenly in the lobby, I was, like –

PIETRA There was some synchronicity there.

JOAN *Totally*. But there was something so sweet and so sad and I felt *so bad* for him. For him, for me, for fuckin every-one... And before he left, I told him I'd help, you know, I said, "whatever you need." I even brought up rehab! I full-on brought it up! I said, "I'll send you to rehab."

PIETRA I think that's great, Joan. That kind of transparency. You let him know you weren't going to enable him. Where did you leave it?

JOAN I gave him my cell. I mean, he's blood, he's my fucking *papaw*. And the man is fucking *tired*. But I'm fuckin tired, too, right? I mean, I got played. Right? By the lawyers and all the fucking parasites who were so-called protecting me... from *who*, Pietra? A broken old man who also happens to be – *happened* to be a brilliant writer, a brilliant novelist? I mean, how pathetic is *that*? Is he really the fuckin villain of the story? Listen: my mother was fucking *nuts*. And I'm supposed to just blindly inherit whatever tangled web of shit she weaved? Well, no more. No fucking more. I might just drop some dollars on 'im – !

PIETRA Before you make a decision like that, let's talk about it firs –

JOAN – I *might* just fuckin do it, Pietra, I am fucking serious. And if I *do*, I'll structure it – you know, have someone oversee – so he can't go out and do whatever crazy shit he does... like, *overdose*. We wouldn't want Grandpa to O.D.! But, like, how long is he gonna live? Doesn't look like long to me! Not from where I'm sitting. Maybe I can give him a few more years. Improve his fucking lifestyle *quality*. He doesn't have anyone to take care of him... if I can get him back to his "fighting weight," you know, make him comfortable and remove some of the fucking stress... get him writing again. He *said* he was writing again, said he's working on a book about his – about *our* family – and it sounds *really fuckin' interesting*. The one thing my parents did, Pietra, the one thing they did that I totally *love* was pledging to give everything away before they died. Did you know I just signed that? Did I tell you I signed the same thing? I met with Mackenzie Bezos – *love* her – and signed the pledge. You can read it online. I'm gonna give everything away, all those fucking ill-gotten gains, and I've sure as shit already started. Millie Bobby Brown gets 5 million for a tortoise sanctuary. Billie Eilish, 25 million to seed a clothing company – she wants 100% of the profits will go to protect at-risk girls. And we're still trying to hammer out a thing with Greta Thunberg, whatever… so why would I *not* give my own grandfather a little something so he can get clean and sober and finish a book about *my* fucking family? And live out his remaining years with some degree of fucking peace and dignity?

PIETRA I think it's a noble pursuit. But let's just make sure that y –

JOAN And you know what? I know how to do this shit. I know how to *structure* it. I was *very* fucking thorough about cleaning house after all the estate shit… the executor tried to fuck me but I went full Thanos on him!

PIETRA I'm so proud of you for doing that – we've discussed it. That was great self-care.

JOAN There is *no* possibility, not *remotely,* of bullshit 5150s or court-ordered permanent conservatorships… I ain't fucking Britney, I'm Thanos. If they dare fuck with me, I snap my fingers and they disappear! Did you know Britney's dad won't let her have a *cellphone*? Hahaha! Well, fuck *him.* Britney and I need to have a little *heart-to-heart.* And you know what? I can burn my money if I want – give it to Steve fucking Bannon or give it to Dr. Now… give it to Britney or Scott fucking Disick, if I want… I can give it to whoever I –

PIETRA [*laughs but acknowledges the uptick in mania by asking:*] How's it going with the new meds?

JOAN – and there's not a fucking thing an executor or anyone can do!

PIETRA Have you seen Dr. Regis? Aren't you due?

JOAN End of the week.

PIETRA And how are you doing with the panic attacks.

JOAN Still happening. But I'm dealing with it.

PIETRA Give it a little time, Joan. The meds can take a moment. Give it some time. But the hour's up – let's talk on Wednesday.

* * *

Some things, she withheld.

Joan didn't tell Pietra the darker aspects of her enthrallment with the Squad – the fantasies of living in a sex commune with Millie, Billie and Greta after their parents had been bloodily dispatched (like Anya's, in *The Witch*) – thoughts that both aroused and tormented, and exacerbated to the point of frenzy when she heard Billie talk on Howard Stern about being "a sex animal." She couldn't share with her therapist those deep meditations on the swirls of hair on their bodies; the memorized freckles, moles, birthmarks and discolorations; the imagined rank, perfumey smells of yawns and holes. She daydreamt of joining Billie on world tour and having stolen make-out sessions in Tokyo and New Zealand, giggling when they were caught by her brother (who so didn't give a shit!)… on *Stranger Things* junkets with Millie, in Australia and the Midwest… of sweaty fumblings with Greta in the dark while on plush sofas of electric busses heading to climate conferences in Lausanne – nor could she mention being stuck in a Thai cave with her Three Virgins, talking them down from despair like a mama bear as the four awaited rescue by scuba-diving medics who soon would come with ampoules of

Versed and Propofol, forcing unconsciousness, binding them together in leather straps, carefully maneuvering the wet, mummified sleeping beauties through oh-so-tight underwater passageways.

Another reverie: with Greta now, in the ancient woodland of Germany's Hambach, Joan at her side as they protested against open-cast mining. Living in a fifty-foot high treehouse, they became human shields, effectively blocking interlopers. (Joan struggled to keep their intimacies to mere mouth kisses.) Sometimes the fantasies took a Michael Jackson Neverland riff, the parents sanguine and pragmatic instead of creepily complicit. *Our daughter loves you and we want her to be happy,* a mom would say. *And we've come to love you as well. That's why we're encouraging you both to have a physical relationship (which, by the way, is legal in the principality you've flown us to) before making a commitment.* How could Joan shut down her brain and stop these travesties?

There was more behind it than moral revulsion. Worse, was the sense that when Joan directed her energy to the Trinity, it was a betrayal of Ali Nell – her beloved, her savior, the Madonna who'd shown her a way out of the maze of confined spaces before laying the stones of the yellow brick road that spiraled toward the Celestial City.

Unlike the others, Ali was *real*.

Ali was in front of her.

It was *Ali* whom the universe chose to be her mate.

Why do I fight it so? Why am I too cowardly to propose?

And yet –

What if the Internet uncovered her lurid agenda of "buying" the baby celebs of her fixation? She'd be labeled a trafficker – Ghislaine Maxwell's demonchild. She had already been vilified so much in her young life for things beyond her control – the murders, the fatness, the overall ugliness – to be judged, and *exposed* as a girl lover would be more than she could bear, even with the cracked shield of Dr. Regis' new drugs. Some of Joan's panic attacks grew horns of paranoia: Saudis using Israeli technology to burrow into her brain like they did Jeff Bezos's cellphone, beaming the hijacked, X-rated pedo-images to the world. That's why she was careful to burn her primitivist montages of the Squad, heads crudely cut and pasted onto bodies culled from her trove of vintage porn. (She never created anything digital, for fear of being hacked.) Joan knew that if she ended up in solitary, she wouldn't have the courage to end her life like Epstein. She couldn't help but think of Jeffrey as sinister uncle and dark overseer – Black Phillip, Anya's goat in *The Witch,* who, in the guise of handsome seducer, suddenly shows himself to be Satan. No, if she were confined to a cell for 23-hours a day, she'd go mad.

She felt the cold, somehow erotic sweat of confinement panic and knew that all the drugs in the world, all the SSRIs and SNRIs, Paxil, Pexeva and Effexor, all the Lithium, Abilify, Metformin, Depakote and Lamictal, all the benzos known to man would never be enough to quell her horror. The only solution was to waste away to "the infinitesimal" – to slip not just between the bars but dissolve into the molecules of the floor itself.

– to become the incredibly shrinking girl.

That way, no rock or underbed space, no jail or coffin cage could vanquish her.

ALI

[*a photo her and Joan at Disneyland*]

14,383 likes

alinell Thank you for the love (you know who you are) and always thank you thank you thank you to @theellen-show for letting me be me. You are always YOU, Elle, so kind and generous and down-to-earth, and we thank God for that. <3<3<3 And to all the haters (love you ANYWAY <3<3<3), all I can say is "the haters gonna hate hate hate hate hate." When I announced on Ellen that I may not have ALS it was not "strategic" but soulful/spontaneous. I am still very VERY sick and most of you reached out with your hearts. But it seems there will always be those who wish to tear down and shout FIRE! in a theater crowded with love. NOTHING has changed, my body is still alter-ing in scary ways, I am afraid every hour of every day – AND I am still a very proud spokesperson for ALS and many orphan diseases. My team's efforts are tireless and will not desist. All of the charities and nonprofit funding that @gammapledge @thezerofoundation @orphancurenow are involved have experienced an INCREASE in donations since @theellenshow appearance, helping thousands if not hundreds of thousands of those who are differently abled and/or challenged by ALS/MS/orphan/auto-immune/facial deformities. Please be kind to one another, it will come back to you like the BEST BOOMERANG EVER! And SO MANY thank yous to @ALSwarriors, @richwilersonjr @dawnchere @jacihermstad @nataliecweaver who talk the talk and walk the long walk/long climb. You remind me not to JUDGE because we are all going to the Celestial City (a beautiful journey we begin at birth), to the place where lovers, not haters thrive! Ms. Louisa May Alcott said it best: " 'Do you remember how you used to play Pilgrims Progress when you were little things? Nothing delighted you more than to have me tie my piece-bags on your backs for burdens, give you hats and sticks and rolls of paper, and let you travel through the house from the cellar, which was the City of Destruction, up, up, to the housetop, where you had all the lovely things you could collect to make a Celestial City.'" Remember always: LOVE IS THE ANSWER. And one day, there will be no questions!

View all 8,913 comments

dawnchere ✛✛✛✛✛ In Jesus FOR Jesus. Only Jesus gives us grace to weather our sorrows. Only Jesus allows us to rest in the eternal Mystery. Only Jesus can shelter us from the ignorant and assure their vanities will be lifted by GRACE. Ali, you're the best girl in town - keep living your best life IN and FOR Jesus! Xx

marvelstudios You ARE Melissa Eerie, every day, in every way! You will NEVER be defeated. All love, all the time, from your forever Marvel Family.

natalieportman ✛✛✛ the dogs bark but the caravan moves on. You are GOLDEN

mingey you've been such a TEACHER, you helped SO MANY. will be in Malibu next weekend & would love to see you and the faboo gammacadabra! Check yr DM

kenzoshmuckface fame whore I hope you DO have ALS and your paralyzed shit-breath ass stays alive and aware FORE VER , your NO GENIUS like Steve Hawking how DARE you place yrself in his company, instead of solving math/world problemz youll just lay in yr own feecees trying to remember

old Bachelor episodes, begging cris jenner to be your mama
& sucking on FATSO's TEATS you lying golddigging fucktwad
CUTN... more

statenislandgal SO many sick people on this thread,
please block! pray they can heal... more

drewbarrymore you got this warriorgirl. You GOT this
<3<3<3<3<3<3<3<3

911thewholetroof I WILL NEVER FORGET how you have
been a constant beacon and and source of light, you have
helped me thru so many dark nites of the soul!!!! still need to
be honest tho, was heartbroken you lied about ALS, please
tell us, is dr. merit cudkowicz at the healey center planning
to sue? (he could not be faulted.) You made millions off those
who loved and believed in you, thinking you had something
you clearly didn't... more

bigblakbutt do not listen to the childish haters!!! you are
Melissa Eerie. pelase get well so you can cameo on Te Deum.
calling all sorceresses, the world needs Melissa!!!!! me myself
and I am an proud afroamerican age 28 with scleroderma,
Currently confined to extension care facility in Daytona
Beach. can you send $$$ or some of the (to expensive for
me) GOOP cream I saw on your Insta... more

reesewitherspoon BRAVE✚ we NEED you in this world
NOW more than ever, NEVER stop, NEVER look back. You
belong to ALL of ... more

MAGAmaggot2020 liar liar DNA on fire! your billion$
brownnose longer than a telephon wire AND longer then
jussie smollets DICK hahahahah... more

rebeccagayheartdane My one and only. My hero. Love
you SO ✚✚✚

JOAN

She was carrying nearly 18 pounds of weight in the skin folds that now hung from her arms and gut. Soon she would undergo the same surgery her treasured *600-lb. Life* fatties had at the hands of Dr. Now. The dermis would be carved off then photographed on the stainless steel tables of the surgical suite like Buffalo Bill's pelts in *The Silence of the Lambs*.

None of the doctors knew how she managed to erase almost 250 pounds in three months, nor could they explain how her organs survived the rapid loss. (Social media accused her of wearing a fat suit all along.) Joan and Ali got hazed – the wacko, now fat-shaming "thrillionaire" and her washed-up consort, a Munchausen By Proxy tease who jacked up her IG numbers with bait-and-switch pity-parties. The narratives of the world were cheap, like colored glass in a toy kaleidoscope.

But as Joanie liked to sing to her love when the going got rough, *Nothing is real. And nothing to get hung about.*

"The maid was complaining of a smell," said Ali as Joan came into the bedroom. "She wears a mask now to work! She says it's for *me*, so I don't 'catch' anything, but I know it's the smell. They're *all* starting to wear masks – "

"You're being paranoid. She's just being thoughtful."

"Do I smell?"

"Of course not!"

"Tell me the truth."

"I just did."

"Because I think it's *me*. The smell is me."

"I mean, the thing on your back – once they took it out, the smell went away."

"You never told me there was a smell," pouted Ali.

"It was so *faint*."

The "lost" earring Joan bought for her had fallen onto the bed sheet and been sucked into a mildewy excrescence on the giftee's lower back while she slept. Even though sterilized after surgical retrieval and shining brighter than ever, Ali felt a measure of guilt for not wanting it anymore.

"I was wondering," said the actress, "if we should maybe just fly to Geneva to the clinic."

"Here we go again."

"Seriously, Joan. I just think it'd be better – for me *and* for you. Better to just end it."

"Stop being so dramatic."

"I just can't take any more of this shit! It's so degrading..." She started to cry. "You don't know what it's like – "

"Oh yes I do," said Joan, holding her. "And it's going to be all right. It *will*. Okay?"

"I was reading this Japanese ghost story," said Ali, her tears already drying, "that reminded me of us. It was about a man who encountered a creature in the middle of the night. He was crossing a bridge and it just lay there, blocking his way. The creature told the man that it came from the ocean and must have committed a crime – though it didn't know what *kind* of crime – because the ruler expelled it from the watery kingdom."

"'Watery kingdom.' I love that."

Ali continued with the story, casually and effectively using her natural-born skills as an actress. Just then, Joan loved her even more.

"The creature said it needed food and shelter or would die. So the man took it home and cared for it."

"Sweet!"

"It lived in a pond next to the house for seven long years. Then one day, the man saw a beautiful girl at the market and fell instantly in love. He learned the girl's parents were offering her for marriage – for a dower of 1,000 jewels. He was poor; there was just no way! He grew lovesick and took to his bed. Now it was the creature's turn to take care of *him*.

"At last, after weeks of going downhill, he told the creature that he was dying. 'It pains me, because when I'm gone, what will happen to you? Who will take care of you? How will my creature live?'

"Seeing how much his benefactor was suffering, the thing began to weep red tears; as they dried, they became rubies. Realizing his problem was solved, he told the creature his predicament and begged him to keep crying so he'd have enough jewels to make the girl his bride."

"Oh, sweet!" said Joan, clapping her hands.

"The creature was terribly offended. 'I'm not a whore! I cannot cry on command!'"

"Well, good for *him*. Yay creature."

"After a sleepless night – the creature was ashamed for being so selfish and knew the man's love for the girl was pure – it came to the bed of the precious being who had saved him. 'Take me to the bridge where you found me,' it said. 'I'll look toward the sea and the place that once was my home. That way, perhaps the tears will come.' So they went to the bridge and the tears came. And soon, the man had enough jewels for the dower."

"*Love* that word 'dower.'"

"As it stared into the horizon, the creature heard a voice – the voice of the king who had exiled him. 'You've been missed! It's time now to come home.' His banishment was lifted."

After a pause, Joan said, "That's *such* a beautiful story. Maybe we could make an animated film, like *Spirited Away...*"

The faraway watery kingdom of Ali's eyes shone. "*I'm* that creature, darling! *I'm* the one you've loved and fed and nurtured, the one you've taken such beautiful care of. And while you were doing that, you fell in love with someone else – a princess, not a creature."

"What are you saying?" Joan asked, nonplussed.

"You fell in love with... *you*. You're getting to know that princess. You're losing the weight that protected her against the world. You're saying goodbye to the fear that was holding you back – "

"Because *you* showed me how!" she protested.

"You're getting stronger and more gorgeous each day – look at you! look how beautiful you are! You're growing up. I think that you found me and took care of me because – I reminded you of the part – the part of you that's dying."

When Joan began to cry herself, Ali suddenly wondered if what she'd just said was even true. She felt a bit like an ingénue at a table read, still searching for her character's core. Still, a deep sorrow came over her. "It's like we met on the bridge, and that's where we should part. Maybe it's time for me to go back home. Wherever that is..."

An actressy, yet earnest sentiment.

"That's so funny," said Joan, smiling through her tears. "When you were telling the story, *I* was the creature and *you* were the bride." She ran her fingers through Ali's oily hair. "But you never asked for rubies, did you? You never asked, knowing I had all the jewels in the world..."

"I didn't *ask*," said Ali, laughing, "but my body *took* one!"

"That was an *emerald*. Your body has good taste!"

"Ha!"

"And you better start wearing that earring again, girl, it's part of your fuckin *dower*." She grew serious again. "Can't you see, babe? *You're* the bride and *I'm* the creature… I always was, and always will be." Her voice cracked but she was luminous. "*You're* the bride. *You're* what was unattainable – and I never thought I'd find you. How lucky am I? And you're wrong about me falling in love, with anyone but you: *you're* the one who's fallen in love with someone else, some*thing* else." She pinned Ali with her eyes. "Don't you see, Ali? It's you who fell in love – with Death." Ali gasped at the savage clarity of Joan's words. "We're *both* on the bridge now. We're both going home… to that watery place! But we're going *together*." In prayer, Joan closed her eyes and said, "You don't *have* to be in love – with me. Be in love with whatever you want, but stay with me – "

"But I do love you! I do – "

Eyes still shut, as if she were speaking aloud, Joan said, "It seems I've been waiting all my life to hear those words." Then: "I wasn't going to ask you this until we got to Arizona."

"Arizona – ?"

"It was going to be a surprise. I had *two* surprises – Arizona was supposed be the first. And when we got there, this was gonna be the second…" Joan shook as she said, "I was going to ask you to be my wife."

Fearing Ali might laugh, Joan's lids slammed shut again, decapitating teardrops. When at last they opened, she saw that Ali had fainted dead away.

In the Penal Colony

ALI

OMG Ripley is SO funny. He was obsessing about who was taller, Sophie Turner or Taylor Swift – but refused to Google! He said he just kept making imaginary red carpet photos in his head of Sophie and Taylor standing next to various celebs, then finally picturing the two side-by-side… he's so BRILLIANT and funny and CRAY and I love him. He's OBSESSED that they're making a *New Mutant* movie, he's always saying horrible things like "I want Stan Lee to be my fuckslut-daddy" (SO horrible!) and was talking yesterday about people who want to save the environment which he says is pointless 'cause the world's gonna end like in 10 years from "the Legacy Virus that killed all the mutants" (!!!!!) I swear he's not even kidding…

But, Diary! I never told you about Joanie's PROPOSAL!!!!

– OR the Painted Desert!!

– OR the Petrified Forest (my soon-to-be nickname, right?)…

Oh, Diary!

I've been so remiss.

So busy & EXCITED but that's NO EXCUSE.

THE PAINTED DESERT & THE PETRIFIED FOREST –
is it possible, Diary of my Heart, there are any three words in
the English language that could ever conjure something more
evocative, more beautiful than those two phrases? (Wonder
if that's where Rick Owens got the amazing wood for Joanie's
desk. Hmmmm.) Well, that's where James Turrell's "Roden"
crater is – my bucket list, remember?!?! – near Flagstaff and
the above-listed supermagical places. Joan said The Painted
Desert was named by a Spanish explorer looking for "The
Seven Cities of Gold." (Why do Spanish explorers always seem
to be lookin for frickin gold?) I think it was – I want to say his
name was Coronado? – which *naturally* made me think of the
Hotel del Coronado in San Diego where Grammie used to take
us. We went there when I wrapped *Arrested Development*, and
at the end of every season of *Te Deum* too; our little tradition.
SUCH an amazing hotel, but YOU remember, don't you, Di?
Course you do…

I do digress!

The Roden Crater is AMAZEBALLS.

And OMG, it's like 400,000 years old!!!

Mister Turrell gave us the tour himself, which he *better*
have, 'cause Joan matched the $10 million Yeezy donated (and
before the tour was over, doubled it). The artist's goal is to
open it to the world in five years, but in order to finish all the
things he has planned, James needs 200 million… it's going to
cost a fortune to build a public road just to get to the place, it's
quite isolated – then you need *bathrooms* and a *restaurant* and
a *gift shop*, whatever. $200 mill does sound like a lot (and is)
but if you put things in context, some people spend more on
super-yachts and crazy penthouse apartments. (And football
teams, which cost so much more.) Roden is something I really

do feel will help heal the planet, unifying "vibratory energies" and bla – you totally feel HIGH when you're there (I know I did!), high on Love and Hope & literally high on LIGHT. That man is such a genius... O, Diary, the light! It pours and pours into the rooms like slivery flashbombs from the Celestial Kingdom... there's, like, kind of smaller "everyday" rooms, then there's GIGANTOR rooms for special celestial events. All these crazy tunnels! And an amazing bronze staircase... the SILENCE and HUMILITY you feel just standing there is "nonpareil" (Grammie's favorite word) –

Diary, I have no words (unlike Grammie).

It was physically quite daunting and I couldn't have done it without Team Ali's Circus Strongmen. They carry me in their arms (when necessary) and are tireless and unflinching and always smiling. When they grunt, they make a joyful noise!

They call me Cleo, as in Patra...

I've been a little scared because my voice is mostly terrible now and a lot of times when I speak no one understands what I'm saying. *Joanie* does, at least about 90% of the time – which is actually kind of a miracle – I guess I need to start using the MIT machine, a tiny little amazing thing that translates and interprets my words. They said it's like 20 generations evolved from the original voicebox Dennis Klatt made for Stephen Hawking. I'm using it to dictate most of THIS (Still too shy to use it in front of people – GET OVER YOURSELF, ALI NELL!) – that's why I sound like the Tin Man of Oz. But you're so sweet not to have said anything. Or maybe you're just happy not to hear my annoying old voice???... just call me the Tin Girl, kk?

Oops! I do digress again.

It's too long and emotional a story but Joan waited for us to be alone then got down on her knees – it was dusk and the crescent moon appeared like a horned halo in the portal above us – and asked me to marry her. Even tho I knew what was coming, I cried and cried and cried because I never felt so loved. So loved and looked after, so protected... I must have done something right, huh Diary? In this, or past lives (the boys *do* call me "Cleo," right?), to have been given this gift from the Universe even though I have so little time left.

I kissed Joan's cheek and saw the little blue box in her hand. Inside was a gigantor canary yellow diamond, the likes of I am told that no one has never seen nor shall ever see again. But that wasn't ALL she had to surprise me with. No, Diary, and you will never ever guess. So, I'll give you a hint...

She gave me a tiara! (So much for hints.)

It was the most ASTONISHING thing...

Sorry for the delay, Diary, I just spent twenty minutes putting it on because I wanted you to see it. Marta begged on helping but I told her to just set it on the pillow. After she left the room I lay on the bed and wiggled my head into it... THERE: can you see? Can you see it? I'll stop jabbering so you can take a good gander...

Isn't it beautiful, Di? Aren't I the blushing bride?

Joan said she got it at auction, that it was Russian but her mom bought it

JOAN

at Sotheby's as a goof, a month before she died. (She remembered Vi using those very words: *a goof.*) It was the most glorious object the 13-year-old child ever beheld. Joan had forgotten about it until she came across the flat, faded-blue box while noodling around in the library hidden behind secret doors.

The executor and everyone else urged her to sell the accursed mansion, suggesting it should be razed first. Joan doggedly resisted. She couldn't bear parting with the library because it served as her mother's sanctuary and safe haven. In the rare times Joan visited, she detoured around the killing rooms, taking solace in the fastness of the dark, book-lined chapel with its high-ceiling'd, pornographic frescoes, its priceless, ribald medieval misercordias. The space was still redolent of Vi's bespoke perfume, making Joan sad-happy; lately, unexpectedly, she'd been aching to be held by her. A thing she loved most about Billie was the singer telling her that whenever she had a bad dream, she still climbed in bed with her mom. Joan and Billie shared so much – both were cutters, both had body dysmorphia, both were home-schooled, both had older brothers. But the most intriguing thing by far was that Billie suffered from sleep paralysis, a condition Joan considered to be a first cousin to her own bondage and confinement fetishes.

She sat in one of the priceless pews, musing, when her eye fell upon a book. Thinner than the surrounding volumes, with no letters on its spine. She climbed the ladder and plucked it out (not far from a copy of *Wild Psalms*) – then gasped, because she knew: the magical tiara. A familiar slip of paper detailing its provenance was enclosed. With speedy heart, Joan read the text as she would a forgotten diary entry of her first love.

The piece was created at the turn of the 20th-century, in Fabergé's St. Petersburg *atelier* – the snow-globe romance of it! – commissioned by the Grand Duchess Anastasia as a gift to her son's bride. The unique design was of forget-me-nots tied with diamond ribbons, each pierced by pear-shaped aquamarine arrows representing Cupid's work. She immediately knew it was meant for Ali; her mother's gift to Joan and her bride, from beyond.

In a burst of reconnoitering energy, she came across something else.

It was one of Vi's teenage journals, from 1985. She would have been thirteen then, the same age as Joan when she first saw the tiara; the same age as Joan as she lay pinned beneath the bed during her mother's execution.

Her magnetic eye fell on the entry about Grandpa Bud:

> Dad said he missed Mom and was so happy it was just the two of us now and that he loved me so much. It was really sweet then he kissed my cheeks and kissed me with his TONGUE in my MOUTH (?!?!?!) and I said DAD what are you DOING???!!! He said he didn't MEAN it, it was a mistake but how COULD it be?!?!?! Diary, UCK YUCK UCK!!!! AND DIARY, YOU BETTER NOT TELL ANYONE. (I am going to throwup)

Reading the entry made her feel queasy, but closer to her papaw, her *zayde*. So *that's* who she got it from – Grandpa Wiggins – the anarchic, joyously errant, disobedient hedonistic impulse, the genetic, careless concupiscence ordering her to bow down at the uncovered feet of the Squad.

Maybe now she could begin to forgive herself.

B U D

"Hello?" said the voice on the other end of Bud's dial.

"Yes?"

"Hi!" said Bud.

"Who is this?"

"Well, who's *this*?" the stoned novelist asked.

"This is Jim Stackpole," said the voice, rather formally.

"Oops! Wrong number, Jimbo."

"Are you looking for Manny Rosen?"

"Yes..." said Bud.

"I'm Manny's agent – "

"Manny has an *agent*," said Bud gleefully. "Will wonders never cease? Editors having agents! Agents having managers! Cats and dogs living together!"

Then the line seemed to go dead.

"Hullo?" said Bud, with sudden desperation. "*Hullo hullo hullo?*"

For weeks he'd been expecting a response from Manny to the *Confessions* excerpt. When nothing came, he started to get nervous, fearing he may had overestimated the chapter's worth. He probably should have waited for the peerless editor's input before sharing the memoir pages with Wylann and Digby – but they were superfans so he wasn't all that worried.

"I'm afraid I have some bad news," said Jimbo. "Manny passed away."

"He what? I didn't hear you – "

"Manny passed away two weeks ago. Sorry you're finding out this way – I have his phone and I've been fielding a lot of calls. I'm actually here in Maine, arranging the sale of the house."

"What happened?"

"Cancer."

"He didn't tell me – "

"For years. His last chemo was in the spring and when it came back, he decided – he just didn't want to go through that again."

* * *

The first few nights after his eviction, Bud was in total shock.

The nightmare had come, in an instant:

Sixty-seven and living in his car.

How could this happen?

He found himself strangely alone in the world. No couch to crash on, no favors to call in. No full-bosomed ladies, old-time or new, to offer their beds, succor and support. There was only Garry Gabe, but something told him it wasn't the time to ask for help.

He wanted to keep that ace in its hole.

He almost phoned Digby but thought it poor form. He was still waiting to see what ol' Dig thought about the excerpt; if he loved it, it would make asking for money easier. Anyway, Digby would probably be calling any day now. When he did, the writer decided that instead of cash, he'd gingerly inquire if there were an unused servant's room that might be put at his disposal.

He only had $600 left and still needed to pay his phone bill. Without a phone, he wouldn't be able to Uber. Without a phone, Wylann and Dig wouldn't be able to reach out.

And nor would Garry Gabe…

When Bud vacated his apartment, he gave Laverne, the building manager, fifty dollars to retrieve his mail and hold onto it until he had a forwarding address. (You never knew what Easter eggs the US Mail might leave in your basket. More importantly, he needed to keep the postal channel open for further communiqués from the State Controller.) Laverne had tears in her eyes when she informed him that the landlord had thrown his worldly goods into the dumpster. Bud shrugged and said, "Fine and dandy." He couldn't get it together to look into renting a cheap storage space. His laptop and manuscripts – the only things of any real importance – were safely stowed in his trunk.

After a few days of splurging on a room at the Sportsman's Lodge, he moved to a cheaper inn, the *Virginia Starr* in Toluca Lake. Tomorrow, as they say, was another day. He welcomed that fluttery, wonderful feeling in his gut that a serious scratcher payday was coming.

On the back of each Big Win ticket, hope sprung eternal:

Odds of winning any prize: 1 in 2.78; cash prize: 1 in 4.13
Odds of winning $10,000,000: 1 in 3,000,000,00

In other words, chances were better than 1-in-3 for *some* kind of win.

It's *all* good… at 1-in-3, how could it not be?

Deep under the passenger seat of his car, he found his ragged copy of Orwell. After a long hot shower at the *Virginia Starr,* Bud lay on the bed and dipped in. Old George really nailed it:

It is a feeling of relief, almost of pleasure, at knowing yourself at last genuinely down and out. You have talked so often of going to the dogs – and well, here are the dogs, and you have reached them, and you can stand it. It takes off a lot of anxiety.

Nailed it!

Hadn't life's petty distractions – its non-essentials – been removed? As by cosmic design, hadn't all the banal obstacles of what his father's generation called the "rat race" been summarily stripped away? Bud certainly thought it no accident that in this convergent moment, he had found his mission: *to finish the memoir.* Like a man in a city blacked out by a violent electrical storm, he looked up to finally see the majesty of the stars.

A pilgrim now, in the City of God...

He understood too that Manny had played his magnificent part. His old friend and editor showed Bud the way, then elegantly left the stage, ushering in the entr'acte.

Bud thought:

Maybe it's this – homelessness – *maybe* that's *the Big Win.*

As if to crown the vagabond king in further glory, he couldn't believe the contents of the package retrieved only hours ago from Laverne, Queen of the Fountain Capri. He was astonished, choked by tears.

He'd read the document a thousand times already:

THE FOUR VIRGINS
DISCRETION, PRUDENCE, PIETY AND CHARITY
request the honor of your presence
AT THE MARRIAGE OF THEIR DAUGHTER

FKA "The Fat Joan"
née Joan Everhart Gamma
to
The Grand Duchess Ali Nell

SATURDAY, THE SEVENTEENTH OF SEPTEMBER
TWO THOUSAND AND NINETEEN

HALF PAST SIX O'CLOCK IN THE EVENING

at

THE PALACE BEAUTIFUL

POINT DUME

Dinner, dancing, and bacchanal to follow

Details to come under separate cover

ALI

The ceremony and festivities were meant to be at Roden Crater but by then, Ali wasn't well enough to travel.

Dr. Pirouette was their sole braintrust now – other medicos on the team grew suspect of his methods and peeled off. The Cambridge fellow, whose bold theories and controversial treatment protocols branded him a charlatan by his peers, was a perfect fit. The three adventurers made a secret pact to sail uncharted seas in search of whatever antidotes, remedies and inoculations could be found in dangerous coves, plain-sight inlets and forgotten archipelagoes whose existence neither captains nor simple sailors had the temerity to imagine.

Joan, puzzlingly shy of a hundred pounds now, became a patient of Dr. P as well. He put her on a regimen of HGH to arrest loss of tissue and bone density. She looked alien and shockingly beautiful. Because the couple spent the last month assiduously out of public and paparazzi eye, wedding guests hardly recognized her. They had a feeling they were being pranked – that the marriage was a sham. They thought Joan hired an actress to "play" herself in a kind of performance art piece.

The nuptials were surreal. Ali was prescribed one of Dr. P's "bomb cyclones" – part-stimulant, part-opiate – to get her through the day. (And suppress discomfort caused by "anomalous molting.") The dreamlike, sheer improbability of circumstances enhanced Ali's feelings of disassociation. If a year ago it had been prophesied, "You will contract an unknown disease that makes you famous beyond your wildest dreams – then marry a 19-year-old billionairess," well, it would have been so absurd that she might have forgotten to laugh.

Vows were exchanged under a billowy white tarp on a bluff recently added to Joan's portfolio for the occasion. Yongey Mingyur Rinpoche, the bestselling author and revered Buddhist tulku, renowned for vanishing from his monastery for five years so he could wander anonymously in the world of *samsara*, performed the ceremony. Ocean and stars needn't bother to compete with the hour-long, spherical Grucci fireworks. Among the privileged who attended were Joan's grandfather, Bud; Billie Eilish (the only member of the Squad who could make it); Mackenzie Bezos; Chris and Katherine Pratt; Elon and Grimes; Bryan and Billie Lourd; Klaus Biesenbach; Abigail Disney; Justine Ludwig; Ryan Jamaal Swain; Anand Giridharadas; Jennifer Pritzker; Lady Gaga; and Ripley, of course.

"Del Taco" was filming in Seattle and unable to attend. Without telling the director too much, Joan confided that her fiancée's illness had caused "some minor facial disfigurement," and asked for his help. Always the gentleman, Guillermo read between the lines – that Joan must be downplaying something far more serious – and unhesitatingly offered to send one of the key makeup artists that worked on *The Shape of Water*. The woman saved the day. She was lavishly paid for her services, which went a long way in getting her over the initial startle of the sight she beheld on wedding day eve: the pastel shadows of a veiled woman, hunched in front of a vanity at the far end of a cathedral-size bedroom, shoulders shrugging in an embarrassed effort to control her tears. When the woman got closer, she thought the bride was wearing some sort of punk headdress (making the tiara that sat precariously upon her head look poignantly clownish), before realizing the spiky, fan-shaped crest of rust-colored feathers, each seemingly dipped in black ink, were attached to her client's skull sans glue or special effect, and rose up organically to mirror the aquamarine stanchions of the Fabergé creation.

When her eyes met Ali's, tears of tender maternal compassion flowed, bonding them in sacred confidentiality. Instantly, the pages-long NDA she signed long before entering the house had been rendered moot.

"Mi corazón!" said the makeup artist. "How *beautiful* you are! And how beautiful you will *be.* Now! Let's get you ready for your big day."

* * *

She lay in bed exhausted.

An old Jimmy Fallon was on.

Brie Larson was the guest.

"You're so amazing," said Jimmy, cockeyed and breathless. "I've been watching all your interviews about the new *Avengers* and I know how *hard* that is. I know how much work that is, those *junkets,* and you've been *so inspiring* in those interviews…"

Brie's answer was drowned out the roar of distant revelries.

The bluff-side hullabaloo gave Ali a voyeur's comforting sense of excitation. She'd loved to have stayed but was glad she didn't; Joan knew how hard the day had been and insisted Ali return to the house. She had an ulterior motive as well – to protect her bride's vanity from prying eyes. Joan purposefully staged the ceremony as a theatrical event, allowing the betrothed to keep the front row of guests far enough away to make it impossible to see Ali's face through the gossamer veil Rick Owens designed and sent from Paris. (Cellphones were quarantined until the afterparty.) She was carried back to the house on a palanquin worthy of Burning Man's finest, an egress that drew the crowd's ovation.

After bathing her, the loyal tribe of Fijian caregivers tucked their charge away under scented Porthault sheets. Joan admonished them *never* to wear facemasks around Ali again; some smeared vapor rub or lavender oil under their nostrils to muzzle the smells, undiminished by discreetly placed silver pots of coffee grounds. Joan had grown up with the congenial, roly-poly nannies – through all her ordeals, they kept her sane. (More than once, she assured Ali that she'd have died without them.) She loved them; they were the only beings she could trust. The Fijians never judged. The stranger that Ali's physicality became, the sweeter, the happier, the *prouder* they seemed, as if watching a daughter change into nubile womanhood. Nothing about her transformation managed to confuse or alarm – not a burnt-orange ruff above the elongation of hard cartilage on her lip, nor the zebra-striped skin on her pelvis, nor the agonized speech that slid into a stammer of cawks, keens and wheezes before busting into a frenzy of joyous birdsong. The only thing that flustered was the persistent odor from her backside, not the anus per se, but the skin surrounding it. The women felt guilty about their struggle to maintain indifference; their animal revulsion was commensurate with the shame at having had such a selfishly personal reaction.

For his part, the plucky Dr. P could barely contain his excitement over Ali's preposterously unclassifiable symptoms. In the weeks following his renunciation of ALS, Pirouette took a stab in the dark and tested her for avian flu, which came back negative. He already ruled out *histoplasmosis*, a condition caused by the inhalation of the spores found in bird droppings; *cryptococcosis*, acquired via starlings' yeasty guts; and the virus called St. Louis Encephalitis, which was usually transmitted by sparrows. The dodgy practitioner was in a frenzy and hardly slept. Detecting the same metallic odor exuded by her grandfather, Joan wondered if the practitioner was fueling himself with amphetamines.

Still, Pirouette captivated, especially when prattling about Aristophanes' play, *The Birds*, about a fellow from Athens who believed the winged creatures to be the original gods, thus deserving to build their Kingdom of Heaven in the sky. (*That's what Ali and I are doing! Just like* Pilgrim's Progress! *We are building a Celestial City – our nest in the heavens!*)

"And did you know," said the vainglorious, scholarly Dr. P. "That lady nightingales have no voice? It's the males who sing."

Around three in the morning, Joan crept in, still
drunk and still dressed.

Ali stirred, smiling when she felt a hand caress her leg.

She meant to say *oooh,* but involuntarily belched *oop! oop! oop!* instead. The comic eructations made them laugh until they cried.

With faltering voice – the meds were wearing off – she asked Joan to turn on the Tiffany lamp at the foot of the bed because she wanted to show her something. The soft light, diffused through roses, lit up the bride's skinscape. It had changed in the hours since the ceremony.

Joan looked then kissed Ali's cheeks.

"I love you," she said, as if it were code for "I don't care what you're becoming." She put a sugar cube under Ali's tongue that was soaked in one of Dr. P's potions – Doxapram, a stimulant given to foals with respiratory issues.

"I'm really becoming like Magik now…"

"How so, babe?"

She inhaled the booze and pot on Joan's breath. "When Magik used her Soulsword, the 'Eldritch armor' appeared – "

"Magik's so fucking hot," said Joan. "I mean, you rocked as Melissa Eerie, but me, Melissa and Magik really need to get *together.*"

"She grew hooves and horns, too…"

"You know, I *totally* relate to Magik – 'cause her brother's parents were murdered. They *were,* right?"

"Joanie! Do you think I have some sort of fucking… *plague*? Like, the X-Men Legacy virus?"

"You know what?" she said drolly. "That may be the *one possibility* Pirouette hasn't looked into yet! I'll tell him he needs to get *on* it."

"I am *serious* – "

"I think all the dope you're taking's makin you a lil bit cray-cray."

"But Magik *died*. You don't want *Wifey* to die, do you, Joanie?"

"Magik died, but she totally came *back*. In fact, she didn't *even* die, she went to frickin *Limbo*. So, if Wifey goes to Limbo like Magik, I'll be all *over* it. I'll be like frickin *Belasco* and bring you back with a powerful spell."

"Promise?" said Ali, utterly sincere.

"Fuck yeah! You'd come back as Darkchilde, right? Isn't that what happened to Magik? I don't know my Marvel shit like you do… but Darkchilde was frickin *hot*. She came back with Karma and Pixie – right? So you'd come back with Karma and Pixie, to fuck with the New Mutants. Then we'd all go to Ibiza and fuck like demons!"

Suddenly, she was fast asleep in Joan's arms.

BUD

The novelist exchanged the minimal comforts of the *Virginia Starr* for those of his roomy 2016 Taurus.

Each time his world grew smaller, he felt liberated. He was amazed by the ideas the social order forced us to carry – the ones that conditioned from infancy, binding like handcuffs. Why was living in one's car even a problem? (Bud was beginning to think that the bigger problem was having a car at all but it was an attachment he still needed to work on.) Like his father used to say, "We've been sold a bill of goods."

You've got to be carefully taught…

Wasn't that how the old song went?

Why didn't everyone live in cars? Easy answer: that'd be gaming the system, which the State didn't like. When thousands of lunatic tent-people with TB and typhus shat the sidewalks and assaulted passers-by, the State could care less. But if you dared find a quiet street where you could sleep overnight, unmolested – in an immaculate vehicle whose payments were up-to-date – look out!

For the first time in his adult life, Bud didn't owe a dime on the first of the month. A slave no more. If he needed to defecate, he just strolled into Gelson's or Starbucks or Bristol Farms and took the biggest, foulest dump he could manage. If he rooster-tailed the bowl, someone eventually came along – some slave – to take care of it. In a stroke of genius, Bud bought a cheap membership at LA Fitness. *Voilà*, he now had a clean, well-lighted place to shit, shave and shower. The clubs were all over the city, so he had his pick. Sometimes he even stepped on a treadmill or grabbed a yoga mat for a few sun salutations.

* * *

"Bud?"

"Wylann?"

"Oh my God, hi!"

"Hi! It's so nice to hear your voice."

"I am so sorry I didn't get back sooner – "

"No, that's – that's fine – it's…"

" – I was on a book tour and you know how crazy that can be."

"Been there, done that," he said, humblebrag playing along.

"Do you have a moment?" she said. "Is this a bad time?"

"No, it's perfect! I've been writing and now I'm at the gym. Doing a little procrastinating before I jump on the elliptical."

"Been there, done that!" she said. "I *so* need to get back to Peloton. I think I gained about twenty pounds on this tour."

"I always gain when I'm hocking a book," he said, throwing fistfuls of bullshit to the wind. Why not push the envelope, for old times' sake? *Wild Psalms* was a critical success but sold less than 5,000 copies. Three West Coast cities comprised his one and only tour; he was lucky if a dozen diehards show up to watch him read.

"Look, this isn't an easy call for me to make." *Oh shit.* "Actually, that's why it took so long to call... but you want me to tell the truth, right? I mean, that's what we do. As *writers*, right? That's what you taught me... and – I know you don't want to even hear this but I read the pages you sent and they were so... wrong! I mean they were – they didn't make *sense*. To me! And that's just *me* – they might make amazing sense to someone else – but I could barely get through them! In fact, I *didn't* – I couldn't even... finish the chapter about your mom where she made the list about the men she'd slept with? You need to take this with a grain of salt! I mean, I'm notorious for not finishing books that go on to become these *amazing bestsellers*. So maybe it's just me! I teach writing now, which is something *you* told me to do by the way, something you *encouraged*, and I'm so grateful. Because I love it! I really love it. So I *teach*, and what you wrote is pretty much everything I tell my students *not* to do! It's crazy! It's crazy for us to be having this conversation! Like – and I don't know how else to put it, but – *the writing just didn't make any sense.* I know I keep saying the same thing... but I couldn't understand what was going on! At all! I know the section is about your mom – the whole book is, kinda, right? – and she – *Dolly* – Dolly sounds so amazing – I remembered her a little from *Wild Psalms* – and *some* of her really shined through – I'm sorry I never met her – though maybe she was at one of the parties I threw for you – was she? – anyway, it was all so… *lurid* – like, you made her into a whore! Oh my God, really, Bud? Do you really – did you really want to even be *saying* that or dishonoring her? Or putting misogynist stuff like that out there? But apart from that 'peccadillo' – ha! – it's just so – *fragmented*, but – [*voices in background*] Can everyone please be *quiet*, Mama's on the *phone*. Sorry about that. Sorry. Anyway, I really have to go, because my daughter's having an epic sleepover tonight and I need to make dinner, but – I know it's not what you wanted to hear, Bud, and I *might be wrong*, I *hope* I'm wrong! – and I'm sorry, but I'd hope you would do the same for me – if ever I sent you something for feedback, which I very well may do, *soon*, because I'm working on – [*shouting away from phone*] I am! I'm coming! Goddammit, your mother is still talking to her friend! Sorry, Bud – anyway, gotta go! But you're okay? You're okay with this? Because I know it wasn't great to hear, what you *wanted* to hear, but I haven't heard you say anything…"

"I'm fine, Wylann!" he said numbly. "No – it's fine. Thank you for your honesty, it's appreciated. I'll try and do better."

A sweaty man who'd been doing kettlebells came and sat nearby, giving Bud the side-eye.

"Okay, good!" said Wylann, sensing his hurt but glad to be off the hook. "That sounded kind of formal but whatever. *Anyway,* take what you want and leave the rest, and all that. And thank *you*. For *thinking* of me, and reaching out. It's so *hard* being a writer, right? But as Hyman Roth said, 'This is the business we chose'! And *please* send anything else – I'd love to see whatever. Because, oh my God, a new work by Bud Wiggins! I want to see that! Okay, gotta go now!"

She hung up. He sat there, immobilized.

The muscle-bound man said, "Are you interested in training?"

"What?"

"In a personal trainer? I do that here. I can cut you a great deal."

* * *

He hadn't thought about Manny, not deeply, but now the sorrow of the loss infected his solitary, car-bound days and nights.

Jimbo the Agent said that he'd stopped his chemo in the spring, around the time Bud first reached out. It hurt that his old friend never confided in him. By default, Manny always let the artist take center stage, yet the itinerant novelist couldn't help but reflect on his own travails, a bonfire of vanities that paled beside the dignified fight of a humble, dying man.

He had a plan.

He'd tell Garry the truth and ask for help.

Then he would do the same with his granddaughter, on a much larger scale. He had a small fear about the new wife having a problem with handouts, but Joan didn't strike him as the henpecked type.

Bud found a cul-de-sac in Cheviot Hills where he felt safe. After a few nights, one of the neighbors approached the Taurus and asked what he was doing there. Bud told the truth. The man nodded thoughtfully, said "Got it," then shuffled off. Telling the truth sometimes got you a Big Win.

He resolved to visit Garry at the studio tomorrow.

The car was parked off Motor. It was a lovely evening and he walked to Beverly Hills, imagining himself a homeowner out for a stroll. In the afternoon, he bought a gram of coke; the connection, Bud's age now, had serviced the writer since both were in their 30s.

He strode into the bar at the Peninsula, feeling like a proper man again. He was turning a corner – he could feel it. He would show that rich, lucky cunt Wylann. He'd show them all. He did a line in the bathroom then returned to the bar and ordered a third whiskey. Within a few minutes, a tattooed young woman took the stool next to him.

That was how he met Reeve Tobrin, the daughter of Elon Musk.

JOAN

[FaceTime]

PIETRA These journals of your mother's that you found –
JOAN They made me so sad! I *cried...* because I – I hadn't actually – it's so weird, because I hadn't actually *thought* about her... ever being that age. And I hadn't been thinking about her *at all*. I mean *really* thinking about her, or Dad, or my brother Tab – Tabula – *any* of them. Oh! My poor little brother! *[Pietra hands her Kleenex]* I *had* thought more about Tab... silly things like how much he would have loved Fortnite – like I randomly burst into tears when I think that he never had the chance to play Fortnite! It's like... for *once* I thought of him, not *myself*, you know, wedged under the

bed. I thought of him – *them* – and what it must have been like… the terror of it! Of what they went through – [sobs]

PIETRA This is an important day, Joan. The day we've been waiting for. The day you can finally start to climb out from under that bed.

JOAN [*laughing and crying*] I don't know if I want to! I don't know if I *want* to, Pietra, I might just want to stay there!

PIETRA I don't think so. I don't think so, Joan. And we don't really have a choice in these matters – I don't even believe we have a choice to be courageous. Which is what you're showing *now*: great courage. Sometimes courage chooses *us*. Can I tell you something else that's remarkable? That I find remarkable? [*Joan nods*] You're building a bridge to your grandfather. Knowing what you know – what you read in your mother's diary – that you're forgiving him, in a sense, *for* Vi. *For* your mother. Only a few months ago, even a few *weeks* ago, that would've been so much harder. It was a kiss, she wrote about a kiss on the mouth. Then it became clear it was far more than that. A kind of rape –

JOAN – and I totally don't feel like cutting myself… I just think – I *believe* – that love – and forgiveness – not just toward others but toward *myself* – is the only thing – not just to "get me through," you know, through whatever past or ongoing trauma of this life – of being alive – but will – is – the only thing with any *meaning*. My whole relationship with Ali, my whole *marriage* is about that – that I bonded with the part of myself – with this gorgeous, amazing, *courageous* woman who's, like, for whatever reason, figurative, literal, or whatever, this woman that's perceived to be… becoming this – they used to call it "sacred monster" – which is what we all are! Right, Pietra? And what we should all be *thankful* to be! *Sacred monsters…* it's French, it comes from the French. My mother used to say it… but isn't that what it's like to be human? Like, isn't that the perfect definition? "Sacred monsters"? *Another* part of me married Ali [*begins to tremble*] – and I haven't – *told* anyone this, I've barely told *myself* –

PIETRA It's okay, Joan. It's safe. You're safe here.

JOAN – I *partially* married Ali because I – and don't freak out! – because I want to… leave – I want to leave the planet when *she* does. I felt so awful – lusting for those – young girls we've talked about, we finally talked about. I realized I've been trying to – *ensnare* them. It made me so sick! To see how sick I was… and I realized when I read what Vi wrote in her diary about my grandfather that I needed to forgive him for *whatever* – whatever sins – *because they were passed on to me too.* I know my parents were up to stuff, they weren't like these "innocents" – I know from talking to people that they were – not "freaks," but… sexual *adventurers.* But I've had enough! And *some* of all this *bullshit* is survivor's guilt, we've talked about that, but some is just – don't freak out – I'm *tired,* Pietra. I've really had enough! Like, the realization that, you know, all this weight loss – a lot of which is *totally mysterious,* like, *no* one, not even Dr. P knows how it's even physically possible… and you're *right* when you say we really don't have a choice in these matters. {*softly crying, resolute*] I just want to disappear with my wife. You know? Right? I want us to be this… incredible shrinking couple! Like a fucking fire sale: *Everything must go.* I want to get rid of it *all,* that's my fucking *pledge* – all the money and all the bodies – the lusting, *mutating* fat and skinny fuckin bodies – all the everything. *Speaking* of which, we're not gonna do *Pilgrim's Progress*, did I tell you? Oh my God, we're gonna remake *Incredible Shrinking Man*, with Guillermo! We got Del Taco! Gonna be our swansong!

* * *

[online]
A COMMITMENT TO PHILANTHROPY

The Giving Pledge is an effort to help address society's most pressing problems by inviting the world's wealthiest individuals and families to commit to giving more than half of their wealth to philanthropy or charitable causes either during their lifetime or in their will. Those who join the Giving Pledge often write a letter explaining their decision to engage deeply and publicly in philanthropy, as well as describing the philanthropic causes to which they are devoted. Signatories give to a diverse range of issues including poverty alleviation, refugee aid, disaster relief, global health, education, women and girls' empowerment, medical research, arts and culture, criminal justice reform, and environmental sustainability.

Joan Gamma
My Giving Pledge

Making the decision to give away my fortune was the easiest and most gratifying thing I've done in my relatively short life – and definitely the most emotional. My parents, Vi and Raphie Gamma, made the Giving Pledge, yet tragic events precluded their wishes from being fulfilled. I choose this path not only as to honor their wishes and legacy as a grateful daughter, but as a grateful human. My wife and I have had many long discussions about this. I won't bore you by citing anodyne Buddhist epigrams of "oneness" or quoting philosophers of old. Instead, I include a monologue from *The Incredible Shrinking Man,* a movie written in 1957 by Richard Matheson and based on his novel of the same name:

> "I looked up, as if somehow I could grasp the heavens, the universe, worlds beyond number. God's silver tapestry spread across the night. And in that moment, I knew the answer to the riddle of the infinite! The trouble was that I'd only been thinking in terms of Man's own limited dimension. I felt my body dwindling, melting, becoming nothing. My fears melted away, and in their place came acceptance. The vast majesty of creation had to mean something – but then I meant something too. To God, there is no zero. I still exist. Suddenly, I knew the infinitesimal and the infinite were just two ends of the same thing. The unbelievably small and the unbelievably vast eventually meet, like the closing of a gigantic circle."

The Bible doesn't say that money is the root of all evil; the *love* of money is what destroys. When I leave this Earth for bluer pastures, I want to be confident that my good fortune will ease the burden of many, even paving the way (through the Zero Foundation that Ali Nell and I am founding) to a broader consciousness, that hopefully will contribute to easing the suffering of so many.

I truly believe that through love – and forgiveness, which leads to love – our journey continues beyond the human experience. It is love that gives us the wings to take flight.

ALI

Dr. P brought an array of chemicals, both traditional and experimental, to the table. He ordered a BiPap, customized to fit the constantly altering bones of Ali's face, to be used at night, palliating the shortness of breath that visited her in the afternoons.

She was lonesome.

Because of her appearance, it was too dangerous to have guests. "Flogs" on the Internet – Joan's word – clickbaited Frankenstein themes 'n' memes, from the tame ("Bride of Dr. Pirouette?") to the cruel (avian porn GIFs). Thankfully, the Fijian helpmeets were exuberant cuddlers; once Joan's saviors, they were now her wife's. Ingesting food had become harder and the boisterous nannies giggled while competing to cook up little treats – plantain and fried grasshopper wraps were Ali's favorite, but for the most part she could only hold down smoothies. She was able to use her voice, unaided by the digital translator, just ten minutes a day.

Ripley, her BFF, was one of the few allowed an audience. Caitlyn Jenner was another. Occasionally, they showed up at the same time and Joan loved it because they made Ali laugh. "You're becoming a righteous *butterfly,* girl," said Caitlyn, in her droll, gun moll way. "Just like me! Time to effing *own* it." Ripley chimed in, "you should go on *The Masked Singer* – come as you are! Put that Donny Osmond peacock to *shame.*" Ali's hilarity soon crescendoed into something grotesque and foreboding; the visit would be cut short as Dr. P was summoned.

One day, Moishe's security people shot down a paparazzi drone hovering a quarter of a mile above the yard – but not before it captured blurry images of Ali sunbathing on her favorite hammock. Her IG page nearly broke from outrage over perceived cultural misappropriation; how dare Ali Nell wear a feathered headdress! (In truth, she was transforming into a bird.) In a duet half-wooden Indian/half-flaming queen, Ripley and Caitlyn read the nasty comments off his iPad, like celebrities reading mean tweets.

"Listen up, Pilgrim!" said Ripley, as he began the scolding thread. "'Pharrell apologized for wearing a WAR BONNET way back in 2014 – have you learned nothing?'" Caitlyn's turn: "'Perhaps your mystery FAKE affliction is giving you BRAIN FOG. It is VERY rare for women in Plains culture to wear such headdresses, and sanction to DO so is HIGHLY RESTRICTED. It is an outrage for you to flaunt that, even in the privacy of your own home!'"

Ali roared, *hooped,* and soiled the bed.

She had 3.5 million followers now.

Despite all efforts, Ali's "wing" still smelled like death. The mattress was changed out three times a day, at the very least. Then Joan cleared up the mystery – though it should be said, exchanged one mystery for another.

After the Fijians swapped the bedding and aired out the room, a swaddled, exhausted actress was trundled back from the solarium. She'd already been bathed, but when the nannies tucked her in, they sponged her crown's plumage for its generally calming effect. Almost instantly, Ali fell asleep. Joan thought she could hear a wheeze and made note to speak with Dr. P about it.

Just then, she got the idea to Google Lens Ali's ruffled diadem. The search returned pictures of the hoopoe – the same bird from the Greek play Dr. P was talking about! – along with the following text:

...the most widespread species of the genus Upupa, native of
Europe, Asia and the northern half of Africa. Characterized by
its splendid crest and plumage, the Eurasian hoopoe has been
adopted as the national bird of Israel.

Breathlessly, Joan learned that the hoopoe enjoyed laying on
the ground, wings and tail spread out, head tilted back – a
"sunbathing stance" identical to the one Ali adopted whenever
they laid her by the pool. She was mesmerized by photos of
the bird's long beak, strong enough to seize much larger prey
and bash them to death against rocks.

Dr. Pirouette excitedly took blood and tissue samples then
conscripted an ornithologist and veterinarian for a house call.
After signing exhaustive NDAs in the breakfast room, they
gave Joan and the physician an impromptu, living room lecture on the cloaca, genital canal and uropygial gland of that
most noble, legendary bird. When they met Ali upstairs, the
ornithologist's nose crinkled at the telltale odor. During breed-
ing season, the vet explained, the hoopoe's gland becomes
swollen, secreting a goo that stank of putrid meat. She coated
herself and the eggs in the concoction ripe with *Enterococcus
faecalis*, a bacterium acting as a shield against any disease that
might threaten the clutch. In a sidebar, they informed that a
week after hatching, the babies instinctively shot streams of
shit at predators, hissed like snakes to scare them away.

The two wives shrugged off the startling revelation. Joan
even managed a joke about Ali "expecting." Dr. Pirouette drily
informed that parthenogenesis – immaculate conception –
was quite common in nature, though less so in birds. The vet
informally added that such a thing *had* occurred, with miti-
gated success, in turkeys and zebra finches.

When everyone left, the couple laughed it off.

"We're all *good*," said Joan. "We'll just spritz you with a little Rose & Cuir when it's 'that time of month.' But, hey: just don't start schmearing my titties with... *gland-filth*. And *do* not friggin' *hiss*. 'Cause *that*, milady, is where I draw the line."

* * *

khloekardashian havent heard from you in awhile baby girl, hope everything's okay. Hit me up we're in palm springs
ripleysbereaveitorknot pretty please DM me my queen, can't reach you, want to know if Saturday is still HAP-HAP-HAPPENING!
freddymercurylover i am in constant pain and struggle daily. my Doctor put me on Paleo Autommune diet. no one knows what I hae either, they thought it was MS then lyme then fibromyalgia, Rheumatoid arthritis and psoriatic arthritis NOT als ever, tho but generalized FND and CRPS can you put me in touch with the brilliant dr. pheddan pirouette,, they are ousting him because he is a genius and genius ALWAYS crucified. My love to joan, GENIUS joan, tell her to start eating,!! I have so many ideas for wellness center for people like us who hae no diagnosis, misdianosis, or diagnosis pending
… more
katebeckinsale SO SO MUCH LOVE
marina.estella.888 este telefono es de uba amiga porque el mio no esta disponible ahora pero mi nombre es benito y quisiera tener una relacion contigo de amistad si tu me to permites soy christiano
C3_pee_ohh the change came at menopause, my doctor said I had symptomless LPTR but 50 PERCENT of women who go into menopause floridly experience LPTR!- 2- and -3. Now

I AM CHANGING TOO and feel SO BLESSED. the psychic in my dream told me YOU are CHANGING, you are so lucky you didn't have to WAIT. It is so beautiful. I FEEL it. I dreamed you were a bird. I am flying HIGHER and HIGHER. i can see you in my ... more

podunk_STAR "We also glory in tribulations, knowing that tribulations produce perseverance; and perseverance, character; and character, hope. Now hope does not disappoint, because the love of God has been poured out in our hearts by the Holy Spirit who was given to us." - Romans 5:3-5

KA.117mosdef I noticed bottleS of Smartwater in yr posts. Is that brand endorsement? I thought you were a HERO but I see you are an INFLUEN$$$ER (don't have emoticons on old phone/pls insert BARFY FACE HERE), checking with Smartwater to see if you have a relationship with ... more

* * *

On most nights, the Fijians carried her to the bluff's grassy overlook, bundled in an Hermès Jeu de Soie shawl. Such a pleasure it was, to lie on the wet ground above the pounding waves! To stare at the cope of stars, knowing *that* was where she belonged, and soon would be traveling...

Her senses were acute: she smelled everything, tasted everything, saw everything –

Was everything.

She had undergone an unspeakable physical transformation. Joan told the caregivers to keep watch from a distance, so her wife would feel less self-conscious. No harm could come; four stories of steel-poled golf netting, hidden in the ground during the day, pneumatically telescoped to the heavens, hemming her in. The protective webbing's presence allowed Joan a semblance of peaceful sleep.

Ali knew she was in a dream but didn't know whose. Evolving night vision enabled her to track dragonflies – those lovely, whirring Art Nouveau creations that zigged and zagged nearby – plucking them from mid-air with the beak she wielded like an entomologist's tweezer. The warriors writhed at its end; she paused to admire the shimmery mosaic of wings, hard-plated exoskeleton and compound eyes before swallowing.

In another part of the dream, she imagined herself ascending to the tarry, supersonic skies until the coast receded, jetting like a witch to Arizona, loitering awhile above Painted Desert and Petrified Forest – then high over the crater where Joan proposed – until the tweezer of God lifted her to the Celestial City where she herself would be ecstatically devoured.

She was aching to fly. Recalling what Joan read aloud – *the glide of the hoopoe is pulsed by short, irregular wing-bursts. The erratic pattern, unique and undulating, makes it resemble a gargantuan butterfly* – she fell into nervous, scattershot reverie. Joan's manic energy had been focused on *The Pilgrim's Progress* film before suddenly pivoting to a remake of *The Incredible Shrinking Man*; it was cool that Guillermo signed on, but the fickleness scared her. Ali couldn't help wondering if *she* were the thing Joan would pivot from next. It sounded petulant but the answer, of course, was that Ali had to leave first. That was actually the *best* thing, and only solution – it would force Joan to take that last step of growing up, a step that Ali prevented so long as she stayed. *I've served my purpose*: a useful, lovely purpose that gave her wife the chance to be selfless and of service, to distract and distance herself from the awful, crippling murders that nearly destroyed her. *And now is the time to disappear...* that's what the Santa Anas whispered as they drew close, rustling her blacker-than-night comb.

She decided, too, that she would die without Joan's help; anything else would be too cruel. She had to do it quickly, before she lost the mental and physical strength.

But how?

Her mind grew disordered.

She thought of her parents – childhood nest in Tulsa – and remembered the strangest things. The stink Daddy made when he left the bathroom on Sunday mornings... the freckly clumps on Mama's right knee that Ali loved to scrutinize whenever watching over the troubled woman's drunken sleep. Her heart suddenly rammed against its cage when she thought of that time Grammie got attacked by a homeless woman outside the 7-Eleven in Toluca Lake –

all her meditations got roughed and ruffled up

Then everything went blank.

After an eternity, she heard shrieking, and felt a weight on her. When she came to, three of the heavier nannies had her pinned like a comic tag-team of Mexican wrestlers. Ali felt like a patient who'd been awakened in the middle of surgery. A faraway Fijian barked orders as Joan's face loomed into view, then Joan was covering her face in kisses. *What the fuck is happening?* Her wife pulled away, bony anorexic cheeks now smeared in blood. Ali speedswiveled her neck and saw the macerated carcass – a ring-tail cat she had her eye on the last few weeks. *It must have tried to get away from me and been trapped by the netting.* Ali tasted something sticky and bittersweet on the long black beak. In sense and memory's time warp, the exsanguinated cat's plaintive cries boomeranged over crashing waves and she recoiled.

The Fijians wrapped her in a duvet and galloped her back to the main house where Dr. Pirouette awaited with powerful sedatives. She had just enough time to look into Joan's eyes and say,

"I can't live, I can't live! Joanie, please don't let me live!"

But it was unintelligible.

B U D

Bud cleaned up with extra care, taking a gym sauna for that touch of his own private "wellness" workshop. Before seeing Garry, he wanted to leach the drugs out of his system.

On the way over, he did a bump of coke to raise his energy and spirits. He stopped at a Sephora to shpritz himself with a medley of perfume. When they hugged, Gigi seemed to appreciate it.

"You smell like my wife!"

"That's right. And we use the same douche."

They were old enough to still have douche jokes in the repertoire.

Garry was riding high. His Netflix show about the Golden State killer just got a slew of Emmy noms and he bought himself a Rolls to celebrate. The new purchase led to memories of the Ferrari showroom on Wilshire where they used to hang after school. The owner kept two Great Danes lolling around, bigger than both boys put together. The floodgates opened and the late-Sixties dominoes dropped: the incensed-up Westwood Boulevard head shops, the "real" lemonade tree inside the toy store on Rodeo, the gingham-uniformed waitresses at the old Ontras Cafeteria over on Dayton Way. From all that, they somehow segued to the more contemporary landmarks of Me Too.

"One of my buddy's shitting bricks," said Garry. "He was at Spring Place, a private club that just moved into the old CAA building. Fucking private clubs are spreading in this town like melanoma. Anyway, he's admiring a woman's bracelet from afar. Maybe admiring the woman too, just a little. *Maybe*. Which is a crime now by the way. So as he leaves, he points to her bracelet and says, 'That's lovely' – she bitches him out! 'Don't *touch* me!' she says – which he *didn't* – touch her, by the way. He said she almost *screamed* it. He looks around – people are staring – he's *embarrassed*. He told me he couldn't even remember what it was like to be embarrassed like that, you know, that hadn't happened since he was *twelve*. And this is a guy who doesn't take shit off *anyone*, right? A few years ago – before all the nonsense – he'd have told her to eat the shit out of his ass. *Now*, he's pussified. So, he points his finger *by way of demonstration* and says, 'I didn't touch, I pointed.' And she says, 'Don't *point*, I don't *know* you!' My friend said the expression on her face was pure *hatred*. He can't sleep – he's not sleeping – he says any day now he's gonna get a call from the *club* or a *lawyer*..."

"I've grown nostalgic for the days when rape was consensual."

Garry belly laughed. "Hey! I forgot to ask! How was the *wedding*?"

"Gigi," said Bud, with a deep sigh of contentment. "It was one of the highlights of my life."

"Isn't that wonderful? I mean, it's a miracle, isn't it? Don't you think it's a miracle?"

"I do. I truly do. It restored my faith. In *everything.*"

"Well, I don't know your granddaughter – I hope to meet her! I really do, Bud – but I *do* know Ali Nell. She's a sweet, sweet soul. I worked with her, you know."

"Really? On what?"

"Her first episode of *Arrested Development.* I directed it."

"Incredible! How did I not know that?"

"'Cause you're a dumbshit. But come on now, tell me more about the wedding! How'd they treat you? Like a VIP? Did Grandpa get a backstage pass?"

"Pretty much."

"Take any pictures?"

"Wasn't allowed – they put everyone's phones under lock and key. Had a videographer though. They're creating a keepsake album. Soon as I have it, I'll shoot it over..." Suddenly, his face went blank. After a pause, he said, "Gigi, I got a serious favor to ask."

"Anything."

"Joanie's about to lay a serious *wad* on her ol' granddad."

"*No shite,*" said Garry, happy Bud's ship came in at last. "It's about time, my friend."

"From all preliminary *discussions* – the intel my lawyers have been able to gather – we expect the number to be in the realm of eight figures."

"Come to Jesus!"

He and Joan hadn't talked specifics, not yet, but Bud was certain he would be taken care of. At last parting, she made sure to show him her heart. She'd even *asked* if he needed money.

"*All that said,* I need a little bridge loan. When I tell you what it's for, you'll understand. And I know you get the irony. You're the *only* one who can appreciate the friggin irony: that sitting before you is an extremely wealthy man, who at the moment is cash poor. Extremely so."

"Understood."

"The arrival of the monies is gonna take three weeks," said Bud, shamelessly adding, "The lawyers just told me, five minutes before I walked in through the door to see you. It's *done,* mon frère, but the parties still need to dot the t's and cross the i's, all that standard rigmarole paper chase bull-shit. When Joan asked how I was fixed, I said I was fine. She wanted to give me something to tide me over, but the hard-headed ol' winemaker said no. Kill me now! Guess it's my friggin trademark *pride,* Gigi, but I just *couldn't.* For years, I tried to get money – to *participate* in the estate – and failed." He grew genuinely emotional. "And now – now that it's *hap-pening* – organically, like I always dreamed it would – I just couldn't bring myself to…"

"Buddy, I love you," said Garry, emotional himself. "And I'm here for you, you know that."

"I know. I know that. And I love you more."

"How can I help? How much do you need?"

"To be honest, I've had a run of miserable luck. This thing with Joan – it's changed my life. *Changed the way I want to live.* The pills and the not-taking-care-of-myself… I haven't shared with you the – "

"No need! No need to explain. *I'm here for you.* And *glad* you're thinking about your health. *So* glad. I never bring it up, Bud, because – "

" – my bullshit, world-class pride! Pride'll kill you every time."

"Yes, yes it will. And blind you. Look: I knew things must be bad, okay? I'm not born yesterday – it's Garry Gabe you're talking to, okay? And we're brothers. All right?" Bud hung his head. "We have the same *history,* the same memories knocking around in our heads, and that's rare. That's a precious, precious thing. I love you, Buddy boy. And *admire* you. Always have. Shit, I wanted to *be* you."

"And I wanted to be *you!*"

"Beautiful," said Garry with a smile. "No one's ever happy with who they are and what they have. Ain't that the way it always is?"

"You know what's funny?" said Bud, eyes shiny now. "This enormous weight got lifted off when I patched it up with my Joanie. Not just money issues – money comes and goes – but the whole... *spiritual* aspect. I don't mean that to sound... the reunion thing with my granddaughter hit me *very,* very hard. I wasn't prepared! How could anyone be prepared for something like that? Of that magnitude? It was like a religious... until it happened, I had no idea there was this *hole* in my life. Gigi, it was the closest I'll ever come to having a religious experience."

"I love it. And you couldn't write it. Well, maybe *you* could..."

"Here's Part Two, and I think you'll appreciate it: the reason I'm asking for a loan isn't for *myself.* 'Cause I'll get by – always have. You know, I can keep doing my Uber and my whatever to pay the bills. I know how to take care of myself. I'm a survivor."

"I know you are," said Garry, humbled. He didn't know Bud was Ubering and briefly wondered what else he was in the dark about.

"The thing is, I haven't gotten them a wedding gift."

"Ah!"

"Didn't have the funds. And now I'm actually staying at their home, they're *hosting* me. In Point Dume. I'm starting to feel awkward. It's crazy, Garry, 'cause I know Joan's not even *thinking* about it, it's the farthest thing from her mind. She and Ali aren't waking up in the morning and grousing, *The bastard never got us a wedding gift.* But it got in my head – those very words! – like in 'The Tell-Tale Heart.' I know I have the traditional year to get them a gift but it doesn't feel right." He became solemn. "The *real* issue is – Gigi, I'm gonna share something with you in *absolute confidence.* Ali's not doing so well. Something is terribly wrong. After the ceremony, they had to carry her back to the house."

"Jesus."

"That's *strictly* between you and me."

"Of course. Of course."

"So, I don't... I don't even know how much time that poor girl has."

"Whatever you need." Garry knew the wedding gift was a smokescreen for a larger ask but didn't mind playing along; he had no worries that his nouveau riche old running partner would make him whole. With a twinkle in his eye, he said, "Get 'em something grand, okay?"

"Thank you," said Bud, wondering how large the check would be.

"Get 'em something grand."

* * *

"I googled you. You really *are* Joan Gamma's grandfather."

Bud sat in a red-booth steakhouse on 8th Street with the tattooed, pale-skinned enigma who sidled up to him at the Peninsula bar.

Initially, he thought she was a whore. He pulled out the heavy artillery on night they first met, confiding his black sheep status in the Gamma Dynasty. She was skeptical but intrigued, fully engaged as she grilled him. Then she made a startling confession, quid pro quo: she was the secret lovechild of Elon Musk. It was Bud's turn to be skeptical (he was already intrigued and fully engaged). Reeve held up her phone and played him a recent home movie. He squinted at the tiny screen and Jesus, yes, there she was, romping with the Tesla King. They must have talked another two hours before she made a Cinderella exit. She wasn't drunk – *he* was – but insisted he "be a gentleman" and walk her out. As they waited for her car, she flirted, kissing the white stubble of his cheeks.

"Take care of yourself, Grandpa Gamma."

"Wiggins, not Gamma. My friends call me Grandpa *Wiggins*."

The valet brought around a new Tesla.

As she drove off, he stared at the license plate – LVCHILD – and was certain he would never see her again. Reeve Tobrin had his cellphone number but he'd forgotten to ask for hers; that's how rusty he was at the game. He fantasized about seeing her again, even coming up with a plan to disabuse her of what she no doubt would have already learned from the Internet: that he lost a years-long court battle. He would tell her that was a lie – he got a lump sum, with a stipulation of the settlement being that the world was never to know. If he had any chance with this woman, it wouldn't be as a bum, but as a man of means, worthy of respect.

The memory of their encounter was dream-smoke until she called to make a date. He had to pinch himself. She wanted to meet at Taylor's, her favorite steak joint. The decrepit novelist was so shocked he could barely stammer out a yes.

It had been a *very* good day. He asked Garry for Five Large but the showrunner had "a better idea." He told his private banker to open an account in Bud's name and put twenty-five thousand in. And now, here he was with Elon Musk's slinky lovechild, having a second rendezvous! As he listened to her talk, Bud did some swift logistical calculations. *What's the closest hotel?* Forget Koreatown, which is where they were... *the Biltmore? or the Bonaventure?* It was a far cry from the usual game he played while out to eat, to pass the time – plotting what hospital was handiest, in case he thought he was having a heart attack. No: it'd been a good day, and he felt fine and dandy; pleasantly drunk, he used alternate hands to feel the outline of the gram of coke in one pocket and the forty Benjamins in the other. He even felt the stirring of an antediluvian hard-on as Reeve made her pitch. Her dad, she said, was developing a "horizontal elevator." For a quarter of a million, she could get Bud in.

"Why me?" he asked.

"I'll tell you why. But I warn you – it's a little California woo-woo."

He talk-sang, "Do that woo-woo that you do so well."

"A shaman in Topanga told me the world is full of cyclic beings. He said that certain people are on the same 'strand of beads' – it's an energy thing. That's you and me. We're on the same strand."

"And how do you know this?"

"Cause I'm a freak. Consider my lineage. I'm my father's child."

"The same strand of beads... like, a curtain?"

"Kind of."

"I hope that doesn't mean it's curtains for us."

"Try not to be so clever."

His age and musty humor were showing. "Sorry. Tell me more about the horizontal elevator." He almost uncleverly added *Then let's go get horizontal* but managed to restrain himself.

She talked and talked but he couldn't focus. There was something in there about Bud coming up with $200,000, with a guaranteed return of at least ten million. *Now that's a very Big Win.* As his attention wavered, her interest waned. In the parking lot, she turned down his clumsy invitation to "join me at a five-star inn." At least she was kind about it; she stroked his fly while bidding adieu. But he was woozy and overexcited and the two Cialis pills he took before dinner failed to launch.

JOAN

[front page, *The New York Post*]
Ali SQUAWKS
... the
bird
FLIPS!

Mrs. Gamma *&?@+#@%!s at drone –
it's FIGHT or
FLIGHT
everybody knows that the bird is the (f-) *word*

* * *

The culprit providing the salacious account to the *Post* – accurate, for the most part, yet more in keeping with bygone tabloid staples such as Big Foot sightings and alien-abduction – was a nurse on Team Ali, recruited by none other than Dr. P. To make matters worse, the woman somehow had avoided signing an NDA. The anguished caregiver confessed that it was the mutilation of the ring-tail that pushed her over the edge, into the verdant Valley of Probity. "It's always upsetting to betray patient confidentiality," she said, "but this story needs to be told" – adding that she had left the field of healthcare to become an antivivisection activist. Any way you cut it, the traitor would be handled.

Moishe himself said, "That piece of shit will be sorry she was ever born." He had Joan's fervent assent.

As it turned out, Guillermo's initial excitement over directing a new version of *The Incredible Shrinking Man* was short-lived. After years of trying, the Mexican visionary was at last filming his *Frankenstein* passion play. Still, when he saw the blurry *Post* cover of a fearsome Ali ("aka Angry Bird") unfolding a claw-like middle finger in the direction of an eye-in-the-sky paparazzo, his curiosity was piqued. He had even heard that Werner Herzog was putting out feelers regarding the strange Point Dume goings-on – which testified to its outlandish veracity. A deeper conversation with the makeup artist he sent to the wedding bore further testimony to the bizarre nature of the story. Perhaps this was no inchoate urban myth after all, but a real, Joseph Campbell-sized one in the making.

He couldn't help but give Joan a call.

"Hey, Sor Juana" – his nickname for her – "has the *New York Post* lost its mind?"

She forced a laugh and said it was "all just fake magical realism news." The deception immediately made her melancholy. "As you know, my wife is very sick – we still don't know what's wrong."

"I'm so sorry, Joan."

In that moment, he knew it all was true.

Joan lapsed into small talk. Guillermo decided not to probe, at least not directly. The conversation tactfully meandered, with the director eventually circling around to the status of *Pilgrim's Progress*. Joan didn't feel like saying the project was dead, so she told him they were waiting on Chris Pratt's first draft instead. When Guillermo realized whom she was talking about, he giggled, epically enthused.

"Star-Lord is writing your movie! Sor Juana, you truly *are* a genius."

"That's why they pay me the big bucks."

"I need to make an amends. You must forgive, because I was never clear – about *Pilgrim*. I think I may have been rude and wish to apologize for never explaining. The reason I did not... that I chose not to become engaged with the project is – it was a bit too *Catholic*. Which, of course, I don't strictly *oppose* because Catholicism is alive and well in *all* fairy tales. I've actually spoken about this quite a bit. In the best fairy tales is this idea of transformation. In the end, the humblest creatures become Gods, it is a metaphor that in my *films* strives to become reality. I suppose – this notion – is behind my obsession with Frankenstein… for me, with Bunyan's book, they *do* reach the Celestial City but my problem is, there is no true transformation. There *is*, yes, but not for *me*. For *Bunyan,* not for me. I could not find it. As director, that is of course up to *me* to make, to *imagine*, but I could not – to my satisfaction. I could not find something beautiful, I could not imagine it, so that is my *failing*. I could not see the proper end, *sor Juana,* which for me is essential. I have said this often, that in the end all vanishes – the honors and awards, property and possessions, the *audience* – and one is simply left in peace. Or in horror. In Buddhism, they say the last thought you have before death determines your next life, good or bad, but I don't believe in next lives! Too Catholic! In the end, the Buddhists are maybe very Catholic too, no? But it could be I am identifying too much with the hero – what was his name? – ah, it's *Christian,* no? How could I forget? Better a hero named 'Christian' than a hero named 'Catholic'! I am identifying too much with *Christian's* travails – he's no 'magic Christian'! – and could not find peace in Bunyanland. I could not find *horror* either, but could not find peace…"

Time to go in for the kill.

"All this business about beautiful Ali – this shit I've been reading – is like a crazy flashback of *Birdman*! Alejandro and I were talking about this! We *talked* because he knows I know you – I hope I am not saying too much, Joan – please stop me if it's too much! – and Alejandro, he too has been aware of this very strange, very… *moving* story. We thought it was just some weird press, some fucking publicity Disney is up to because that wonderful character of hers – *Melissa Eerie,* in *Te Deum,* had feathers – Marvel is doing a reboot, no? Three days ago, I received a call from CAA that Disney is asking for me to somehow be *involved*. But you're saying no, you have no knowledge, that Ali has no involvement? So what I ask of you, I will just say it, because we are such strong friends, what I ask is that you tell me the *truth* of what has been occurring, Corazon, because my heart tells me *your* heart is desperate to have a confidant, to stand with, to talk with, to whisper to if it must – ..."

* * *

She wanted things settled with her grandfather, and her lawyers knew better than to challenge her wishes.

Bud Wiggins would be the recipient of a $25 million trust, as long as he agreed the following: a) He must undergo detox and a comprehensive physical exam overseen by Dr. Phedan Pirouette; b) He must successfully complete a 90-day rehab at a treatment center in Malibu; c) He must attend at least two AA meetings a week for the rest of his natural life; d) He must consent to having a live-in sober companion for a period of no less than three years (but not capped); a panel of addiction experts will assess his progress in monthly reviews. As long as he remained clean and sober, he would receive $50,000 a month in living expenses (with no say in how the principal was invested). Finally, out of that sum, he must hire an editor to help complete his memoir and ready it for publication. If Bud "slipped" – if he drank or used again – the contract's terms would be suspended until at least 90 days of rehab were completed and the panel deemed his privileges should be restored.

When she tried to call, his phone was disconnected – which didn't surprise. Someone in the room was tasked to

find the old man. Joan stressed the urgency, fearing he may
have overdosed, or collapsed from "whatever other issues."
The first thing she suggested was that they get in touch with
his old friend, the producer Garry Gabe Vicker. If they had
no luck, she would turn to Moishe, head of the crack team
that guarded her after her family was killed. But just now, she
needed Moishe's full attention on something else.

Something special, that she could entrust to no one but
him.

At the end of the meeting, one of the senior attorneys
walked her out. He made a comment about her precipitous
weight loss.

"It's glandular," she huffed. "I'm handling it."

After she left, in an aside to a colleague, he said

"She couldn't be more than 80 pounds."

* * *

As soon as she got home, Joan checked on her wife.

Ali was deeply depressed. She stopped speaking through
the device provided by MIT and didn't watch television anymore. They used to watch *Botched*, joking about making an
appearance together – "Dr. Nassif, *please* fix my long beak!" –
that ritual was gone. In their last, meaningful conversation,
Ali expressed how much she'd been hurt by the vicious, slan-
derous backlash over her ALS misdiagnosis. She could take
almost anything – anything but the hateful accusations that
she was a fraud who targeted Joan's fortune. It broke her spirit.
Through the voicebox, came the stuttering digital plea: *joan-
joan joan whathappening to my fans whathappening joan i love you
joanjoanjoan do you know whathappening*

Joan had no answer.

Soon, none of it would matter.

Moishe knew her plan, and all was nearly in place. The love of her life had become a circus freak – was she supposed to keep shooting down drones and submitting her to Dr. P's miracle drugs/procedures of the week? Helicoptering her to far-flung experimental clinics in a steel cage, sedated, as Joan watched bluish tears roll down her viscous, hard-feathered cheek? How many useless hematopoietic stem cell transplants must Ali endure?

There was no dignity in it for either of them.

And besides, Joan wondered how much time she had left herself.

When the Fijians came for Ali's sponge bath, Joan kissed her goodnight then hovered in the hall to eavesdrop on the happy-faced nannies while they ministered.

"You look so pretty tonight, Miss Oops! You getting more and more *beeyootiful*. You are *too* beeyootiful, Miss Oops! No Marvel hero keep up with you... you saw Disney Legends on the television, Miss Ali? We were watching, and they talk about *you*! They talk about return of Miss Melissa Eerie! They are wanting your voice for new movie! Miss Joanie no tell you? They are *animating*, so you can *do* it, Miss Ali! You are going to? You must do it! You make the recording right here in bedroom! You use your machine to talk! Miss Joanie she take care *everything*. You *must* be Disney legend! You *are* Disney Legend! Like Mr. Favreau and Miss Aguilera... you *legend*, and they invite you to DisneyMarvel Theme Park! We come with you! We take care of you at DisneyMarvel Theme Park! They build now the Stark Industries at California Adventure, they build the Iron Man Tony Stark 'HQ'! Do you know what Miss Christina Aguilera say she is most proud? We hear it when she come on the Disney

Legends show! Miss Christina she say she proud *not about the highlights*, she say, *but to stand back up when she fall down from the hardships.* To stand up after she fall – that is what *you* do, Miss Oops! It is *already* what you do! And you can teach her *more*! You can teach the *peoples* how to stand up when they are fallen!"

* * *

Joan couldn't sleep.

She noticed that the door to the bedside cabinet where she kept her mother's journals was ajar. Vi's notebooks were intact – but Joan's sketchbook was gone. The one filled with pornographic drawings and pasted photo montages of herself with Millie, Billie and Greta, separately and in groups. She had whimsically labeled the portfolio "Squad Goals."

And now it belonged to the larcenous nurse.

B U D

He lay in the backseat of his car on the Cheviot Hills cul-de-sac. It'd been a while since he bathed, and the vinyl stuck to his skin as he bobbed like a cork on the vast, mysterious Sea of Probability. Amphetamine salts captained the yacht, navigating aquamarine, saltwater depths; amphetamine, seraphic patron of algorithms real and imagined, enabled him to identify and observe oceanic numerical patterns in all their glory. The hallucinations, a kind of volcanic woolgathering, were an everyday thing now. Sometimes he visited Dolly, to sate the longing that he experienced in the recurring dream of her abandonment; other times, he saw his daughter Vi running away. He hadn't caught up to her yet but she smiled back in a manner he interpreted as both fetching and forgiving.

But usually he just found himself on deck, an old salt entranced by the red tide made from the effloresced calculus of scratchers odds.

As Bud drifted, his whole being languorously ruffled by the soft, evocative trade winds of *South Pacific* (Dolly's favorite musical), he stared out at the beds of data-kelp carpeting the mainframe of the membranous deep. Often at this dusky hour, he found himself dwelling on that gallingly "legendary" axiom born in a Monte Carlo casino in 1913, ironically named "The Gambler's Fallacy" – for it was a fallacy itself. Originally pertaining to dice, the Fallacy, reframed, posited that if one lost 99 scratchers in a row, one was *no more likely to win on the 100th ticket than the ninety-nine that came before.* In other words, each buy was statistically independent, which Bud knew to be an obscene, dangerous notion. If the Fallacy *were* true, why did the back of Big Win tickets assert, "Odds of winning any prize: 1:2.78; cash prize 1:4.13. Odds of winning $10,000,000: 1 in 3,000,000.00." Why wouldn't it simply say

Odds of winning any prize: EVEN; cash prize: EVEN
Odds of winning $10,000,000: EVEN

Such imperious, small-minded propositions came from a dead, nonspiritual bureau born of the social order. The architects of the Fallacy had no way of parsing the sorrowful ghosts that roved the world, magnificently, tragically sacred… nor was it capable of balancing the Book of Dreams, the Book of Death, the Book of the Eternal. Could the Fallacy's logic dare accept the proposition that the living were the same as the dead? How might it even begin to categorize the heartrending mysticism of the Santa Anas that *on this against-all-odds night* gently rocked the HMS Taurus as it maundered on the Cheviot seas? What *rule* did it have that governed the numinous, beaded strand he shared with Reeve Tobrin? Like an automaton, the Fallacy swept the unthinkable Big Win of Bud's reunion with his granddaughter away. The supernal has no interest in the cretinous commandments of social order statisticians. In the spiritual realm, there is no such thing as "statistical independence."

All things are interconnected...

In this life, Bud knew the nature of his karma – to sample *luck* and *unluckiness* in the extreme. (Most went to the grave without experiencing either.) He had great critical success with a novel, followed by years of anonymity and writer's block; the birth of a daughter brought intoxicating joy, and her estrangement tremendous suffering; he embarked on a quixotic, protracted court battle that failed – only to have the ruling reversed, and Love bequeathed, by the grandchild he thought had literally disowned him. Bud was certain that the Fallacy, unable to compass the immanence of a Big Win *deus ex machina*, was hell-bent on refuting his own magnificently tragic, sacred journey. The trick was to see everything for what it was: a grand illusion. Both sides of the coin – *luck* and *unluckiness* – were the same, which meant there were no sides at all. The "coin" itself was an invention of the social order.

He leaned from the backseat, turned the radio to a classical station, and continued his scold.

The "Gambler's Fallacy" actually wanted him to *believe* that he could take $10 million of Joan's money, buy a *million* ten-dollar scratchers – and *never, ever win*. Not once! A million scratcher losses in a row!

The Fallacy had been drawn up by the same cabal of dream-killers he had faced all of his life, with answers for everything.

Bud was tired of answers.

Answers were an invention of the social order.

Yesterday he stole a Buddhist book from the library. Now he lay back in the sea-spray, opening it to "The Unanswered Questions."

The phrase *unanswered questions* or *undeclared questions* (Sanskrit avyākṛta, Pali: avyākata – "unfathomable, unexpounded") refers to a set of common philosophical questions that Buddha refused to answer. The Pali texts give only ten, the Sanskrit texts fourteen questions.

Is the world eternal – or not? Both? Or neither? Is it finite – or not? Both or neither? Is the Self identical with the body? Or different from the body? Does the Buddha exist after death – or not? Both? Or neither?

A few pages later:

What am I? How am I? Am I? Am I not? Did I exist in the past? Did I not exist in the past? What was I in the past? How was I in the past? Having been what, did I become what in the past? Shall I exist in future? Shall I not exist in future? What shall I be in future? How shall I be in future? Having been what, shall I become what in future? Whence came this person? Whither will he go?

They need not be answered…

His reveries were interrupted by a burst of light, emanating from under the passenger seat – his missing iPhone. He was glad because he hadn't been able to find it for a few days.

The screen said

MISSED CALL, DIGBY COLT

He listened to the voicemail.

"Hey, Bud – it's Dig. I, uhm, sorry I didn't get back to you, uhm, sooner, but I've been up to my proverbial *teats* teaching prose in Idyllwild." The novelist winced at the mannered, anachronistic diction – Digby's trademark, which he no doubt thought made him memorable. "Rather brutal! They're not bad *kids*, but they *are* bad *writers*. Not bad, *terrible*. Some of them – well, most of them. My work's cut out for me! *Anyway*, look… I *actually* didn't want to leave a *message* but the wife and I are on our way to Maui-wowee so I think I'm gonna *have* to. I actually read the pages you sent and was… rather mortified! Or do I mean revolted… albeit, *some* of it's kinda funny but I guess *part* of what I'm saying, maybe the *main* part, is that it felt a little 'try-hardy.' The words on the page kept saying 'Look at me!' but never really lit *up*. It's always about the words on the page, isn't it, Bud? I'm always telling my students about the *words*, the *words*, the *words* – do they light up the room? And if they *do*, is it candlelight? Is it neon? Or is it *sterno*? Or did the frickin' power go out! *Another* thing I have to say, Bud, is that it was *confusing*. I know you like the nonlinear thing but the magic of *Wild Psalms* just ain't there, brotha. Or if it *was*, well, you could see the trick – how the naked lady was sawed in half. I wanted to saw those pages in half!

Just joking – that was harsh. Sorry. I have great respect... but just couldn't follow a lot of what was going on. Maybe things got clearer along the way... maybe I'm just getting *old* but as I told the wife, 'If I can't sort out page *five,* how'm I going to look on page *300?* Will I be Linda Blair, with my head spinning and vomit spewing?' I hope this is okay. I feel bad because it was actually so good to hear from you. But I never sugarcoated stuff *then* and I'm not going to start *now*. I think you know there's *lots* of stuff I wished you would've cut from *Psalms*... John Updike and I had a little difference of opinion! (My apologies, Johnny Boy.) Far be it from *me*! But I'm always happy to admit I'm wrong, and I *was* wrong about *Psalms* – mostly! – so maybe I'm wrong about this. I kinda don't *think* so... but, uhm, thanks for the read (I *guess*) and call me back! Please? Or don't. Maybe we can have lunch sometime at the new Formosa. Or not. Haven't been to the new old Formosa yet, and I'm *muy curioso*. We used to go there when we were youngsters, remember?"

* * *

This time, Reeve suggested the Pacific Dining Car downtown. The gal had a thing for plushy steakhouses.

He hadn't slept in days. Before their date, he took more opiates and benzos than usual to wrangle the amphetamines. She made a comment about his state of disarray that may or may not have been snide; he wasn't in any shape to assess. The ribeyes were $70 each but that was okay – the results of the memoirist's afternoon scratcher binge still left a balance of about $8,000 in "Garry's" account. He felt jauntily hopeful: even the Fallacy would have to concede that the probability of

Bud increasing that number a thousand-fold (a Big Win) fell into just three distinct categories: high, low, average.

In the middle of dinner, she spied an old friend at a far-away booth.

"Oh my God, it's *Albie*. He's a crazy genius…" She found something on her phone then handed it to Bud. "Read this! I'm gonna walk him over."

He watched her stroll to a distant booth where an attractive young man rose to embrace her.

It was difficult to focus but he started reading the Wikipedia entry that she pulled up.

Albie Rausch (born January 17, 1987) is an American entre-preneur with an estimated worth of $3.9 billion. An early "angel" investor in Facebook, Snapchat and Uber, he is now a silent partner of Elon Musk, overseeing the technologist and designer's ventures in private and governmental sectors –

Just then, Reeve and her friend arrived.

To Bud's relief, the addition of a third party made it eas-ier to "maintain." Albie was easygoing and articulate – and had actually read *Wild Psalms,* which he called a "coruscating primer that should be mandatory reading for anyone foolish enough to want to 'go Hollywood.'" The novelist smiled and kept quiet, soaking in the adulation.

When Reeve excused herself to the ladies room, Albie took the opportunity to compliment him on his good fortune. "She said there was something about you that she *trusted* right away – and meeting you, I get it, I can see what she saw. So I'm not really surprised she told you about her *dad*. Still, that's a pretty big deal for her. So keep all that to yourself, 'kay?"

"I wouldn't ever say anything..."

"Good! She's fuckin funny. Part of her *hates* being Elon Musk's daughter – and part of her full-on *loves* it. But anyhoo, you know what? I stopped trying to understand the Reeve algorithm a long time ago."

"You've known her a while?"

"For ten years. Elon's like a big brother – or a father, whatever. They're as close to family as I'll ever get. *You*, my friend, just got the Golden Ticket. Get ready for Mrs. Toad's wild ride. She's like the Tinder genie – a sex freak that can also make you *very*, very rich." Then he brought up the horizontal elevator, telling Bud, "I myself only got recently involved. In that way, you and I are exactly alike – we're both on the ground floor. *An even playing field.* And you know what? I *am* shocked she told you about *that.* But you know what they say: Don't look a gift elevator in the mouth. How much you gonna throw in?"

The novelist licked his dry lips and reached for his drink with a trembling hand. "I think," said Bud, "I'll give her a million. She asked for three-fifty but I'd be foolish not to go all in. Don't you think? Tell me – do you agree? Do you think a million's enough or should it be more? I can probably go as high as *three*, but that's probably going to be my limit."

* * *

Before they met for dinner, he rented a suite at the Bonaventure. When they walked in, the curtains were drawn, as he'd left them. It was pitch dark and he told her not to turn on the lights.

"My eyes were dilated this afternoon. For glaucoma. I don't have it but they wanted to take a look."

When she returned from the bathroom, Bud surprised her. He knew the check looked a little bogus – it was a temporary one from "Garry's" account. Still, he wanted to present it as an act of good faith. After they slept together, he'd cancel it. He would tell the bank manager that it was drunken gag and they'd have a good laugh.

"What's this?" she said. She read aloud, theatrically: "'Pay to the Order of Reeve Tobrin. Five hundred thousand dollars and zero-zero cents.'"

Bud smiled and said, "Five hundred now and five hundred after Joan's lawyers – *my* lawyers – look at the contract."

"This is dated two months from now."

"That's when the funds will be available."

"No can do, bubbalah. Has to be cash."

"I can't get that much just now."

"Then get *less* – get two hundred. Get a *hundred. Cash.* And *no one knows about this,* right? I *told* you – right? Not your *grand*daughter, not your granddaughter's *attorneys, no one.* My father would fucking disown me if he thought you were spreading his shit all over town."

"No! I haven't told a soul. I *wouldn't...*"

Reeve pulled him toward her.

"Look, I appreciate the gesture, really I do, but if this is going to work, you *have* to get me two hundred in *cash.* Because we're closing on this, like, *yesterday.* I *might* be able to push it 48 hours, but the window is *closing.* Can you do that? Because you know what this is going to return, don't you? Didn't Albie say? In three months, you'll have *one hundred times your investment.* That's *twenty million dollars.*" She pushed him onto the bed. "Just tell *Joan* that Grandpa needs *cash* – two-hundred-thousand is *mad money* for her. Pull on her heartstrings. Tell her it's for good works. That you had a dream about starting a foundation for the struggling families of dead first responders. Tell her *anything*. You can do that, can't you, Bud?"

"Yes. I can do it. I'll do it."

"Because when you come back to her in three months with that kind of *multiple*, she'll be *seriously* impressed. So will the lawyers! Then you *can* start a fucking foundation – if you want. Okay?"

As if to seal the deal, she lifted her skirt and pulled off her panties, pushing Bud's head between her legs. He licked then gagged. The room spun and he passed out (sometimes that happened when he mixed blood pressure meds with too much Cialis).

When he came to, Reeve was in the midst of pulling the shirt over Bud's head. "You're burning up!" Then she looked at his chest and recoiled in horror. "What are those… *sores?*" All he could do was grunt. "Are they – cigarette burns?" She took a closer look. "Oh my God, no they're *not*. What are those disgusting *sores?*"

"I won!" he said boyishly. "I finally won."

"What the fuck are you talking about?"

He swept a hand over the wounds like a game show hostess showing prizes on the board. "*I* am the scratcher. *I am* the ticket…"

"Oh my God, I can't believe this. You're out of your mind."

"Look closer – "

When he forced her head down to see, she slapped him hard across the face, punched his stomach, and fled.

He threw up.

He would do as Reeve said and go to the wedding house in Point Dume. His body would be his collateral. He wore a sport coat over his bare chest, so that Joan could easily see the *real* Golden Ticket, with the hundreds of perfectly etched circles that Reeve had beheld.

Beneath one of them – one was all it took – he had finally found the grail of

Big

Win

Winner take all.

DENOUEMENT

Time was lost on her now and it was a liberation.

She stopped bothering to communicate.

Alien senses, spookily heightened.

DM'd by birds, DM'd by humans – each undecipherable.

Still in that between-place.

Yet she could feel the profundity of Love: its voluptuousness surged, soaking and spattering the Fijians, and even Dr. Pirouette as he put the needle in. When it came to her wife, *always* swallowing, embracing, wingbeating, surrounding, as Joan's face changed into stones then ferns then rabbit noses – now Joan was Katy Perry! now, Melissa Eerie! now, Grammie! – then into all the black shiny faces of Kanye's Calabasas chorale gathered in a bubble-eyed dome like that of the dragonflies she once coveted. Her watery sensoria receded, leaving her marooned on the shore of adolescent memory, night-hunting grunion at the beach house of an *Arrested Development* producer – until awakening in the ruins of the Smokehouse amidst the seaweed necklaces and sun-burnt crew of *Te Deum*... and the grain-of-sand souls (in the millions! That's how many followers Ripley once told her she had) who loved her then turned on her but would love her again. Somewhere in the shadows of the shadows of her shadow, she could *feel* the fans still thinking of her, dreaming of her each night and day. The faces of her parents were less frequent, oddly supplanted by random Tulsa parishioners she once focused on as a child, from her pew, yes – and sex thoughts swooped, carrying her off – from her very first kiss to her last, semi-invalidic gangbang – to Joan's relentless mouth-fucking.

What a beautiful farce was this life, how could she know

her caregivers put music on, suggested by a Crow shaman Joan flew in from Sedona – Vaughn-Williams' "Lark Ascending," Grieg's "Little Bird," Ravel's "Oiseaux Tristes," all if it so on-the-nose corny Joan couldn't bear it so she tried some Kanye church music (which seemed to get Ali super-agitated, lol) and finally some of Billie's E.'s gothy ballads before settling on Lana Del Rey, Lana was always Ali's fave in sadsexyhappier times. Mrs. Ali Nell-Gamma toggled between states of hypnagogic ecstasy and unutterable unbearable panic, a hell of confusion and horrorpain no different than torture by love and by fire, hundreds of times a day brought to the brink of death and emotional madness again, a lurching swooping cycle of joy and cruelty, agony and relief

diehard loyal Ripley left in charge of maintaining her Instagram, pretending for the world that Ali was sequestered but still her same old self, through queer eye torrents of tears he posted *#WomenCrushWednesday* pics of Jean Seberg, the young Liv Ullman, the young Michelle Obama, the young Mia Farrow (the Grammie too!)... Joan wasn't sure if the subterfuge was a good idea but didn't intervene – what difference did it

make if he/they were found out,
what difference? She didn't stop
him even when Ali's account
was hacked by shamers of the
deformed and differently-abled,
by anti-Semitic birdwatchers,
trans-baiters, witch hunters and
Joan-targeted anorexophobes –

*PLEASE GRAMMIE PLEASE! i so scare – where perfume where
old perfume of yours i love to smell – where papa sunday morning shitstink where mommy make nest eggs for breffast? mama put
papashit on eggs to protect*

the whole

congregation

she felt herself fucking; being fucked; watching friends watch. In this fatal, swollen mating
season, beaksnatched memories – babysitter's
hand down little Ali's pants? Saw her mother
Barbara Ann brazenly drunkfucking, parishioners brought home while daddy... & now
saw papa fuck too, fucked by boyish men,
bearish men, criminal men – the whole world
fucking/being fucked, the hole world congregation hunting, hunted, dirtyass clutching,
cuntsmeared and clutched – whole world congregation hate-commenting, funny-kittening,
product-sponsoring on Insta – then *soaring*,
butterfly soaring, *that's* what Ali wanted most,
Wifey read to her from hoopoe wiki and *said*

one day she would – but impossible just now to soar, impossible still! Impossible ever? *Pinned*, she was pinned here and now, *Joanie* was pinning her! Ripley and her followers were pinning her! Dr. P, who kept injecting & injecting & injecting was pinning her... *why why why!* She wanted to kill, fly, eat, clutch, love, be loved – the 10,000[th] hallucination yanked her to the *Arrested* set again, a writer from *People* knockknockknocking at the trailer door for an interview... *with Grammie now, at the Smokehouse, celebrating, eating cooked birds, Ali eating one of her own and loving it! LOL... at the memory of her enjoyment of the burned wingèd creature, her impulse to humanlaugh caused an avalanche of panic and she sprayed a Fijian who was feeding her from a bucket of cicadas and oh! oh! oh how she missed her friends missed her luscious actress body missed all her own human smells and sorrows* OH *the delight tho when one of the bolder caregivers dangled a frog and Ali gulped it like a zoofish piercing the water as Wifey came in reeking of alcohol and boisterously singing Sly's*

Everybody is a star!
I can feel it when you shine on me!
I love you for who you are!
Not the one you feel you need to be!

and Wifey shouted Come sing with me! Come
sing! Come sing! *and the Fijians said* don't shout
at her you're shouting at her it's hurting her *and
Wifey said* I don't care! I don't fucking care *and
for a moment Ali understood, that was the worst
part, for a moment she understood the nannies'
caution and their fear, of Wifey's rage, of Wifey's
terror and frustration, and Ali prayed for death to
take her –*

"Do you want me to read to you?" Wifey asked through weeping bathos, like an actress onstage.

I don't care said Ali, I don't fucking care, she said, she echoed, or thought she did, tho she hadn't said a word, nor even sprayed.

"Huh sweetheart? Want me to? Do you want me to read – ?" Ali just blinked, struggling with the lovesick urge to impale Wifey with beak, & devour like birdsong, like birdseed and Joan said to the Fijians, "Get the fuck out!" and settled herself to read the part from *Little Women* where Beth says

I read in Pilgrim's Progress today how, after many troubles, Christian and Hopeful came to a pleasant green meadow where lilies bloomed all year round, and there they rested happily, as we do now, before they went on to their journey's end …

Oh YES! *said Ali, or thought, or felt. The Celestial City! Grammie read her the exact same passage when she was a girl, Ali knew one day she would go there, Grammie said she would, why wouldn't she believe her – and now Grammie was waiting there for her to come but Ali was pinned how how how can I get to the Celestial City when I am pinned*

Then someone entered the room.

Joan snapped rudely at the interruption but was overruled by Moishe's men's voices and quickly left. The Fijians poured in to tend her but Ali swiveled her head protectively toward Wifey, she flew from the bedroom after Joan, screeching

oo-poo! Oo-*poo!* Oooo-oooop. Ooob-oob.
Oooo-pooo!

Oob-oob!
Oob-oob!
Oob-oob!
Oob-oob!
Oob-oob!

OOO-POO!

* * *

Luckily, Bud carried the follow-up invitation with the address of the wedding in his pocket like a talisman. He'd even written his name on the back, as the Lottery office recommended with any jackpot scratcher. The Bonaventure doorman put him in a cab. Point Dume was 45 minutes away.

The old man felt like a cog in a subatomic machine, a participant in the manipulation of chance and molecular matter. The apparatus of breath and consciousness revolved around incalculables and unanswerable questions... the odds for and against *this* moment, *this* breath – the infinity of moments that led to him meeting *that* woman, Reeve – and *this* hurtling from *that* hotel, toward *his* granddaughter (the only granddaughter who *could* be his, who carried her own infinity of moments) in *this* cab at *this* time on *this* day-night, as *that* wind blew through *that* passenger-side window... and *that* smell – was it jasmine? – infused Bud's mind and memory with that seminal moment when, as a boy, biking home from the dark playground on *those* dark suburban streets with *those* wind-whirled sentinel trees, the scent associated itself with the algorithms of love and a dim recognition of the infinite. He'd gotten *very lucky* – again – for he knew it was a miracle to have a righteous plan, to have any plan at all. It was miraculous to be able to swim in the Sea of Probability and not drown.

He felt so blessed. What would he say to Joan? He wasn't sure; best not to think too much. Words would be provided.

He was made from the flesh of the soft machine, and where he was heading there were no answers or questions.

* * *

Hours before she'd been interrupted by one of Moishe's men as she read to her wife from *Little Women*, Joan received some unpleasant news.

The nurse who stole the "Squad Goals" sketchbook got in touch with Joan directly, asking a ransom of $5 million for the return of the portfolio, "to avoid damaging exposure in the media." As part of "our agreement," a galling caveat insisted the heiress "seek professional help for your pedophilic issues." She wasn't rattled (at 63 pounds, there wasn't much to rattle). Besides, Joan would rather hang in the court of public opinion than be pushed around by a felonious, amateur-hour cunt. Moishe told her to begin negotiations, buying time for him to find her. She suddenly found herself not caring, not even for postmortem vengeance.

For tomorrow, if all went to plan, she would be dead.

* * *

The taxi left Bud at the gate.

Guards recognized him from the wedding. Disheveled and bizarre, he was still her grandfather. Ms. Gamma should definitely be alerted.

Joan gave the word to bring him in.

When Bud saw her, his eyes widened like those of a boy who'd been naughty – then he smiled.

Two of Moishe's dead-eyed men bracketed him, for Joan's safety.

"Bud," she said. "What is it? What's happened?"

"I'm so sorry, Joanie – I know it's late!"

"What *is* it? *Tell* me. What's wrong?"

"I wanted you to be the first to know." He stared shyly at the floor. "I *won* – the Big Win scratcher. I won all prizes – "

"I don't understand. What are you saying…"

"The problem is, I can't collect, because the regional office takes two months to pay. They don't take state taxes by the way, only federal. Joan…" Again, he stared at the floor, this time in shame. "There's something I didn't tell you. I meant to, but... see, the truth is that I was engaged to write something about the family, *through your eyes*. A 'reimagining' is what they call it... and I said no! For *years,* I said no – But then I said *yes...* because I was desperate! And Joan, I'm so sorry! But I'm here now to tell you I'm not going to do it, I was *never* going to do it! It was what they call a fallacy! A fallacy! And now I've won *all the prizes* and don't need to! I'm set for life! I was going to tell you that time I came to your office, that's the real reason – among others! – that I wanted to see you. But somehow I couldn't... I know I should have tried, but I got scared – and I knew I wasn't going to write it anyway, so I burned it when I got home, I burned all the pages! I knew I wasn't going to write it, Joanie, you have to believe me, I wouldn't have given them that book even if I *hadn't* won all the prizes! The only book I'm doing, the only one I *care* about is the memoir about your great-grandma Dolly... *that's* the book, *that's* the one. Wylann Partland already gave me a blurb – "

"Bud," said Joan gravely. "I want you to listen to me." She took his hands. "You need to go to the hospital."

"You don't understand – "

"Papaw, *listen.* Listen to your *granddaughter,* okay? You need to be in an environment where you can get well – where you can get help. I will totally do that for you. I told you that before and I meant it."

"Joanie, Joanie, Joanie! The odds are there – *here* – in this moment, this whatever, the odds that the entire lottery system – in the infinity of probability presenting itself that coalesced for us to share DNA – the odds *are* or *can* or *could* be, Joan, that the entire lottery system, the cosmology of it, the cosmology of *scratchers* only came into existence for... *me* – for *Bud Wiggins!* – so that *at this moment,* I could show you... look – !"

He opened his coat, revealing the stippled, star-spangled wounds.

"Jesus," said Joanie, turning her head to a protector. "Can someone please call 911?"

Bud was softly crying. "*This* is the book, Joan – *this* is the memoir." He pointed, one by one, to the small circles scraped on his skin. "Look! Look what's written under this one – *there*. Can you see? Can you see the letters? Can you see the 'Big Win'? It means I won all the prizes..."

Eyes rolling back in his head, he collapsed.

She knelt beside him. Her touch awakened Bud from his trance and he instinctively reached out, seizing Joan in his terror. Both were off-balance and changed places; now she lay underneath him.

A gust and ear-piercing shriek swept through the room. One of the guards was hurled against a wall, shattering a mirror. With lightning speed, Ali's beak entered the author's mouth. As he stared unblinking into the orangish iris of his executioner, his own eyes bulged; his look was that of pleasant surprise. An overpowering stench filled the air.

"Ali, stop!" cried Joan. "Ali, no! No! No! No!"

Joan clung to her wife, who was now passive, as if willing them both to awaken from a dream. Slowly, almost penitently, Ali withdrew from sheath of his throat.

Briefly, Joan feared she'd been run through herself, then understood: Ali must have thought she was being attacked. The look in her mate's eyes was of heartbreak and supplication.

Then she whooshed back upstairs like a dervish, leaving a trail of gore on the Moroccan carpet runner.

* * *

Moishe had been out of town, making preparations, when he got the call. He had trained his men well: no outside agency had been alerted to what transpired – not 911, not even Dr. Pirouette. (The Fijians knew everything but were trusted implicitly.) As Moishe flew home on a private plane, the body was removed while a crew ripped out the carpet, sanitized the foyer, and generally restored things to order.

Ali was heavily sedated and would remain so until they reached their destination.

At 5AM, he and Joan shared a coffee in the solarium. She looked ravaged, oracular, serene. Estimating her weight at 30 kilos, Moishe had the uncanny sense she was shrinking before his eyes. He wondered if she'd even survive the journey. Who would die first, Joan or her wife?

"We need to leave *now*," said Joan. "I mean, obviously."

"Not until nightfall – it has to be night." She nodded her assent. "Joan, are you certain you don't want to fly? It would make things easier."

"I already told you." Exhaustion made her testy. "Ali and I talked about it – once she's up in the air, she wants to *stay* there. She made me promise."

"The van will be here in the afternoon. We're using a different medical team. When it's over, they fly straight back to Haifa. There won't even be a record of them ever having been in this country."

"As long as we're where we're supposed to be, before dawn."

"Don't worry. You will be."

"There's a document on the desk in my office. It's already signed and notarized, witnessed by you. It lists dispersal amounts – to the Fijians, to Dr. Pirouette and the people on his team, even to Ripley. I don't want him writing a tell-all. With the amount he's getting, believe me, he won't."

"There's probably a more effective way to do all this."

"But not a more beautiful one."

She touched his hand and smiled.

"I'll give you that," he said, smiling back.

* * *

It was a small, escape caravan, the type Moishe had spent a lifetime organizing for a hundred operations, in a hundred cities, villages and wildernesses, used by exiled royalty, Russian and Saudi dissenters marked for death, and those who'd been kidnapped by cartels. Just three vehicles: "Father" (Moishe, a driver, and two assassins), followed by "Mother" (principals, medics, two gunmen) and "the Children" (more assassins) bringing up the rear. Anything could go wrong and it was Moishe's art to anticipate the unscripted. A Department of Public Safety insider minimized the chance of being stopped by law enforcement. Still, a fourth team ("Chaperone") shadowed the vehicles from a mile away, ready to pull focus by whatever means necessary.

When they got to the desert, the motorcade left the highway and extinguished its lights. The soldiers donned infrared goggles.

Joan nodded out, the hand of her twig-like arm resting on her wife's body like a widow's upon the coffin of the departed. She'd been losing five pounds a day despite Dr. Pirouette's valiant efforts; the process would only accelerate now that his radical potions had been withdrawn. Ali, encased in a wet cotton cocoon, was in a twilight sleep induced by an anesthesiologist who also happened to be a world-class avian veterinarian. Between nods, Joan kept whispering "we're on our way," though wasn't sure her wife understood. (Joan hardly understood herself.) It was so quiet in the van, except for Ali's soothing respirations – until she wheezed and Joan jerked awake in distress.

The vet smiled and said, "She's just dreaming."

"I wonder what about."

"Well," he said, almost wryly. "That was a courtship sound."

"Like she's having a sex dream?" asked Joan impishly.

"Maybe," he replied. "Did you know that hoopoes are monogamous for life?" She liked hearing that. Just then, Ali hissed in alarm. "I'm going to give her something to help her into a deeper sleep." He injected a sedative into IV. After a moment, a high-pitched *tiiiii* sound emerged from the swaddling, muffled.

"Is she crying?" said Joan, concerned.

The doctor wore a look of curiosity. "No – it sounds like – chicks, when they're hungry."

That made Joan sad.

Lulled to sleep by the soft, sure tread of tires ferrying them over sandy pastel floors, she found herself under the bed again, but this time Papaw was the one being butchered in the living room… as consciousness flickered, she thought how funny it was that she would soon be embalmed in a volcanic cone yet feared nothing! Just hours away now from a sacred place of immobilized bondage that she once associated with eternal panic. Eons would pass until the rocks crumbled and the ashes of her dry bones rose up to join Infinity's cold black space: the ultimate Giving Pledge.

When she woke up, they were there.

A few weeks ago, she provided Moishe with detailed blueprints. They were easy to get; as a major donor, she had carte blanche. He designed a VR program replicating every detail and dimension of the crater's interior. Joan knew exactly where he was to leave them – past the East Portal and golden stairs, toward the skyspace framing the crater's eye.

She meticulously arranged things in such a way that there would be no controversy surrounding their passing; no dark clouds could darken Mr. Turrell's stunning creation. The artist was in Europe for at least ten days. During that time, the crater would be depopulated of workers. She instructed Moishe to meet with James in person on his return and to be transparent about the trespass. In her heart, she believed James would understand and appreciate what he would be told. For the imaginative yet uninvited intrusion, Moishe would inform Mr. Turrell of the half-billion dollar gift, an amount guaranteeing not only the expansion of his vision, but the maintenance of his creation in perpetuity.

It was cold inside.

Even colder, it seemed, after everyone left.

She felt herself getting smaller and smaller.

They were in the South Space, where Joan, her eyesight failing, still had a clear view of the North Star.

Winter solstice, just as planned – the coming of the light!

When she had asked Moishe what time it was, he said, "Three hours before dawn." He always spoke quite formally when overcome.

She said, *Thank you, Moishe. I love you.*

He kissed her cheek – cool, razored sliver of cheek – and walked out.

Joan was naked, her skin and very cells now dissolving off her into a fine mist. She had just enough energy to crawl to her wife. She needed to reach her soon, before becoming too small, and the journey too long.

Ali, unwrapped now, lay on a comforter. The drugs were slowly wearing off. Not yet awake, she looked so beautiful, so radiant, so alive. Perhaps she'd never come to consciousness.

Would that be so terrible?

Then – were those rattles Joan heard?

Her vision was fading but it seemed Ali's body was elongating, searching out the cool corridor like a tendril, then, like a root that thickened in time-lapse. A soundless voice rose in Joan's throat of birds and said morning star! creator of books, of wind, corn, chakras, cosmos…

in the Pleiades, the Pleiades, the

Pleiades

maybe she's already seeing her Grammie, high in the floating

City.

and as Joan began to make her laborious, wiggling slither, she thought, *Je ne regrette rien* (Mommy used to sing that)… *je ne regrette* (sang Joan) *les monstres sacrés* –

Midway through the crab-crawl to the sepulcher – now the hard bed of her beloved wife – Joan felt a stab to her wafer-sized heart. What if I can't get to her – if I don't have the strength? Random thoughts flitted then drizzled down: Kanye told her the 808 drumbeat hit the lowest chakra, the sex chakra… she thought of Star-Lord, and wished him well… I missed – did I miss it? Billie Eilish's birthday? When? December 18th? Oh no, tell me I didn't miss it please please please ... another paper airplane thought came: an article in the *Daily Mail* about people suffering as they die: they called it the "end-of-life agony index" ... I'm so glad Marvel attached Millie to *The Eternals*. But I pray for her – she's doing too much. I should have said, "Mills, you don't need everyone to love you, you don't need to be an entrepreneurial Mistress of the Universe" ... with a dreadful shame-pang, she thought of the nurse who stole her #squadgoals porn and in the same thought-breath forgave her, sending out a fragile wish to Moishe that he leave her be and not hunt her down ... *another* pang as she tried to throttle the horror-clown image of her speared, startled Papaw that suddenly photobombed her own end-of-life experience. In the final leg of the grueling, Herculean exodus to her wife, she ruminated on the Squad. Joan bequeathed $50 million to each through the Zero Foundation: to Billie's homeless/spectrum youth initiatives – to Millie's Olivia Hope Foundation, named for a friend who died from leukemia at the age of 12 – and to dear, *dearest* Greta's brand new rainforest awareness campaign. Joan entrusted Mackenzie Bezos to disperse the rest of her fortune, with a personal note urging the monies be used for public health initiatives and carbon neutrality. *OH –*

...so, so cold now!

Idly, she wondered how small she had become. *Must get to Ali before some fucking rodent or itty-bitty insect devours me* ... and felt so terrible when she remembered that the incredible shrinking man had no wife to crawl home to. Poor soul!

So alone, alone, alone –

A hair under a foot-long, she propelled herself onto Ali's thorax...

...and at last, she was wedged, in the salty, rank, plumed, heaving bosom of her twin soul.

Soon she heard a deep rumble-stir, like the warm-up jets of a launchpad rocket. The catacomb reverberated with Ali's poignant vocalizations – a feathered dragon-like wheeze-roar beneath chick-panicked *tiiiiiii* might easily have knocked Joan from her bride but instead, atomized, she sank down into her beloved's flesh and become One.

The orb of skyspace lightened imperceptibly; her near nonexistent eyes now so exquisitely sensitive that it blinded, and she went sightless.

Transcendent sorrow pumped through her huge, minis-cule heart.

Joan's penultimate thought was an Instagram account she followed of a mom celebrating the short life of her daughter. The girl died from a syndrome that made her face look like a cantaloupe with teeth. The mother wrote *Because of her my life is better. I know what true happiness is.*

Her last thought:
To God, there is no zero.
Her last feeling ––––––––

Love.

POSTMORTEM

A strange thing happened.

At least, strange in the sense that Moishe, who was preternaturally cautious and methodical, failed to make a contingency plan in case of his own debilitation or sudden death. Joan's strange illness and subsequent suicide mission played havoc with his emotions. Now in her thirties, his daughter struggled with a nearly fatal anorexia when she was Joan's age; at the time of the Roden caper, the young woman was in Israel having chemo for a cancer that eventually went into remission. The convergence of twin-starred crises resulted in the unthinkable – Moishe got sloppy.

After the mission, he went to Jerusalem to be with her but was there for less than a week. Three days before James Turrell was due back from Europe, Moishe returned to Arizona. From his hotel room in Scottsdale, he called the artist to say that he had "a message from Joan" and it was important they spoke in person. He would meet James at the airport when he landed. Moishe's people were still onsite, to make sure crater groupies and Burning Man-types stayed away – an accidental discovery of the bodies just wouldn't do. A caretaker circled the property on an ATV but rarely went inside the structures, and most of the staff had been given time off while James was away. Now they were beginning to trickle in. Shooing off hippie trespassers was one thing; denying access to the Roden staff was another.

Moishe was on his way to the airport when a cyclonic headache struck. It was an aneurysm. Later, the doctors marveled that he managed to drive himself to the emergency room. The bleed was quickly treated but he lay in hospital, insensible.

Forty-eight hours after the missed appointment, he finally gathered his wits. First and foremost, he feared the bodies were already found. Before even calling his crew, he went on the Internet – nothing. After his people reported the same, he immediately called James to explain why he failed to show up for their appointment. He'd just left the hospital, he said, "against medical orders" and was on his way.

Moishe was compelled to share on the phone some of what he originally planned to say face-to-face; he couldn't risk the possibility of the artist making the horrific discovery by himself, during rounds. He dropped the preplanned-narrative bombshell: last week, the couple, plagued by terminal medical conditions, committed suicide at a clinic in Switzerland. In a document found on her desk (which Moishe dutifully produced), Joan expressed their last wishes – to be buried together beneath the crater. Moishe quickly added, "Just now, though, I'm afraid that they're pretty much out in the open. As you can read in the letter, it was part of what they wanted." After a minute of silent shock, the artist shared that he believed he knew exactly where "out in the open" was – the place Joan kept circling back to when he took them on their one and only tour. "When you look up, it's all about the North Star." He was right.

Moishe added it was imperative to keep the staff embargoed from the South Space until he arrived, and the bodies moved to "their final resting place, under the volcano."

As they drove to the site, Moishe informed him of Joan's gift, "all of which has been wired, and is immediately available." The artist gasped. Moishe said that his client was emphatic about "protecting your reputation and vision," assuring that scrupulous provisions had been put in place to that effect. "She of course asked you to select the place of burial," adding that Joan had told him there was no doubt in her mind that "James would appreciate the operatic gesture." The artist smiled when he heard that.

When they got to the end of the vaulted, oval-apertured chamber, the bodies were gone. All that remained was the stained, quilted comforter, and a few orange, black-tipped feathers left like pilgrim's alms. The mucosal trail left by Joan as she dragged herself to her wife's breast was by then invisible to the naked eye, as was the smear on the rim of the high-up hole made by something ecstatic during its rough escape.

* * *

A rumor was leaked to the media.

It mushroomed on social media, culminating in an article in the *New York Times*. A euthanasia clinic in Switzerland was the focal point of the piece. A journalist (and Moishe operative) interviewed a "long-time spokesperson" (also an operative) of the suicide co-op; certain spectacular fiscal arrangements had been arranged that paved the way for an airtight fiction about the last days and hours of the doomed couple. An autopsy revealed that Ali Nell had ALS after all (Joan's sardonic parting touch.) The coup de grace was that Joan Everhart Gamma had been closely guarding a tragic secret; shortly after their marriage, she had been diagnosed with a particularly aggressive form of the same disease as her wife. The couple made a pact to die together; such was the heart-wrenching, impossibly romantic motive behind their vows. The article said they were cremated and the ashes dispersed "somewhere in India."

Two urgent matters remained.

The RN who stole from Joan was hiding out at an Airbnb in Wyoming, with the original sketchbook; its only copy was in a safety deposit box in Los Angeles. The blackmailer and both manuscripts were burnt on the same day.

The second matter – that Joan and Ali impossibly evanesced from the chamber and were thus unburied – tormented Moishe for the rest of his life. He considered his inability to solve the mystery the single failure of his career. Beset by nightmares of the bodies' desecration, he waited to be contacted by ransomers.

He had just turned 80 when he died. It was only then, on his deathbed, as his daughter stared into his eyes, that he understood, and himself ascended.

* * *

Wylann Partland occasionally thought of their last phone call, wondering if she'd been too harsh. Each time she thought she should pick up the phone and apologize, her husband lobbied against it. "If anything, you're always too nice," he lectured. "You don't own him anything but the truth! You were so good to him, Wy! All those parties we threw! And let me tell you something: *he's* not responsible for your success, *you* are! You're a *better writer* than Bud Wiggins ever was, and you've got to stop feeling *guilty* about that. Whatever talent he once had, he *lost* – he's someone else now! And that has *nothing* to do with *you!*" She instantly felt better. Besides, her life was too full to stress about it. She was *already* upset about having to suspend her master class in fiction during the third leg of a tour for her most recent bestseller.

Without the distraction of a tour – or earning a living – Digby Colt taught his pro bono memoir workshop all year round. Wishing to share Bud's pages with his students, he reached out to his old friend, without luck. After a few weeks of mulling, he decided the educational benefits derived from the study of the pages Bud sent him was for the greater good of his fledgling autobiographers, outweighing any moral qualms that might accrue for not having gotten the author's permission. The excerpt – from a "work-in-progress, by Anonymous" – served as a cautionary tale.

Bud's work became a part of a study guide, and carried the playful heading: *What's Wrong With This Picture?*

Then:

List 5 Things (Okay, 10!!!)

* * *

The apartment manager for Keith Moon got a beat-up package in the mail, addressed to the former tenant in a shaky hand. It was from Maine, postmarked three months back, and she had no idea why it took such a tortuous path. She hadn't heard from Bud since early December; in the time since, Laverne went from worry to indifference. The delivery sent her back to worry again.

Impulsively, she opened it and found a sheaf of typewritten pages. Sharpied across the top was

This is absolutely marvelous! MORE, please. xManny

A detached Post-it read, "Wylann said she's gonna blurb!"

She sat down a moment to read. Laverne didn't understand what she was reading, but a yenta's curiosity bade her finish the pages before throwing them in the trash.

After the divorce, Dad wrote a letter that Dolly kept in the night-stand for almost fifty years.

"Take a good long look in the mirror," it said. "Know what you'll see? An old, dried-up cunt."

She reignited her hatred by reading the sentences whenever she felt herself starting to love him again. Maybe it excited her. In my early twenties, I was snooping around and found a vibrator lying across it like a paperweight. I reflexively picked it up to sniff. It was sweet and sour.

I was eleven when their dance of death became brutally syncopated. My scapegoat ears ached from decoding the progress of their bedroom firefights because I knew what was coming: a crescendo of ragged sobs, muttered entreaties and pounding foot-steps as Mom made the long shag carpet hajj to my room. I would already be propped up in bed like a meerkat, frozen prey as she burst in, an unhinged diva soliciting my futile protection. In an instant she was off and running while I trailed her to the main event in my pj bottoms. Dad awaited in navy blue bikini briefs on a gilt-edge Louis XIV knockoff chair, his feet tucked beneath, both concubine and strongman, swirling a snifter of scotch while ogling his double conquest.

"Your father hit me!" she shouted, as if to judge and bailiff. "I'm black and blue! Your father is sick, Bud! Your father's a sick, sick man!"

"*Leave! Her! Alone,*" I shouted, throwing my body against him, pounding away with tiny fists – the same hands that practiced a Chopin scherzo hours ago – his flesh an implacable wall of hard, hairy rubber. He pretend-fell, grunting as we tussled, faking defeat like a professional wrestler in a charity match with a disabled child.

All to a soundtrack of Mantovani.

During the WrestleMania years, Dad evicted himself to a series of boutiquey hotels called the Beverly This, the Beverly That. I made pilgrimages to visit after school and thought how glamorous they were with their perfect little pools. He stayed away a while and seemed happy. Finally, I could sleep. Holding me tight, she'd say, Without you, I'd kill myself, a chorus repeated day and night, sometimes with actressy, Strindbergian passion, other times singsongy and infantile.

A few days after each fracas, the doorbell rang. As the new husband, it was my job to answer. Father stood there with roses. The first time, I thought they were for me. My confusion gave him a hard-on; I know this now, recalling his sinister look. Dolly puttered in the bathroom, grooming herself for sex. (At 80, she confessed, "I stopped loving him around the time you were born. But the sex was so good, I couldn't walk away.") She clapped up the flowers, kissed his mouth, and coquettishly disappeared.

He hung back and leered.

"Did you know I slept with your mother every time the police left? Did you know that, Bud? And I'm going to sleep with her now. Do you have a problem with that?" I wasn't really sure what he meant. "Will that be a problem for you, Bud? Because I know you have so many problems."

I wondered if she still hated him. He was long dead. She lay in hospice, afloat in the sheltered bay of dementia whose waters would soon carry her to nameless emerald seas.

Cleaning out her apartment, I found a letter that was far different than the one of Dad's that she'd saved. She sent it to him in her early twenties, when they were courting:

Darling, darling – I can't go on without you – damn the Army. I am going to marry you in September, do you hear? And you'll be my husby & I'll be your little wifey & you know what? We'll have separate bedrooms and I'll have a big bad lock on my door – on the outside. And you'll have the key.

BOOK TWO

SUICIDE SQUAD VS. THE BELOVED CHILD

a DC/Marvel MASHUP

A ragged urchin, aimless and alone,
Loitered about that vacancy; a bird
Flew up to safety from his well-aimed stone:
That girls are raped, that two boys knife a third,
Were axioms to him, who'd never heard
Of any world where promises were kept,
Or one could weep because another wept.

– Auden

SOMETIME LATER

THERE WAS Portia Coldstream, seriously coiffed and neck-tatted, in a Delevingne-vibe patchwork of new/vintage Chanel – plus silver Margiela Tabi split-toe ankle boots stolen under the nose of a Dover Street Market DTLA employee who was obsessed with her cunt (and the electro-bluish white dyed bush it lived in) – the ends of her shockblue Hermés scarf caressing the cold onyx floor as she sat inside the sealed crypt of the resort toilet, her dilated eyes glued to a luxe-retro flip phone, the du jour accessory of hypebeast assholes. The secondhand waft of the lavatory's atomized public space *parfum* commingled with dainty stall-stank, creating a bespoke scent. As a venue for her shenanigans, the Montage Laguna Beach was brand new. Her ten-month winning streak had nearly ended in arrest – at the Sharia-shunned Bev Hills Hotel *and* the Peninsula bar – so she prudently self-imposed a moratorium on LA proper.

Blasting *Blue Neighborhood* as she rocketed to Laguna, the warmth of grifter's hope stirred anew, like a brushfire seen through stained glass.

After gifting Cage (the trusty manager of Exxxotica Rentacar, West Holly) with a middle toe-size tube of blow, she swapped her banged-up Alfa for a Model X, throwing a blow-job in for goodwill and general juju. Cage certainly appreciated the gesture; he was one happy glamper. Post-suck, the man even took great pleasure screwing on the specialty plates she brought. He never failed to dumbjoke, "Maybe you should take a Porsche, Portia."

Better hoof it before he gets hard again...

Back to the marble closet of the Montage, where she cokeshat while googling the mark's name: it was Arnold, as in Arnold Neidhoff Auto Parts – then linked to his wife's FB page – pics of wifey with Happy Boy at car auctions and

sundry corporate events – BBQs with their gawky tween progeny, usually in Spidey get-ups – *looks kinda twappy* – she wondered if Petey Parker was special needs. An "Arnold Neidhoff
Net Worth" search led to a Bloomberg Businessweek header:
Cleveland's Neidhoff Acquired by Traton Industries for $95 mill.

Ooooooh! *Too* fucking perfect...

She whisper-sang the theme from *Botched!* – *"I wanna be
purrrfect..."* – then clipped a turd.

*A car guy! Fucking nuts. Oh Arnie, I am gonna make you my
bitch.*

As she oozed back into the booth, Arnold said,

"I was about to call a search party."

"Mighta got ugly."

"You think?"

"I don't think, I know."

"You do look like a gal who can handle herself."

"Handle with care or beware."

"Wouldn't have it any other way."

He was fat-faced and ruddy, though not unhandsome. A
sweetness about him: a self-made, mid-life, Midwestern horn-
dog-type with enough jolly ch'i to put some serious skin in the
game once he was twisted around one of her beringed, tatted
fingers.

"*Reeve's* an interesting name," he said, after ordering
another round.

"It's my father's middle," she lied.

"He give it to you? Or did you steal it?"

Oh, Daddy! Out of the mouths of babes and marks.

"Well you know what they say, Arnold. Thou shalt not
steal but thou sure as shit may borrow."

He barked a laugh; a mote of scotchspittle flew to her chin. "That mean I can borrow *you?*"

She almost let the remark go – he was lit and over his head – but zapped him with a raised eyebrow. Suitably chastised, he winced, contritely showing his gooey middle.

Oh, *this* one.

This one's gonna give me the farm...

Let the games begin!

"You said you're out here on business."

"Except for tonight," he said. "Tonight is for play."

"Well look at *you*, you baller. Where are you from?"

"Cleveland. Not too sexy, I know."

"Cleveland's in the eye of the beholder."

Tan lines made the absence of a wedding band rubeishly obvious that it was boy's night out. Pretending she'd just noticed, Portia said, "You're married."

"A little bit. Does it matter?"

"It can. It might."

She needed him to believe she had scruples.

"Actually, I'm separated."

Arnold saw that she was going to keep mum until he said something more so he bought himself time by finishing his drink and staring over her shoulder into space.

Awkward.

Then:

"We're separated."

"What kind of business you in, Separated Man?"

He grinned with relief and said, "Automobile."

She smiled and subtly shook her head. "I can't seem to get away from men who play with cars."

"How so?"

"Oh, Daddy's in the business."

"Is that right? Maybe I know him – it's a small world."

"He makes the Tesla. Among other things."

"Ah – the manufacturing end. What's his name?"

"Elon."

"As in Musk?" he said, jokily.

"Yup."

"Heh heh. No fucking way."

"What can I say."

"Are you telling me your father is Elon Musk?"

"Uh huh."

"You're shitting me."

"I need to know you a little better before I do that."

"How did *that* happen?"

"Is that a trick question?"

"No – but you are *not*."

"Okay."

It was her turn to stare into space.

"Seriously?" he said.

This was the part of the Game she loved, the high she was always chasing – the part where they didn't believe her. The part where they thought it was still within their power to bail. The part where they believed they finally had the upper hand because they were dealing with some kind of psycho. The part where she watched them risk-assess with lightning speed whether falling into bed with an unstable woman was worth it. (Always a resounding *yes*.) The part where the body didn't yet know she'd cut off its head.

"Well," began the practiced explanation. "When Daddy was 18, he moved to Canada – "

"I thought Musk was South African."

"Born in Pretoria," she nodded, dragging from a cigarette. "Went to school in Pennsylvania when he was 19. Had a fling with a Wharton girl – that would be Mama – and *voila*, the rest is secret history."

"Now *that* – is just fucking amazing!"

His drunken, too loud, whizbang WTF-overwhelm provided a stagey outlet for all that oafish Ohioan horndoggery.

"Google it," she said, "and you won't find a word about me. *Ima lovechild.*"

"But does he – this is crazy! Does he… 'acknowledge' you?"

"Yup. Still talks to Mom, like, every day. That's the way she wants it. That's the way *I* want it. Life's too frickin insane *without* Daddy being Elon Musk. We're super close though."

She flashed on returning to the head for another bump.

"I'm struggling to believe you," he said gallantly.

Arnold squinted at her, trying to find traces of Elon. But the woman across from him looked like the gal from his favorite Tarantino movie, *Jackie Brown*.

Peter Fonda's daughter – what was her name?

Portia's fingers speed-twitched her phone screen then handed him the device. He gaped at a seamless home video of father and daughter.

"Wow… whoa – this is *crazy*. That is so cool!"

"By the way, I usually don't tell people about the 'love connection.'"

"And to what do I owe this honor?"

"Welp, I'll tell ya… it's a little California woo-woo but I think you can handle it. A shaman in Topanga told me the world's full of 'cyclic beings.' He said that certain people are on the same strand of beads. Whole *groups* are connected, like *beaded curtains*. That's you and me – *maybe*. Time will tell."

"OK – all right – OK." He grew quiet, earnestly mulling the canyon mysticism. He was in a lather. "Hey, can I ask a personal question?"

"Always the best kind."

"I don't mean this to be crass – so tell me if I'm being an asshole, okay? But are you... taken care of? I mean, did he *provide*?"

"I don't have any worries, Arnold," she said, smiling demurely.

"Nice!" He was genuinely, hornily happy for her. "I mean, *really* glad to hear that. I mean, it's *good* – sounds like he's a good man, your father." His use of *the f-word* cued Portia that if he didn't yet believe her, he was starting to entertain the notion. He stared bashfully into his glass. "Honestly? I thought you might have been 'working' tonight."

"Flatterer."

"Oh shit!" he snapped, as if stung by a jellyfish. "Sorry. *That* was fucking stupid. Dumb, dumb, *dumb*."

Oh, he is lit.

"Hey, don't beat yourself up. Let *me* find people to do that."

He laughed and laughed.

"Reeve, will you forgive me?"

"Hey, the hick jumped out – NBD. Look. I like *people*, Arnold, that's all. Talking to people. Guess I get that from my dad. Sometimes L.A. starts to feel like a giant fucked-up private club. And when it *does*, I like to get outta Dodge. Hotel bars are great places to meet folks like you – "

"Hicks?" he said with a smile.

"I call em 'non-members.' Non-members are *way* more interesting."

"Reeve Musk," he said, arching his head in horny, titillated abandon at the provenance of his liaison. "I certainly didn't see *that* coming. That I'd be having a drink with 'the daughter of.'"

"I *never* use that name," she reprimanded. "It's Tobrin. Reeve Tobrin."

"Duly noted. Man, I *loved* that thing he did with the astronaut driving the Tesla in space."

"Guess whose idea that was."

"Yours? Really?"

"He was gonna use 'Across the Universe' but I said *hell the fuck* no. Gotta be Bowie."

They waited under the canopy for the valet.

Drunk Arnold had already made a few clumsy, non-member, non-baller attempts to get her back to his room. Seeing that wasn't going to happen, he defaulted to romcom guilelessness.

"You know, I'd really like to see you again."

He was almost teary-eyed about it.

"That can be arranged. How long are you here?"

"Long as you want me to be."

"Right answer. What are you doing Wednesday night?"

(It was only Friday. How could he wait until Wednesday? But making him wait was part of the Game.)

Peaking on booze and hornaciousness, he went for it:

"I'd like to do *you* Wednesday night."

It was so retarded that she laughed out loud.

"*Easy*, Separated Man. Promise to behave and on Wednesday I'll tell you about a crazy deal Elon's really excited about. Spoiler alert: it's a horizontal elevator. Tim Cook wants to retrofit them into the rings of the Apple mothership. The Pentagon wants em too, if Trump doesn't kill the contract, like he likes to kill everything. You a Trump guy?"

"Pretty much."

"I can work with that," she said impishly.

And there it came, as if by teleportation: the loaned-out falcon-winged Model X, a silent angel with screwed-on wings. The plate said

LVCHILD

My finest work.

After her auspicious labors with Ohio Arnold, Portia pit-stopped at Playa Vista, delivering GBH to the gamers that texted right as she left the Montage. (An agent at WME gave them her cell.) By the time she returned the Tesla to Exxxotica it was 3:30AM. Cage was so janky and dramaqueen angry over the broken curfew that she made an exxxecutive decision to give his asshole a spa treatment while she blew him; it helped that she was super high. He was vital to her ongoing enterprise – what was a girl to do? The operation took more time than she'd have liked, thanks to a lazy, indurate prostate and an even lazier dick. Glancing up at him as she struggled to breathe through her snotnose, Portia was reminded of a museum Old Master she saw during a high school outing: a dirty, snaggled-toothed old peasant, ecstatic eyes rolling back in his rheumy head as he paid the mortal price of those who dared look directly into the face of God.

On the 405 back home, she felt Gladys Knight's song in her heart again and gave it full throat:

> Ooh, that man is fine
> What's even better – the man is mine

Which he was.

Witchy witchy was –

* * *

Trix faked that she was sleeping when her mother peeked in. One time, as her mom dropped her off at school, Trixanna espied the LVCHILD plates on the Alfa's littered backseat floor. When she asked what it meant, Portia smirked, "*Lovechild.* Duh!" – which Trixanna liked, because a loved child was an amazing message to put on the back of your car.

She knew those plates were meant for *her* because Trix had a dream about Professor Charles Francis Xavier telling her to always to be sure to "look for the extraordinary within the ordinary." The motto of the school he founded – the Xavier Institute for Mutant Education and Outreach – was *Mutatis Mutandis*: "change only that which needs to be changed," and when she saw the wooden sign that Portia bought as a gift for her AA home group, Dr. Xavier's proverb came back to her:

GRANT ME THE SERENITY
TO ACCEPT THE THINGS I CANNOT CHANGE
THE COURAGE TO CHANGE THE THINGS I CAN
AND THE WISDOM TO KNOW THE DIFFERENCE

Trixanna knew nothing about her dad; Portia rarely mentioned him, but *had* said some key things – one of them being that "he looked like Forest Whitaker." When she googled the actor, Trix was shocked to learn he had actually played Zuri, keeper of the heart-shaped herb native to Wakanda. Portia was careful never to disclose his name. Another thing she said was that everyone used to call him Old Boy, and that he died before she was born.

The little girl was sure *that* was a lie.

Trixanna was green-eyed and light-skinned but not Meghan Markle- or Cardi B- or the Zoës-light (Saldana and

Kravitz). Whenever online strangers asked what movie star she looked like, Trix usually said Shuri, from *Black Panther.* "Sometimes," she texted, "I look like Laura, in *Logan,*" adding "from the X-Men movie" for the uninitiated. That's who she *really* wanted to be: not Shuri or Meghan or even a Kardashian daughter, but "Laura Kinney" aka X-23, the feral child cloned from her father – the dying, 200-year-old Wolverine. *That's* who she dreamed she already was or at least would grow into: the warrior Laura, who, as someone on a fan site perfectly put it, was "the samurai sword trying to become a little girl." Each day, she painfully directed the cells of her body to mutate. Each day, she made a prayer to Professor Charles Francis Xavier and the Marvel Universe to send indestructible adamantium that would meld with her bones as she slept. In time, the spring-loaded knives would erupt from her extremities but first she would need to soak in adamantium too if she were to become immortal. Portia's origin story of Old Boy dying in a car crash was just so *dumb*. Trix knew the only thing that could kill her dad were adamantium bullets – or the drugs that Transigen was flooding the food supply with, fatal only to mutants…

The comic books said her *real* mother was an Omega-level mutant named Jean Grey aka Marvel Girl. But if that were true, who was Portia? A Transigen spy? An assassin? A member of the Reavers? (The cyborgs that were sent by Transigen to exterminate any mutants living undercover after the purge.) The movie that held all the answers was called *Logan*. Hugh Jackman played the hero, Old Man Logan, the aging Wolverine – and it hadn't been lost on her how close his name was to "Old Boy." Slowly, she fit together the puzzle pieces… The most *astonishing* part was that Old Man had been tasked with ushering his cloned daughter Laura to a place in North Dakota called Eden, after she and her mutant friends escaped certain death from a hospital run by Transigen. (Trix was convinced it must be Valley Vista, in Oakland, where Portia had sent her not too long ago.) In *Logan,* the creator of the X-Men, Professor Charles Francis Xavier, told Laura that she was the only one who could save him from the suicidal depression brought on by poisons the Reavers put in his body.

She never told anyone about her transformation, especially not the psychiatrist at Valley Vista where Trix had been hospitalized after attacking a teacher with scissors. Just like in *Logan*, the nurses there were sympathetic to the children, and helped them escape. But Portia contradicted her. "You did not *escape,* Trixanna. What happened was they *released* you and you waited with a nurse in the front of the hospital and I picked you up. So stop the fantasies, okay? The fantasies are what got you there in the first place." When they fled to L.A., Portia took her to another therapist who prescribed pills that took away her superpowers. They neutralized the adamantium and stopped it from coating her skeleton when she slept. She needed to have full strength if she were to reunite with fellow escapees – Old Boy (that's what she called Old Man Logan now) needed to be strong too because the children couldn't make the journey without him. When the war was over, and the Reavers defeated, they would carry her father to Eden. There, he would heal.

That's why she stopped taking the meds.

That night, while the impostor who called itself her mother was at the Montage Laguna Beach, Trixanna tripped on an edible that she stole from Portia's stash. She was supposed to be writing an essay on Meghan Markle, "the Duchess of Success" – she came up with that herself and wanted to make a TikTok, dancing in a t-shirt with ~~SUSSEX~~ replaced with SUCCESS. Instead, she watched tit-toks of half-naked anorexic schoolgirls doing pantomimes, inflating their tummies then pretending to let the air out until the belly button caved and touched the spine.

Then she got bored and binged on videos of obese cats in Spiderman cosplay. Tabasco, her orange calico, wasn't all that interested.

Trixanna switched to her laptop and watched *Lockup*. (When Portia and Jaxx got stoned, they only watched *Swamp People*. She always heard them laughing and fucking.) She learned a lot from that show, like how prisoners talked to each other by dropping notes attached to strings called "kites." "Shot callers" were gang leaders who could order the murders of people in jail, or even in faraway cities. If you were in your cell and threw doody or cum juice on a guard, they called that "gassing." Trix had a fleeting thought that maybe she should change the Meghan assignment to an essay about *Lockup*...

She was streaming an episode where the guards prepared for an "extraction," i.e. the removal a violent prisoner from his cell. All of them were white, with acne and baby fat. They shook with fear as they strapped on padded armor; they wore swimmer's goggles and held plastic shields to protect them from being gassed. It reminded her of that time in Oakland when the Reavers put her in restraints, leaving Trix in a quiet room "to think about what you'd do differently the next time." But all she *could* think about was the savagery she would rain down on her captors one day, and how she would help her fellow mutant inmates escape.

The man on-camera was famous for having had the most extractions of any prisoner nationwide. Even one of the pudgy pigs called him "a legend." The next day, when the Extraction King was interviewed by the *Lockup* crew, he had a twinkle in his eye. "It's about winning," he said. "As long as you fight, you win."

Just then his name appeared at the bottom of the screen:

REGINALD RONALD "OLD BOY" WHITE,
SERIAL MURDER,
LIFE WITHOUT PAROLE

She gasped.

Her heart did a fluttery, blackout thump-dance, making Trix think of something from the Internet about scientists finding a black hole that ate a sun every two days. And of *course* she thought of Thanos and his daughter Gamora and their complicated love, and of *course* she thought of Laura, cloned from her father, Old Man Logan –

A voice instantly warned her not to tell Portia about her discovery.

Now I finally know. I finally know where you are.

She pressed pause, googling the words on the screen:

Pelican Bay State Prison
Crescent City
Del Norte County, CA.

Just a half-day's drive away!

She flung herself on the bed and stared at a ceiling pasted over with photo collages of Kims and Kanyes, of Princess

Meghans and Laura animé, all sexy and switchblade-knuck-led with deadpool eyes. Her mind wandered to the license plate *Beloved Child*. That's what Trixanna was: a beloved child everlasting, an adamantium child whom her father would *know* from the moment he saw her. She couldn't imagine what hell he'd gone through. God only knew what the show *hadn't* filmed – or the footage Transigen suppressed. God only knew what the Reavers had done to his mind and body to make sure he would *never* be reunited with the daughter that was his! She saw from his eyes that he'd gone mad and was dying.

I will travel to Pelican Bay and extract him.

Then she would find her friends. With Old Man's guid-ance, they make the perilous journey to North Dakota and cross over to Eden.

She didn't know how to email him but anyway thought that writing a letter was the safest way. At the top of the page, she carefully wrote

Not only a hello! In this leter I will soon speak of one of the 3 GEMS that will free you! And most importantly, of the SHIELD which will SOON be in my possession, because Dr. CHARLES FRANCIS XAVIER told me it has been HIDING IN PLANE SIGHT and is actually STRONGER then the SHIELD of CAPTAIN AMERICA!!!

Then
    Dearest Father,
    It is I, your long lost dauhgter.
    I am 12 now.
    My true name is LAURA.

I am wandering if you have seen the movie called LOGAN. I do not know if they give the akkused killers TV to watch or how many chanels are available but LOGAN definitly is streeming on netflix.

'They' SAY you are a killer but if it is true you were only doing so to protec yourself and those you Loved and Lost. Also you probably killed only RIEVERS, who are NOT human, so dont even count. So you are forggiven.

You most probably would not know who I am because 1) you may not know any thing about me or that I was clonned from you 2) you may know but maybe forgot due to the poison that Pelican/Transigen are leeching into your adamantium bones 3) if you DO know you have a childe, you may not have ANY idea of its gender and most certainly probably would not know its name.

{If you have forgot or been poisoned so that you would forget and you do not have access to Marvel books or movies, you ALSO may not know.}

The woman who calls herself my "Mother" told me you were dead (which I DID NOT believe). Perhaps you may not even ever have met or heard of her.

My full name is Trixanna Coldstream. (It is actually in truth Trixanna White, & I hearbye ask your legal permission to make it your sir-name.) I do not know where "Coldstream" came from but am thinking of a BBC show that "mother" is fond of, or prhaps from the name of a contestent on the Shark Tank, which Portia likes to watch as well. (+ Swamp Thing, which she watches with her bf.) Anyway, "mother" said she liked the cereal "Trix" when she was little and that her own mother was called Anna, so she made a collab of the 2 to name me.

If you need further identifaction, the woman who takes care of me as "mother" is named PORTIA COLDSTREAM, I promise not to mention her again because you may have hardened feelings against her. She has always rongfully declared you to be dead by a car crash, but is respeckful in all other ways. She does not throw shade. Maybe she still loves you more than she would say because she is proud. Maybe you left her or hurt her.

I saw you on <u>Lockup</u>. You were being X-tracted.

I do not even know if you can recieve this because the people who guard over you do not seem to be very bright or helpful, I have seen them on TV, they dont even abidding by the rules of such an institute, even if it is to tensionally keep you from this letter, which is against the law. I found you by myself {tho I cannot help but believe it was arranged by Marvel} because I would not wish you to think "Mother" betrayed you in any way. I was watching LOCKUP and there you were, so brave to be fighting the men who thought they were warriers when they are ackually just pighead RIEVERS. I too have been X-tracted but in a hospital setting in Oakland, not jail. I was punnished for attempting to destroy a Riever nurse with scissorblades that sprung from my hand. (I was not yet strong enough or she would be ded.) I proudly agree with your thoughts about Fighting and Winning, as you aired on <u>Lockup</u>, & it is True. If we do not fight we can not win, I beleive I am in that way very much my fathers daughter.

I will be 14 at Christmas.

I know you are very sick, not just from the adamantium but the food additives that the RIEVERS, under supervission of Dr. ZANDER RICE have placed in the trays slipped into your cell. {{I do not indorse gassing btw. I believe it is GROSS, and do not think you do it. But would understand if you did.}}

Prhaps youve forgotten, with the poor diet and the poisons, who you ARE. As your daughter, my destiny is to remind you:

You are LOGAN, the WOLVERINE.
<u>and WE THE CHILDREN need your HELP!!!</u>

We are traveling to EDEN, just above North Dakota, where we will all settle and live. You will get better there, Daddy. The poisons will leave your system. I may or may not buy us a boat but may have to steel a car.

LOVE   xxxxxxxxxxxxxxXXXXXXXXXXXXXXXXXX
Trixanna Coldstream White (& Laura Kinney/X-23)
They ALSO call ME "Wolverine"!!!!

PS - I wish you could get TikTok it is so funny and you would laugh. I will show, when we are together! Right now I am watching cos-play of cats and wolverines.

PSS - btw my plan to X-tract you involves THE SHIELD (which I will BURY in the BACKYARD of our house because DIRT {{of all things!!!}} is the PERFECT INVVISIBILITY CLOAK) and will ALSO be helped by 3 out of 6 GEMS that still remain on this Earth. Espeshally the TIME STONE, which currently belongs of DR STRANGE.

IT WILL GIVE US COMPLEATE CONTROL OVER TIME!!!!!!!!!!! and make X-traction very easy and carefree

But if Dr. Strange wont let me borrow, I will do some X-tracting of my own, to get it back. Like a black hole., Thanos tried to EAT & X-stinguish every single SUN-STAR but WE, dear-est FATHER, will SHINE SHINE SHINE ;D

* * *

While her daughter wrote the clandestine dispatch, Portia smoked weed and watched a *Twilight Zone*. The shows were usually amazing, but this one was a dud.

On the way to the kitchen for Kombucha, she busted Trixanna.

"Why aren't you fucking asleep?"

"What does it *matter.* Tomorrow's *Saturday.* You were gone *all night.*"

Portia snatched the iPad away and said, "Lights out, lovechild."

"You are *so mean.*"

"Yeah well, mean girls get mean moms. Nightie-night."

Portia took a long soak with her favorite Lush bath bombs, all glittery and gory red. Submerged to the neck, she had a feeling in her gut and cervix that Arnold Neidhoff was the *man.* Maybe she could finally buy herself a hillside bungalow in Eagle Rock or Highland Park – some fantabulous *treehouse* – even wind up an owner right cheer in Echo Park. Or a split-level abode overlooking the Silver Lake Reservoir, like the one belonging to Kick Kennedy. (Portia saw her house on the gram when JFK's grandniece sent out pleas to find her missing cat.) It'd be *so nice* not to be renting a grotty wannabe condo, to feel *human* instead of like a permanent piece-of-shit scrounging slave.

Eyes shut and way, way high, Portia stirred in the pearlescent scarlet water having happy thoughts about the king of auto parts as she used her waterproof Lelo to probe... for climaximal effect, she jimmied a basic bitch dildo into her rear-end and got the usual, post-orgasm giggles.

It was some kind of reflex.

Back in bed, she checked her phone messages, listening to each just a few seconds before deleting. Two from Jaxx (all love-dovey), three from Cage (pre-blowjob and pissed, wondering *where the fuck are you*), and three from Trixanna. *Mama where* are *you? You better come home* NOW!

She saved the UNKNOWN one for last.

Hi, Ruthanne! I'm *hoping* this is Ruthanne – Ruthanne Davies?

(A knife slid into Portia's heart. That was her name in another world, another life, when she was being hunted and haunted on a zombie planet.)

> This is Kim Kardashian. It's really *me* [laughs], and kind of a long story why I'm reaching out. I'm going to give you a number to call...

A pause, before "Kim" intoned *425 771 5187*, repeating it twice more like they do in commercials before going on.

> That's my mom's production company, Jenner Communications. So when you call back, you can see it's really me! Just tell whoever answers that 'Kiki' left you a message, that 'Kiki' called you *directly*. They'll put you right through to Rhapsody, my assistant. It's really import-ant you call, Ruthanne! I'm so hoping that it's you... and I'd really love to – I can't wait to meet you! I'd really love to have lunch. Okay – and thank you. Hoping you and your daughter are well, and have a *wonderful* evening... see soon. Bye!

Portia immediately dialed the number and listened to a recorded message from "Jenner Productions."

At first, she thought it was some kind of brazen hus-tle. (A bit of professional admiration in there, too, for the creative chutzpah.) It was easy to have a drop – Portia'd done that before herself – a dummy office number with a credible "employee" answering. But something told her that Kim was the real deal, and gave her that same, giddy, Arnold feeling.

The adrenaline made it hard to sleep.

She started masturbating again but stopped, suddenly panicked by Kim's throwaway signoff:

Hoping you and your daughter are well…

WTF?

Her head went every which way, scattering like some fucked up herd when a lion steps onto the veldt. If it *wasn't* the real Kim, what was behind it? She thought maybe some blackmail deal over her long-ago foray into porn? But that didn't make sense… a heart-jolt made her think of the "influencer" scam Jaxx helped her with, right when he got out of prison: Portia created fake IG accounts and in exchange for hyping their brands, solicited companies to send free clothes and beauty shit to a P.O. in Weho. If it *were* the real Kim, that didn't make sense either, not only because it would have been a fucking *lawyer* calling, not Mrs. Kanye, but because she and Jaxx *never* would have involved the Kardashians – it was just a small-timey, short-lived hack, targeting Instas with less than 250,000 followers. *Kim had 150 million…* unless it was a stunt for *KUWTK*, and everything on KK's end was being filmed.

No way. Tooooo fuckin crazy.

Portia kept stripping her gears.

She lit some loud and drifted a hand down to her puss while puzzling over *hoping you and your daughter are well*. Why bring Trixanna into it? She texted Jaxx but of course he was sleeping. Or maybe not. A stab of jealousy, wondering what he was up to, who he might be fucking.

She couldn't help circling back to the impossible idea that the call was legit. As she gently fingered her clit, she thought:

Kimmy K wants to have lunch!

Then she veered dark again, wondering if "Kim" was a kop. One of those dragnet stings, trying to arrest her for some old or newish crime –

Still, any random thing she dredged up, dead-ended.

She listened to the vmail, over and over.

Hi, Ruthanne! I'm *hoping* this is Ruthanne – Ruthanne Davies?

Hi, Ruthanne! I'm *hoping* this is Ruthanne – Ruthanne Davies?

Hi, Ruthanne! I'm *hoping* this is Ruthanne – Ruthanne Davies?...

She'd had a thousand names but not even Jaxx knew that one. Her birth name.

* * *

When she told the girl "Kiki called me directly," Portia was transferred to a gal who cheerfully introduced herself as Rhapsody, who officiously said, "Hold for Kim." When the connection didn't happen, she apologized profusely. "Kim's having a little emergency with one of the kids – nothing serious! But I know that she *really* wants to meet you. Do you think you can *tomorrow*? I know it's short notice but her schedule's *so* crazy right now. She's leaving for Wyoming on Wednesday – "

It spooked her that the meeting was in a Century City conference room. She'd hoped it would be at the famous house in Calabasas or Nobu or even Craig's – not a soulless silver building that stank of lawyers. The AC was cranked so high, she felt like she was on the shelf of a Sub-Zero. Portia dressed like she had a gazillion followers, her outfit a gajillion likes. Another fantasy was, the camera crew for *KUWTK* would be there, and as she signed a release, Kim and her mom would say, "We are totally going to make you a star!" It would take her less than half a season to pry Scott Disick away from Kourtney for good, and marry into the mob.

When Kim swept in, it took her breath away. Portia liked that she ditched her entourage; it showed respect. She was way more beautiful than she looked on television.

"You're so gorgeous!" said Kim, taking her visitor aback.

"Oh my God, thank you!"

She scanned Portia's oversized flannel shirt, a Gosha x Burberry collab. "Did you get that at Dover Street?"

"Yes!" said Portia, tongue-tied.

"Oh my God, I *saw* that there and wanted to get it! Khloé said no, but I should have! Don't you *love* that place?"

"It's amazing. But *crazy* expensive."

"I know!" said Kim, like some bff who was also on a budget.

It went on like that, with Portia getting comfortable enough to ask about the new ranch in Wyoming. (She wouldn't have thought to if Rhapsody hadn't mentioned it). When an older, silver-haired man came in, Portia instantly got the willies. He vibed reality show fuzz.

"This is Richie Raskin," said Kim.

"It's a pleasure," he said, shaking Portia's hand.

At least he didn't cuff me heh heh.

"*Thank you* for coming on such short notice," said Kim. "So, I want to clear the air of *mystery*, okay? Because you must have been totally wondering, like, 'What the *fuck*. Why am I here?' Right?"

"A little," smiled Portia.

"You may or may not know I've been doing a lot of work with prisoners. *Some* of the cases I'm helping with are high profile – but most are *way* below the radar. It's not political, *per se*. I'm not really a political person, but I'll do what has to be done. I even went to the White House to – "

"I know!" blurted Portia, regretting she cut her off.

"One thing I've learned never to do is to assume that anyone knows anything about me – it's healthier that way! I'm actually getting my license to practice law. That's something I've always secretly wanted to do. My dad was a lawyer" – Portia nodded, without blurting – "so I guess it's in my genes. Anyway, there's a man who's been in jail for thirteen years here in California... Reginald Ronald White." Seemingly gauging her reaction, Kim let it sink in. "Is that name familiar to you?"

Portia blanched. She stuttered *Old Boy*, half to herself.

"Yes! That's his nickname. He said the two of you went a long way back but hadn't been in touch for a long, long time." Portia shook her head in agreement, to which Kim responded with the non sequitur, "Perfect." "He *never* should have been convicted," she went on. "I've looked into a number of wrongful convictions and *this* one's probably the most egregious. I'm doing everything I can to get him released. It's urgent now because he's" – Kim glanced at Richie – "dying. Cancer. It's spread. And the reason we got in touch" – again, she looked toward her colleague – "the reason I asked Richie to find you was because Reginald said you were a *very* important person in his life, and asked for my help. His request wasn't public so I don't want you to think your name is out there *in any way*. Reginald believes that Trixanna – that's your daughter, isn't it? You have a daughter named Trixanna?"

"Yes."

"An amazing name, by the way. I *love* it."

"Your kids have pretty amazing names too."

"Thank you. *We* think so, anyway," she smiled. Kim paused, now staring at Portia through steely, unblinking eyes. "Reginald believes he's the father. He said that he wanted to meet Trixanna before he dies. Of course, you'd first want to make sure that what he's *thinking* is *true!*"

"A simple blood test," said Richie.

"Only if you agree," said Kim, before looking at Richie again.

"Of course," said the detective. "That's your prerogative. And there would be no need for your daughter to know what the test was for."

"If it *is* true he's the dad," said Kim, "well, you're the *mother*, so everything would be up to you. Whether to have them meet, or even to *tell* her. As a mom, I don't even *know* what I'd do." Portia liked that Kim said that – it was real. "One thing I *can* say, knowing Reginald the way I do, even for the short time it's been, is I'm one hundred per cent certain that 'demanding' a meeting is something he would never do."

"Which of course he cannot, legally," said the detective.

"And something I would *never* support or encourage," said Kim. "*It's in your hands.* And he's fully aware, Ruthanne, that even if it *is* true, you may not want anything to do with him. You *or* Trixanna. Because of course I wanted to talk to him about that, and he's already told me he would be fully in acceptance of your wishes." She smiled and said, "Look: I don't know anything about what Reginald was like. *Back in the day.* None of the prisoners I work with are angels – no one is! – but he's a remarkable man. He's become that, that's his journey. He's actually a monk now."

"What?" said Portia.

"Maybe not a 'full' monk yet, but pretty close."

"Really," said Portia, oversaturated.

"A Buddhist," said Richie. "I'm a little skeptical of the ones that find Jesus, but the crazy ones *never* find the Buddha."

Kim gave him a mildly disapproving side-eye. "Reginald's been doing the training for years."

"Long before the cancer," added the detective, as if to erase his snide remark.

"He's taking the vows. There's a whole process. I think it's, like, a hundred-thousand prostrations? Or *something* like that – all kinds of things. He has a teacher who visits from a retreat center that's not too far from the prison. His teacher has a monastery in Nepal too... I'm just learning more. Reginald's a gentle man, a *spiritual* man – he's *become* that – who wants to do no harm. Not to you, not to anyone. Especially not your daughter."

"When there's so little time left," chimed Richie, solemnly.

"It's a lot to process, I know!" said Kim. "And I *also* want you to know that I'm making a documentary. Which – knock on wood – will include Reginald's release."

"Wow," said Portia.

"He'd be going directly to hospice. We're not sure if his journey – the documentary – is going to be the focus, or part of a larger narrative. It may be just his story or may be one of three. But if things 'work out,' I'd love you to be part of it. And Trixanna."

"Well," said Richie. "That's a bit premature."

"Right!" laughed Kim, unguardedly. "There I go, rushing forward – my husband's always accusing me of that. *He's* one to talk, right?" Portia liked her more and more. Signaling the meeting's end, Kim exuberantly said, "I'm so happy to meet you, Ruthanne!"

She stood and they hugged.

"Can I just ask y'all one thing?" said Portia.

The hosts girded themselves for the worst. From what Richie Raskin unearthed (he had shared his intel with Kim, of course), they were dealing with a potentially untrustworthy, volatile woman whom for all they knew was about to demand money – or tell them to go fuck themselves.

"Can y'all please call me Portia? I friggin' *hate* 'Ruthanne'."

"Oh *hell* yeah!" laughed Kim, relieved. "Portia's *so* much better."

* * *

In Pelican Bay

The cyclical travesty of it...

Saṃsāra can be such a farce.

...and all of the accused were Black.

How vexing were the algorithms of the material world!

Old Boy's personal mandala was made of these sand-drawn tableaux:

From the mid-60s to mid-70s, L.A.'s "Skid Row Slasher" bloodily ruled. By the time they caught up to him, eleven victims had been claimed. In 1978, his successor was clumsily dubbed the Skid Row Stabber. Oddly, almost unbelievably, he had eleven victims too...

In 2004, karma's recondite board game demanded a third sacrifice, anointing a third African man, bloodthirsty for downtown transients. *This* one's name was Reginald Ronald "Old Boy" White.

During nearly fifteen years of incarceration, Old Boy (erstwhile known as the Extraction King) gave his predicament a great deal of thought – to wit, whether one's guilt or innocence mattered at all. The notion overtook him like a slow and steady marathon runner. He'd come a long way since those days when it took ten gladiators to tear him from the cell; now, he had a more graceful strategy of escape, for soon he would be dead. Long before his diagnosis, he was blessed with a Buddhist's perspective. He understood how the wrongly convicted had the habit of being poisoned by righteous martyrdom, which always redounded to great trauma and karmic disadvantage.

And yet, he began to believe that even karma was an illusion.

Sitting on the concrete floor of his cell in half-lotus, a thin pillow tucked beneath his failing, pain-wracked body, Old Boy mused...

Didn't Saṃsāra decree the activities of *any* being that hadn't yet escaped the Wheel of Life to be ephemeral and without meaning? Weren't all temporal experiences commensurate to a dream within the dream? To think anything else was simply the intoxicated heresy of being human.

In 1961, Reggie White, a precocious five-year-old in foster care, dream child of an infinity of deaths and rebirths, would of course have no idea his current incarnation would end in a life sentence for a crime he didn't commit. He knew nothing of karma and its mercilessness. Young Old Boy worked on ships and lived in Europe a while, even studying philosophy at a junior college before becoming a bookie and a pimp who enjoyed robbing smalltime dope dealers. His cerebral side appealed to the ladies (especially Ruthanne Davies) almost as much as his rugged good looks.

2006: five homeless men are knifed on Skid Row. Police and politicos are desperate. Old Boy, busted on a trafficking charge, winds up in a cell with a notorious jailhouse rat. Months later, using embellished details gleaned from the news, the snitch claims Reginald confessed to the murders. Old Boy's arrested in the parking lot of Yang Chow, a Chinatown restaurant still favored by undercover cops. A long dagger kept handy for the occasional unruly john is found in his car. Its serrations are close *enough* to match the photographed wounds of one of the dead; his palm print close *enough* to the latent found on a bus bench near another victim.

It's an election year.

A wag in the precinct dubbed him "Wolverine." Tabloids and TV news went wild for it. But Marvel doesn't think the association is good for the brand so the moniker's scrapped, and Old Boy is prosaically baptized the Skid Row Ripper.

He's acquitted on two murders. The jury can't reach a decision on six others. They convict on one count of homicide. He gets life. It happens with a nightmare's dizzying speed.

Everything in this life repeats, from noblest birth to lowliest death.

Saṃsāra can be such a farce...

He's 53 when he goes in, an old boy indeed. By then, he knew himself well. His temperament was cool and unshakeable. Yet in the first few years, something he thought was impossible happened: he went crazy. The temporary cure was to bring hellfire to the guards, who rushed into his cage so often that he grew immune to beatings and pepper spray. Instead of unraveling, the stints in solitary wrapped him tighter. Alone in ad seg, 23 hours a day, his blurry self dripped into stones and crevices and spidery ceiling cracks, down steel sinks and toilet pipes. Rioting was the infernal calisthenic that kept him sane.

All of the battles occurred in a void – until *Lockup*.

The defunct MSNBC docuseries featured him twice, on *Lockup Supermax: Pelican Bay* and *Lockup Raw: Inmates Gone Wild*. The violently choreographed extractions went viral, with hundreds of thousands of views. Groupies sent mash notes, begging to marry and bear his children. *Anyone who uses a knife like that*, a woman wrote, *would be a perfect protector, a perfect husband, a perfect father.* He threw their letters away.

One year, between stays in the hole, a visitor came in saffron robes.

Chökyi Nyingma Rinpoche was the abbot of a monastery in Nepal. He was also the spiritual director of a meditation and retreat center three-hours south of Pelican Bay. He was nothing like a guru or learned man, at least not the sort Old Boy imagined; rather, he was droll and disarming. He came straight to the point, revealing a detail that the prisoner, having heard it from his public defender in the early days of the trial, had long forgotten. He said that "a victim of this crime" was his student, a young monk on a year-long, wandering retreat. Old Boy stiffened at the words, expecting condemnation to follow but the rinpoche elegantly assured that he wasn't accusing him of committing any crimes. Instead, the abbot said he'd simply come to offer a blessing. Trembling with passion, the red-faced convict insisted he'd never murdered the student or anyone else. The rinpoche looked in his eyes without judgment, anger or blame. "It doesn't matter," he said, with a warm smile. Then he enunciated the words of *metanoia* that would alter the remainder of Old Boy's life:

"Everything changes. The prisoner becomes rinpoche; rinpoche becomes the prisoner. *We are the same.*"

A few days later, a guard brought some books to Old Boy's cell. One was called *Liberation in the Palm of Your Hand.* Stained and dog-eared, it was filled with highlighted passages and excitable, fervent jottings in the margins. A note from the abbot said that it had belonged to his murdered student and to "please accept this gift from him."

He turned to an underscored paragraph.

An old couple had a son. The son and his wife gave them a grandchild, and the family lived together in a big house. The old man loved to eat fish that he caught in a pond on the property. He was so attached to his routine that when he died, he was reborn as a fish in the pond. His widow was so attached to the house that when she died not long after, she was reborn as the family dog because she couldn't bear to leave. Their son, daughter-in-law and grandchild now lived there, alone. While the son was away on business, an admirer of his wife broke in and raped her. He was quickly caught and executed for the crime. Because he was so attached to his victim, the rapist was reborn as the couple's infant daughter. One afternoon, the son caught a fish in the pond; while he chewed its meat, the dog stole the fish bones from his plate and was beaten for it. When the son resumed eating, the tittering infant clambered onto his knee.

Śhāriputra said: "The son eats his father's flesh as the widow gnaws her husband's bones. He beats his mother while his wife's rapist sits on his lap, laughing in delight. Saṃsāra can be such a farce!"

Old Boy brought his attention to the second book, a biography of a man named Aṅgulimāla. Aṅgulimāla was an ardent student of Buddhism and a favorite of his teacher. His jealous peers wickedly convinced the teacher that Aṅgulimāla was plotting to seduce his wife. Unable to confront Aṅgulimāla directly without losing face, the imaginary cuckold sent his prize scholar on a perversely impossible task which he knew would be fatal. He told Aṅgulimāla that a "traditional goodbye gift to one's teacher is certain to bring enlightenment." The gift, said the teacher, would be 1,000 severed fingers from 1,000 different beings. Aṅgulimāla was a kindhearted young man so it took some convincing. In the end, he believed that obedience to his teacher served the highest purpose. Aṅgulimāla became a monster. He ambushed whoever entered the valley, stealing their lives then their fingers. People began avoiding the roads and he dragged them from their houses. Whole villages were abandoned. Wherever Aṅgulimāla stored the appendages, birds found and devoured them. To solve the problem, he wore them around his neck. (Aṅgulimāla means "necklace of fingers.") When his mother learned that the King was sending an army to kill her son, she came to the valley to dissuade him. She would be Aṅgulimāla's thousandth victim.

That was when the Buddha intervened.

The Perfect Master had a vision that as long as Aṅgulimāla was stopped before committing matricide, it would still be possible for him to become a monk and reach nirvana. When the deranged student saw the Buddha approaching, he rushed toward him with a sword yet such was the Awakened One's power that the brigand was converted on the spot.

On his way to kill the fiend of the Valley, the King stopped at the Buddha's monastery to pay homage. When he was introduced to the Aṅgulimāla – now a baldheaded monk-in-training – the stunned monarch immediately granted amnesty.

Months later, Aṅgulimāla encountered a pregnant woman in difficult labor. Overcome by compassion, he felt helpless. He went to the Buddha and asked how he might be of service. "Tell her," said his final teacher, "that since the moment you were born, you have never deprived a person of life. Hearing such a truth, she and her baby will be well." When Aṅgulimāla refused to deceive her, the Buddha revised his words. "Then tell her *since the moment you were born into noble birth,* you have never deprived anyone of life," thus, converting a lie to an *act of truth.* He did as he was told; when a healthy girl was born, Aṅgulimāla became the patron saint of childbirth.

That's what got Old Boy to remembering Ruthanne Davies – and the little girl he knew was his.

Chōkyi Nyingma Rinpoche kept up his visits. Whenever he was in Tibet, others came in his place, monks who lived at the nearby retreat in Leggett. Others belonged to an overseas group that ministered to prisoners, named after Aṅgulimāla himself. In time, Old Boy was given lessons by a former drug dealer who'd begun his journey in federal prison. (He completed his *ngöndro* – the foundational practices that precede becoming a monk – by doing prostrations in his cell.) He told Reginald that he too had the blessed privilege of being visited by a rinpoche while in prison. Upon release, he was ordained as a Zen monk.

Old Boy was an exceptional student. He was often called on by guards to defuse volatile situations. As a show of respect, the inmates stopped calling him Wolverine.

Now they called him Dr. Strange.

The cancer visited his lungs like a traditional goodbye gift. He was all right with dying, even excited by it. But then he began to have neurotic fears about the idea of not having enough time to study the dharma. What if when his body finally gave out, he wasn't ready? Rinpoche laughed and said, "*Moksha* not like school! We don't graduate! *Moksha* comes in *different* way. No homework! *Yes,* do homework, *but not like that.* The ladder of freedom has 10,000 rungs – can also have only five! When the body gives up, you may already be on *fourth* rung, stepping onto last."

Enter Kim Kardashian.

The woman had enough clout that she was allowed to visit him in his cell. She was the daughter of the man who defended O.J. – that's all he knew. A prisoner that Old Boy was teaching how to meditate said she was married to a rapper "who got Donald's ear. Gonna spring you for *reals,* Dr. Strange, bitch got *all* kindsa Get Outta Jail Free cards tucked in that pussy."

She arrived with a crew of advocates and attorneys. They'd been busy – not only had "Team Old Boy" ratified that at the time of his trial, the State's star witness, now dead, was indicted for perjury in a separate case, but had found, processed and matched "lost" DNA samples from the fingernails of two Ripper victims with a man currently in jail in Alabama.

A few days ago, he made a full confession to Kim's people.

I am hopeful, read Kim's public statement, *that Reginald will be fully exonerated. I'm grateful to Governor Newsom for ending capital punishment in California and considering our petition. We are optimistic that the 9th Circuit Court of Appeals will soon overturn the convictions and effect a compassionate release for medical reasons.*

She came out of nowhere and smelled like a forest.

A vision came as he lay in the prison hospital.

A palace hung before him like a celestial chandelier.

The fierce Buddhist deities and "destroyers of obstacles" lived within its brilliant, blinding light. Old Boy moved toward it now – toward the child he created with Ruthanne and been separated from all these years.

For she was in the lights as well.

He thought of his jailhouse meditation student solemnly presenting him with the gift of a Dr. Strange comic, and laughed. Who were the wisdom kings, if not superheroes? Who were the Yidams, the Buddhas and Bodhisattvas, if not super-heroes? Who were the protectors – the Devas and Asuras, the Garudas and the Nāgas, the Yakshas and Gandharvas – if not comic book gods? Who were the Lokapālas, or "Four Heavenly Kings," that hung from the palace belonging to

* * *

a friendly competitor from back home. Just yesterday, a snarky colleague sent a link to the "titanic estate on a prime parcel in the Malibu Hills" that Pat "Playboy" James "scooped up" for $23 million. Arnold's flamboyant colleague was from Chagrin Falls, a name whose comical irony he never got enough of. (They were about the same age and grew up together in Auto World.) Not too long ago, Arnold outplayed him by acquiring a coveted manufacturing plant. When Pat saw he'd been checkmated, he fedexed over a giant screw.

The day before their dinner date, Reeve finally called with the details. When Arnold heard the message, he stayed hard for two hours. She wanted to go to Geoffrey's, "a corny, fun roadside joint up the coast." His business in Orange County and L.A. being done, he decided to take a day trip and kill two birds – he could do a little Geoffrey's recon then take a sojourn to scope out Playboy Patrick's new digs. He wanted to see for himself just what twenty-three mill would buy you up there, 'case he suddenly wanted to go Hollywood. (He might have to get a divorce first.) He laughed out loud at his brain for sending a picture of him standing beneath a canopy, looking over his shoulder as Elon Musk walked Lovechild down the aisle to join Arnold in marriage everlasting.

He parked outside the "titanic estate" and reread the link:

From Pacific Coast Highway, towering gates swing open to reveal a long drive that meanders past guesthouses and orchards to a formal motor court. Inside, a double-height foyer is sure to mesmerize the pizza delivery person with its stunning ocean views. Other luxury spaces include a media room and wood-paneled library that is – a rarity in Lotusland – actually filled with books. The 1.7-acre blufftop lot has painstakingly maintained grounds that include vast lawns, formal gardens, an oversized swimming pool, and stairs leading down to coveted Malibu Road, home to some of the city's best surf spots. And this being Malibu, it's a given that many of the nearby neighbors are exceptionally famous. Folks within sugar-borrowing distance include Cher, Jane Seymour (who happens to live right next door) and Simon Cowell.

He was feelin' the vibe . . .

Why not?

Then his wife and son intruded on the brain-pic, stabbing him in the eye with those guilt-icepicks. He shook it off and drove down to a beach called Matador. Pretty romantic name. He hiked down to a hidden cove, running barefoot on the beach until he exhausted himself. He thought about eating but wanted to stay trim for Reeve. He needed to lose a few pounds but didn't look too bad for 53.

He stopped at Erewhon in the Palisades to buy sushi. It felt good to roam. He was like a blessed pilgrim, a spy in the city of God – a city suffused with Reeve's energy, laugh, smells. He drove down a long residential street that deadended at a bluff. He parked and took a stroll in the soft sun and bright wind. *I could get used to this town.* The houses looked older, stately, sedate, as if still having their original owners; you could almost see the ghosts of 40s movie stars rambling inside. He stood at a low wooden fence and stared at the magnificent ocean's red tide. How strange and wondrous this world, how lucky he was! He took a gander toward Malibu to see if he could spot Pat's house.

Six feet outside the barrier, something caught his eye, a charming little altar of rock cairns and seashells, flower stalks, and an elephant figurine. He squinted at what might have been a photo of a guru but couldn't see that far and wasn't about to walk out on the cliff.

Beside it was a message carved onto driftwood.

THIS IS A SYMBOL OF MY GRATITUDE. THANKS.

Arnold's feelings, exactly.

He was in sync with the universe.

He sat on a bench with a breathtaking view of the coast. He thought about fucking Reeve and got hard again. When he stood to go, he idly reviewed the bronze plaque on the back of his seat: "The Sun Never Sets On Love." A little on-the-spot googling said the bench and its view were dedicated to a young man from a legendary showbiz family who died of melanoma. He loved that about L.A. – fame and death were always intertwined.

He grunted, thinking of the wife and kid. He missed them terribly; loved them terribly; but in the last week, maybe for the first time in his life he felt truly, terribly alive. He had never been unfaithful to Raleigh, not strictly so. He'd come close. Once, he necked with a middle-aged waitress in the parking lot of Barnaby's, a restaurant in Nashville – another time, in Boca, during a convivial conversation with a gal at the Mint Lounge. She put her hand on his crotch and left it there like it'd fallen asleep. Flirtations always happened on the road, except that time in Cleveland at the Apple store when a Genius Bar girl with a pierced nose actually came onto him. Arnold's heart almost attacked him as he pretended to shop for phone cases but every time that he looked back she was making eye contact. He finally got the courage to slip her a note with his number. She left a voicemail apologizing for the delay (it wasn't much of one), explaining how she had to wait until she got home – the store apparently knew when employees texted customers that were in the database. Or something like that. She said she was *really* glad he gave her his number. "I thought, wow, what a cool-looking older man!" Some Daddy issues there, no doubt, not that he gave a shit; his marriage was a sexual dead zone, further enervated by Cammy, their adopted, "differently abled" son. Raleigh's full-time job was healthcare management – the boy had heart issues on top of autism – so the Apple girl's attentions made Arnold feel super-stoned. He never called back though, even deleting the number so as not to be tempted. It felt good to be so righteous, so disciplined. But he knew that all he was doing was buying an indulgence, getting pre-approved amnesty for future adulteries.

What if I fall in love with Reeve Musk?

* * *

Back at the hotel now.

Three o'clock LA time, six o'clock Cleveland.

Raleigh was FaceTiming but he didn't answer. He was at the pool and didn't want his wife to see him sunbathing, see him musing, see him dreaming of escape. Didn't want her to see the new, hedonistic, free-falling Arnold building castles in the sky. Didn't want her to sense he was rising up, or *might* be...

The palace revolt gave him a frisson of panicky delight.

Reeve, Reeve, Reeve, Reeve, Reeve...

He trudged to his room so he could FaceTime her back.

When she answered, he looked and thought, *How pretty she is.*

His heart broke again, over what they once had.

"Hi babe."

"*There* you are," she said.

"Sorry I couldn't pick up. Was on a call."

"How's it going?"

"Good – actually, great."

"Have you gone Hollywood yet?"

He flinched at the phrase, like she'd somehow got inside his head.

"Not *yet*. But I've sure gone Laguna Beach. How are things? Cammy good?"

"Well," she said gravely. "All *hell's* broken loose here."

"What happened?"

"I'm kidding. I just liked hearing myself say that."

"Jesus, Raleigh," he sighed. "I forgot you're a comedian."

"*Oh my God*, Arn, I saw this gal on Netflix last night – I couldn't sleep. I can't remember her name, but she was *so funny*. She's Asian – 'Mustang'! *That's* her name, like the car... she spent an *hour* talking about blowjobs – I mean, I kept waiting for her to *move on*, but it was like her entire *special*."

He was surprised because she was usually pretty careful not to talk about sex stuff. Neither one of them wanted to throw light on what they were missing out on. "You trying to tell me something?"

"*Maybe*. We'll see about that when you come home."

"Ready, willing and able."

The banter was bullshit but it was easier to just play along.

"And by the *way*, when *are* you coming home?"

He sighed and said, "Probably not for another week."

"Oh, Arn!" she said, disappointed. "Do ya mean it?"

"Yup."

"You won't be home for Hallowe'en?"

"Not looking that great right now."

"But you *have* to be. I mean, seriously?"

"Probably the Monday after."

"Cammy's gonna be so upset."

"I know. I'll talk to him. How's he doing?"

"You can see for yourself in a minute. Arn, can't you just come home and Skype whatever big shot you're seeing out there?"

"I *could*... if the CEO wasn't a paranoid, closet conspiracy freak who actually believes cellphones have been hijacked by the Deep State."

"Is that for real?"

"*Oh* yeah. The guy seriously needs to be medicated. If I Skyped from Ohio, he'd be convinced he was talking to a reptile."

"Now that gives me pause – show me your tongue."

He stuck it out and they both laughed.

Offstage, their son gurgled with anticipatory delight.

"Someone wants to talk to you," said Raleigh, with a wink.

"Papa! Papa!"

"Hey there, Cameron! What's that you're wearing?"

Usually he was in a Spidey outfit but this was something else entirely. Raleigh bopped into the frame to chime in. "I told him we had to wait for Hallowe'en but he tortured me so I caved."

"Whoa! Hey now! Is that Thanos?" said Arnold, like a fanboy.

"*Thanos, Thanos, Thanos!*" cried the boy.

"Holy shit."

"Holy shit, holy shit, holy shit!" echoed Cammy.

"Now that *is* impressive."

"It's the 'deluxe,'" she said. "You don't even want to *know* how much it cost. I mean, isn't Marvel making enough already with the movies?"

The boy thrust a jewel-gloved hand in front of the lens.

"In-finty Stones!" he shouted.

"Well they sure *are*," said Arnold, admiring the bright-colored gems welded into a glove's hardware. "Bet you couldn't find *those* at the bottom of a Crackerjack box."

"Crackerjack! Crackerjack! Crackerjack!"

The doorbell rang.

"It's Phyllis and the gals," said Raleigh. "Bridge night. Say goodnight to Daddy, Cam." She left to answer the door.

"*Say* it!" shouted Cammy into the phone. "*Say* it!"

"I will," said Arnold. "But remember, buddy, *you* have to say it first."

It was a game they played ever since they saw *Avengers: Endgame* at the Shaker Square multiplex. In the scene where Iron Man dies, Thanos is convinced of his triumph. "I am inevitable," he proclaims. "And *I*," says Tony Stark, "am *Iron Man*." He kills Thanos, before succumbing himself.

Cammy got serious.

"*I*," he intoned, like a ham actor. "Am *inevitable*."

"And *I...*" said Arnold, "am *Iron Man*."

His son howled with glee.

Raleigh walked back in with a caregiver. "Okay, Mr. Thanos, bath time. Ronald's gonna escort you, and he's got a surprise."

"What's the surprise?"

"Infinity Stone soap!"

"O boy o boy o boy o boy – "

"More money for Marvel," she said, winking again at Arnold. "And after your little lizard convention, *call* me."

"It's inevitable. Love you, babe."

She puckered up and kissed the lens.

He spent the night drinking and masturbating, trying not to text Reeve. He wondered what she was doing. Maybe she was with her dad...

He was proud for having the fortitude not to text.

He smiled to himself – he felt like a schoolboy again.

He was randy and cabin feverish. Probably a good idea to leave the room before he went and texted something dipshitty like *can't wait to see you.* He took a quick shower and dressed for success.

Arnold was more loaded than he thought. In the elevator, he said *feelin no pain,* out loud. Striding across the lobby, he shook his head and muttered *amazing the power a woman has.* In no time, he was at the bar sipping a $400 Remy. He wondered (some more and some more and some more) how sex with Reeve would go down. Worried about being so turned on that he wouldn't be able to perform. Glad he brought his Cialis stash. *If it conks out on me, no biggie. I'll just do the ol alphabet trick, gets em every time.*

He saw an attractive woman at the end of the bar and wondered if he should send a drink over. Everything was Reeve foreplay. Just when he was about to ask the bartender what the lady was drinking, her boyfriend joined her. (No one was wearing wedding bands.) Arnold realized he saw the two at brunch.

A salvo of raucous laughter came from two couples in a booth.

The gal at the bar looked over and said, "It's him."

"No way," said her companion.

"It *is,* it *is.*" She was drunk.

He looked toward the booth and said, "Well you may be right."

"Not *may, am* – not *may,* okay? *Am.* Oh my God, I am *obsessed.* The Greatest Fucking Showman!"

"The greatest fucking showman to *you,*" said the boyfriend or whatever. "But to *me,* he'll always be the *Wolverine.*"

Arnold looked to see what they were fussing over.

Hugh Jackman – holy shit.

Wait'll I tell Cammy.

"Why don't you just go over?" said the man.

"Are you fucking *serious*?"

"Celebrities love that."

"I would *never*," she said, in outrage.

"They love it!"

"They *pretend* to but they *hate* it. It's so fucking *rude*."

"Then *I'll* go over," he said, without budging.

"You *do* and you can fuck someone else tonight."

The bartender liked that one; she caught his smile and liked it too.

"Sounds like a plan," said her man.

On impulse, Arnold stood. Walking past them, he said, "I'll go over for you." The woman stared blankly as he strode to the booth.

The tuxedoed men looked up with half-smiles.

"I have a wife and son back home," said Arnold, directing his remarks to Jackman. "My boy's disabled. My wife is too – no, she isn't, that's a bad joke, and I apologize for it. But my son is autistic – he's got other problems too – and my wife's a total hero. *Both* of them think the world of you. As do I. I can't wait to tell my boy I met Wolverine."

He doffed a phantom top hat, bowed, and apologized for barging in.

"Please join us," said Jackman.

He introduced his wife, Deborra-Lee, and the other couple (who weren't together) – Jean Trebek, the wife of the game show host, and Wolfgang Puck. They'd just come from a benefit for his and Deborra-Lee's foundation. Ten minutes in, thinking he'd overstayed, Arnold felt so expansive that he pulled an emergency check from his wallet and wrote out the sum of $150,000 to *Promises Kept: the Orphans Alliance.* Hugh and Deborra-Lee were gobsmacked. Arnold assured his impromptu hosts that he could afford it. "My eleemosynary impulse is not due to drunkenness but because you, sir, and your lady – and you, chef Wolfgang, and you, Mrs. Trebek – and this marvelous foundation – terribly moves me."

All were seriously touched by the gesture.

"My only wish," he went on, "is the gift be made in my son's name – no – my wife and son. In their names." He doffed the ghost cap again as he left. "I *thank* you, sirs and ladies. And to all a goodnight."

* * *

When her mom came in, Trixanna was watching a YouTube of Kim Kardashian on *Ellen*. It was annoying because Portia said, "Oh, there's Kim," like they were old friends or something, and sat down to watch.

Ellen was saying that Kim had probably met every famous person who ever lived but wanted to know if there was still someone on her wish list. "Greta Thunberg," replied Kim. Trixanna found the clip because she was writing a paper for school about the Swedish firebrand and the "new mutants," trying to decode the agenda behind Greta's cover as a climate crusader. (Environmental issues had zero effect on X-Men.) She *did* understand the fiery impulse to "heal," but Old Boy was the only thing Trix wanted to save. Not the Earth, not ocean or sky... just Old Boy.

"Greta's amazing," said Kim. "And so *brave* to stand up to grown-ups – that can be really scary. For her to be so honest is exactly what we need to hear. She's such a role model for my daughters."

Portia abruptly grabbed Trixanna's jaw and peered into her mouth.

"Ow!" said Trix, jerking away. "What are you *doing*?"

Her mother tightened her grip and said, "*Just hold still.*"

She took a stick and swabbed the inside of her cheek.

"*Stop* it – "

"All done!"

"What is that?" she said, as Portia tucked the swab into an envelope.

"It's a pre-test – for the HPV vaccine."

"What's HPV?"

"Papillomavirus."

"You are so *crazy*!"

"Don't *worry* about it, *all* the kids are getting tested. Now brush your teeth and get dressed. Mama has a busy day and needs to take you to school early."

All day long in class, she replayed the disturbing incident of the swab, which stirred up the questions that already haunted:

Is this woman really my mother? Or is she on a mission to pinpoint my mutant strain so that Transigen can find a way to neutralize the adamantium that is slowly but surely making me indestructible?

She was glad she stopped taking the new pills.

On the way home from school, she sat on a bench watching a young couple pedal around Echo Park Lake in a swan boat. Trixanna had no friends; the kids called her Psycho but always behaved when her mom dropped her off. Something deep in their nervous systems told them not to fuck with the wildcardy Ms. Coldstream. She spent a lot of time scanning other students in hopes of finding fellow mutants from the hospital in Oakland, who for some reason she may not have met. A prime candidate was Joey Levender – he didn't have any friends either. The meaner boys called him "Get Out" and joked to his face about how he was going to become the first Black school shooter. When they passed him in the hall, they whispered *Don't fuck with us, Parkland, we got bulletproof backpacks.*

One day at lunch, Trixanna surprised herself by plunking down beside him at a cafeteria table. Joey gave a little start.

"Look!" said a nasty boy. "Jay Z and Blue Ivy!"

"Get Out finally got himself a second shooter!"

She waited for them to move on.

"Are you doing a paper?" she shyly asked.

"Uhm, we *have* to," he said defensively. "That's the *assignment.*"

She knew a girl who was writing a paper about the history of *Dancing With the Stars.* Another student was doing one about young celebs with business empires, like Kylie Jenner, the Olsen Twins, and Millie Bobby Brown. Originally, Trix was going to write about Meghan Markle but knew that her interest in the Duchess came from her non-mutant side; after her father was revealed to be the Wolverine, she switched to Greta, in hopes she might learn something from the X-Force activist's strategies that would help free him.

"What are you writing about?" she said, her initial boldness fading.

After a nervous hesitation, Joey said, "Elon Musk."

"Oh," said Trix. "Who's that?"

"You mean, you don't know?"

Embarrassed, she looked at her shoes and shook her head.

"*SpaceX,*" he said disdainfully. "And the *Tesla.*"

"Oh."

"I was going to do Jeff Bezos but I think Elon's actually *way* more interesting." She was happy he got chatty. And the more he spoke, the more certain she was that Joey was an X-Child. "Not to minimize Jeff's accomplishments, which are pretty amazing. Did I say 'amazing'? I meant Ama-*zon*." He snort-laughed, pleased at the quip. "I mean, Jeff's richer than Elon *by far* but probably not for *long*. See, the outer space game is a *bit* more complicated than getting same-day delivery of a Dyson fan. If you know what I mean. *My* money's on Mr. Musk. Jeff has a rocket company too, but I think he's in it for the *commerce*. Like, if you *really* need that Dyson vacuum delivered to your summer place in the *lunar* colony, for that pesky build-up of moon dust. Elon has a *visionary* approach. In the end, the nonbinaries *win*. Plus, he wants to go to Mars because he thinks Earth isn't going to last much longer."

"That's what Greta says."

"Who's that?"

"You mean, you don't know?" she said, impishly throwing back his own words. She could be funny when she wanted to. "The school striker! The Swedish climate crusader." She almost said *and new mutant*.

"Elon got bullied in school," said Joey, ignoring her. "According to Wikipedia. According to Wikipedia, he actually had to go to the hospital after some *assholes* broke his nose and threw him down the stairs."

"Oh," said Trix, blanching. "That's terrible." Though she didn't know who Elon was, her lip trembled with a tender empathy that wasn't lost on her new acquaintance. "So," she said, without sarcasm. "He's going to Mars to escape the bullies?"

"*No*, not *really*, though you just may have a point. A point Mr. Musk may not necessarily *appreciate* – and a point *I* certainly would never bring up *if* I am ever lucky enough to find myself conversing with the man. In, say, a Joe Rogan podcast situation."

"Mars *is* kind of like Eden, I guess. Elon *does* sound a little like Logan – well, I mean, *sort* of." The comparison was definitely a stretch but Trix was enjoying her convo with a mutant boy. Besides, she felt safe saying what she did because he wasn't paying attention.

Wrong.

"Who's Logan?" he asked.

"Oh!" Flummoxed, she said, "I don't know!"

"You're *very* strange. Anyone ever tell you that? It's *okay*, I don't *mind*, they tell *me* that all the time. And when they don't say it, they're thinking it. What's your name?"

"Trixanna."

"What kind of name is that?"

She was going to go into it, but just shrugged.

"My name's Joey."

"I know." He took that in. Some kids made kissy sounds at them from across the room. "Mars is far away," she said, apropos of nothing, unable to help herself. "But Eden's really close." She rambled when she got nervous. "It's in North Dakota."

"What are you *talking* about?"

"Did you ever see *Logan*? About the Wolverine? He's dying – poisoned by Dr. Zander Rice and the Transigen people. His daughter Laura and her mutant friends escape from a special hospital because the the Reavers are trying to kill them. Logan helps them get to the one place they'll be safe."

The outburst made her contrite and she ended by whispering, "That place is called Eden."

Something in Joey stirred. "That's from a comic book?" Trix nodded, even though it was so much more. "I don't watch movies from comics. I guess I don't really see too many movies, *period*," he amended, not wanting to be mean. "But actually, I hear that one's pretty good."

Trixanna's heart fluttered as he joined her on a bench at the lake's rim. The swan boats languished in the dock. A fountain in the middle of the lotuses was in full-tilt geyser mode. A huge bird appeared, startling her.

"A pelican!" said Joey. "They don't come here too often. See how the babies aren't afraid?" A row of tiny ducks suddenly lined up behind it. "It's adopted them – see? They think he's Mommy!"

It was a sign. With all her strength, she summoned the courage to tell him about Old Boy, the prisoner of Pelican Bay, but no words came.

"Pelicans are actually interesting," he said. "If their babies are starving and there's no food, they stab their breast so the chicks can drink. Actually, I'm not sure that pelican babies are *called* chicks. I'll have to google that."

"They stab… and milk comes out?"

"Blood!"

"That's *gross*."

"Blood's really *nourishing*. My dad said Christ was a pelican."

"Do you live with him?"

The question, born of father-longing, burst from her mouth.

"No," he said. "But we go to church every other weekend. That's when I see him – every other weekend. He said Christ isn't really a pelican but a *symbol* of one. Because Jesus actually supposedly fed hungry children from his breast. Not sure if he stabbed himself, though. Maybe he *did*, like, with his crown of thorns."

The last, another quip, went over Trixanna's head.

Without warning, Joey leaned over to kiss her cheek. Her skin flushed pink; sweat sprung from his brow.

"We can watch a movie if you want. At the house. We can even watch the *Logan* movie."

"You mean now?" she asked, flustered.

"It's one of Dad's weekends but he doesn't have me 'cause he's at a conference. So you could sleep over. We have lots of extra rooms."

She would wait until then to tell him the truth about Old Boy.

Joey was *so smart* – maybe he'd even help with the letter she was sending to Pelican Bay. She felt that weird blackout thump-dance in her chest and was overcome, but this time everything felt different.

Trixanna was in love.

* * *

Portia thought the house was perfect.

It was way down on Sunset, on Via De La Paz. Palatial but not showy, traditional yet with unexpectedly stylish touches, she could see Kendall Jenner living there. Soft around the edges, with tons of roses and a seriously pruned hedge, it totally worked as the high-end, hide-in-plain-sight bivouac of Reeve Musk: a billionaire Daddy's gift to his wild child daughter. A tender trap in the complacent bastion of Pacific Palisades.

A few months ago, as part of the pre-con, Portia got herself hired as a home-arranger temp. The manse had been on the market too long. Averse to flash, the owner finally caved and hired Faustino "the Pharaoh" Blanco, the legendary Westside realtor with his own reality show. *BDW – Billion Dollar World!* was in its fourth season.

The first thing Faustino did was enlist his go-to home stager because the place was empty as a mausoleum. After 48 hours of Trudy doing her thing, he swept in with two personal assistants and surveyed.

"Yes yes *yes*," said the Pharaoh. "It is beginning to look *genuis*." He drew his hands together, pressing them against nose and mouth in contemplative prayer, then sniffed his fingertips like Benedict Cumberbatch having a meta-moment. "More furniture *please*, Trudy!" A ringmaster calling, *More tigers! More trapezes! More dancing bears!* "Listen and *learn*, from the Pharaoh. The *reason* this home didn't sell is that the *previous idiot realtors* were fresh out of *fucks* and fresh out of *furniture*. As you know, Trudy, because you have been *tutelaged* by the Pharaoh, the three most important factors in selling houses are not *location, location, location*. The three most important factors are *furniture, furniture, furniture!*"

"You want more? You got it!" said Trudy.

"Paintings, paintings, paintings! More paintings! More framed little pictures! Little framed pictures of little framed *people* we are *pretending* still live here! Little framed pictures on the *piano*, little framed pictures on the fireplace *mantle*, little framed pictures *everywhere*! Ándale, Ándale, Ándale!"

Just then, Portia walked in.

She wore a head wrap and held a cobalt blue ceramic pitcher at her hip like Hockney's take on a Vermeer Millennial. Trudy had a crush on her from Day One and it was in Portia's business interests to keep that flame burning. Trudy loved how Portia cruelly shamed the furniture movers who hit on her. One of the lamer suitors was Jerzy, a charmless Tom Hardy wannabe with a hipster-hoodlum demeanor. He wore cheap, Schott-knockoff biker leathers sold at stalls along Venice Beach. Jerzy was a jerk, but he was dependable, so Trudy kept him working. Whenever he saw Portia, he always played it like they might have hooked up once, tilting his head and squinting his eyes.

"You never did the online dating thing?"

"Yeah," she'd answer, tits-out and bored. "I was working, undercover – you know that show *To Catch a Predator*? I pretended to be a horny eight-year-old. So we actually might have texted."

"You're funny," smirked Jerzy. "How long you been doing this?"

She couldn't believe the piece of shit was still trying to engage.

"It's been a dream of mine since I was a little. I didn't want to settle for being a house sitter or a dog walker so I worked hard and became a home stager instead. God works in mysterious ways."

Later, she traipsed to the distant master bath, for a privacy shit. The door was half open; Jerzy hunched by the toilet, showing something to a coworker. He looked up at her.

"It's *you, hell* yeah! It's her! I knew it! I *knew* I fuckin knew you!"

He stiff-armed the phone for Portia to see one of the old "improv" porns of her getting ass-fucked by Jaxx. She snatched

it from his hand and threw it in the bowl. The coworker burst
out laughing. Jerzy raised a hand to strike her but held back.

"Oh, *please*," said Portia. "*Please* fucking hit me so I can
kill you."

Backing off, he said, "The phone's waterproof, you cunt."

He fished it out of the yellow water as she split.

At the end of the workday, she strolled to her Alfa and grabbed
a sack of sugar kept in the trunk for such occasions. With an
eye on the house, she emptied it into the tank of Jersey's wannabe Harley.

On the way to the Grove, she stopped at Exxxotica to give
Cage the impression she made from the key in the mansion's
lockbox. Then she went to Zara and put $800 on a stolen
credit card.

She came, rolled off him, and lit a joint.

Jaxx looked like a petite Elvis. But Portia thought the sexiest, most random thing about him was his tech-head genius.
They'd been living together for a year when he got busted for
using dark web malware to lock up PCs for ransom. He wound
up doing 23 months. Since Jaxx's release, his primary source
of income was freelance work, mostly creating synthetic porn
for clients of his old friend Cage. Somehow, Cage got hooked
up with a billionaire teen who paid big money for all kinds of
silly shit – deepfake, X-rated films of Greta Thunberg getting it
on with plus-sizers like Lizzo and Ashley Graham. Jaxx took a
25% cut. When "Fat Joan" vanished from the face of the Earth,
wallets everywhere took a major hit.

Before his conviction, Jaxx and Portia were starting to get
noticed in the newish category of "alt-porn." They were part

of a new wave of amateurs with a relatable, mumblecore millennial vibe that some adult film producers thought looked like the future. It was fun because they actually considered themselves to be aspiring actors and sometimes did ten minutes of improv before the sex even started. Their specialty was playing brother and sister. In one of their videos, Portia came home early from college and confessed that she'd played a drunk, disastrous game of truth or consequences with her sorority sisters. They went around the room asking each girl about their secret crush; when she said "my brother," everyone recoiled. Portia goes on to tell Jaxx that she had to drop out because she was so embarrassed. After a while, she nervously suggests that "maybe we should try it? Like, just once?" Her bro gets mucho uncomfortable and Portia's embarrassed all over again. Of course, they wind up getting it on but until they did, things were awkward and super-real. Portia was proud of it; she thought the acting was as good as any in a topnotch verité-style indie. They even won an award for it in Vegas.

When she finally told him about her meeting with Kim, Jaxx was more excited than she was. "That's fucking *insane*. I mean, do you even understand what this *is*? How *major*? I cannot *believe*... do you know how fucking *large* this could be, Porsh?"

"I don't know. It's all *so* crazy."

"But – do you think – do you really think the dude's Trixanna's fucking *baby daddy*?"

"*Maybeeeeee*."

"Fuck!"

"I don't know. *Prolly?* Naw, I'm shittin you. *Way* doubtful. I was so loaded back then, I mean, *all the time* – Old Boy saw to that. So who the fuck knows. And it wasn't like we were *exclusive*. He was my pimp."

"This is such a trip! So, why do they even want to know?"

"She's trying to get him out of prison."

"*Whoa.*"

"He's, like, dying. Of cancer. And he wants – if Trix is *his*, he just wants to meet her. Wants *her* to meet *him*. Whatever."

"Epic."

"For a documentary they're doing. Like, it's the money-shot – you know, when I bring our *daughter* to the prison or hospital or wherever, and they hug it out for the *Keeping Up With the Kardash* cameras."

"Can't you just *say* she is? Because if she *isn't*, Kim's like gonna have *no need…*"

Portia shook her head. "They're doing – they want Trixanna's DNA. I already swabbed her."

"And if she *is*," said Jaxx. "Then, there's money?"

"We'd be in the documentary."

"That's *nuts*."

"You know, like, Kim's gonna be a lawyer. And the film would be about, I don't know, her whole free-the-slaves trip or whatever."

"So you'd get paid."

"I don't *think* so. But – maybe there's, like, maybe some *scholarship* Kim would give to Trix so like when he… after he dies – "

"*Fuck* all that, *you're* the one who should get the scholarship!"

"I just don't think it's gonna go down like that, Jaxx. I mean, even if she does turn out to be his. That's why we need to go heavy on Arnold before he trots his ass back to Cleveland."

"Do *both*. Can't you fucking multi-task?"

"What's *effed up* is I googled Richie 'Snoop' Raskin and he's LAPD. Retired homicide."

"Who *is* that?"

"Like, *Detective Snoop* is fucking *real*."

"*Who's Detective Snoop*."

"The motherfucker who *found* me. He was in the fucking *room* – in Century City – with Kim. The man's written *books*, Jaxx, he had a freakin *reality* show… I don't even want to *think* about what the dude actually knows about me. It's got to be *everything*, though, right? And he would have had to have told *Kim* whatever he found out, right? I mean, the man *works* for her. But she's, like – she was classy. She has this amazing, beautiful poker face and *never* lets on what she knows, like, whatever he told her, because she wouldn't want to just, throw something in my face. She's *already* probably worried about the sketchy shit, like, worried I won't want to *participate*. Maybe I should have played harder to get. Then, maybe she would have thrown some *money* at me… but you so do *not* want to have Richie fucking Snoop's eyes on you, Jaxx! You seriously *don't*. So I'm not real happy about that."

"You just have to play along. Do what you need to do – whatever they fucking *want*. Kim'll protect you. Trust me, she don't care about your larcenous shit. Look, Portia, it's totally not in her *interest* to st – "

"Who the fuck *knows* what's in her interest, Jaxx! She's Kim fucking Kardashian! Those women are all fucking killers! Prolly even *Kendall's* a fucking killer! And the 'momager'? Don't *even*. Kris Jenner is Suge fucking Knight."

"Kris would for sure be sucking Suge's dick if he was out."

"Heh heh."

"Okay, *listen*. Kim gets him out, right? Gets him freed. And she *will*, too, 'cause whatever Kimmy wants, Kimmy gets. Okay? So she gets 'Old Boy' out, then *guess what*. Your baby daddy's gonna be owed a shit-ton by the state. They incarcerate an innocent man for what, 13 years? That's no joke, babe. They might settle out for three, four million. Maybe five. And let's say – with your input and encouragement – *Kim's* input and encouragement – Old Boy agrees to leave *all* of it or *most* of it to *Trix*."

"*Mayyyy*-be."

He had her attention.

"You might not even have to *wait* for him to get out. If he's fucking dying, he could just put his wishes in a will. If he's as sick as Kim says he is, he might not even make it *out*. Right? Might fucking die *tomorrow*. Maybe it can be worked that he'll leave the settlement money to *both* of you. See where I'm heading? And let's say you *agree* to be in the documentary she's making. I mean, if Trix actually turns out to be his kid, yadda yadda. That doc is gonna blow *up*. Shit's gonna be seen by millions of *eyeballs*. 'Cause the Kardashians are master marketeers, right? Film festivals, HBO, Netflix, *wherever...* and all that genius PR cross-pollinating on their show, cause you *know* they're gonna talk about it every episode, Porsh. You'll be on the fucking show, Portia! *Keeping Up With the Kardashians featuring Portia Coldstream*! Kim ain't stupid, that's one thing she's not. None of 'em are. They got a about a billion followers on the gram between em. She won't make herself the center of attention, you know, the classic *humblebrag* move is to bring you and Trixanna in for a tug at the fucking heartstrings. 'Cause they know they need to keep it real once in a while, people get tired of them bitching each other out in the Maldives. On the periods and shit on private planes... I swear to you, Trix'll become best friends for life with Kim's daughters! What are those little cunts' names? North and Chicago? And that fucked up-looking Disick brood? You *know* that's going to happen, Porsh. In a few years, Trix could *marry in*. Like, marry one of Scott Disick's kids. Or Kanye's boys... or if Trix is a dyke and one of the Kardashian or Jenner kids is a dyke, they could hook up! But *whatever*, this doc is gonna win *awards* – and *bam*, you're in film festivals all over Europe. Because remember, Kim's advised by Kanye, right? He, like, fucking runs her life. He designed the *house*, picks out her *clothes*, she *admits* that. He's a bipolar fucking control freak. Which means he's gonna make sure she hires the best person to direct it – they'll *buy* the best person. Spike Jonze, Spike Lee, Spike Whomever. You could even get cast in a real fucking *movie* off that. Like, a feature! They might even wind up making a movie about *you*. Yes! Wouldn't you like to be played by Margot Robbie?"

She spit out her kombucha and howled with laughter.

"Come *on*, Portia, weirder shit's happened! The *worst* thing that can happen is you get massive fucking exposure." With a wolfish smile, he added, "Then Ohio Arnold recognizes you and wants his money back!"

"That's no joke, bubba. Don't think it didn't enter my mind."

"Not gonna *happen*. Guaranteed. Because every 'Arnold' you've ever hustled is too fucking *embarrassed* to come forward. Not just because they're gullible dipshits but 'cause they're *married* dipshits, with dipshit *children*." He had a brain skid. "Hey! Didja ever show Mister Ohio my home movie masterpiece? Of you and Elon?"

"Oh *hell* yeah, it sealed the deal! How did you *do* that, you're a fucking *genius*, even *I* thought it was real." She kissed him and said, "And you put Geoffrey's in your calendar, right?"

"When is that?"

"Fucking Wednesday, *dipshit*." She swatted him. "*Oh my God,* you're *coming*, right, Jaxx?"

"Yeah yeah yeah…"

"And you need to bring *Cage*. You *both* have to be there – "

"I said I would be, Margot, so can you chill?"

Jaxx scanned the images of online booking agencies for a lookalike of Elon Musk. There was a surfeit of Post Malones, Brad Pitts, Joe Bidens and John Legends – but no Elons, which kind of surprised him.

Leaving Starbucks, he saw a stack of *LA Weekly*s resting in a windowless, rusted-out newspaper container like an exhibit in a dead media museum. He grabbed one, randomly opening to

Sunday Night!
Improv @ the KTown Kollective
ADELE COBAIN (AdeleCobain – YouTube)
KEVIN LEE (Jimmy Kimmel's very own 'Elon Musk')

He googled "Kevin Lee" and "Kevin Lee Jimmy Kimmel" but couldn't find video of the guy. But "Kevin Lee Elon Musk" yielded a few blurry thumbnails that looked half-promising.

That night, stoned, he drove to the club in the Falcon convertible Cage helped him find at auction. The warm wind felt good against his face and he imagined himself flying. His mind kept gnawing on the whole Portia/Kim K phenomenon, like a dog on a golden bone.

The "kollective" was actually comprised of wall-to-wall karaoke rooms, with a lounge in back for plastered patrons who decided to try their hand at open mic. Twice a week, it featured standups and sketch comedy. When Jaxx walked in, his quarry was already onstage.

The lookalike was pale white, and Korean, which actually worked because @therealElonMusk's eyes vibed Asiatic, especially when the impish genius deployed that charming, low-kilowatt grin. The hair was perfect too. He was in the middle of a doing a routine with tonight's other featured player, Adele Cobain. The stacked comedienne wore oversized purple glasses and a tight, sweat-soaked #mejew t-shirt.

"Mr. Musk!" she said breathlessly. "There's something Adele needs to *know*. Why the *fuck* did you keep marrying and divorcing the *same woman*?"

"Practice makes perfect," said the Elon.

(Not the greatest but Jaxx wasn't looking for Shia LaBeouf.)

In an aside to the audience, she said, "Can you *believe* that Elon Musk married the same woman three times? *Three times*. It's on Wikipedia, which is my fucking bible." Abandoning the unresponsive crowd with a shrug of disgust, she resumed the routine. "I wonder what *that* was like – for *her*, not *you*, Elon. Guess she's kinda like that gal who got run over last year by a Tesla on autopilot, huh. Except she comes back from the dead and gets hit again! But *you'll* invent a way to reanimate her, *won't* you? She'll say, 'Oh my God! Elon! I was dead AF – *twice*. And now that I'm alive, the first thing I want to do is get married again! To *you*!'"

"Third time's the charm," beamed the dullwitted double, who was starting to look more like the real thing to Jaxx than ever.

As if she'd had enough of the fiasco, Adele Cobain abruptly turned to the crowd. "Thanks for finding your way to this ratfuck K-town firetrap. *Jackasses.* And if you're in the mood for love, remember: Lyft drivers are *way* better rapists than Ubers, trust me, I know from experience. Their hygiene's better and they tend to be less... Armenian? But hey, that's just one happy victim's opinion! And as you leave the club, don't forget to wave to the birthday boy – that would be the bald, terminal kid nodding out in one of the karaoke rooms while Mom and Dad do their 'Old Town Road' duet. A real fucking crowd pleaser!" Before the mic drop, she told them all to eat shit and die. Jaxx thought it was actually pretty funny.

He bought the lookalike a drink and laid out his proposition: a close, "gullible" tekkie friend worshipped the ground Musk walked on. "I told my bud that I met Elon at a convention a few months ago – I've been planning this! If he actually *sees* us together, from a distance (I'll make sure he doesn't get too close), he will *freak.*"

The gentleman was a little bewildered but when Jaxx said he'd get $300 for 10 minutes work, any confusion cleared.

* * *

Early the next morning came a pair of startling events.

Team Old Boy had found Ruthanne Davies, but Kim cautioned against getting too hopeful. "Mom's still the decider" – it was up to "Portia" whether to allow a visit from the girl, or let sleeping dogs lie. In any case, the matter was on hold until the results of the paternity test came in.

Yet, there it was: the letter.

The childish penmanship was weirdly ornate. Calling herself both Trixanna and "Laura/X-23," she wrote about coming to Pelican Bay to "X-tract" him. The prisoner was flummoxed. It didn't help that Reginald wasn't feeling well – he vomited blood twice during the night – or that a banner at the top of the page announced, "I will soon speak of one of the 3 GEMS that will free you!" His mind was muddled. *How could she know? Who would have told her of "the Triple Gem" – the Buddha, the Dharma, the Sangha – that I took refuge in?* She seemed to know that he was sick too, and now Old Boy thought he finally understood. He gave Kim permission to tell Ruthanne about the cancer, to lend urgency to his wish for a compassionate rendezvous with their child. To paint a softer picture of the prisoner (for both Ruthanne *and* Trixanna), Kim may even have shared that he would soon to be ordained as a Buddhist monk... which would explain the girl's mention of "the 3 gems." He theorized that Ruthanne, impatient for the DNA results and already certain of what they'd reveal, impetuously told Trixanna everything.

And to pack a little bag for a surprise visit to papa.

The child, bless her heart, jumped the gun!

His heart danced: joy and rank nausea changed partners.

He wept between ragged breaths – *so blessed.*

– a letter! A letter from his lost, beloved babygirl...

She called him "Wolverine" and it hurt to think she must have read on her computer about that terrible name the press had given him... he couldn't wait to tell her that everything was a lie.

He scrutinized the pages like a scholar parsing an ancient scroll. She was only a child, unformed and unruly and hard-headed (*got that from me,* he thought), but Old Boy appre-hended something else (no – yes?): that his raving, ravenous baby girl was damaged in some way. It made sense because Ruthanne would have been taking so much dope all through the gestation… yet all that mattered was that they'd found one another. She kept saying "Portia" wasn't her real mom, but he thought it normal for a girl her age to cleave toward the father, especially one she had never known.

With trembling hand, he returned to the dizzyingly esoteric manuscript, *almost* able to make sense of the Logans and Edens, the cold streams and Reavers, the time stones and the adamantium bones –

But the only thing that needed to make sense was Her.

The mixed, messy blessing of words, the volcanic *all* of it made Reginald Ronald White's headheart swim before drowning – dead in his cell by the time a guard rushed in.

It was better that way. Better not to hear what Snoop conveyed to Team Old Boy only a few hours later:

Trixanna Coldstream wasn't his.

He was 58 and Ruthanne was 19. Like some gypsy, Old Boy knew she was pregnant before she did, but never let on. She was afraid it belonged to a trick. (Years later, she died of shame when she made the connection between tricks and Trixanna.) Ruthanne didn't want to be with johns anymore – at least, not while she was expecting – and was certain Old Boy would punish her for that. Then she started to worry about him being the father; it filled her with dread because how could she ever tell her child daddy made his living selling mama's body to strangers? Still, she didn't want an abortion. (Ruthanne kept surprising herself with the promises she broke, 'cause she had four abortions after Trixanna.) To get away from Old Boy and the Life, she made plans to disappear in the middle of the night – back to Santa Fe or Casper or Clearwater or even Seattle – that became moot when Reginald got arrested. For being a serial killer! That was some bizarre impossible bullshit so she kept on expecting him to be released. It was crazy when he got convicted but anyhow she was glad because the whole whatever problem went away. She felt bad for him because she knew he never could have killed those men. She never went to see him in jail but did write, only once, to tell him she had a kid. He wrote back but she threw his letters away and then she moved and never gave the post office a forwarding address. When Trix was born, she took one look and said: "it's his." Not just the skin and something in her eyes, but the feet – the feet! Trixanna had feet like her dad, it was crazy. Ruthanne loved closing a book and it was easy to close the Old Boy book when they gave him a life sentence. Over the years, she thought of telling him more about their beloved child but what would be the point? Jaxx was already a father to her and the little girl loved him. One day, to her surprise, she told Trix his name. Ruthanne (she'd been Portia for a hundred years now) couldn't believe it spilled from her mouth but it felt right. Her eyes bugged out cartoon-style and she raced around the room in tight circles, gleefully shouting, "Old Boy? Old Boy? Old Boy! Old Boy!"

Every child should know their father's name…

*and when they put him away, Old Boy closed the book to –
closed everything that was open, until he met Rinpoche*

*& read about Aṅgulimāla, the madman who became a monk
& oversaw the perilous birth of an infant girl
& became the patron saint of childbirth.*

After Ruthanne wrote to him about the birth (cruelly with-holding Trixanna's name), Old Boy visualized a golden-brown child sitting beside a buddha as part of his Vajrayana medi-tation practice. He did that for more than a decade. At first, the image sustained him. But he came to worry it was some kind of desecration, that he was *using* the girl to benefit his own practice. What was worse – exploiting her for spiritual gain or allowing himself to indulge his deeply human emotions? Either way, Reggie believed his *attachment* (to practice, to daughter) clouded mind and motive. He pushed Trix away by wondering, *Is it Ruthanne I really love? Is it Ruthanne I miss? Is pride projecting my love for Ruthanne upon the girl?* He didn't know if the child was even alive. He anguished over this spectral being becoming too large, a great shadow that blotted out the dharma sun nourishing his eventual release from the Great Wheel of Saṃsāra. Before even knowing of the cancer, Old Boy feared that his daughter-attachment, his *obsession*, would demolish all the painstaking bardo work he had done to prevent himself from panicking at the moment it was time to leave his body. As Chökyi Nyingma Rinpoche said, so many hardships accompanied the dissolution of the elements! Such challenges, horrors and hallucinations! When the moment of death came, every iota of a warrior's sobriety and discipline were required to vanquish the dark forces working against liberation, seducing one into another futile rebirth.

Rinpoche said that when dying, one is either realized or confused, and Old Boy did *not* want to be confused. With enormous effort he managed to dampen his worshipfulness until the child became distant thunder. When Kim Kardashian came into his world, Old Boy was so much farther along in his practice. *Well, what harm can come by seeking her?* After all, he was dying. When she'd been found and he was told her name – "Trixanna" – all discipline was instantly erased. As if struck by lightning, he was consumed anew, and ashamed. He couldn't bring himself to confide in Chökyi Nyingma Rinpoche, fearing his teacher's disappointment.

Holding the girl's letter, his fears vanished. Everything was clear. Here he was now, holding the pages – cradling the body of his child – swimming in the debris-strewn wordsea of his long-lost beloved.

A sea of love!

He was interrupted by the sound of jet engines in his cell. The letter fell to the floor, wafting under the bunk like a paper plane itself.

Time now for the most exciting thing –

All at once, he knew something else:

He would not escape the Wheel – not this time *my teacher will forgive me* in an instant he no longer cared about the consequence of his failure, nor consider the form and nature of upcoming rebirth. He might become the moth that alit on his sink yesterday and dustily died or the dog one of the convicts was training in the Yard for adoption on the outside or a sea urchin washed up like a tiny satellite on the shore of Pelican Bay Beach or he might enter the spirit of the guard that used to be a frightened member of the extraction team but had become Old Boy's dearest friend…

His mother's voice suddenly filled the cell like a crushed cathedral, singing the hymn she cherished, *Love is strong as death*. He never understood what that meant, he puzzled over it for years as a nonsensical cliché, it seemed he'd never under-stood *any* of the teachings he received – not Rinpoche's, not Mother's, not anyone's. Her words rang out, "Set me as a seal on your heart, as a seal on your arm: for love is strong as death; jealousy is cruel as the grave." For the first time he understood, especially about jealousy –

> *I've been so jealous of the world, a world my beloved child lived in without me, a world she'll continue to enjoy – without me. Until she dies*
>
> > *without me.*

But how extraordinary it would be
> to wake up on the other side

of that world –

the same one Trixanna lives in, to awake in a body that's her same age – a
12-year-old novice monk sitting on a stool in open air, in the forest, trembling
while his head is shaved, his robes and the crowns of trees blown by black sky
star wind! – or reborn as a wanderer, a śramaṇa like the murdered student
of my teacher…

might I be

> nun or Rinpoche

visiting a wrongly accused man in a faraway cell to give him a book about
Aṅgulimāla – I am Aṅgulimāla

NO

– I am one of his 999 victims – NO – how long would it take to be reborn
as each one? – no! A bird, I am a bird – a sacred hoopoe – pecking at the
hidden hoard of severed fingers belonging to Aṅgulimāla's hapless wayfarers
before he made them into a necklace…

no

i shall be King

> the king who tried to stop him

> – NO –

> a soldier in the king's army, or
> insect on a leaf of the tree Aṅgulimāla hid behind in the rain
> I shall be the mother he almost killed.

(Śhāriputra said: "The son eats his father's flesh as the widow gnaws
her husband's bones. He beats his mother while his wife's rapist sits
on his lap, laughing in delight. Saṃsāra can be such a farce!")

– NO –

no – wait for it – wait –

i am the woman of pain, almost dead from the childbirth he
oversaw –

NO! NO!

       NO

trixanna!

yes

I am Trixanna, awakening from

* * *

          her sleepover, which was
handy, because Portia was having an overnight at Jaxx's. When
she dropped off her daughter at a huge old home in Angelino
Heights, she met the new friend Joey, a Poindexter-type, and
his two gay moms.

Geoffrey's was the perfect beachy shithole for a hustle.
The dumb, "classy" tourist trap attracted the occasional Young
Hollywood superstar (there on an Instagram goof) or stoned,
aged-out Malibu celeb slumming for rubbernecks. Portia made
sure to be nearly an hour late; she wanted Arnold to be jan-
gly when she got there. Which he was. For the first few minutes he was like an actor trying different approaches to a role,
until finally settling into the character of Alpha Male Shows
Dominance By Not Giving Two Fucks. She almost laughed
in his face because the man was an open book. Portia knew
that he just couldn't believe a woman who walked, talked and
smelled like she did would give him the time of day, let alone
hold out the promise she might deign to sit on his face.

And on top of it all, she was a Musk!

Occasionally, she glanced at the window table where Jaxx
and Cage were already having dinner. She could hear the zombie waves pounding dead-alive and fibrous black against the

set-decorated rocks, garishly lit to satisfy its customers' kitschy fantasies of livin' large.

"So, when you goin' back?" she asked, turning her full attention back to the mark. "Has Cleveland filed a missing persons report yet?"

"I extended my stay," he said coquettishly.

"Ah. Won't Mrs. Neidhoff be pining for you?"

"She's pretty much moved on, Reeve. We both have."

"Okay," she said, easing up. "I get it." Strategically, she needed Arnold to think that his soon-to-be single status was finally registering.

"I'm almost a bachelor. In three months, it's official."

He was so cheesily earnest that Portia was surprised he didn't drop to a knee and pop an engagement ring alongside that nonstop boner.

"Well, I'm a bachelorette. Should I give you a rose?" His face glitched and she laughed. "Guess you don't watch the show, huh." It was time. "Oh my God," she exclaimed, staring off-camera. "Is that who I think – what the fuck is *he* doing here?"

Arnold turned to look. "Someone you know?"

"You *have* to meet him, he's a fucking *genius.*"

He got a gnawy feeling in his stomach that the handsome young man by the window was an old flame. Portia scribbled a name on a napkin: TAMBLYN JUNEAU – and pushed it toward him as she went to greet her friend. "Google him! He's *totally* under the radar – he has, like, *teams* of people scrubbing his name off the Internet 24/7, but there's prolly still a Wikipedia page up. Be right back!"

Watching her go, he did what he was told.

The first few lines read:

Tamblyn Leroy Juneau (born March 4, 1987) is a technology entrepreneur and venture capitalist.[4][5][6] An early investor in Facebook, Snapchat, PayPal and Uber, he is a close friend of Elon Musk[7] and silent co-founder of Neuralink, an American neurotechnology company founded by Musk.[10] He has a net worth of $2.3 billion and is listed as #87 in the annual *Forbes* list of Angels and Influenc

When Arnold glanced up to check their progress, he was alarmed to see that Portia and her friend were almost on top of him. Nervously flipping his phone facedown, he stood to shake Jaxx's hand.

"Arnold from Ohio?" said Portia. "Meet Tamblyn from Tiburon – *and* Lalaland *and* Maui and fucking *beyond*."

"A pleasure!" said the auto parts king with startled jolly.

"Alan Schaaf's from Ohio," said Jaxx. "He founded Imgur."

"Yes! We've met. I don't know him, but we've met."

"A *crazyman*," said Jaxx. "And about as smart as they come."

Portia pretended to get a call, checked the screen then abruptly stood. She was drunk and made sure Arnold saw her lips bump against her boyfriend's ear as she loudly whispered, "Mr. Ohio *knows* – I told him *all* about Daddy." She threw the Ohioan a conspiratorial wink and left.

The men admired the view as she sashayed off.

"Where'd you get that fairy dust you sprinkled on her?" said Jaxx.

"What do you mean?"

"She told you about Elon?"

"She did."

"That's a fairly heavy thing for her to share." Jaxx giggled, playing at being more loaded than he was. "I mean y'all just met, right?"

"I kind of... picked her up at a bar."

They laughed about that, macho-bonding.

"Well-done!"

"We're just having fun," said Arnold.

He didn't want to be boastful – didn't want to queer the deal, on the sex *or* business side – and besides, nothing had happened (yet) to be boastful *about*. Plus, he didn't know the history of their relationship; for all he knew, they might be *in* a relationship. Better to play it safe.

"You know to keep that to yourself, right?" said Jaxx.

"About picking her up?" said the rube.

Jaxx laughed. "About *Elon*, dummy. Tell *no one*, is that understood?"

"Of course – " stammered Arnold.

"Under penalty of *extreme prejudice*." In a drunken tone of silly-billy, remonstrating lawyerese, Jaxx added, "*Nor* shall you disclose in *casual conversation with friends,* nor *on social media* that she, Reeve Tobrin, is in actuality and perpetuity his rightful *daughter* and *issue*."

"Yes! Of course! Absolutely."

"You're the *man*." They toasted glasses. "I don't get protective about too many things, Arnold," he said humorlessly. "But Reeve's my *little sister*. If you *talk* about this, *any* of it, there are some very powerful people – myself included – who'll make sure you..."

Arnold was getting uncomfortable. "I would never – talk. About it. Honestly!" *Had* he mentioned it to anyone? A quick, paranoid google search of his head confirmed he was in the clear.

"Good. Just keep that head and ass wired together or I *will* take a giant shit on you."

"What?"

"That's from *Full Metal Jacket*. Fucking love that movie."

"I want you to know I can be completely trusted, Mr. Tamblyn."

"Juneau. Juneau's the surname."

"Mr. *Juneau.*"

"Cut the mister and call me Tamblyn."

He put an avuncular hand on Arnold's shoulder and gently massaged, as if a storm had passed and they were blood brothers now. Jaxx saw the look that never failed to excite: the mark as hungry cultist and dizzy newborn, the mark as seeker and terminal schmuck.

"It doesn't surprise me," said Jaxx, "that she told you about her dad. I can see that you're cool. And she's done it before – it's *rare*, but she's done it. Anyhoo, know what? I stopped trying to understand the Reeve algorithm a long time ago."

"You've known her a while?"

"Ten years. Her dad's like a big brother. Or father, whatever. They're as close to family as I'll ever get. She's a wild ride. But *you*, my Ohioan friend, just got the Golden Ticket."

"How so?"

"Reeve's like the Tinder genie: a sex freak who can also make you very, very rich."

Arnold choked on the remark as Portia returned.

"That was Daddy," she said. Ignoring her date, she said to Jaxx, "So – are you in on the elevator dillio? Come on, Baby Shark. Come on, Baby Shark Tank. Are you Mark Cuban-*in* or are you Mr. Wonderful-*out*?"

"I'm as 'in' as Elon lets me, sugarplum. I wanted to give him thirty million but the man will only take fifteen."

"Are you talking about the horizontal elevator?" said Arnold exuberantly.

"Jesus," said Jaxx to Portia, with mock outrage. "Is there *anything* you haven't told this dude?"

"Aw *c'mon*, Tamblyn, Arnold's cool." Rubbing the mark's arm, she said, "He's *very* cool," then winked. "We're beads on the same strand."

"I'm not even going to *touch* that," said Jaxx. He turned to address the mark, in a tone both intimate and heartfelt. "The thing about *Elon*... I guess Ashton – Kutcher – had the best definition of 'disrupters' I've heard yet. Ashton said *visionaries* have crazy data nodes about overturning the given. See, in ten years, horizontal elevators will be a *necessary* part of our experiential vocabulary. It's not a world-changer – it ain't rockets or neurolinks – but one of these *niches* Elon uses like a safety valve to distract himself from the epic sci-fi shit going through his head on any Sunday. It's kinda like Picasso doodling. But hey: works for *me*. When Elon gets a niche, I'm gonna scratch it. Or try, anyway. My Get Niche Quick scheme!"

Apart from the chase (the promise of life-altering sex), Arnold was ecstatic to find himself in such unlikely, exalted company. It was surreal – he wasn't just out of town, he was light-years from home. He'd only read about people like this in books or seen them in movies or on the nightly news. There was something dangerous about it, in a good way. He felt lucky and *alive*.

Like having drinks with Harley Quinn and Iron Man.

His phone vibrated, popping the bubble. He glanced down and saw that his wife was FaceTiming. Arnold fretted as he pressed *decline* – maybe there was something wrong, something with Cammy.

"Be right back," he said.

When he stepped outside, the valets jerked to attention before standing at ease. Warm Santa Anas pillowed PCH.

"Hey there, honcho," said Raleigh. "Where are you?"

"A very boring business dinner."

"*Better* be," said the wife, with the sass that seduced him nearly twenty years back. "Paintin the town red, huh?"

"Hardly."

"And who may I ask has the pleasure of your company?"

"Some Autozone folks – Jay Galworth and a new hire. They're picking my brain."

"That's gotta hurt."

"Is Cammy okay?"

"He was a handful today – kept snapping his fingers and hoping I'll disappear. Thanos is *not* my friend."

It went on like that, with Arnold breaking the news that he was definitely going to miss Hallowe'en.

Inside, Portia rubbed Jaxx's crotch as he checked his phone. Cage kept an eye on them from afar, snorting coke from a black bullet.

"I just took down the wiki page," said Jaxx. "When he looks me up again, Tamblyn Leroy Juneau will be gone gone gone."

"Oh, he'll be fine. I already told him Nazi web-hunters scrub your shit ASAP."

"Hope he's stupider than he looks."

Arnold slinked back to the table and said, "One of my suppliers had a little emergency." It was lame – Portia knew who had called, but didn't want to fuck with him. Besides, he was past the point of no return.

Jaxx stood and extended a hand.

"Great to meet you, Arnold."

"Thank you!" stuttered Ohio.

"Can you and Elon drop by the house Friday night?"

"Might be tough," said Jaxx. "We're having dinner in Point Dume with Dylan. Supposedly."

"Thanks for inviting me," said Portia.

In an aside to Arnold, he said, "Bob Dylan and Jim Carrey. *There's* a pair to draw to."

"Then come *before*," she pleaded, stoned and kittenish. "Pretty pretty *please*, Tamby? Come *before,* just to say hey." She put a hand on Arnold's arm again and looked in his eyes. "Are you free, babe? Will you still be here on Friday or do you have to run back to Cleveland?"

She couldn't help the jibe.

"I will *totally* be here," Arnold exulted, before self-consciously turning down the volume. "I have business straight to the end of the week."

"We'll try to make it, Reeve," said the elusive, debonair billionaire.

"You *better*," said Portia. "And it'd be fun for Arnold to meet Elon!"

"All right, kids," said Jaxx. "See you Monday. 'The Fairy Dust Kids' – that's your new name." On his way back to Cage and the window seat, he murmured in Arnold's ear, "*Try not to fall in love.*"

When he left, Portia girlishly asked, "What'd he say?"

"Nothing," said Arnold, demurely.

"*You better tell me*," she said, grinning wide.

"That you were a pain in the ass but totally worth it."

"He did not!"

"Naw, you're right. He said, 'Try not to fall in love.'"

"He did *not.*"

"Actually, he did – exactly that. 'Try not to fall in love.'"

"How's that working out for you?"
The pianist started to play "Killing Me Softly."
Too perfect.

* * *

Trixanna was excited about her stayover at Joey's.

She wanted to be courageous, not shy, so she stood in front of the bedroom mirror and practiced saying, *How dare you!* – just like Greta when she made fiery speeches in front of the politicians that were letting the world die. But Trixanna's only cause at the moment was not to embarrass herself with Joey Levender, at least no more than she already had. Mostly, she prayed she wouldn't talk too much or be weird because she wanted him to love her back.

She thought some more about the Swedish mutant, wondering why they'd never met in Oakland, when both were inmates. There was so much she wanted to know! Like, how Greta had escaped, and *when*... Those school strikes she was always busy with were obviously about something else entirely; Greta's *real* purpose was to identify children who attended the Xavier Institute for Mutant Education and Outreach so she could round them up for the pilgrimage to Eden. As powerful as Greta was, Trixanna knew something her counterpart seemed strangely blind to: that such a journey would inevitably fail without the help of the Wolverine aka Reginald Ronald "Old Boy" Logan aka *my father*. She was certain Greta was seeking answers too, and that her trip to L.A. had been organized solely for them to meet. Trix planned to identify herself by the words *Mutatis Mutandis* – "change only that which needs to be changed" – but on the very day the braided mutant spoke to thousands at City Hall, Transigen's powerful forces intervened, setting fires in Malibu and Calabasas that made their rendezvous impossible.

Joey's mom took her on a tour of the ginormous house. Loretta said it was "a Victorian," without explaining what she meant. But Trix had a warm feeling because it really did feel like the kind of place where mutant children might take refuge while on the run.

Loretta's girlfriend was called Cheyenne and both of them crushed on her mom when she dropped Trix off. Portia was a big flirt. The couple kept staring at her like she was some amazing new Netflix show.

After dinner, his moms went out, and they watched TV in the living room. Joey suddenly seemed edgy without parental supervision. Trix thought it was sweet that he'd prepared a few things to show her – like a video of his hero Elon Musk smoking dope during an interview with another hero, Joe Rogan. When Joey saw that she was bored (she wasn't but knew her nervousness made it look that way), he did something totally unexpected: he put on *Logan*. She thought he was just being nice, but they ended up watching the whole movie and he said he really enjoyed it. Then he said he wanted to show her something else but they had to go to his room to see it.

It was obvious he prepared this clip too.

Trixanna stared at the laptop and went numb. He said it was animation from Japan called "hent-eye." She'd seen regular porn before but not like this. One time when she walked into her mom's room, Portia and Jaxx were passed out in front of the muted TV. They'd been watching a YouPorn of themselves fucking. With *hent-eye*, everything was so perfect and bright and slurpy and weird, you knew a computer made it but after a while it was just like watching real people. Joey had another hent-eye synced up, about Logan and his daughter. Logan and Laura were in bed and his claws were out but hers weren't. She squirmed beneath him then the knives shot from her hands and feet, and water gushed out. It was hard for Trix to watch but she didn't want to offend her host, so she closed her eyes. Joey must have seen her reaction because he switched to something else.

"See this? It's called *deep fake*," he said conspiratorially. Joey said the people were real – "sort of." She didn't recognize the men onscreen. "That's Elon having sex with Elton John. Have you ever seen *Rocketman*? I watched it with Loretta and Cheyenne. It was great. Elton's really great." He refocused on the clip. "It's kinda gay but not really, 'cause it isn't real. Now Elon's having sex with Bezos – that's Jeff Bezos. See?" She recognized everyone in the next one: Greta, Billie Eilish, Millie Bobby Brown. They were all sandwiched together, moaning and crying. Trixanna closed her eyes again, struggling not to cry herself. That was when she felt Joey's hot breath and a small, cold hand wriggling down her underwear. Thank God his moms came home right then, calling out his name. He jumped and shouted "Hi!" then shut off the computer.

"Let's go downstairs for ice cream," he said affectlessly. "I usually have Rocky Road but tonight I'm having strawberry. They've been out of Rocky Road."

In the morning, she lay awake in the guest room wondering if the letter had found its way to her father's cell. (She regretted not asking Joey for help but couldn't wait to send it. Time was of the essence.) The same powerful forces that could prevent her note from being delivered were also the same ones that might make *certain* it wound up in Old Boy's hands – diabolically laying a trap for mutant father and daughter.

At least now, Old Boy would know she was on her way.

Trixanna googled Pelican Bay State Prison (again). 5905 Lake Earl Drive, Crescent City – 739 miles straight up the I-5, 11 hours and 56 minutes away by car. There were lots of different ways to get there, in case she was being followed. She could even walk; she pulled up an app that said it would "comfortably" take about two weeks.

Trixanna heard the sound of the moms laughing in the kitchen. She had to pee. She felt wet down there and let out a shriek. Loretta rushed in and saw her frozen and whimpering on bloody sheets. When Joey appeared, Loretta shooed him away and slammed the door. She stayed with her while Cheyenne got a tampon. Loretta showed her how to use it. Then she kissed her cheek and told her not to worry, it was "wonderful." She said to go ahead and shower and come down for breakfast.

As the water beat down, Trix thought she would be embarrassed but wasn't. What could have been more embarrassing than those awful things Joey showed her? (He was probably worried she would tell.) No – she felt powerful, and saved. The blood was a sign that her body was being purged of poison and foul matter.

A sign that adamantium was bonding with her bones and soon she would have enough strength to make the journey north to free her father.

* * *

On the way home from Geoffrey's, she listened to her voicemail.

"Hi, Ruthanne, it's Rhapsody from Kim's office. Can you call, first thing?"

She assumed they had the test results.

It was closer to noon when she phoned Rhapsody back. She was hung over; they partied till five in the morning, in celebration of Arnold's promise to bring $200,000 in cash to the next assignation. (On All Hallows' Eve, no less.) Any way you sliced it, Kim was her ace in the hole; she already had a winning hand with the King of All Auto Parts and could afford to play it cool with the Reality Show Queen. Jaxx said it was best not to seem too eager, especially about the documentary.

They even rehearsed her little speech, like they used to do improv before shooting porn:

I've just been mindful, she'd tell Kim, *of putting our daughter's face – and life – out there. I mean, it's amazing and beautiful, and I'm so glad she can maybe meet her dad – and it's for an* amazing *cause, I think what you're doing is so amazing – you're amazing – but we can't forget – and I know you get this, because you have beautiful daughters of your own – we can't forget that* Trixanna *is the most important thing. She's at that fragile, vulnerable age – she just got her period! – and I just want to make sure she isn't overwhelmed... blah blah blah.* Of *course* Kim would understand, and respect her even more as a fellow tiger mom. Jaxx said there wasn't a downside in playing hard to get. The *upside* being, money might be offered as further, compassionate persuasion.

Rhapsody said Kim was in Armenia and abruptly put her through to the detective.

"Hi!" said Richie.

"Hi! How are you?"

"I'm well, thank you."

"I was going to call, but things have been *crazy* – crazy, but great. Did you guys get the test results back?"

He began to talk but was distracted by a voice. He shouted, "I will have to call them *back*." Kinda harsh. After apologizing to Portia, he said, "I don't have a lot of time. But I wanted to share two things."

"O-*kay*," she said, her guard suddenly up.

"Old Boy died yesterday morning."

"Oh my God."

"It's about to be on the news and I wanted you to know first-hand. Kim was going to call you herself but she's overseas – "

"How?"

"It was the cancer. He was very, very sick – as you know. It was both expected and unexpected."

"That's so *awful*."

"And – as it turns out – he isn't the father." Correcting himself, he said, "Wasn't the father."

"You're saying that he – "

"The paternity test was negative."

"Are you sure?"

"One hundred per cent."

"That's *crazy*." He talked some more but she wasn't listening. After a moment, she said, "Is Kim still making the documentary?"

The question took him aback. "That I don't know."

"I was just wondering. Because if she is, I could still – we could still be in it. Or – maybe not Trixanna, just me. You know, as the woman… the woman he *thought* was the mother of his child."

The detective winced.

"If that's the case, Ruthanne, and Kim wants to pursue, I assure that I'll be in touch."

Six o'clock and already dark.

Only a few days ago, she realized how dumb it was to be doing this on Hallowe'en. (*What was I thinking? How stoned was I?*) All they needed was to have trick-or-treaters knocking at the door to fuck up their shit. As usual, Jaxx chilled her out and said to just call Arnold and push the meeting time to 9:30. "Little shits'll be gone by then." Actually, the change in plan added a nice flavor because the new story was, "They're not coming till around 8:30 and I want some alone-time with Daddy before I introduce you – need to *inform* him that you know about the elevator. He can be finicky but once he sees you, he'll fuckin love ya. Tamblyn's gonna chime in that you're a good egg, blah. Tam *really* liked you by the way."

For hours, she weirdly obsessed about getting a Witch's Brew Frappuccino, but the Palisades Starbucks was closed. *I'll just make myself an iced coffee up at the house.* She drove down Via De La Paz and parked a few long blocks away. Portia had to take the Alfa because she couldn't find the LVCHILD plates, which pissed her off no end. As it turned out, the street was dark and deserted.

Not a dress-up slut or superhero in sight.

She took the duffel from her trunk and strode up the walkway to the lockbox. Her heart skip-thumped when she realized she'd forgotten to test the duplicate key Cage made. It worked like a charm. She swiveled a potted plant in front of the box, to camouflage. She always planned her crimes so carefully. The uncharacteristic lack of follow-through – not trying the key beforehand – gave Portia a creeped-out, doomy feeling.

She got there early so she'd have time to mess things up, for that lived-in look. She loved sinking into role-play. Paying special attention to the upstairs master suite, she roughed up the sheets. Then she put on what Jaxx called her lucky "felony bra" for the occasion, a La Perla she superstitiously kept unwashed since buying it five years ago. In the duffel were shampoos, clothes and miscellanea: framed photos of her and Elon to be placed in strategic spots around the house, especially the nightstand, where Arnold was sure to see. It carried her "rape-kit" (Jaxx again) too: lube, condoms, weed, coke, mace. By the time the Lamborghini backed into the drive, Portia would already have bathed, slipping into her lucky vintage emerald green Jil Sander coat, acquired a few years ago at The RealReal. For a final, haphazard touch, she threw a bunch of Louboutins on the floor.

Sitting in the backyard, meditating on it all, Portia realized she was depressed. *Oops. Guess it's official.* The detective's one-two punch did more of a number on her than she expected. Gone were the fantasies of becoming part of the extended Kardashian family. Gone were the fantasies of Trixanna marrying into the klan, which Portia actually started to believe could happen, because it made perfect sense – any of Kim's sons would have inherited Kanye's crazy brain and want a crazy-brained 'bitch to crash through reality shows with. *That would be Trix.* She and Jaxx had even been dreaming up a concept that Kim and Kris could endorse on *KUWTK* or their Instagram, something upright and modestly sensible like Rob Kardashian's sock business. Belts they could sell at Target or wherever.

All that was gone now.

Jaxx wouldn't be there until nine. He'd been dispatched to pick up the Elon because there was no way Portia was leaving the lookalike's arrival to chance. Just then, he texted *the elon has landed*: the decoy was safely ensconced in a borrowed Lambo, courtesy of Exxxotica. They had to come up with two hundred more dollars than agreed because the Elon *also* forgot it was Hallowe'en, the one day of the year that he said was "guaranteed" to fetch a higher price for his important work.

Jaxx pulled in, leaving the Elon in the vehicle as per plan.

When Portia told him the Kardashian kaper was off, he shrugged like it was nbd. She loved that about him. He was one of the few people who could instantly chill her out and make her feel hopeful all at once.

"Fuck all that noise," he said. "And *fuck* the *Kardashians*. No money there, any*how* – just pussyjuice and promises. The money's *here*, Reeve. Ohio's *bringin* it, and Kimmy sure as shit *ain't*."

"Maybe we'll move to London after this," said Portia. She did some coke off the back of her hand and passed him the vial.

"I don't think my P.O. would be too happy about that."

"Your P.O. would be p.o.'d, huh. But seriously, joker, we could make hella money in the UK. Meghan's totally paved the way for the American hustle!"

"*American Hustle* – greatest film *ever*. Right?"

"Not greater than *Joker*, joker."

* * *

Arnold left Laguna in the late afternoon.

An early start on his drinking was a new habit. He wasn't meeting Reeve till nighttime but there were a coupla things he had to do, like get the money from Chase, in Century City. It wasn't going to be the two hundred Reeve asked for – *not gonna happen* – but she'd get over it. She'd have to. The hard negotiator came out at last. If he gave her the whole thing, it'd be like tattooing I'M YOUR BITCH on his forehead. (*Which I am,* he laughed.) He didn't want her to forget that he was the Man. Until now, Arnold hadn't much of an opportunity to show that side of himself... anyway, she knew he was a tough, canny businessman – like her father – and would expect nothing less than a little gamesmanship.

The amount that felt right was 35K.

The cashier put the c-notes in a stiff, old-timey brown envelope that reminded him of the ones he'd seen in film noirs. He left the bank with a spring in his step and a bright, half-confused sense of purpose. *Now* what to do? Just bop around and go where his nose led him, a slow meander toward his final destination in the Palisades. He was playing hooky from his life. He hot-rodded down Olympic, wondering whether he should duck into a movie or get a frozen yogurt.

Without warning, the car rocked from a little earthquake of second thoughts. He pulled over and called Reeve. She picked up right away.

There was an open, sunny catch in her voice, as if she were prepared for anything – to cancel their dinner or talk *him* out of canceling. Arnold lied and said he was still at Chase. *Why is it,* he asked, *that it needs to be cash? It's so much easier to wire it.* She was sweet and patient, for which he was grateful; he wasn't in the mood to be ragged on. Stepping outside her usual voice, she sounded like a podcast historian talking anecdotally about the early days of venture capitalism. She said that Tamblyn started the cash-only tradition "with his own 'circle of angels' back in the early Paypal days.

That's why Dad calls our investment club The Greenery. Kinda *mafia*, right? Cash became a good luck thing." Then she laughed, in the way she did, that made him want to blow up his life and everyone else's if that's what it took to have her. When he asked what was funny, she said, "Stop thinking vertically, Arnold! Start thinking *horizontally,* like the fucking elevator!"

He chuckled and said, "Is there anything I should bring?"

"Just your hot body. And your sweet Cleveland self."

That caught him off-guard because he thought she'd have said something like *Don't forget the money* – and was glad she didn't.

He migrated west to kill a few hours on the Promenade. Outside a shuttered Barnes & Noble, a fountain adorned with bad metal art wasn't running; it belonged to the homeless now. They clustered on its stone steps but at least were behaving. He decided to have a bite at a Mexican joint on Santa Monica Boulevard. Nothing too heavy – half a tostada to absorb the morning booze. Waiting for the food, dark thoughts infiltrated his jittery, horn-dog head. What if when he got to the house, someone cracked him on the head, took his money, stole his I.D. and left him in a coma? Raleigh would fly out, losing her mind from the stress of keeping a bedside vigil while managing Cammy's caregivers from long-distance. The agony of their son not knowing where his parents were! He shrugged off the fanta-sia with a shiver. Trouble was, he'd watched too much television last night. On an episode of *The First 48*, a gal lured a john to a motel where he was robbed and killed by her boyfriend. Tamblyn Juneau wasn't exactly the strong, violent type, but *still…* maybe she was working alone. Maybe she was gonna drug him – reality show cops called that "trick-rolling." He tried to calm himself, thinking, *If that's what she was up to, she wouldn't have asked me over — she'd have insisted we meet at the hotel.* Anyway, it would already have happened! It'd have happened the first night we met. *Hey, you were dying to get her back to your room, remember, Dummy? But she wouldn't go for it. My Rolex was hers to lose. Stop being such a dummy, Dummy.* He laughed at his paranoia before it boomeranged and another temblor came. His head filled with dialogue mimicked from movies he liked to watch back home in the den after Raleigh and Cammy were fast asleep. *The Grifters,* and old Mamets like *House of Games* and *The Spanish Prisoner. She's playing for keeps. They're running a 'long con' — smart!* He flashed on the video of Reeve and Elon. Guess it could have been doctored. Could be fake news. Tamblyn's Wikipedia page disappeared right after they met at Geoffrey's, just like Reeve said it would. Looking back, it seemed a little too convenient. He'd randomly asked a few colleagues about Mr. Juneau but no one'd ever heard of him. Not that anyone necessarily would have; every time he read the Forbes billionaire list, there were shitloads of folks on it he'd never heard of... still, there wasn't anything on Google about "Tamblyn Juneau." Not *a thing —*

But now *I'm on my way to meet Musk himself. Can't fake that.*

Pussy crowded out further ratiocination.

All part of the adventure, he mused. Pee Wee's Big Lalaland Adventure... *if it don't work out, I'll survive. Hell, if a man never gets his heart stomped on, he ain't a man. No harm, no foul. Tuck my tongue back in my mouth and my tail between my legs and fly like a bird back home. Renew my vows with Raleigh and slap some fresh white paint on the picket fence.*

He was early.

It was dark but the terrain seemed familiar.

When he saw that Via De La Paz dead-ended, he didn't go any further, just in case Reeve and Elon were loitering out front. *That'd be awkward.* Suddenly, he realized that she lived on the same street he walked down a few days ago, bringing him to the bench memorial on the bluff. Sometimes the world liked to show you how small it was.

He looped back to the local CVS. A mom with two kids was flirting with the security guard. When they kissed on the mouth, Arnold realized it was her husband, in costume. Their daughter, a skeleton/punk-girl hybrid of around seven, held the hand of her baby brother. He was dressed as Spidey and it broke Arnold's heart. He thought of Cammy and was gut-punched by shame, guilt and worry. *What the fuck am I doing? I don't belong here. I'm about to pay $35,000 for some 'strange.' It's still not too late to go home…* Earlier, he FaceTimed with Raleigh from the hotel. It was already 3PM in Cleveland and she was about to take their son trick-or-treating. (Cammy got over-stimulated after dark and was subject to violent tantrums.) Arnold called to check in but made the rookie mistake of telling Raleigh to make sure to stay away from unwrapped candy because he saw something on the news about an anti-vaxxer – an RN giving the gift of "lifetime immunity" via lollipops laced with chickenpox virus. Nothing was more sinful than a fake helicopter dad. Raleigh gave him stink-eye. She was already in a quiet rage about him still being in L.A., though it never would have occurred to her that he was fooling around.

She put Cammy on. He was in his pricey Thanos costume, and so excited about trick-or-treating that he looked terrified. When Arnold asked to speak to Mom again, he heard his wife's pissed-off voice. "Tell your father we'll talk tomorrow. Got my hands full, Arnold! And thanks!"

Raleigh snatched the phone and hung up.

He drove down a parallel street to the bluff, to clear his head. He sat on the memorial bench again with his helicoptering hard-on. He kept flashing on being naked with Reeve – his heart skipped all kinds of beats. Then his thoughts turned to the money. Should I leave it in the car or bring it in? *Probably bring it.* If he left it in the vehicle, he might have to deal with more stink-eye. Best to get it over with. He knew he was overthinking, as usual – she'd *love* that he kept his word and wouldn't give six fucks if he left the money in the glove box, chucked it over the fence, dropped it from a tree or pitched it through a window. Maybe it was all just a test to prove he was worthy of future riches, that he was worthy of being a devotee, of joining the Inner Circle of Angel Investors or the fucking *Greenery*... that he – *they* – were meant to be. Cyclic beings, like she'd said. Beads on the same strand... maybe Reeve hadn't been expecting him to trust her at *all* and by bringing the money (even if it weren't the full amount), he had already passed a test that so many others had failed. As a reward, she might just kneel down and blow him the minute he came through the door.

Or maybe that's when I'll be killed –

That one made him laugh out loud.

The hour snuck up on him and he bolted from bench to car.

When he got to the house, he looked for the Tesla with the LVCHILD plates but didn't see it. It was probably in the garage.

Watching the street from her darkened second-story lookout, she quickly told Jaxx to hurry to the driveway.

She saw Arnold retrieve something from the passenger side and put it in his coat.

Yeah baby yeah. There's the money, honey –

Downstairs now, she waited for Jaxx to start up the Lambo before buzzing Arnold in, then flung the front door open, shouting,

"*There* he is!"

The automated driveway gate slowly swept out to the street. Jaxx mischievously revved the engine as the car inched forward.

"Tamblyn!" she screamed. "Would you please fuckin *stop*?"

Arnold beheld the miracle in the passenger seat: *Elon Musk was beaming at him from no more than ten feet away.*

Jaxx locked eyes with Arnold and said, "There's the *man*. The man of the hour!"

"Daddy?" said Portia. "This is Arnold Neidhoff, one of the 'horizontal angels' we were telling you about."

The Elon extended his arm through the window and shook Arnold's hand while Jaxx beamed at the mise-en-scène.

Portia had been nervous about this part but instantly knew that her boyfriend was right. "Arnold's the Manchurian Candidate," he had said. (Whatever that meant.) Jaxx told her the mark would be desperate to believe his lyin' eyes, and whomever he was looking at *must* appear to be the real thing. "It's human psychology." With all the fantasized buildup, all the *investment,* the moment he shook the Elon's hand, the illusion was cemented. Even Portia forgot about the impersonator Kevin Lee. Alt-reality became real world; deepfake, deep real.

Stepping from the ground-hugging racecar, Jaxx popped up like a soigné Jaxx-in-the-box while the lookalike stayed put. It was important to keep distracting the mark, as insurance against those lyin' eyes suddenly becoming truth-tellers.

"Elon, this is the gent we've been hyping. When in Cleveland, visit Arnold Neidhoff *first* – the Museum of Rock 'n' Roll *second!*"

"Nice to meet you," said the cordial if inscrutable genius-billionaire.

"It is definitely an honor, Mr. Musk," said Arnold, starstruck.

"Oh, Daddy *loves* when people fawn over him!" said Portia.

"Arnold," said Elon, with an elfin smile. "Make sure to press 'penthouse,' not 'garage.' When you get in. To the elevator!"

Kevin muffed his one and only line but it worked out in the end.

"We're on our way to Florida for a launch," said Jaxx.

"The ladies who launch," said Portia.

"SpaceX!" said Arnold orgiastically.

"And Ohio," Jaxx went on. "We might be having a little party next month for the 'horizontal angels.' Your presence is politely requested."

"Hope you can fly in," said Portia, winking at the mark.

"I *will*," said Arnold, sweating. "And thank you! That's amazing!"

Jaxx climbed back in the car. Taking the cue, Elon stared at Arnold with twinkling eyes, improvising "Have a good one."

Elon Musk just told him to have a good one! His words almost had the same effect Reeve's hand did when it brushed Arnold's prick that first night in Laguna – accidentally on purpose.

Then, as if in a dream, the Lambo vanished.

"They're such dicks!" she said, walking him into the living room where a fire was going. "We were supposed to be having a business meeting but all they did was drink and talk smack. They're like children."

"It was amazing to meet him, though. *Thank you.*"

"He fucking googled you! He called you a 'factory guy' – which, coming from my Dad, who likes to fucking *sleep* on factory floors, is a high compliment. He *loves* successful people who get their hands dirty."

"Haven't got my hands dirty in a while, I'm afraid."

"We can fix that," she said licentiously. She nodded toward the foyer where he'd set his bag. "So what's in the satchel, Bubba?"

Arnold panicked, suddenly wishing he'd brought the full amount. When he said he only had $35,000, the light drained from her eyes like a just-killed person transitioning to zombie on Cammy's favorite show, *The Walking Dead.* He quickly lied, saying the bank had issues with handing over two-hundred-thousand in cash but were already in touch with his home branch in Cleveland. He would bring the rest tomorrow.

Portia heard Jaxx's calming voice in her head. *Be chill,* it whispered. *We're there, we're already there. It's all happening, it's all gonna happen.* Thirty-five in the hand was still worth 200K in the bush. Yet – out of nowhere – she watched herself stand and strut to the front door.

"Take your thirty-five," she watched herself say, "and fly away like the untrusting shitbird hick you are. Okay? Fly back to Ass-wad, Ohio. You think I'm playing, Arnold? That this is some kind of fucking game?"

"No, Reeve, no I don't!"

"Get out! *Get out!*"

"Reeve, wait! Listen to me, I'm *sorry!* I – "

"Do you *know* how many people would fucking *kill* to trade places with you? What is that, your kid's *allowance?* Do you think I *need* your fucking – *petty cash?* It's so insulting! *I'm* the one taking a chance, not you! Fucking embarrass me in front of my *father...* you have no idea how lucky you are – *were* – because we are *done*. Get the fuck out. Now!"

"Reeve, please! Please! Reeve, I'll have it in the morning, I promise!" She held the door open for him to walk through. "It's just a bank thing, Reeve... they'll release the funds in the morning, and I'll bring it to you!"

Like an android responding to remote command, Portia's features immediately softened. In a programmed burlesque, she slipped off the coat and let it drop to the ground. He gaped at her body – her nipples went hard with the adrenaline of dominance and fury.

"You are such a dumbshit," she said, shaking off the spite like a dog that was finally let inside after a downpour. "Wanna have a drink? Come on, Mr. *Izza Bank Thang*, let's have a drink. Let's get turnt up. Would you like that, Mr. Ass-wad Ohio Numbnuts? Wanna get turnt up, Mr. I'll Bring It? Mr. Bring It In The Morning?"

She kissed his frightened, bad-breath mouth, resting a hand on his crotch. Limp down there – her tirade put him in an altered state. (Sometimes you had to bring a mark to heel.) Though he was dollar-short, she made the executive decision to bonus him out with an unscheduled fuck. A woman less sure of herself would have waited for him to deliver the balance, but Portia knew what she was worth.

Last week, "the Pharaoh" Faustino was in New York for the Project ALS gala, sharing a table at Cipriani 42nd Street with

Ben Stiller, Ben's ex-, and their gorgeous daughter, Ella (back when they were married, he found them two properties in the Bird Streets); a few nights ago, it was the Montage in Laguna for Promises Kept, Hugh Jackman's orphan charity; now, he was at the Beverly Wilshire Four Seasons for the ALS Association Golden West Chapter's Hallowe'en Ball.

The famous realtor couldn't understand why ALS was such a gold standard staple on the Sad Disease Circuit because hardly anyone but one or two celebs actually seemed have it. Anyway, it was what the Pharaoh called a "zero-hoper" – you may as well have burned the money raised for research because there would never, ever be a cure. Faustino thought it was a disgusting waste of resources. Sometimes you just had to say, *Ladies, we must put a fork in this one. Moving on!* Where was the shame? The only ones benefiting from ALS were the hotels that threw the galas and the florists providing centerpieces. A million times more people had lupus or scleroderma and a zillion more with endometriosis, Parkinson's, *whatever.* Why pin the tail on a rotting donkey? How long could you wheel out Nanci Ryder and bullshit about her being a warrior-princess? Answer: *until she dies.* Even *that* wouldn't stop them. Renée and Courteney would probably pull a *My Weekend At Bernie's* stunt – that fantastic movie he saw for the first time on Netflix last week – where they jack up a corpse to make it look alive.

In truth, the Pharaoh enjoyed himself pink at the high-end mortality hoedowns. They were good hunting grounds for fat cats looking to beef up their property portfolios. But *this* could be his last ALS outing, because he'd done something very naughty; henceforward, Faustino might be declared persona non grata. It being a costume ball, he'd spent five hours and a small fortune transforming himself into an obscene, grotesquely costumed version of his departed, all-time Hall of Famer client, "the Fat Joan" Gamma. (*Joanie* would have definitely gotten the joke.) Yet because he was outrageously, wickedly funny, because he was *Faustino Blanco,* the *Pharaoh,* he seemed to have gotten away with it – for now. In the ballroom, when people first laid eyes on him, there was a lot of jaw-dropping, explosive laughter. It didn't hurt that he was sitting at Patricia Arquette's table – who famously loved the Fat Joan – garnering her raucous stamp of approval, which went a long way with the toadying twitterati. Those assholes always made sure to take the PC temperature of the VIPs in the room before blasting out their witless or fawning critiques. He wanted to believe he had performed a public service by breaking the taboo of referencing her, dispelling the bad vibes that continued to surround the tragic billionairess. Her reputation had been besmirched when her sweet, fragile wife *dared* to say she may have been misdiagnosed and didn't have ALS after all. Even after her death – and the stunning double revelation that not only did Ali Nell have the disease, but *Joan* did *too* – the benighted orphan remained a controversial figure in the research and fundraising sector. *Oh, those little minds!* Faustino thought that was as hypocritical as it was moronic because Joanie continued to give tens of millions to the cause, *posthumously!* Where was the shame, anyway? Where was the shame in a "misdiagnosis" that in the end turned out to be bullshit? People were so dreadful! They jumped on poor Ali Nell as if she were some fraudulent poseur and when the autopsies showed the world how wrong it was, the institutions benefitting didn't even have the grace or common decency to make a public apology.

How disgusting!

As he waited for the valet to bring his Phantom Drophead Coupe, a couple approached. The middle-aged woman was dressed like a sexy snail. Her partner, an elderly Chinese man, wore a normal business suit. In a thick accent, she complimented Faustino on his costume, but he had no energy to explain.

When he introduced himself, she reeled back, agog.

"Faustino! The Pharaoh! *Billion Dollar World!* My Gawd, my Gawd!" She turned to her husband and repeated the same. The man grinned back indulgently. "You are Faustino!" she emoted. "Pharaoh of West Side!"

"The very one," he said courteously, praying his car would come.

"I cannot believe it is him! I watch all episodes!"

"Well aren't you a dear. You're Mantis, no? From *Guardians of the Galaxy?*"

"Yes! Yes! Mantis!" she said, almost tearfully.

Faustino turned to the husband and said, "And who are *we* tonight?"

He beamed, thrilled to be asked.

"I! Have! Come! As! *Laurence Li.*"

Faustino instantly got the joke, which wasn't a bad one at all. Li was the famous industrialist and casino operator. The man had come as himself.

He told Mr. Li that he had many clients from the Mainland, asking if he knew Jack Ma. Mr. Li said *Jack Ma very good friend* and Faustino informed that when Mr. Ma's son graduated Berkeley, he put him in a Wallace Neff in Trousdale. Searching the night's image trove, Faustino said, "Weren't you two sitting with Reese?"

Ping – Laurence's inamorata – excitedly said, "Yes! Reese close friend! We neighbors in Carpinteria!" before blurting out that they wanted to find a house for their daughter, "Close to Reese, in Palisades! She Hancock Park now! Close to Reese in Palisades our dream!"

When Faustino said, "I actually sold Reese that house," Ping nearly collapsed.

"Oh my God! Reese our daughter godmother!"

The valet pulled up in his Roller. Ping suddenly looked so sad and prepared herself for goodbyes. Instead, Faustino threw open the back door with a flourish, catching the polyurethane of his costume and inadvertently tearing off a pound of flesh.

"Allow me to take you to the dream," he said.

"Oh my God," said Ping.

"Allow me to show you your daughter's new home."

Ping's snail antennae sprung this way and that, electrified. As she implored her grinning husband, Faustino interrupted, parroting a Chinese phrase he learned for Jack Ma.

"Be afraid only of standing still," said the sententious Pharaoh.

"He know proverbs!" shouted Ping. "You not Pharaoh of West Side, you emperor!" She turned to Mr. Li. "He not pharaoh, he emperor!"

Top down, Santa Anas blowing cool-hot, the Fatsuit Joan Gamma shanghaied his charges, ferrying them from Wilshire to Beverly Glen then up to Sunset. As they wound their way to Via De La Paz. Faustino could smell the wire transfer. He'd been doing this long enough to know he would close on the sale – *tonight*. As part of the deal, Ping might insist to be on *Billion Dollar World!* (which would be good for the show) but the secretive Mr. Li would likely put the kibosh on her guest star aspirations.

He wished a camera crew were along for the ride. It'd make great television. *This is what it's all about! I love my life.* A pioneer of reality "listing" shows, he was very rich, and he was a star. Most importantly, he never compromised – he was always joyously, disruptively, unapologetically Faustino Blanco. He made people feel special, which of course everyone was, especially in the case of all-cash offers with no inspections and barely-there escrows.

When he saw the lights were on in the house, Faustino thought he had the wrong address. In milliseconds, other thoughts intruded: Is Trudy the Home Stager working overtime? That didn't make sense… *is she partying?* But that didn't make sense either –

He told his clients to stay in the car while he went to ask the owners "if we can take a peek."

Moving the plant aside and seeing the half-open lockbox, his adrenaline got carbonated. He saw that he didn't need a key; the front door was ajar. Entering, he heard music and smelled weed.

WTF –

The teenage daughter of the sellers? He felt like he was in a dream – maybe he was one who was trespassing.

"Hello? *Hel-lo-oh.* Hello!"

Faustino took the stairs.

Coke and booze, potentiated by the arrival of an unexpected freight of guilt, were *not* a cock's friend. Getting him hard wasn't strictly necessary but the woman was on a mission. She climbed on top, jamming Arnold's soft, scorched helmet a third of the way in. He looked *way* pallid, and his skin hot and dry; Portia conjured a GIF of the mark lying dead in bed.

Ha!

Well that's okay too cause that's a $35,000 hump right there. I'll take it.

Just then, his eyes widened and his body went rigid – she thought he *was* dying. She arched her head to see what he was looking at.

An angry apparition stood in the bedroom door.

Clearly a man, but *tall*, dressed like some kind of… swollen tumor –

"What is this!" boomed the creature. "Who the fuck *are* you!"

Arnold tumbled her over and leapt to his feet, grabbing shoes and clothes before running naked out the door. With an almost comical measure of horror and disbelief, the accent told her it was Trudy's boss.

"I know who you are! You're the fucking home stager!"

"I have permission," she stammered. "Trudy said it was okay – "

"*Bullshit bullshit bullshit!* Leave *now*, piece of shit! Do you *know* what kind of fucking trouble you are in? I am calling 911!"

Gathering purse and negligee – all she had on was her lucky La Perla – Portia sprinted from the room.

She needed to get that money.

She ran downstairs past a startled woman with bobbing antennae. The front door gaped open and Arnold was nowhere in sight. Worse, the envelope was gone from the entry table. Faustino galloped down after her, shouting, "Trespasser!" From the living room, Laurence Li grinned at the goings-on like a yokel watching dinner theater – he assumed it was all part of the inventive realtor's show.

"Oh my God," clapped Ping. "Is so fantastic!"

Outside, Arnold clambered into his car, naked and fumbling at the inside-out pants for keys. Portia materialized barefoot at the driver's side door and lurched for the envelope he'd thrown on the dash. A tug-of-war ensued.

"*Give* it to me!" she shouted. "That's *my* fuckin money!"

With a burst of strength, he managed to shove her out of the car onto the ground. Like a sci-fi spider, she click-clacked into the passenger seat just before he careened the rental in reverse.

Faustino was out on the lawn now but abandoned his pursuit, Walking back in, he literally closed the door on the randy interlopers. (Recounting the tale to his sales gang, he said, "That was the most sex I've had in a year! The Pharaoh may now cancel his Raya! His GoFuckMe page! His Lickstarter!") The stager and her consort were tiny fish to fry, especially when he was about to roast himself a whole Year of the Pig. He would deal with Trudy and her delinquent employee tomorrow; if nothing was damaged or stolen, he might not deal with it at all. In twenty years of selling houses, the Faustino had seen everything – this was *maybe* Number 7 of his Top Ten. Regaining full composure, he brushed off the incident as fortuitously anecdotal; it would live forever, burnishing the legend.

"Squatters," he shrugged, to the ever-delighted Ping. "What can I say? Everyone wants to live in the Palisades! Now: let Faustino give you *le Grand Tour*. Prepare to experience most favorable feng sui!"

Meanwhile, Portia snatched the money and leapt from the moving car. Stoned, shocky, and no longer in his body, Arnold stupidly gave chase. Holding her purse in one hand and the envelope in the other, she tried orienting herself to find the Alfa but had gone in the wrong direction, toward the bluff. He caught up and flipped her around.

"Give me the money or I'll go to the police!"

"Fuck you!"

She slapped him hard and he punched her face.

Portia was stunned. Her nose was bleeding – she hadn't thought he was capable of that. In a stagey, little girl voice, she said, "You *hit* me." He picked up the envelope from the ground. He felt bad that he struck her. *You hurt me,* she quietly repeated, stalling for time by appealing to chivalry. When he asked if she was okay, she kneed him in the balls, grabbed the money and ran past the memorial bench.

He caught her again and trance-pounded her stomach, her breasts, her face – for what must have been five minutes, bleating all the while like some folkloric monkey-goat. He only stopped when his arms could no longer move. In time, he had the strength to drag the macerated body to the edge of the bluff and push it off.

Walking back to his car, he was amazed at how quiet it was and how dark were the houses.

It was like leaving an abandoned movie set.

He needed to get back to Laguna but that was all he knew.

His heart hurt and he checked his arms for the telltale signs of irradiating pain. Arnold considered throwing himself off the cliff too, but his calculus was rudely interrupted by the same animal bleating he had heard while wrestling – that was the word he used internally, "wrestling" – with Reeve. He looked outside to see where it was coming from; with a shock

of repulsed recognition, he realized the caterwauls poured
from his mouth.

The sound of the car starting made him feel hopeful he
might escape. He took comfort that it was a dream he could
will himself to awaken from, an old trope as reliable as the
terminal impulse to pray.

The pungent stink of Reeve's blood and dragged-body
shit-smear dressed the abrasions from the pummeling of her
bones. He vomited into his lap then drove back to Sunset,
down Chautauqua to PCH. He had to use the toilet (all systems crashing) but didn't want to go anywhere with a surveil-
lance camera. *Good luck with that!* He looked like hell, but it
was Hallowe'en – he would just be another zombie or slasher
movie victim...

What did any of it matter? They could already place him at
the scene. He'd watched enough *First 48*'s to know that time-
stamped locations could be triangulated through cell tower
pings and subpoenaed phone records. So he did the only thing
that made sense to a fried brain.

He took her purse and its belongings with him.

* * *

The streets were filled with little Wonder Womans, Billie
Eilishes and Meghan Markles, bad-boy Jokers and Pennywises.
Trixanna went as the mutant Greta (Joey got an endless kick
out of saying "Trix-or-treat!"), wearing pigtail extensions that
Portia snagged at a shop in Silver Lake.

For weeks, Joey had been saying he wanted to go as
Elon but Loretta said "no one's gonna get it" so he went as a
Tesla coil instead. Weeks ago, a neighborhood engineer and

hobbyist with a crush on Cheyenne secretly started working on a kitschy, harnessed apparatus; all Joey had to do was flick a switch for the spidery, crowd-pleasing electrical effect.

His moms went as Tony Stark and "Pepper" Potts.

Trixanna was sleepy, due to the effects of half a crushed-up Ativan that Portia snuck into her thermos of Diet Dr. Pepper. Lately, the girl had been acting out and just now, Portia couldn't deal. She couldn't afford to get a frantic call from the sleepover parents to come and get her; she had way too much going on, what with Ohio Arnold, the Kardashian kluster-fuck, et al. Committing her daughter on a 5185 would put a serious crimp in her income. She'd deal with it after the mark left town.

The next morning, Portia was supposed to pick her up at 11. Loretta kept calling but she didn't answer.

* * *

By chance, the woman who created the This Is A Symbol of My Gratitude altar came to see it early the next morning. A friend from college was in town and before they went surfing she wanted to proudly show him the "guerrilla bodhicitta pop-up" sitting illegally outside the guardrail.

She was shocked to see it in violent disarray – driftwood gone, rocks and candles scattered, Ganesha overturned. The glass on the little photo of Chokyi Nyingma Rinpoche was shattered. Probably Hallowe'en marauders, though this was hardly the neighborhood for that.

When she climbed over the low fence to fix it, she screamed at the nude body caught upside-down on the lip of the ridge.

* * *

Around 10AM, he phoned Trudy to tell her he'd just sold the house on Via De La Paz. He was spreading the good news to everyone in his posse.

Kidnapping "Ping and Pong" from the ALS shindig and closing the deal ten minutes into the tour was a good story, and vintage Faustino. It was also vintage Faustino to bury the lead – in this case, what he called "coitus trespasserruptus." A natural storyteller, he teased out the *second* buried lead: one of the intruders was a home stager. Trudy was enjoying the rough-and-tumble tale so much that she didn't immediately grasp what he was saying. Then it slowly crystallized: an employee of hers had – *wha?* – broken into the house to *fuck.* No, no, no! She knew right away that he was talking about her dangerous crush, Portia Coldstream. Spooked about possible repercussions, she evinced more outrage than she actually felt. She wanted to keep her profitable relationship with the Pharaoh intact.

"Did you call the police?" she said, stagily alarmed.

"Faustino is his own swat team! Quite *forcefully*, he *dismissed* the disgusting couple. They ran for their pathetic, dirty-ass lives!"

"Oh my God, Faustino, I am *so sorry.* I cannot believe – "

"I must tell you, Trudy," he said, lowering his voice for dramatic effect. "Seeing those two in bed... *was the most sex the Pharaoh has had in two years.*"

He horse-laughed, and she did too, mostly in relief that her boss had kept his famous sense of humor. It so easily could have gone the other way.

"Is there anything I should do? Do you want me to call the police?"

"Personally, my darling, I am fresh out of fucks. The house is sold for twelve-point-eight, a record for the bluff!"

"You are *so amazing*," she said, in joyful-slave mode.

"But Faustino was slightly *inebriato*. After he made his little sale, he *fled the crime scene* – of course he had to drive Ping-Pong back to their hotel. So would it be *possible*, my love, for you to go *back* to the house and check for *le damage?* or *les* stolen items? Find nothing, and the bitch shall not be *prosecuted*. She will become part of the Faustino Legend. But if Trudy gets *moody* – if Missy finds something *amiss* – you *must* call the authorities to hunt down your former employee like the filthy whoring squatter she is."

* * *

On her way to Via De La Paz, she kept calling but only got Portia's voicemail. Trudy had to park further down because the end of the street was filled with cop cars. She wondered if Faustino called them after all. *Fuckin overkill for a bullshit B and E. Fuckin drama queens.* When she saw a news van, she figured something else was going on but wasn't curious. She was focused on getting inside the house.

As she stepped from the car, she noticed Portia's Alfa Romeo.

Now that's fuckin weird.

The house smelled of weed but nothing else jumped out. She went upstairs – there were all kinds of shoes on the floor and the bed sheets were yuck. Out of jealousy, she started getting pissed at the woman she'd been masturbating over the last few months. Her eyes idly lit on the nightstand and rested there, waiting for Trudy to pay attention:

A framed selfie of Portia and… *Elon Musk?*

The doorbell rang.

She ran downstairs, thinking for a moment it was Portia, coming to make amends.

A man was stood there in a suit.

Detective So-and-So asked if she'd been home last night. She told him she didn't live there, no one did, and it wasn't her house, she worked for the realtor who just sold it. When she asked *What's this about?* he said that a body had been found on the bluff and they were asking the neighbors if they'd seen or heard anything. She heard herself say, *Is it a woman?* That got his interest. Trudy started to shake. *Is it still there? Can I see it?* He walked her to the scene, sat her down and said he'd be right back. She noticed a plaque on the bench: "The Sun Never Sets On Love."

Returning, he said, "Do you think you'd recognize tattoos?"

He held up his phone and showed an image.

"That's Portia," she said, crumpling in tears.

He put a hand on her shoulder like she was the widow.

* * *

Detective Matias Marengo spoke to Faustino, who described, to the best of his abilities, the man he had caught in bed with the victim.

"He ran like a bat from hell, so I didn't see much. If memory *serves,* he was a bit... *unattractive.* Late forties, early fifties. On the chubby side." The Pharaoh closed his eyes in meditation. "I believe you may safely eliminate George Clooney and Brad Pitt from your list of suspects."

Marengo said, "My wife loves your show."

* * *

Because Trudy mentioned to the detective Portia's little run-in with a coworker, Marengo had a chat with Jerzy.

"The cunt was wack," he told the investigator. "She poured sugar in the gas tank of my motorcycle – had to rebuild the engine. All because she was pissed I recognized her from some shit porn. She was *horrible* in it, a skank with no tits. So fuck *her*, hope she suffered."

* * *

After they left the Palisades, Jaxx dropped the lookalike at his place in Koreatown and drove the Lambo back to Exxxotica. He sat in the office watching TV and doing coke with Cage and his sister Utopia, waiting for Portia to check in sometime between midnight and 1AM.

Utopia's hustle was to call a bunch of hotels until she found one that didn't allow emotional support animals. When that happened, she called her emotional support addict-attorney, who sued the hostelry under the American Disability Act. She was a big-boned girl but kind of sexy. Cage liked to call her "roomy," doing his best Hannibal Lecter from *Silence of the Lambs*.

At two-thirty, Jaxx went home. It was a little strange that he hadn't heard from her but he wasn't too concerned. As fucked up as Portia could get, she was a pro. She knew the drill: minimize the time spent "inside" with a mark. Kick him out sometime après-sex then clean the place up and leave – *with the money, honey.* She already told him about Arnold's magic satchel, so Jaxx had no worries they'd been stiffed.

He sent a *you good?* text then went to sleep.

At 7:45AM he checked his phone and panicked. There wasn't a single missed call or message.

Just then, Cage called about a body being found in the Palisades. It was on the news.

* * *

Fingerprints further identified Ruthanne Davies. (Five listed aliases.)

PRIORS

shoplifting, larceny, prostitution.

TATTOOS

back of neck (gothic letters): PROP. OF JAXX S.

between breasts: skull with roses in eye sockets

between belly button and pubis: SCROLL DOWN

left bicep (above arrow thru heart): TRIXANNA

right arm: vines with thorns

knuckles (left hand): LUST

knuckles (right hand): LOVE

small of back: YER WELCOME

Last known address:

[three rentals ago]

* * *

Arnold told the top-dog valet at the Montage that a friend puked the rentacar during Hallowe'en revelries. He palmed him $200 to have his crew detail it out before noon. There was still a faint smell of vomit. On the way to return it, he bombed the seats and carpets with deodorizer.

His head flashed with the image of being interrogated. On reality shows, homicide detectives always wanted to check the suspect's hands for fresh cuts or scabbing. Arnold thought he might "pass" because he didn't have any of those. But a closer examination might reveal he'd used his fists like hammers; the heels were bruised and already turning bluish green...

Hand-thoughts led him to what he knew would be his downfall: fingerprints. Arnold inventoried what he had touched. Not the front door: it was open when he came in *and* when he ran out. (The man who discovered them must have forgotten to close it.) He remembered being too excited to use the bathroom at *all*, even before the aborted romp. The only thing Arnold remembered touching was a glass he shared with Reeve. Maybe her prints would obscure his. He was less worried about DNA. *Forensic Files* and *The First 48* both made it clear that the probability of him being in the database was doubtful. That he hadn't left a print or any other kind of trace-able evidence was farfetched but he allowed himself to feel hopeful. Arnold needed that respite.

He asked his assistant to arrange a Netjets flight and told her not to let Raleigh know because he wanted his homecom-ing to be a surprise. After dropping off the car, he ubered to a private airport in Van Nuys called Million Air. He had the driver stop at a liquor store to buy cigarettes. Even though he'd quit 20 years ago, he had the sudden, strong impulse to smoke.

A charismatic, tousle-haired woman was in line ahead of him. It was obvious from her banter with the clerk that she was an old customer. She half-turned to make eye contact with Arnold, as if including him in their repartee. She smiled and he smiled back. He was amazed by her beauty and shocked by his resilience. The gonads die hard. He turned to watch those long legs leave and the chatty clerk watched too.

"Know who that was?" he said. "Lisa – *Lisa Linde*. She was married to Cyclops, from *X-Men*. He left her for another woman, can you believe it? Who would leave Lisa? Who, who, who?"

He bought a pack of Marlboros and a scratcher.

As the plane took off, he felt relief, even if it was counterfeit.

He went through her purse.

"Ruthanne Davis" – so that was her real name.

Online, he found a mugshot from 2010. *Las Vegas Metropolitan Police.*

He had already dismantled her phone and thrown it in a curbside drain; he'd shred her license and credit cards once he got to Cleveland. His google searches could be subpoenaed so it probably wasn't such a bright idea to be hunting around, but what difference did it make? The noose was waiting whether they found his prints or not. He shuddered when he thought of Tamblyn – "Reeve's" co-conspirator – and Elon Musk! It was *brilliant*. He was right: a "long con" after all. Wow! Even the guy Tamblyn was having dinner with at Geoffrey's was part of it... a whole fucking *ring*. They'd go to the police and say, "Arnold Neidhoff is your man!" Would they, though? (*Maybe*, if there was a giant reward. But giant rewards were usually reserved for cartel guys and Ten Most Wanteds.) Turning him in would be like snitching on themselves...

They're street. They'll come after me directly, for revenge. They know where I live, they know everything about me. They know about Raleigh and Cammy –

He shook it off and used a coin on the ten-dollar scratcher.

It returned $500.

* * *

Kim Kardashian took it hard when Richie told her about the murder. (She was still overseas.) Her heart went out to the daughter.

"What's going to happen to her now? Where will she go?"

"Unless there's living relatives, she'll enter the system."

"I'd like to help," she said. "Do we know where she is?"

"I'll look into that."

"When did you and Ruthanne last talk?"

"Yesterday. When I told her the results of the paternity test."

"And now she's dead – how *crazy* is that, Snoop? Does anyone know what happened?"

"An old friend of mine is working the case. I'll find out what I can."

"It's so horrible."

"She wasn't a stranger to the game. Sometimes you end up with a mark who doesn't want to play. The bill usually comes when you're not expecting it."

"It was so *inappropriate* for her to tell her daughter to write to him – "

"She was a wildcard, to say the least."

" – I mean, before she even *knew* anything, before she knew the *results*. Did you ask her about that?"

"I didn't. Didn't see the benefit. To tell the truth, when we got the results, I was just happy we could wash our hands of her."

Kim sighed. "I'm still reeling over Old Boy, and now *this*… it's just so *sad*. I want to pay the funeral costs. Are there any arrangements?"

"Too soon. Once the coroner does a report, the body will be released."

"To *who*?" she asked.

"Let me find out."

"I really want to help the little girl. In *some* way. Poor Trixanna!"

"Let's see if there's anything we can do. And that's very generous, by the way."

* * *

The address listed on the Alfa's registration was of no help to the police. But among the debris of fast food wrappers, there was a utility bill for what looked like a current residence. Two days after Portia was found, Matias Marengo went to Echo Park with a search warrant. While he and a police officer rooted around, there was a noisy knock at the front door.

As it slowly opened, a voice tentatively inquired,

"Hello? Portia? Is that you? *Hello –* "

That was how Joey's mom found out.

After a good cry, Loretta told the detective how frantic she'd been – Portia's daughter had been staying with them since Hallowe'en and she was about to file a missing person report. Marengo wanted to know where the girl was. "She's at school." When he asked if she'd be willing to keep Trixanna a few more days, Loretta scrunched her face and said, "I really don't think so." In a whisper, as if worried she might be overheard, she added, "Something's *wrong* with her. I'm just not comfortable having her in the house anymore. That's why I came today – here – to see if Portia was home, before going to the police."

A policewoman and a lady from DCFS accompanied Marengo to Logan Street Elementary. The caseworker told Trixanna that something happened to her mom and they were going to take her to "a safe place." When the girl started to shake, the caseworker reached out to comfort her – that's when Trixanna took hands from pockets and lashed out. Her fingers were taped with penknives and broken scissor blades.

"Reavers!" she shouted as they disarmed her, binding her with plastic cuffs. "You killed my *real* mom! Portia isn't my mom, my *real* mom was dead all along! You and the Reavers and Transigen killed her! When I extract the Wolverine from Pelican Bay, you will all die, die, die, die!"

"This one," said the caseworker matter-of-factly, "needs to go to the hospital."

* * *

Jaxx called the Montage Laguna Beach, on speaker.

"Arnold Neidhoff please."

"Is he a guest?"

"Yes."

"That party checked out."

"Right," he said, clicking off.

"That *schmuck*?" said Cage, in disbelief. "He *couldn't* have, he's a straight-up *pussy*. I can't fucking believe it."

"Well you better."

"What happened to the fuckin bread?"

"We don't know if he even brought it."

"Portia would have got it *first thing*, he *must* have. Fuck! But dude, what *happened* – "

"No fuckin idea. Maybe it was a sex-gone-bad deal. Maybe 'Ohio' was a rage-fucker..."

"Jesus! But the *cliff*... what were they doing *outside* on the *cliff*, bro?"

"No clue, bro."

"And she's, like, what – buck naked? Bro, what the fuck is *that* all about? I still don't get *why*."

"Maybe she told him he had a tiny dick."

"You know what we should do? I'll *tell* you what we should do. We should go to the fuckin police."

"Oh, right, our *friends*. Our friends the police."

"We could do it *anonymously*."

"I gotta better idea."

"And what about the *Elon*?"

"What about him?"

"What if he calls the cops?"

"And why would he do that?"

"What if, like, more details come out…"

"Like what."

"What if he hears it on the news, bro? Like, there's a picture of Portia on the news and the *Elon* puts it all together – that he was there on the night it *happened*?"

"He's retarded. There's no way."

Cage had a point but Jaxx needed to triage.

At the top of his stress list was Portia's cellphone. He knew the cops didn't have possession because he'd have heard from them. No doubt they were already getting her phone records but that would take a moment. He was careful about his texts, but Portia was reckless – her side of the conversation would definitely be incriminating. Jaxx accepted that he'd be going back to prison but didn't care. All he cared about was inflicting maximum pain on the asshole who pulverized his baby.

It took three hours to hack into Arnold's phone.

Jaxx searched the recently deleted file, and there it was: a blurry, reeling funhouse of naked disarray and raucous laughter in the bedroom on Via De La Paz. (Though Portia was still in her felony bra). Arnold held a phone to the sliding wardrobe mirror while she playfully tried to grab it.

The video ended and Jaxx went to the next.

This one, shot by Portia like a POV porn, had her filming while on top. "How does it feel?" she said, off-camera. "You like that? Is it too tight? Huh? Too tightie-tight, like a tiny little girl? Like a tiny little girl's butt?" Arnold grabbed the phone, turning it on her as she rode him. "Nice fat cock," said Portia, eyes half-closed. "*Hmmmm*... nice fat Cleveland cock... you all the way hard, honey? Such a tease! *Please* don't get all the way hard cause this tiny tiny girl cannot fucking *take* it. Oh, oh, holy *shit*, can I squirt? Wanna see me squirt, hon? Can I squirt on that baby boy? Wait – wait – we're gonna need a towel..."

Jaxx mirrored the video on the widescreen, jerking off to the last part.

* * *

There weren't any beds in L.A. for someone Trixanna's age. The social worker was glad; generally, county placements were nightmarish. She'd sent kids to Big Bear Behavioral Health Center before and was impressed. BB/BHC was in Redlands, not far from Patton State Hospital, where a lot of Big Bear kids' parents cycled through. Patton's original name was Southern California State Asylum for the Insane and Inebriates.

They doped her up the first two days and she lived on a cotton candy cloud. Most of the time she heard a thrum; her whole body vibrated while she imagined being lost in the bowels of a great ocean liner like in the YouTubes she loved of Shirley Temple in *Stowaway* and *Captain January*. *But where's my mommy? What did they do with Mommy!* Sometimes she cried and other times watched funny TrixToks she made up in her head (while the very real ghost of Tabasco sat on her lap), as she waited for Portia to come home. To pass the time, she conjured the photomontage of superheroes pasted onto the ceiling of the old bedroom in Echo Park. Meghan Markle floated over her and she wondered what was taking so long for the Duchess of Success to be made queen.

She never stopped thinking about her father.

Old Boy Logan would make them *pay* for what they did to Portia. (She still got mixed up about who was her real mom.) She started another letter in her head. When she escaped, she would find a nice library where she could write it all down.

Dearest Father,

I am writing this to you from yet another Transigen facillity. But do not depair, I am making plans to X-tract myself SOON. When this ocurrs, I will be on my way for YOUR X-traction.

I am thinking all this will take 3 days or ONE WEEK.

So Much has happenned!

For an X-ample: I am a bleeding woman now. And They have killed your wife and my Mama. (The woman who made such a clame.)

I am getting stronger now because now I am not taking the Rx. It was hard not to take the Rx at first because they were carefully watching me but now it is easier and I am gettinhg SO MUCH StRONGER.

The adamantium was sleeping but now it is awake.

* * *

Old Boy's ashes were released to Chökyi Nyingma Rinpoche. In a note discovered in his cell, he requested that his cremains be scattered on the walking mediation grounds of Ka-Nying Shedrub Ling Monastery in Kathmandu, where his teacher was abbot. He also wanted some of the ashes to be given to his dear friend and ally, Kim Kardashian.

He and Kim had talked a lot about the ranch that she and her husband bought in Wyoming – Old Boy loved its name, "Monster Lake" – and he joked about always wanting to be a "zen Black cowboy." She promised that when he was released from prison, he could live out the remainder of his days in the godly, wide-open spaces if he wished.

She brought the ashes there. The Rinpoche, unable to attend, sent three monks. She asked them if it would be all right to film the ceremony, "Not for my show, but for a documentary I'm making about Old Boy and the system that failed him." They smiled and nodded. Afterward, one of the crew approached the monks with a clipboard. "What's that?" said Kim, interrupting. "Releases," said the young man. Kim took the clipboard and handed it back.

"You don't have to sign anything," she said to the monks.

She needed to speak to Rinpoche first. She wanted his benediction.

With a huge smile, one of them said, "No – we sign! We sign! So *happy* to be on *KUWTK* with Mrs. Kardashian-West!"

* * *

A week into Trixanna's Big Bear stay, the fog lifted. Her appetite came back and she tried out a few giggles. The nurses smiled at the breakthrough-sun of her face.

They finally let her out of her room.

The television was in a cage and always set to cartoons, but a genius named Gem (for Gemini) knew how to change the channel. He called it "my superpower." (He pretended to do it with his mind but Trix saw him secretly fiddling with something in his pocket.) He reminded her of Joey, only thinner and taller and older and more handsome. Gem fiddled with his pocket again and the cartoon changed to a man in a Wolverine costume posing for tourists. A newsperson was saying how beloved he was and how he came to L.A. to be an actor but only found work as a busboy. When people kept saying how much he looked like Hugh Jackman, he decided to make money by dressing up as the Wolverine in front of a Chinese theatre. Then he got beat up and never recovered. Thugs burned his costume and he became homeless. The newsperson said he had a heart attack and fell into a dumpster in Van Nuys while rummaging for donated clothes. They were doing a Kickstarter to bury him at Hollywood Forever.

Gem said he would help her escape, but she'd have to help him too. He said she was really cute and how they would make a really cute couple. And besides, he said, because they were both in a facility, "statutory's non-applicable." He told her that he was sixteen and

* * *

Jaxx drove down to Baja. He didn't have to check in with his P.O. for another two weeks. He thought about going to the desert to chill – Joshua Tree, wherever – but it didn't feel far away enough.

He *definitely* didn't want to be in L.A. when the police got hold of Portia's phone records. Jaxx's entire plan hinged on them still having no suspect – but for all he knew, Arnold had been print-ID'd and the fuzz were already on the midnight train to Cleveland. If so, it was game over and Jaxx lost his chance to plea bargain. A fancy lawyer would no doubt paint Arnold Neidhoff as a hapless, fish-out-of-water family man, hoodwinked and tortured by yours truly, ringleader of a cabal of slick sociopathic Hollywood swindlers that drove his client to madness and murder. He could easily find himself on the wrong end of twenty years. But a conspiracy charge probably wouldn't stick; Portia died before properly fleecing the fat fuck. It was moot, anyhow, because homicide always trumped hustle. The only thing they could nail him on was possession of a smartphone and PC, violations of his parole. Still, all that bad press had a way of tacking on beaucoup time.

He needed to work fast.

He walked the Ensenadan beach, thinking of her.

He never expected such agony.

He picked up a girl at a cybercafé. They went back to the Airbnb and got drunk. Jaxx carefully smeared her skin with black watercolor; she didn't know he was replicating the ghost tattoos that belonged to his love. (He couldn't bring himself to daub PROP. OF JAXX S on the back of her neck.) In the acrylic, moonlit room, he imagined Portia under him. He cried when he came and when the girl saw that, she cried too, thinking

Por fin he encontrado mi amor.

When they were done, they listened to Jaxx's playlist. Sinatra randomly sang, "It's not her smile, but such a lovely smile that it's all right with me," and he began to laugh, knowingly, then wildly, and she laughed too. A dreaded sense of aloneness, sorrow and dislocation descended. Of spiritual desolation... she gathered him in her arms like a mother, which he allowed. He would *never* let Portia do that, he was always the one to make such a gesture, *he* was the one yes *he was the one* – a sudden pang as he wondered if he'd been selfish, if the reason he loved Portia was merely because they were so much alike.

Jaxx hadn't cried like that before, about anything or anyone. It made him feel alive, and loved – by *Her* – the warm, ectoplasmic embrace of a dead soul attended by the gooey, transcendent apprehension that she would stay, just as long as he kept loving her the way that he did: with infinite, cyclonic force. He never had that sense about his mom when she passed, nor his closest friend (who died of Hodgkin's when they were both 12), nor any of the beloved family dogs that departed.

It both comforted and filled with insatiate rage.

While the wrong smile slept beside him, Jaxx sent off a few texts. The first was

wanna see me squirt?

Then,

i am SO fucked, arnie! you killed me dead, but I'm still horny!

In the morning, he'd send the Via de la Paz sex video to Matias Marengo, detective of record. Even if they already knew the name of the killer, Jaxx figured he still might get points toward leniency.

At the same time Marengo got it, so would all of Raleigh Neidhoff's Facebook friends.

* * *

A friend invited him to Dayton. There was another mass shooting and Dave Chappelle was having a Sunday memorial, for locals only. Folks like Stevie Wonder, Chris Rock and Alicia Keys were going to perform. Kanye West and his Sunday choir were coming too.

It was a three-hour drive from Cleveland and whenever he looked over at his wife, Arnold practically blushed with an old feeling he thought he would never recapture: the blissful days of their courtship. When he first got back, Raleigh begged him to see a doctor. His hands were puffy and bluish and when she googled, she got scared because edema was a sign of so many things, like kidney disease or congestive heart failure.

Then suddenly he was the picture of health – and more. He made love to her in a different way and it felt like she was cheating. It excited her more than she would ever admit. Raleigh wasn't sure what happened in California, but *something* did; she nearly asked if he'd had an affair but held her tongue because she almost didn't care, as long as the new "them" stayed a while. Their bedroom sessions were down to once a month, and only when their son was in daycare. But now they fucked while Cammy was in the house, even when they heard a physical therapist or schoolteacher giving him lessons in another room. She couldn't believe it when he ate her ass. They got so down and dirty that Raleigh couldn't even bring herself to tell her best girlfriend what they were up to.

Dayton was astonishing. Dave Chappelle was so smart and funny and poignant that Arnold just sobbed and sobbed. Kanye and his people shouted out beautiful hymns and Stevie Wonder sang a song called "They Won't Go When I Go" that brought the couple to their knees. All that death, all that

celebration! That's where Arnold lived now: in death and celebration. The brittle, horrorshow flashbacks of the Palisades
bluff crept in during calm, unlikely moments, the stuff of a
nauseating dream, but he was of the living and needed to celebrate. Eerily reborn, he pushed away the eventuality of an
arrest.

Surviving – any and everything – was his new superpower.

He read about it online. Still no suspects. *Must not have
found a usable print.* But he knew from the cop shows that
sooner or later his texts would be discovered on Reeve's
phone… and yet, even knowing it was a matter of time before
the knock came at the door didn't stop Arnold from feeling
invincible. Besides, what could he be charged with? He started
to rehearse a defense. He would tell them they were in the
house together and heard noises, that Reeve told him some
bad people were after her – folks she'd ripped off. *I got really
scared and ran.* That when he got in his car and took off, he
never saw or heard from her again. Though maybe it was better not to say anything until he got an attorney… maybe this
was a no-brainer rage-insanity defense. *Your Honor, my client
made some mistakes, for which he feels contrite, and the consequences of those mistakes will live with him to the end of his days.
His first mistake was being human. An attractive, seductive young
woman caught his eye while he was out of town on a business trip,
one of a thousand trips he'd made in the past to earn money in
support of his precious family. Your Honor, my client is from Ohio.
He is a good man, a church-going man. And he is a wealthy man,
but not worldly – but, Your Honor, he is a man. A vain man, in the
middle-life of his years. Who allowed himself to be flattered and
manipulated by a provocative woman, a career criminal, who was
far, far out of his league. By doing so, he betrayed the one person*

that meant everything to him – his wife and childhood sweetheart. And forgive me for this, ladies and gentlemen of the jury, but I hope you'll understand: Raleigh Neidhoff is a woman he would quite literally kill for. He betrayed not only his wife, but their beloved, differently abled son Cammy. His second mistake was losing his mind – that's right, losing his mind! Seduced by a liar! A hardened poseur! A predator! Trampled on by a gang of thieves that plotted to rob him of $200,000 and threatened to expose him. Not just to his wife but to his longtime business associates and the whole world. We've already had several experts talk to the court – and jury – about the physical and emotional mechanism of threat. A person can black out, just as my client did, when presented with an intolerable *threat – and let's not pretend for a moment that he wasn't threatened, even with death by their hands! Just yesterday, we heard an esteemed psychiatrist speak of –*

Sometimes now, making love to his wife, he pretended the act would end in her death – both their deaths – and got jolted by a surge of power. If he *were* arrested, he was certain Raleigh would forgive, and stand beside him. They were busy finding the love they once had and could get through anything, even the public disgrace of a trial. He dared to feel hopeful about his legal prospects – he had enough money to hire Dershowitz or Boies, he could hire them *both* – and after he was exonerated, he'd sell his company and move the family to Europe. The world was ending anyway. The billionaires were buying up land in New Zealand and building high-tech bunkers, maybe that's where they'd go, to New Zealand or Iceland or Geneva or Scotland, some cold and isolated place where they could dream a new dream.

When they returned from Dayton, Cammy was asleep. He sent the caregiver home while Raleigh showered, then watched TV in the den.

A show was on about Hugh Jackman. His wife Deborra-Lee sat in for the interview. *Hey now, I know those people.* Just like Raleigh and Arnold, the couple suffered miscarriages and tried IVF before finally adopting – Ava, their youngest, was Cammy's age. "I don't think of them as adopted," Hugh said. "They're our children. Deb and I are believers in... I suppose you could call it destiny. We feel things happened the way they are meant to. Obviously, biologically wasn't the way we were meant to have kids."

Arnold almost forgot about the $150,000 check. Tomorrow, he would share the whole encounter with Raleigh. She'd be so moved the donation was given in mother and son's name. They would have a little meeting with Cammy to share the news that Dad was helping the Wolverine with a wonderful cause – and how the Wolverine *himself* was looking forward to meeting him.

He climbed in with Raleigh then dreamed he was back in the house on Via De La Paz, in bed with Reeve. But Cammy was somewhere downstairs and suddenly his wife was FaceTiming. When Reeve mischievously grabbed the phone from his hand to answer, Arnold screamed inside the dream but no sound came out. When he awakened, Raleigh was trying to soothe him and she

* * *

helped Gemini like she had promised. Trixanna was still looking for other mutant children and made the mistake of oversharing that she was actually Laura, the cloned daughter of her imprisoned father, aka the Wolverine. She told Gem about her adamantium bones too and gossiped about the coming exodus to Eden from Pelican Bay. With respectful seriousness, as if to show he believed her, Gem said that he wished he had claws too. Trix knew he had a sympathetic heart, even if it wasn't in the right place.

A few days after they met, he pointed out a pretty nurse's aide from the Dominican, the one who always playfully rolled her eyes whenever she saw Gem and Trix whispering together. "That's my girlfriend," he said. "She's got one in the oven – knocked her up on the second week of my admit. We're gonna get a little apartment when I get out." Trix thought he was lying but hoped that he wasn't because he kept saying things like, "She's gonna help spring you 'cause she likes you. (She likes me more, heh heh)" and "*Mostly* she's gonna help you *escape* 'cause the girl is *fuckin bored*" and "Yuli's on *staff* but she don't care if she get caught. Yuli just wanna go *west*. Yuli wants to go to Hollywood and be a *star!*"

Then one night, Gem told her to be ready at 1AM – "grab your shoes, coat and hat, 'cause Yuli's workin *graveyard*."

The door cracked open at the appointed time and Trixanna waited a moment before stepping into the deserted fluorescent hall. At the end of the corridor, Yuli smiled and made a swift nod toward an unmarked door. She dropped some money on the ground for Trix to see and disappeared.

She picked two twenties off the floor and was suddenly outside in the cold, starry air. She walk-ran for miles and miles, avoiding areas lit by moon- or streetlight. She found an encampment under the freeway and lay down on a discarded sleeping bag. At dawn, she awakened to a stinky drunk lady going through her pockets. *What you got there little bitch what you got.* All kinds of dogs started barking and as Trix scrambled out, a thousand arms and hands reached out to grab her like a horror movie.

Before journeying to Crescent City, she first had to go home. If she didn't retrieve the weaponshield from the backyard where it was buried, she would never be able to free her father. Echo Park was only an hour-and-a-half away by car – but who would drive an unescorted child? She needed a miracle.

It came outside an old supermarket.

Trixanna sat atop an unmoving mechanical horse, just like the scene with Laura and the Wolverine in *Logan*. She couldn't keep her eyes open and thought it was safe to nap in the saddle because that was a kid thing to do and wouldn't draw attention. A woman appeared with a little girl, and spoke to her like they were peers. Right away, Trix knew something was wrong. *Who is she working for who is she pretending to be.* But Trix had no other choice than to say that her parents had an argument and she needed a ride back to Echo Park. The woman said she could only take her as far as County General, where she had an appointment for a CT scan. For the whole ride, the woman smiled as she softly sang to herself, and the little girl stared wide-eyed at their guest. By the time she was dropped off, Trixanna was convinced the pair were angels, sent by Greta.

She was a two-hour walk from home now.

She hid in the park where she used to sit on the bench with Joey because it wasn't safe to go home until it after dark. She looked for the pelican and its tiny, orphaned ducks but they weren't there anymore. When she finally got to the house it was locked and foreboding. *The Reavers have already been here.* What she came for was buried in the yard but Trixanna was curious; she broke a back window and climbed in. She turned on a light and made number two in the hallway then stood in the doorway of Portia's room barefoot. She stared at the bed, trying to conjure her mother's snoring body. In her own room, photos of Queen Meghan, Laura/X-23 and Shuri still graced the ceiling like church frescoes. She was so tired but there was no time to rest. It wasn't safe to stay. That's why she didn't use the toilet – in Pelican Bay, prisoners talked to each other through the bathroom pipes, which meant that the army of Reavers hiding in local safe houses would totally be able to listen in and learn what she was up to. Time to go.

If she were to free her father, she had to dig up the weaponshield.

The police shone a floodlight into the yard.

A lady who lived next door saw a burglar moving furtively around the house and called 911. Of course, everyone in the neighborhood knew about the murder; everyone felt terrible for the little girl.

Trixanna didn't run.

She had the shield now and knew it would protect her.

She raised it high as one of the officers unholstered his gun. It was a lucky thing she wasn't shot.

"Mutatis Mutandis!" she shouted, as they closed in.

But on the way to the precinct, the cries became *Momma!*

* * *

Richie "Snoop" Raskin was in the news again, thanks to his association with Kim Kardashian and the unfortunate turn of events surrounding Reginald Ronald "Old Boy" White. He never really left the public eye, even after *The Snoop Files* went off the air. He was his own press agent, and a good one, cultivating a Ray Donovan vibe, which, in younger days, wasn't far from the truth. All the recent attention was a blessing. He was already approached by ID and Hulu about a reboot of the old show.

More than a week had passed since the murder and he'd been meaning to get in touch with his homeboy, Matias Marengo. The plan was to hook him up with Kim, who wanted to meet the man in charge of the Ruthanne Davies homicide. (Kim was a crime show addict and fangirl of *The Snoop Files,* which was why she hired Richie in the first place.) Before *Files* was canceled, Matias consulted on an episode about "Fat" Joan Gamma, the notorious billionaire, and had also been looking into the disappearance of her grandfather, a once-famous novelist.

"Well, *you've* been a busy boy," said Marengo. "You oughta do a show called *Keeping Up With Snoop Raskin.*"

"The yacht ain't gonna pay for itself."

They always broke each other's balls.

"I thought Kim would have *given* you a boat by now."

"Who knows?" said Richie. "Maybe it'll be under the tree for Christmas. Might have to find me a sequoia or two though."

"Christmas is too far away. Just sit on your ass and wait for Kanye to go bipolar. He'll buy you a boat *and* a jet. And throw in a sequoia."

"Oh, I won't have to wait, my friend. Yeezy's bipolar 24-7."

"He can *walk* you to your boat. You've got two choices: he can part the sea or you can both walk on water."

"Oh, he'll be fine. But I might need a flotation device."

"If you really want to rough it – "

"Well *that* don't sound fun."

" – just switch to a dinghy like the rest of us."

"Any swingin' dinghy'll do."

"But you're too fancy for that now, huh."

"Matty, I was born with a dinghy between my legs. But the minute I got rich, all the ladies started calling it a super-yacht."

Marengo laughed like hell.

Snoop talked about his oddball connection to the vic – how he and Ruthanne once met, in Century City.

"All roads lead back to Kimmy K," said Marengo.

He said that he didn't have any leads and was still waiting on phone records. It would probably take another week or so.

"No prints at the scene?" asked Richie.

"About ten thousand – the place was for sale and all the furniture was rented. Moved around hither and thither."

"After being tasked to find Ms. Davies, I did a bit of a deep dive. Kim was thinking of putting her in a documentary and I had to see if that was viable. Colorful lady! Ran hustles out of five-star hotels."

"I knew that."

"Very *imaginative* shakedowns."

"Mr. Musk was sorely abused," said Marengo.

"Meaning?"

"Oh, we found a picture in a frame... it's probably nothing."

"Have you talked to Jaxx?"

"Who dat?"

"The boyfriend."

"Tell me more, Yoda."

"Ruthanne's partner in crime. They did porn together too."

"Ooh, Yoda! Send me a link!"

"He's on parole for cyber-crimes."

"You think he was involved in the hijinks?"

"They like a caper," said Richie.

"Would Yoda happen to know his whereabouts?"

"Tell you what. I'll share my intel if you agree to 'co-star' on the pilot for my *Snoop Files* redo."

"That's what you said on the Wiggins deal."

"Well, we didn't find a body on that one. Not very sexy. "

"I want *serious* screen time. I want to be Meryl Marengo."

"I'll put it in writing," said Richie. "Of course, we'll need to wait till we get a conviction. You know the drill."

"*Deal*. Just get me out of a dinghy and into a super-yacht, okay?"

"Aye-aye, Cap'n. And if you're *real* good, I might even introduce you to Kanye."

"Praise Jesus!"

"Only his close friends call him that."

* * *

Arnold was at the office when he got the first text your life is OVER, bitch then another the horizontal elevator is actually... a COFFIN. For YOU, you fat murdering piece of shit and another sending this on BLAST to LAPD and Raleigh's FB! then sending to you NOW and to wifey & cops LATER then want you to see it FIRST and FEEL the PAIN and get ready to suck M-13 COCK in jail/HELL

It was strange for Arnold to see the X-rated video because it felt like he'd already lived and died multiple lives since then. He and Reeve seemed like actors – *bad actors,* in the phrase of the day – faraway from what was real, faraway from the consequences of their actions.

Sitting at his desk, he got sick like he did that night in the car right after but this time the throw-up mostly stayed in his mouth.

When he came home from work, she didn't say anything – it was obvious nothing had been sent – and now it was 10PM and Raleigh was sleeping.

He wondered if Jaxx was bluffing.

(He assumed it was Jaxx who sent the texts.)

Her phone was right there but Arnold didn't know how to check her Facebook.

He wondered about prison –

I think I could survive there.

He thought about waking her up, to confess. Then ask her to drive him to the police station…

He went to the den and turned on the TV. It was the middle of a *20/20*, featuring Kim Kardashian. She was talking about what it was like to be in Texas visiting a prisoner on death row, right when they got word of a stay of execution. The hope and jubilation. *Maybe she could join the legal team. Put on some blackface to get her attention.* She said she had been on her way to Dayton, where her husband was doing a Sunday Service at a memorial that Dave Chappelle was organizing. The program took a darker turn when it showed Kim in conversation with Reginald Ronald "Old Boy" White, another prisoner she'd advocated for. Wrongly convicted, he died in his cell before being released. Kim told the interviewer it broke her heart that she couldn't get him out. "He had cancer and was going to live out his days at our ranch in Wyoming." They showed footage from his early years of incarceration, being extracted from his cell. A real badass.

He went to the bedroom and touched Raleigh's shoulder.

He lifted the sheet off and kissed her bush.

He licked it and she groaned.

Some part of her brain said *Guess this is the new normal.* She laughingly told one of her galfriends, "I think Arnold's got a tumor – pressing against his dick gland."

Some part of her brain said…

He climbed on top and kissed her mouth, already rank with sleep. When she started to come, he reached for the gun he slipped under the bed but reached too far and fell off her. Startled, she said *Oh honey! You okay?* and he shot her in the face then shot her again in the heart.

He put on a robe and went to Cammy's room.

Peered in.

The boy was listening to music on his headphones.

Arnold went to the library.

His hands were shaking.

He wrote something on a sheet of paper then signed and dated it. He was hoping the court or whoever would rule that he was in fact in his right mind at the time of the wishes he had just expressed. He thought twice, copied the same words, and backdated the document by a week. He put the earlier draft in an ashtray and watched it burn.

When Cammy saw his dad, he lit up and took off the headset.

"Dad! Dad!"

"Hel-lo, Winter Soldier."

"Your face wet, your face wet! You crying! Dad why you crying?"

"Because I'm so happy to see you, my son."

Cammy thought that was hysterical.

"Hey, buddy," said Arnold. "Do you want to play the game?"

"The game! The game!"

"Yeah! Come on, buddy, let's play the game."

"The game, the game! *Say* it!" exclaimed Cammy. "*Say* it!"

"I will," said Arnold. "But *you* have to say it *first*. Remember?"

Cammy shrieked and tittered – he couldn't believe he wasn't being told to turn out the lights and go to sleep.

That Daddy wanted to play the *game*.

"I... am... inevitable!"

"Good," said Arnold.

"I am inevitable! I am inevitable!"

"Close your eyes. Go ahead now, son. Close'm."

Cammy did what he was told, whispering, *I am inevitable.*

"And I

said Arnold, taking the gun from the terrycloth pocket and stroking his son's silky hair with his free hand

am Iron Man."

* * *

Minutes after getting the boyfriend lead, Matias Marengo drove to the address Snoop provided. His phone dinged. The detective pulled over to look at an encrypted skinflick, taken in what looked to be the Via De La Paz bedroom. The vitals (home address, cellphone) of one Arnold Neidhoff, Cleveland, OH, followed.

The little movie was captioned too: LAST TO SEE HER ALIVE
The end of the note read

in mex, back in l.a. tomorrow. i'll come see you. Jaxx Snowcroft.

Marengo googled *Arnold Neidhoff*: all in all, Ruthanne hooked a pretty big fish. Sold his business not too long ago for close to a hundred mill.

Might be smoke and mirrors – who said Neidhoff was the last to see her? The boyfriend, that's who. One possible scenario was that he caught Portia and Arnold in bed and in the heat of passion, forgot they were playing a long money game. Or Peeping Tom'd, lay in wait for Neidhoff to leave, then chased her down. Could've chased her down in *front* of the frightened mark – who ran like hell.

He needed to talk to Jaxx but for now Arnold Neidhoff would definitely do.

He dialed the 216 prefix.

"Hello?"

"Arnold?"

"Who's this?" said the voice.

"Detective Matias Marengo, LAPD. With who am I speaking?"

"Clyde Jooler, Cleveland Homicide."

"Did he kill himself?"

"Oh, that and then some."

* * *

From his south-of-the-border bolthole, Jaxx suddenly had qualms about sending the sex video to Raleigh Neidhoff's FB page. It didn't sit well with him to punish the woman for her husband's sins; more so, because he was reluctant to expose his lover to the postmortem blue light amber of the web. For him, it had become a snuff film.

The laughing exhibitionist in her would have wanted to go viral. But the abused little girl, who sobbed in his arms when too stoned or not stoned enough, would have died all over again. In the end, Jaxx couldn't throw Portia to the hounds of 4chan and Reddit, or body-dump her at XXX sites like DaftPorn and Humoron. He still ran the risk of it being hacked or leaked by the cops themselves but that was a risk he was willing to take. All that mattered was making Arnold Neidhoff accountable. Make him suffer. Make him live with what he had done. Anything else would have left the chapel of Jaxx's love like Tiffany's after a smash and grab.

When he heard about the double murder and suicide on the news, he grew calm. Jaxx wondered why he had never even considered such possibility. *Now*, it made perfect sense; *now*, it seemed inevitable. But why take the lives of his own wife and child? *Just wired that way I guess.* Knowing the carnage was triggered by his texts, he still felt no guilt.

Only closure.

* * *

Seeing that he was genuinely aggrieved over his loss, the detective shifted his tone. The young man expressed remorse over the deaths of the perpetrator's wife and child, and that too seemed genuine.

"We're grateful for all your help," said Marengo, and meant it.

It more or less played out like Jaxx thought it would. He got a year for his violations but did six months. He stayed clean in jail, and upon release, became a warrior in the rooms of Narcotics Anonymous.

* * *

Marengo kept in touch and became a mentor of sorts. He had the idea that the kid would do well lecturing at the Academy about computer hacking. He was right. Jaxx was funny and personable and one thing led to another until he found himself the star of a small, burgeoning network of cyber-security trolls who crossed over to the good side.

One day, Jaxx idly asked how Portia's daughter was doing. The detective, sensing there was still healing to be done, made a few calls.

"Trixanna's doing great," he said.

"Oh, cool. Where is she?"

"In Redlands."

"Living with a family?"

"No – in kind of a halfway house. It's part of the hospital she was being treated at."

"Can I go visit?"

"I don't see why not."

* * *

It started in prison – an aching, almost primal need to see her.

They had a rollicking, devilish rapport. Whenever Portia saw them behaving like co-conspirators, she called them "Jaxanna." "Look at you," she'd say. "All thick as thieves."

When Trix got spooky and began acting out, he worried about Portia's sketchy maternal instincts. He didn't think she had what it took to deal. Anyway, Jaxx was at an impasse because the bottom line was that he didn't really want to get involved. What the fuck could he do for Trixanna Coldstream anyway? What could *anyone* do? He'd always felt guilty about that.

Over the last few months, he found himself fantasizing about who Trixanna's father could be – strange in itself, because he had never given it a thought, not before nor after Kim Kardashian came along with the fake news of Old Boy being the alleged dad. He began wondering what sort of man would abandon his child. If her real father could be located – if he could secretly be introduced to Trix and saw how *amazing* she was – what would he do? Go on his merry, shitty way? Could he even be able to claim her, legally? Jaxx remembered his weird sense of relief when Portia announced that Reginald Ronald "Old Boy" White wasn't the one. He finally had to admit how jealous he'd been of the possibility.

He realized that his growing interest in her patrimony stemmed from the fear that her biological father might come out of the woodwork.

– and do what?

Snatch her away.

But from whom?

From me!

Slowly, he unraveled the quixotic dream of adopting her. It was an absurd notion, yet when such thoughts arrived, he let them stay a while.

* * *

It was Christmastime when he saw her.

They talked a few times on the phone beforehand. (She refused to FaceTime.) She spoke in a monotone and Jaxx assumed she was medicated. She usually loosened up toward the end of their conversations and showed him glints of the old Trixanna. Still, there was something different about her that he couldn't put his finger on.

Then it came to him: she wasn't crazy anymore.

On the day of his visit, he talked to the nurse in charge.

"She sounds so grown up," he said. "So... mellow."

"She's our Wonder Girl," said Cappy.

"I can see that – it's in her voice. Is it because she's taking her meds? I know it used to be challenging for her mom to get her to do that."

"We're pretty aggressive about teaching them the importance of *swallowing* what the doctor prescribes. But I think a lot of how well she's doing is because of the ECT. We have a new clinical head and he's a real advocate. We've just had *amazing* results with our cubs, across the board."

"What is that?"

"Oh, sorry! Electroconvulsive therapy."

"Right," said Jaxx. "I've known people who've had that. I just didn't know they used it on kids."

"It's *super-safe* for cubs. It's like having your tonsils or wisdom teeth out – they're sleeping when we do it. They're in hibernation! It's *so* effective for depression. That's mostly when we use it but it really helps with her psychosis. There was always a taboo, out of ignorance more than anything else. You know: 'No ECT for the kiddies, please!' Which is *totally* unjustified – as you'll see by the results."

Big Bear Behavioral Health Center had a residential wing across the street from hospital, mostly for nonviolent kids transitioning to foster care. The living spaces were called Cub Cottages and each unit was presided over by a designated Mama or Papa Bear RN. (The dens were *a* through *h*; Trixanna was in *e*-Den.) Jaxx was surprised at how quiet and empty the place was. Maybe everyone was in school or on a field trip.

An aide brought her out. Trix knew he was coming but stared blankly before looking away. Jaxx thought she was probably just nervous and hoped that would burn off. They shook hands like polite strangers and went to sit in the dining room. She looked beautiful – luminous and spirited, like her mother. He wanted to hug her. He got emotional, and tamped the feelings down.

As she tore open the birthday gift box, Jaxx thought he made a terrible mistake. It was a floppy cat and he feared she'd suddenly tantrum over the real tabby she had lost. Instead, Trix gasped in pleasure. She closed her eyes and rocked, holding it close.

"He's just like Tabasco!" she exclaimed, without a hint of sadness.

He decided it was best to leave the whole topic alone.

She just turned fourteen. She wore pigtails in that complicated way Portia taught her, "for special occasions." He didn't know what to talk about and tried to relate by asking if she liked Billie Eilish. She shrugged. "What do you think about Meghan Markle maybe moving to L.A.?" She shrugged again. Jaxx already decided not to bring up Portia – he'd save that for another day, if there was one. He *did* say he wasn't using drugs anymore and had a job as a consultant, helping the same people who were responsible for putting him in jail. *That* tickled her funny bone.

He asked when she thought she might be leaving here. Trixanna said she'd already been there longer than anyone and would move to a group home in the next few weeks "if no one buys me." She told him the Mama Bears took her to adoption carnivals on the weekends where she met families who were looking for kids. She called them "auctions" and her mordant smile reminded him of Portia.

When it came time to go, he asked if he could visit again. She nodded, smiling at her shoes as she clicked them together. "If you're not here," he smirked, "I'll track down your 'buyers.'"

She laughed, suddenly taking his hand. "Want to see my room?"

She led him to a clean, sunlit space with two beds. She said that "my cellie" left a few days ago and it was nice to be alone.

Just then, Cappy the Mama Bear bounced into the room.

"Hey there, Trix! Giving your friend the royal tour?"

"*Yes*," she said. "But now I want to take a nap."

"Well all *rightie* then," said Cappy, winking at Jaxx. "Whatever Lola wants, Lola gets. A beauty rest it shall be."

Trix raced to the bed, holding her new cat close.

"Now, where did you get *that* fine feline?"

"Jaxx gave it to me!"

"He *did*? Wasn't that sweet of him?"

"Jaxx was in jail!" she tittered.

The Mama Bear, having spoken first with Detective Marengo, already knew. Still, a gentle reprimand was in order. "Now honey, that's not something your friend may want to broadcast to the world!"

"He's not my *friend*, he's *Jaxx*."

"It's okay," he said, winking. "Everyone knows I'm a jailbird."

They all had a laugh.

Cappy said, "I see he gave you that wonderful kitty. But did *you* give him *your* gift?"

Trixanna looked perplexed, then erupted in giggles. "I forgot!"

"It's lucky *I* didn't!" said the nurse.

Trix reached under the bed and pulled out a shoebox wrapped in paper made from magazine photos of young celebrities. With pride, she handed it to Jaxx. He opened it and froze, staring at what was inside.

"Now I don't know *why* it was so important she give this to you," said Cappy. "Or what it all *means*. But around here, we just do as Trix tells us to."

It was the license plate from the Elon scam – he remembered how pissed Portia was that she couldn't find it that Hallowe'en night. He held the battered metal in his hands like a dangerous, priceless object.

"What's this?" said Jaxx.

"I *buried* it. In the *yard*." Her eyes gleamed mischievously. "Back when I was *crazy*. I thought it was a *shield*, to *protect* me. I thought I could *use* it to save the *world*. I was going to free my father from *Pelican Bay*."

He was gutted.

Portia must have told her about Old Boy after all; she'd probably been too excited about the prospect of joining the Kardashian clan to contain herself. But had she given Trix the update that he *wasn't* her father, as well? Did her daughter even know he was dead?

Playing dumb, he said, "Your dad's in Pelican Bay?"

"Not anymore – he died. It was on the Internet. Do you like it?"

He realized Trix was talking about her gift to him.

"Yes!" he stammered. "*Very* much. And thank you."

Stricken with bashfulness, she raced to the bed and hid beneath the covers. She peeked out naughtily, then ran back to Jaxx and hugged his waist. Cappy looked startled but glad, as if never having seen the girl demonstrate such affection. Jaxx felt awkward but gradually succumbed, leaning over to hold her. She just wouldn't let go. He full-on ugly-cried and Trixanna's cheeks were wet with tears.

The nurse let them be.

* * *

In the weeks that followed the funerals, no one in the extended Neidhoff family came forward to contest his hastily scribbled endgame wishes – a bequeathal of $25 million to Promises Kept. There *was* some controversy amongst the foundation's board over whether to accept the tainted benefaction – yet it couldn't be argued that many, many children's lives would be bettered, if not outright saved. In the end, Hugh and Deborra-Lee decided to allow the gift to grow into a great, nourishing oak, albeit one that had been planted on a blood-soaked battleground.

Scholarship candidates were submitted in a lottery. The selection of Trixanna Coldstream was entirely coinciden-tal. She was among a group of beneficiaries in the first batch of "Guardian Angel" grants, each presented with stipends amounting (over time) to roughly $200,000 – the figure Arnold was meant to bring to his swindlers on that fateful night.

There was a reason the committee didn't make the connection between the girl and the endowment's provenance. On the same page that outlined the bequest, Arnold scrawled an unselfish afterthought: knowing his association to the charity would be radioactive, he stipulated that the source of the monies should remain anonymous for a cooling-off period of five years – after which, the identity of the grantors must be revealed and memorialized. Accordingly, it wasn't until Trixanna came of age that the curious, morbid link between she and her benefactors was made known. The Dickensian twist – her mother's killer making amends from beyond the grave – was revealed on Season Four of *The Snoop Files*, causing a stir on the Internet that culminated in the orphan's poignant appearance on the *Ellen Show*.

Just now, it was better no one knew.

It might be too soon for Jaxx to discover that Trixanna's emergency needs, future education and general welfare were "made possible by a gift from Raleigh and Cammy Neidhoff." Better not to know the truth about Trixanna's "angels" – for now – because it may have been a bit much.

Sometimes a thing can be too much.

He would talk to Matias in the morning about the adoption. The detective would write a glowing letter of recommendation. None of it would be easy – he was a single man with a criminal record. But Jaxx knew with utter certainty what was coming. He would raise this child as if she were his own, for she was beloved.

BOOK THREE

ENDGAME

Season Finale

CURRENT AFFAIRS

Though as a ghost, I shall lightly tread the summer fields.

- Hokusai

Garry Gabe

Nonconsensual Karma

Vaccinated by the indifference of a long, unblemished career, he was deaf to the pain and panic experienced by those for whom the Internet tolled. Until one day it tolled, trolled, and scrolled down – for him.

GG, as he was affectionately known in the industry, was a peer of Chuck Lorre, whom he considered to be a kind of cancer. Garry's hero and mentor was James Burrows, the eightysomething pioneer that launched a thousand shitcoms from *Laverne & Shirley* to *Cheers* to *3rd Rock,* and directed every single episode of *Will & Grace.* The difference between Lorre and Burrows was that Jimmy never aspired to be more than the workaday craftsman he was. Chuck had the gall to think of himself as an *artiste.* He wasn't even fit to polish Norman Lear's coffin.

One morning, out of the blue, Garry Gabe Vicker got ambushed in *The Reporter.* Women whose names and faces he didn't recognize came forward to denounce him as a sexual predator. The beloved showrunner's loyalists mobilized; GG's cheerleaders dutifully shook their pompoms, albeit with increasing lethargy toward week's end. Still friendly with a few canceled men, he knew what was coming. The bell had tolled but the squall of Google Alerts evoked a different metaphor: the apparatus from Kafka's "In the Penal Colony." A favorite of Garry's precocious adolescent bookworm years, the short story featured a torture machine that carved the letter of the law onto the backs of the condemned. The mutilation proved fatal within hours – but the targets of Time's Up had time to burn.

The luckiest of them had boats, beach houses and brownstones where they could properly isolate. Implosions of reputation, career and social status left more than one King Leer with a surprising sense of relief. *Free at last!* Free to do some serious meditating (wives, daughters and mistresses – not to mention David Lynch himself – had been gently trying to shove TM down their throats for years)... free now to make the most of that $300,000 in-house sushi bar, carving fish alongside a famous *itamae* flown in from Nagoya... free to strum the theremin instructor (the one with the cliché pale skin and Louise Brooks bob), after pre-paying a full year of caregivers for her special needs kid... free to visit Cuba or Mustique or St. Petersburg or Utah's Amangiri with whoever was tutoring Japanese or Hebrew or Catalan during breaks between anilingus at sundry UNESCO World Heritage Sites and seven-star hotels – at least till they got home and could fornicate in the birthday gifted Playa del Rey or Ventura or Rancho Mirage condo.

Free, free, free!

...to pretend to be testing the waters for a life partner, insinuating they were open to having more children (without mentioning the vasectomy). Free to fuck throwaway protégés on private planes and sloping Bel-Air lawns dotted by Nevelson spiders, Serra monstrosities, and marble, water seal-smooth Henry Moores – free to tongue the squeaky-clean manicured privates of indentured interns, bodyworkers, and anorexic desperadoes, on perfumed Santa Ana-blown nights.

The *unlucky* Time's Uppers went broke trying to put out consecutive fires of fresh allegations. To make things worse, their children were still in the penal colony of progressive middle schools, where bullies and mean girls got busy tattooing the sins of the fathers on their flesh, mind, spirit. Even favorite teachers were caught giving the shamed progeny side-eye.

After *Golden State*'s windfall Emmy sweep, Garry made an overall deal with Netflix in the low (very) nine figures. He had two ideas for his next project. One was about the "Hollywood Ripper," a case that tweaked public consciousness when Ashton Kutcher took the stand to testify that he'd dated one of the victims. The other proposal, far closer to his heart, explored the curious life and times of "The Fat Joan" Gamma and her wife, actress Ali Nell. The epic tale, magnificently strange and beautiful, seemed impossible to approach, but Garry finally found a way in.

As luck would have it, his boyhood chum was Joan's grandfather. Once an acclaimed novelist, Bud Wiggins fell into addiction and obscurity yet still managed to give lie to the adage there are no second acts in American lives – by suing Joan for a piece of the billions she inherited when her parents were murdered. A few weeks before Joan and Ali's deaths were made public, Bud went missing and was now presumed dead as well. Garry's epiphany was to have his old friend narrate the story from beyond the grave, like Bill Holden in *Sunset Boulevard*. The conceit would give both writer and audience sufficient distance from a story that in spite of being so contemporary had already become mythic. Bud would be the loser, the dreamer, the wounded Everyman overtaken by grief, failure and destiny. A bonus would be to rescue the brilliant, hapless writer from footnote status in the drama of a superstar couple that ended their lives at a clinic in Switzerland; in an avalanche, it isn't missing sherpas (or aged-out literary men) who captivate the world, but the entitled mountaineers that bucket-listed their way to the summit before littering the snowscape with their Moncler-clad wellness bodies. He'd always thought that Bud was a genius who had been misunderstood, forgotten, unfairly maligned; the series Garry planned not only had a chance to bestow the dignity that escaped him in life but to restore his only novel, *Wild Psalms,* to its rightful place in the canon.

While researching *Golden State,* Garry met Matias Marengo, who later became the homicide detective in charge of the Wiggins case. Foul play had been suspected but never proved; the blood in the car that Bud left at the Bonaventure turned out to be the novelist's own. To his chagrin, Marengo was never able to track down the stylish, tattooed woman on CCTV footage shown leaving his hotel room on the night he disappeared.

When Garry began to research the Fat Joan project, Matias led him to a dubious Israeli "contractor" named Moishe Fineman. Fineman had a long history as Vi and Raphie Gamma's security chief but wasn't working for them when they died. After the murders, he became Joan's guardian and de facto father figure. He lived in Israel – so he said – but was often in L.A. tending to nameless clients. When they met for coffee at a Dunkin' Donuts in La Crescenta, he told Garry a detail that Marengo notably withheld: Bud's last recorded act was to take a Lyft ride from the Bonaventure to Joan's house in Point Dume. When Garry tried to put a finer point on it, Fineman deflected, rambling about "the Great Game, as Kipling called it." The spymaster manqué was what they used to call a colorful character. In flights of screenwriter fantasy, Garry surmised that the Israeli was far more involved in the case than he would ever let on.

Much had already been written about the flamboyant, improbable folk hero Joan and her glamorous actress-invalid wife, ranging from slapdash instabooks to pretentious oral histories. An animated half-hour about the couple by the creator of *BoJack Horseman* was about to debut on Adult Swim and just this month, Alison Bechdel's graphic novel, "Saint Joan," was shortlisted for an important literary prize. Two "insider" tell-alls floated up from muddy depths before hastily returning to oblivion – an innocuous memoir penned by Ripley Labrador, Ali Nell's vulgarly witty stylist (now Andy Cohen's BFF), that was all about Ripley and nothing about the doomed actress; and a "remembrance" from the controversial, ink-stained hand of the debonair Dr. Phedan Pirouette. The unorthodox clinician's contention that Ali's ALS had been misdiagnosed (an untruth, as it turned out) provoked her ill-conceived announcement on the *Ellen Show*. Ever the showman, the announcement of the suspension of Pirouette's California medical license coincided with his book's release. He no longer lived on the Point Dume property, which had been acquired from the estate by a trust belonging to Post Malone. A Beanie Feldstein indie, "Bigger Than Life," flopped after being bought at Sundance for $8 million. A feature by Robert Eggers, the director of Joan's favorite film, *The Witch,* was in preproduction. Alex Gibney was doing a signature HBO doc and rumor had it Werner Herzog was halfway through his own. (Rumor also had it that Herzog had already abandoned his efforts.) Elton John denied composing songs for a musical, inciting Aaron Sorkin to deny he was writing the book for same. Depending on the media outlet, Amy

Schumer, Rebel Wilson and Patricia Arquette were negotiating to play Joan in filmographies directed by Phoebe Waller-Bridge, Peter Farrelly and Bong Joon-ho; no less than three operas were planned, with Kristin Stewart, Marina Rebeka and Billie Eilish agreeing to portray Ali Nell. Or so it was said.

But Garry wasn't dissuaded. He was certain that the zeitgeisty saga of Ali and Joan was on the cusp of being transformed – by someone, somewhere, *somehow* – into a towering work of art. How could it not be? The right person would inevitably come along to make a poetic, apocalyptic cautionary showbiz tale, satirical, tragic, transcendent: think *Joker* crossed with Cocteau by way of (dare he say it) Ryan Murphy. The *Succession* folks might sink their grandiose, nauseatingly clever hooks into it... anything was possible. With *Golden State,* Garry already achieved the miraculous: a lateral, hyperspace move that broke the sitcom showrunner box the Industry expected him to be buried in. *Fat Joan and the Phoenix* was essential to his late-blooming journey as a major artist. The outlandish urban legend that wanted to believe Ali Nell metamorphosed into a bird was balderdash – though he *would* embrace an element of magical realism. He was utterly captivated. The series would be his dreamwork and chef-d'oeuvre, his capstone and eulogy, his epitaph and goodbye.

Garry had no real premonition of his own mortality but was superstitious. He remembered talking on the phone with his friend Wes Craven a few months before he died of the brain cancer that had been in remission. The director spoke animatedly of a smorgasbord of development deals – as if they were a shield against what Wes knew was coming. But that wasn't Garry's style. He would focus solely on *Fat Joan,* with the *Ripper* as a back-up.

Two weeks after the *Reporter* exposé, just when the contract was set to close, Netflix informed that Ryan Murphy had decided to pursue the saga of Joan and Ali. The executive – the same who greenlit *Golden State* – hemmed and hawed, using the sickening phrase, "My bad." He told Garry, "Ryan 'officially' told us of his interest months ago but until yesterday, it was radio silence. We're contractually compelled."

Today is the first day of the rest of your cancelled life.

Garry wanted to sue but his lawyer advised against it.

"They paid you a *lot* of money and to bite the hand isn't a good look. Plus, we don't have grounds. They had 'first look' so you're free to shop it. Actually gives us more leverage to push *Ripper*. Netflix is going to want to play nice."

But Ryan got that one too, for *American Crime Story.*

In an unguarded moment, Garry said to one of his interns, "'You've Been Canceled' is the new 'You've Got Mail.'"

The boy smiled, pretending to know what he was talking about.

† † †

In 1987, Garry Gabe Vicker – the prolific director of hundreds of half hours, now enjoying an unlikely renaissance as *netflixauteur* – raped Summer Cobain, his married assistant. At the time, he was also married (and remains so, to the same woman). Not too long after the 18-month "affair" ended, Ms. Cobain killed herself; from then on, he clutched the horror like a rosary, clacking and worrying the beads, praying the talisman would provide redemption.

It wasn't until she died that he realized how much he loved her. He wasn't sure if it were guilt, or the primal, idyllic notion of irretrievably lost love that unhinged him. Whatever it was, GG panicked, like someone who finds himself in a stalled, smoky elevator. For the first time in his life, unthinkably, he smelled the fumes of madness itself. If it *was* guilt, that would have been shabby but easier. The alternative – to have let something rare, majestic, and eternal slip away – was too damning.

Even though it was Summer who had been dumped, the pretentious soundtrack of his life became Schubert's *lieder* of broken young men as they set out on marathon death marches away from home, banished by the ladies that spurned them. He was ashamed at his pretensions; to salve a guilty conscience, he had the audacity to compare himself to Kierkegaard, who'd pushed away his fiancé Regine Olsen because he couldn't be unfaithful to his true calling: his writing work. He became a connoisseur of masochistic romance, devouring haunted anthologies of poems about lost love, impossible love, mangled love. His studies went deep. He gave himself a PhD in Roland Barthes' scientific encyclopedia of heartbreak, *A Lover's Discourse*, and reread books from college including *The Sorrows Of Young Werther*, a thin, overheated 18th-century melodrama of suicide and unrequited romance. He self-soothed with the late poems of Thomas Hardy, who after his wife's death rode a horse to visit all the places they intimately came to know during courtship – then asked that his heart be removed before cremation and buried with her (and it was) – and drew solace that Robert Graves threw himself from the window above the one his lover had leapt from moments before.

GG wished he had the balls.

Instead, he made an uneasy pact with Summer's spirit, postponing the consequences of what he had done until a horse arrived to carry him, heart and hat in hand, to her grave.

† † †

"We're vetting them," said Marmal, of the *Reporter* accusers.

Garry's first impulse was to hire Donna Rotunno but his daughter talked him out of it. "Lawyering up with Harvey Weinstein's gal is *super*-shitty optics," said Regan. He said he thought it was important to be repped by a woman, but she talked him out of that too. "It's gonna look like a *move*, Dad. Look, whatever you do, you can't win, okay? And if you can't *win*, you may as well hire Sammy Marmal. He's probably the only one who's tough and smart as Donna, anyway." Last night, Regan sent him a photo of a t-shirt with I BELIEVE HER... AND HER, AND HER AND HER written across the front. She was trying to lift his mood, but it sent him into a rage of impotence.

Of the two women featured in the exposé, he *almost* remembered Khloe – and was *certain* he never met Dianne. Both were lying through their teeth, that much he knew. He understood that memory was fungible but when Summer died, the rules governing his life instantly became rigid and absolute; as an amends, he grew devoutly, assiduously virtuous in his behavior and actions toward women. Reflexive reparations, muttered like devotions while fingering the ghostly rosary of remorse, demanded he take the mantle of *le misérable*, though as one who'd stolen a life, not a loaf. (His own Inspector Javert, Summer Cobain, nipped at his heels from the grave.) Ever after, he was known as a *menimist* – that dreaded word signaling a privileged white male hobbyist – renowned as an equal rights éminence grise and full-throated women's advocate. His bonafides were duly noted by historians of the Industry and acknowledged on the national stage.

Garry hired a publicist and asked her to sit in on the meeting with his attorney. She specialized in disgraced, horny showbizzers.

"It's easier to discredit women like this, or *can* be, when they ask for money," said Marmal. "Unfortunately, shaking the money tree is *not* the trend of the day."

"*Attention* is the new money," said the publicist, trying to earn her keep. "Everybody wants *attention*."

"If it was he-said-she-said..." interjected Garry, before trailing off, exasperated. "But how do you fight this? How can I fight *she-said-she-said*?"

"You don't," said Marmal. "If you fight, you lose, because we have a knife but they're bringing guns. So, we *don't* fight – we overcome. It's Aikido at the O.K Corral. We bend, not break. We let *them* break."

"In these narratives, it's the memory game," said the publicist, sounding more like a therapist now – or forensic shrink. "It's *Rashomon*."

"Great movie," said Marmal.

"A lot of what I do," she said, "is whittle away at perceptions. I bring a little gray to a black-and-white picture. Sometimes a *lot* of gray! That's what we did with Jeffrey."

"Epstein?" said Garry, recoiling.

"Tambor." So much water and so many bodies had floated under the #MeToo bridge that if she hadn't sent the link last night to Tambor's interview in the *Reporter*, Garry wouldn't have even remembered the dustup ending in the actor's dismissal from *Transparent*. "A measured response like Jeffrey's might be something to consider."

Garry caught himself looking at her toned body as she spoke.

"But he *knew* those women!" he barked. "And Jeff was nasty, he was *mean*, he *said* that he was! Those women worked for him!"

"*With* him," she corrected, already grooming her client for the interrogations to come, should he agree to go the high-class interview route that she would suggest. "Some of this might be 'copycat' – it's *crazy* how many women came forward this month. It's like 2017 again!"

"This... *person* – this *Khloe*" – the name was like dirt in his mouth – "this *makeup artist* I spent *two seconds* with in my life... *apparently* I said to her, 'Hey, take a look at this great big penis! Wouldn't you like this blue-veined monster to go deep inside of you?' I *paraphrase* but it's not far from the truth – you cannot *write* the kind of shit she said. And then I'm nude! Chasing her down the street like Leatherface! Why did she leave out the chainsaw? Huh, Sammy? Why'd she leave out that I was wielding a fucking chainsaw! But oh she *will*, you better *believe* she'll recover *that* detail after a little hypnosis. Jesus *Christ* – fucking ludicrous. It'd be laughable if it weren't so craven and pathetic. And 'Dianne,' whoever *that* is, *Dianne* says I patted her leg under a table 40 years ago – 40 years ago! – which caused her to spend the rest of her life alone, depressed, addicted and fucking suicidal..."

The infelicitous mention of the S-word evoked another one – *Summer* – promptly sending him back to the penal colony. But this time, the etching machine was even more diabolical: though now wrongly accused, his original sin made martyrdom moot. Each time GG dared raise his voice against how he'd been wronged, his woof was silenced by a painful jolt, like a dog in a shock collar. He was fucked, even if Summer Cobain never existed: she-said-she-said was a superbug that no drug nor protestation of innocence could kill.

He could tell that Sammy'd had enough of the publicist but was being courteous. She seemed to feel the vibe as well.

"We have a few options," she said, in wrap-up mode. "The best one, I think, is to release a short, elegant denial of the accusations, expressing compassion for *all* victims who've had the bravery to come forward. A few days later, we follow up with an open letter of support from friends. *Women.* Actresses, writers, colleagues. A second option is do nothing – for now. And take the temperature at the end of the week."

Garry had a more pressing to-do list:

1. He immediately had to call Netflix and tell them the accusations were bogus. He would talk more with Sammy about the likelihood of his contract's "rescission" – as CBS had effected with Les Mooves – which would nullify tens of millions still owed;

2. In a few months, Women In Media was giving him a special award at the Paley Center Gala. Garry needed to get ahead of that and call them directly, to bow out. The publicist would draft a press release explaining that he didn't want to be a distraction "for this wonderful organization that has been such an amazing champion – as have I – for women's rights, equal pay," &tc. (She later advised that it would be better to omit the *as have I.* He scrawled in the margin, *I'm on the board of a number of groups that mentor women. How to deal with shitstorm?* So many shitstorms to come!)

3. For the last six months, he was having trouble writing
   in longhand. His internist said it was probably what they
   call an intentional tremor but the neurologist at Cedars
   confirmed it was Parkinson's. He hadn't told his wife and
   daughter.

Marmal stood to shake her hand. Both watched her ass as
she walked out the door. "I like her," said the attorney.

"Sorry – I should have told you I was bringing her."

"No worries. The more the merrier."

"The more *accusers*, the merrier."

A little gallows humor.

"I'm not worried about these two Jane Does," said Marmal.

"They're Jane Does? They're not using their real names?"

"*Of course* they are but I don't give a shit. At the end of the
day, they're *Jane* fucking *Does*. No one will remember their
names." His face pinched. "I did get a call this morning from a
lawyer I've never heard of in San Diego – 'Maynard C. Krebs.'
At first I thought it was a joke, you *cannot* make this shit up.
He said he has a client coming forward… with allegations."

"Please. Please tell me you are fucking kidding me."

"When it rains, it pours. This one may be more of a
problem."

"I'm trapped in the first season of *Black Mirror*!"

"Her name," he said, looking at a note, "is Imogen Waldorf-
Windsor. Sounds like *she's* trapped in *The Crown* – or *Fleabag*."
He handed Garry the Facebook printout of a dolled-up, over-
weight woman in her fifties. "Ever seen her before?" GG softly
shook his head. He was in shock and no longer inhabited the
room. "She wants a million to go away. Which actually works
for us. I went through the same thing with Ryan."

"Murphy?"

"Seacrest. She *alleges* that she met you in Vegas, at something called… the ScreenTime convention." He glanced at his notes again. "In 2008. Said you invited her to your room for a drink. Says her drink tasted funny."

"Jesus God."

"Dame Waldorf Salad claims she woke up on the floor next to the bed. Her words: 'He stood over me in his robe. When I got home, I noticed I was bruised.' Let's see… she goes on, you this, you that, yadda yadda," he said, riffling the notes. "Oh, here it is: 'DNA was visible on my chest.' Her words – not semen, not spluge, not fun-spunk, but *DNA*. 'He stood over me and said, "You look like you need a cup of coffee."' And that was when – she alleges – you forced cunnilingus. 'I was too scared and disoriented to leave…'"

"Bullshit! Bullshit! Bullshit! Okay, I'm done. I'm not going to do this, Sammy! I am not going to be blackmailed!"

"*Of course not.* But you need to calm down, all right, Garry? Because we are at the *beginning* of a long and winding road. We *will* get to where we want to be but it's going to take a minute. Okay? It's going to take a minute and it's going to take nerves of steel. So *you*, my friend, need to meditate or do yoga or smoke one of those marijuana pens or *whatever* – and prepare yourself for battle. Because I need you to go back and see if you were ever at the ScreenTime convention in Las Vegas." Garry started to interrupt but Sammy raised a hand. "Don't say anything! Don't say anything *now*. When you get home, I want you to take a look at your calendar. My office can help. I have a crack team of cyberheroes that can do a deep forensic dive into your digital life. If you *were* there, I want to know the *hotel* you were at, who you were *with*, what your *schedule* was, what you had for fucking *breakfast*, okay? – whatever's documented or whatever you can remember. Take these home," he said, handing him an envelope. "And pour yourself a stiff drink. Treat yourself to one of those Percocets you've been hoarding from the dentist."

"How'd you know."

"We *all* hoard Percocet from the dentist. And don't worry. If you worry, they win. Snoop will sort it out. He's looking into *Lady Windsor-Waldorf* as we speak. You must know Snoop – Richie Raskin?"

"I do. He's a friend of a detective I know."

"I figured you might have met him in your research travels."

"Is there going to be a press conference?" said Garry.

"There's always a press conference."

Adele

Living with IBS

"*How* – how – HOW is that unfunny twat doing the new Marvel? Wha? Like, you're telling me *Mustang* is actually starring in the new – "

Adele Cobain was shocked and outraged. The bulletin had been delivered courtesy of a vanilla standup named Coral Pelz as they stood in the closet-sized dressing room of The LaffTrack, a grotty cyst of a club nestled in the groin of that Disney-fed terminus called Anaheim.

"Who even told you that?" asked Adele.

"I don't know," sighed Coral, wishing she never mentioned it.

"But like *what* Marvel movie? An *Avengers*?"

"Isn't *The Avengers*, like, *over*? Didn't Robert Downey die?"

"Those movies are never fucking over!"

"It's maybe something called 'Shang'-something? I think Awkwafina's in it and one of the *Mulan* stars – "

"*Shang*? What the fuck is that, like, a Kung Fu?"

"Google it, Adele," she said, rolling her eyes.

"Fuck *you*, Coral. If this is fake news..."

Mustang and Adele were on the same poverty train comedy club circuit. Well, *not anymore*. Two years ago they got drunk and Addie ate her out in the green room of a Boston rathole called HAHAHA, an act of kindness for which Tammy Tang – nicknamed Mustang by school friends when her parents Sweet Sixteen'd her with an old GT (or so the phony origin story went) – never evinced one ounce of gratitude, even though the bitch had to cram a fist in her own mouth so as not to scream when she came.

The past year, Mustang was pretty much MIA, an absence that started to make sense if what Coral was telling her were true. For a while there'd been gossip that Tammy supplemented her go-nowhere jester income with part-time gigs like voiceovers and crappy regional TV ads that no one ever saw. Which is why Adele diss-dubbed her "Miss Taskrabbit, Work For Hire." Actually, she pivoted between Taskrabbit and "Sandra *Whoa*" – owing to Mustang's ugly-sexy look, a cheap knockoff of the *Killing Eve* star's charismatically cubist face. The bottom line was that Adele thought Taskrabbit deserved all the shit she could sling at her, having committed the original sin of... *not being funny!* If you were funny, Adele forgave everything. If you weren't, you were fair game for a neverending, backstabby roast.

Taskrabbit was supposedly sober but Adele never saw her at meetings, except once at a woman's stag in the Valley, just a few months after licking her ungrateful puss. A Twelve-Step yenta started whispering about how "Mustang's making a *fortune* doing commercials in the red states." Typical AA bullshit. Then one night at 4AM, there she was, in a low-rent insurance ad – some Aflac rip-off requiring an off-beat, off-white mug. She didn't have any lines, so the *making a fortune* part had to be another lie because you couldn't score those residuals if you didn't open your fucking mouth. No one ever got rich being a SAG-defined "featured extra," though maybe there were some exceptions… Adele auditioned for the role of an angry bowel last year that would have had a giant payday (or so her agent implied). She never got called back. Sure enough, a few weeks after seeing her nemesis in the wannabe Aflac, Sandra *Whoa* appeared in the very same IBS spot Adele tried out for, her homely face ticcing and shticking above a fat tube of intestine before suddenly giving chase to a Boomer lady in a park. Adele had to admit that an inflamed, Crip-walking bowel was actually kind of funny.

Good job, Taskrabbit!

The laughs ended when she started seeing the ad sixty times a day.

Adele struggled to push the breaking news of Mustang's marvel out of her head, otherwise it would seriously fuck with her act. Thank God Judd Apatow wasn't in the audience tonight or Jeff Ross or Whitney Cummings… or David Spade – she *so* wanted to be asked on *Lights Out*. In the months since he found his groove, David was really starting to give back. Local comics were doing guest spots all the time. When his scouts saw a standup they liked, the unknown was invited to tape a "tight five." If you did well, David might ask you to join the panel. You'd go from total obscurity to being on television, Whitney on one side and Nikki Glaser on the other. Adele knew if she got the chance to do a tight five, she'd *rock*.

But tonight, she was over it.

There was barely an audience at all...

Trooper that she was, Adele went out there on autopilot, doing her tried and true *anal du jour* – teachers giving lessons in anal to middle school hotties, nursing home folks getting their crusty asses invaded by transgender orderlies, Jeffrey Epstein getting reamed in Hell by Steve Irwin, Liberace, whomever. *Anal this, anal that, anal all the livelong day.* She segued to her Hinge profile: "loves cuddling after abortions." The crowd was so sparse that there weren't even the usual groans, which was actually perfect because it reminded Adele the transgressive material just wasn't working anymore. Thousands of desperate, potty-mouthed comediennes were doing the exact same thing; the envelope had been pushed out further than a vaginal prolapse, the latter being another thematic fave of all the punch-drunk, punchline "funny ladies." *It worked for Sarah Silverman and Amy Schumer – but that was then, and this is now.* Adele disgusted herself. She knew the only way forward was to talk about her own life, to be more "actress" than standup. That's how Mustang started getting noticed. Still, the prospect bored her. *I will not exploit my mother's suicide by sharing it with the shitty, indifferent world. I will not honor my father's abandonment of me and Celeste.* To monologue about your banal sorrows – to be "uproariously moving," as the critics loved to lie – was the stuff of podcasts and failed memoirs, concomitant to admitting defeat. Adele thought what she *really* needed was something to set her apart from all the clit-baiting, rusty trombone/blowjob-obsessed Nikki knockoffs, something to catch the eye of an Apatow or *Lights Out* co-producer, for real – one of those golden tickets that hip, slumming *NYT* journalists made a hobby of "discovering" like truffle-snorting pigs. Say, a nice, non-fatal Tig Notaro cancer or a confession of MS: deadpan observational comedy delivered in the quaver of spasmodic dysphonia, ya know, Seinfeld with a harder edge. Maybe she could cultivate some kind of droll, Aspergerian pathology, a Hannah Gadsby spectrum-vibe that let the performer off the hook of having to actually be funny because a cerebral Ted Talk-style act hoodwinked the audience into believing they were watching something revolutionary, something bigger than comedy and life itself. Something...

...*uproariously moving.*

Sadly, all Adele had was anger issues and a few maraschino cherry-sized fibroid tumors that she *could* upgrade to endometriosis – but Lena Dunham already beat her to it, and beat it to death.

She launched into her trademark brutalist trollfest:

I wish I'd slept with Robin Williams... when he had dementia. Oh my God, that'd have been *so* cool. Like, for once I wouldn't have had to worry, "Does he think I'm funny?" Cause when you sleep with a comedian – by the way, I try to sleep mostly with black comics because they have the biggest jokes, their jokes are fuckin *scary*. They refuse to give head, but *man* do they make up for it with those girthy, uncut, purple-headed jokes... seriously though, when you sleep with a standup, there's always a subtext: *Who's funnier?* At the end, Robin didn't know what funny *was* anymore, bless his soul. His tongue had trouble forming words – which I'd be totally okay with, as long as it could find my asshole. *Mork & Mindy...* I never even *watched* that shitty show! I wonder if in the end Robin couldn't remember what "Nanu Nanu" was. Imagine trying to explain *Nanu Nanu* to someone with Lewy Body Dementia. Such a weird name for a disease. Maybe they meant "Louis CK Body Dementia." "*Well*, Robin, ya see, the phrase 'Nanu Nanu' is actually an Orkan greeting..." And I know I totally would have fucked him like a dude – like, only focused on taking care of my own needs. Wham bam thank you Mork! *Especially* if I knew that his *thing* turned out to be instead of smoking a cigarette after, like his thing was to *hang* himself... if I knew *that* was the plan, I'd *definitely* have made the sex last longer – I mean, so the world could have had him a few minutes longer. You know, try to straight-up come again. Oh, look! They're leaving – did I cross the line? Is it too soon? He's been dead ten fucking years, is that too soon? There's only three people in this comedy Chernobyl and two are leaving! *Congrats, bitches.* I'm shocked and actually kinda impressed you lasted this long. Buh-*bye!* Hey, it's okay. I don't think they were comedy aficionados, anyway. Fucking dumb MAGA fascists. Though maybe not – who am I to judge? Maybe they rushed out so they wouldn't miss Colbert. Maybe they were in a hurry to catch Bill Maher on *Real Time.* Or catch that 90th *amazing* Dave Chappelle Netflix special... or didn't want to miss *Lights Out!* That's right! Spade freaks! None of em know how to record shit on their DVR. Naw... they're probably just killing time till that text from 24-hour Walgreens lights up their stolen iPhone. *Dear Customer, your Oxycontin and Adderall is now ready.* Live it up, you MAGA pieces of shit. Pick up your Walgreen dope and splurge on those *awesome* twirling Chicken Ranch taquitos 7-Eleven keeps in that dirty aquarium on the counter. Hurry back to your room and post encrypted dark web "America's Funniest Motel 6 Videos," the ones where people pay to see you and the wife jack off your developmentally disabled toddler. MAGA family fun!

† † †

Driving back to Silver Lake where Adele roomed with Big Sis, she circled back to the bejeweled vomit of Mustang's good fortune. Getting cast in a Marvel movie was like winning a billion-dollar Powerball – it didn't make *sense*, in the way the outside world no longer made sense to a deeply grieving or incarcerated person. Why, *how*, would the universe conspire to make that happen? If only she too could find a way to break the code. If Addie could alter her abysmal fate – which *might* still be possible (she prayed), if her path was fluid and not fixed.

What I would give to be announced in a new Marvel! What I would give –

Home now, in bed with her airbook, stoned and overcome. Flooded by the sensuous glory and golden religion of breaking through to the other side, her cynicism melted away: to star or costar in a Marvel became a cellular soak, the new Hero's journey, a prospect both frightening and ennobling, impossibly possible, like pulling a sword from a rock.

In an instant, Mustang became the beacon that would light the way. Hadn't destiny thrown them together, sealing their pact in the cellar of a dingy Boston laugh club? Adele surrendered to the hungry, cosmic need of being a Marvel family member, a voluptuous, primal yearning that must have been close to what

Mustang herself experienced prior to her initiation. After musing about her adoption into the MCU, Adele binged on other fantasias, ecstatically live-streaming the royal fallout that came from being crowned Marvelous: an anointment by Howard Stern (as he had anointed Amy and Sarah and Nikki and so many others); guest-hosting *Ellen* while the host was in Africa; headlining *SNL* and loitering onstage while the end credits famously rolled. Hooking up with some of the show's musical guests, getting her ovaries tongued-tied by Halsey and DaBaby and Billie Eilish, while Finneas tripped and rolled blunts.

She boned up on the Marvel character "Shang-Chi," a mortal and martial artist who somehow managed to join the Avengers. His dad was a Thanos/Darth Vader-type and his archenemy was "The Mandarin." The usual cockamamie, nerdy stroke book dumbfuckery – but *obviously* there was something she'd been missing all these years because so many people Adele admired and secretly coveted were busy enlisting.

> This is Angelina Jolie's first foray into the Marvel Cinematic Universe. She surprised fans by showing up to the official cast announcement at San Diego's Comic Con on July 20. Wearing a sexy LBD, the superstar told the packed hall, "I'm so excited to be here! I think of what it means to be a part of the MCU, what it means to be an Eternal, what it means to be in this family. We've all read the script and we know what the task is and so we are going to work very, very hard."

Everyone was always humbled and grateful to be chosen. It didn't matter if they'd won Academy Awards or done Lear at the Royal National Theatre – each rapturously recommitted to the passion and monastic discipline of their craft, to the certainty of a world audience's unconditional adulation. *I would work hard too,* thought Adele tearfully. (The edible kicked in.) *Harder than anyone!*

The cliché was true: family was everything. Being an MCU family member would save her, like the dying boy on Channel 7 whose parents had already signed off on organ harvesting – when suddenly he woke up. The only thing the kid said he remembered was standing in an open field.

That's where Adele wanted to be: a biblical open field, snatched from the comedy club caravan as she crisscrossed this dying, unfunny nation. She had paid her dues, and would finally be finished, she was done! The MCU would teleport her to a grassy, empyrean plain with wheatstalks and bulrushes: barefoot and godsmelling, seared yet cleansed, she'd stand tall, royal, gorgeous, immortal – like Evan Rachel Wood in *Westworld*, or unshackled Meghan, back on the hiking trail in L.A. with her Archie. Free, lustrous, lustful, beaming! God's breath on her nape, Addie saw herself as the adventuress on the mesmerizing cover of an old sci-fi paperback that once belonged to their mother. Summer was a big reader of Asimov and Heinlein. Dirty-cheeked, wounded, in a scant, bosomy leather vest, the cosmic diva stared up at a seven-mooned sky ready for battle, the broken rocket ship far behind her. *Good riddance.* What did superheroes need of rocket ships? Adele closed her eyes to imagine herself exhausted, walking smoky intergalactic fields after an interstellar clash, alien mud squooshing up between her toes – the brave new world somehow smelling like the head of a newborn.

All suffering would at last be lifted…

She hadn't been this stoned in a long, long time.

I don't have Musty's email, should I just send a text? I wonder if she still has the same number… oh *shit,* what if she heard I've been calling her mean names? Or ghosts me because she thinks I'm gonna say something about having had sex with her on Twitter and she doesn't want the studio to find out – which would be *dumb*, because Marvel was finally getting woke or trying to and anyway, fans would *love* finding out Musty was ambisexual, genderqueer, whatever... the MCU would be so supportive and encourage her to tell all. She strained her brain wondering what specific role Mustang was cast in. There was all this stuff on the Internet about Shang Chi but nothing about what part Mustang was going to play. What if it isn't comedic? What if it's a breakout dramatic turn as a god or bodhisattva and they make her *beautiful*, what if she's one of those people the camera just loves, the quirkier you look, the more amazing you *present*... what if it's not a "character" role, what if she's one of the leads, with superpowers greater than Brie or Scarlett or any who came before her –

No doubt the headstrong Mustang would have special "ideas" to contribute to the project. No doubt she'd give the studio notes and the notes would be welcomed and embraced. No doubt she'd end up on talkshows riffing about how the process was a "true collaboration with my MCU family." She would charmingly share about her pre-Marvel life and how she once played an angry bowel to make ends meet ("My very first superhero role!"), which the fans would totally love and *relate* to because everyone has their struggles, though none but a lucky few would ever experience a leap to immortality such as hers, nor could ever fathom the beatitude and riches the Marvel Universe conferred –

How I pray, thought Adele, nodding out, *that my destiny isn't fixed.*

Celeste

Crisis Actor

In 1988, when Celeste was six, her mother hanged herself four months after giving birth to Adele. Years later, Celeste's therapist guessed that Summer Cobain was suffering from postpartum depression; back then, the mood disorder hadn't fully entered the pop lexicon. After her death, Dad stayed in the apartment on Lillian Way and Fountain, moving them in with his folks in Van Nuys. An electrician on a long-running sitcom, Conrad was slowly falling apart. He got fired for being drunk at a live show, cashed out his pension, and lost every penny at Hollywood Park. A flat-earth adherent, he fell off the edge not long after.

The memories were growing dim, but she could recall him bringing her to the studio when her mom was still alive. She loved it because the cast and crew fussed over her; she was mascot for the day. Celeste didn't have an actress bone in her body but over the years convinced herself that "the business" was in her blood. After years of failed auditions, she got steady work as a movie extra and even had a SAG card. It was a fun way to keep a foot in the glamour door and make a little money too. (When their grandparents died, they left the sisters $85,000 but that was three years ago and the money was all gone.) If she had trouble paying the rent, she supplemented her work as an extra by doing rideshare.

Last week on a movie set, Celeste was talking with a gal – they were listed on the call sheet as "Persons In A Crowd" – about the crazy jobs they'd taken to get by.

"I even thought of getting a job as a crab fisher on *Deadliest Catch*," said the new friend. "Another thing I'm thinking is to become a dealer."

"A drug dealer?" said Celeste, shocked.

"Ha! I wish! A *card* dealer. Though maybe drug dealing is *next*. Ha! What's great is, once you learn how to deal – blackjack or whatever – I think you make the most money dealing baccarat – you can get a job at *any* of the casinos. There's one in Hawaiian Gardens, a half-hour from my house! I don't think they play *baccarat* there, but they play a lot of other weird games… there's Morongo and of course Vegas. *Anywhere*. Once you're trained, you pretty much have carte blanche. There's always a shortage of dealers." For now, she was exploring another vocation: closet organizer. "You can make $300 a day for arranging rich ladies' shoes."

"Nice work, if you can get it," said Celeste with a twinkle, adding that it "might be fun – for neatness freaks like myself."

† † †

When she read the article online, Celeste was triggered:

The Hollywood Reporter

7:22 AM 1/3/2020 by **Jake Desmoines**

Garry Gabe Vicker, multi-hyphenate creator of the acclaimed limited series *Golden State,* has been accused of sexual assault in incidents dating back over three decades. Before his Emmy-winning dramatic turn for Netflix, the showrunner was a prolific television director known for classic sitcoms starring empowered, unconventional women.

Dianne Delongpre told the *Reporter* that Vicker touched her thigh under the table at a restaurant in New York in 1983. "It was made worse," she said, "because I was sitting next to my husband at the time. This wasn't a drunken grope – which would have been inexcusable, because that kind of behavior is never okay – it was more like a premeditated assault. His hand kept moving up. I dug my nails in, to make him stop but he just laughed at me. I was so shaken that I told my husband I wasn't feeling well, and we left."

In the most serious allegation, Khloe Kerrigan, a former makeup artist, said she met Vicker at a party in Malibu in 1991.

"He invited me to his home. He said he was unhappy with the skin tone of some of the characters on *Angela*," said Kerrigan. "It was late, and yes, we'd had a few drinks, but I was absolutely not inebriated. I respected his work and as far as I was concerned there was no reason to believe it was going to be anything but a totally professional business meeting. Within seconds of being inside the door, he took his clothes off and grabbed me between the legs, bruising me. 'Look at my penis!' he shouted. 'Isn't it big? You want my big penis, don't you? You must not resist!' I was in shock and said, 'I do not want that. It is inappropriate. I am here for a professional meeting.' He was like Jekyll and Hyde. I ran crying from the house, and he chased me into the street, naked. He was screaming. 'You must do this or your career will go away! With a snap of my fingers, I can make that happen.' I was in shock but remember saying to myself, 'Is this real? Can this really be happening?' I didn't leave my bed for two weeks. I stopped eating and bathing. I was afraid to tell my therapist but did end up telling a girlfriend. She told me not to report it because he was so powerful, and no one would believe me. She said it wasn't worth it and I should just move on. But I was so traumatized, I never really did."

When Celeste was a day player on *Community*, she actually spent some time with Khloe, then a makeup artist on the show. (She had just two lines – in a gag with Donald Glover! – but it was cut. Two lines was still her personal best.) They bonded in a trailer on the parking lot of LA City College while Khloe applied a funny nose prosthetic for the scene.

And of course she knew "GG."

When she graduated from Occidental as a Theater Arts major, Grandma suggested she call "Mr. Vicker."

"He was the best boss your mother ever had, so you never know. He might hire you for a big part on one of his shows! Were you aware," she said, with wet eyes, "that he paid for her funeral?" She brushed away a tear. "I'm sure he'd like to help. You might be the one doing *him* a favor."

She got up the courage to call – that would have been sometime in the early 2000s – and Garry couldn't have been nicer. They had lunch on the Warner Brothers lot. When the talk came around to Summer, he winced the saddest of smiles, eyes like tiny frozen ponds. He asked about Conrad and was genuinely upset when she told him about the man's troubles in the wake of his wife's death. "My sister and I don't even know if he's alive." GG asked about Adele *pro forma* and was delighted when Celeste said that she was starting to do open mics at comedy clubs. And of course, she told him about her theater studies. As they left the commissary, Garry said he would see about getting her some work. True to his word, two weeks later a casting person on *Pixietown* hired her for a walk-on. (Another role that was cut but she had so much fun.) In the months that followed, she auditioned a few times at GG's behest. Nothing ever came of it but they stayed in touch. To this day, she got the random holiday or friendship postcard.

The article in the *Reporter* left a bad taste. Celeste had read this sort of Me Too laundry list before and considered herself an amateur necromancer, fancying that she could separate the legitimately aggrieved from the gold diggers and attention whores. The funny thing was, she remembered really *liking* Khloe. While Celeste sat in the *Community* makeup chair, the woman's outrageous monologue was still vivid. The theme was always the same: women needed to "do what's necessary." *It's your own damn fault if you sleep your way to the bottom instead of the top.* She had the kind of snarky-dark Adele humor that put Celeste in hysterics.

Well, one of them was lying and it for sure wasn't Garry.

Reading such awful things about him hurt her stomach. He paid for Mom's funeral! And was always a perfect gentleman, doing his best to throw work her way. But apart from all that, Celeste knew in her heart that he was a good man, a decent man, a caring, giving soul. She hated seeing *anyone* wronged. She decided to act on her impulse to call – it really did feel like the right thing. He might not welcome it, but even the smallest of gestures could make a difference.

Her grandma told her so.

† † †

Celeste got cast as a "Random Person, Running" in a Marvel prequel. During a lunch break, one of the extras told her about a side gig that sounded outlandish but intriguing. The woman was already getting paid much more than Celeste because she wore a policewoman's uniform and spent the day shouting commands at Random, Running Persons as they fled from whatever green screen menace.

She told Celeste there were special schools that helped train doctors and social workers. What they did was provide surrogates for them to interview or examine, as a way of gaining experience.

"You make $25 an hour and it's fun! All you do is impersonate a patient. They show you how. It's pretty easy. You can make up to *sixty-five an hour* for breast and pelvic exams. Kinda like hooking up online," she laughed. "Just kidding. It's totally legit."

Celeste went for an interview with the clinical director the next day.

"I see you're a theater major," he said, giving her application a once-over. His office was in an adjunct building of a college in Inglewood. "We get a lot of those but sometimes it's a hindrance. It's interesting – most of the people who do really well for us are engineers and accountants. We *strongly* discourage 'overacting.' In the world of Standardized Patients, less is definitely more."

It wasn't just "disease simulation" that was required. Rape victims and battered women were also popular staples of the growing role-play repertoire of patient-healthcare worker interaction. He told Celeste she might even have a scene partner – "something you may already have experienced in an acting class situation." For example, the director said she could find herself paired with a "husband" when a sensitivity training scenario called for educating students on how to inform a nervous "waiting room couple" that their baby had passed away. Sometimes, he said, SPs worked from scripts. The whole thing was mind-blowing. Celeste thought it might even rekindle her passion for acting.

The training period included a checklist of the basics that Standardized Patients needed to be conversant in, so they could "grade" their students: the proper way vital signs were taken, the art of palpation, the four places of the heart that had to be covered during auscultation – that sort of thing. After each exam, the surrogates were charged with telling their supervisor which signs and clues were missed or glossed over. The doctors-in-training were allowed to give feedback too, thus becoming part of the "creative" process. That was something not even actresses were allowed, unless they were famous.

Celeste was a natural. Uncannily mirroring the symptoms of whatever ailment or syndrome was required, she was empathic and gently articulate in her comments as well. To one student, she said, "When I told you I was having trouble getting my landlord to repair the ceiling, I was hoping you would have explored that. I'd have told you there was mold." To another, "I *loved* how you responded when I said that my brother died last month. You were so warm and caring! It made it so much easier to open up about my physical issues." And another: "You established good rapport, but I wondered why you didn't ask more about the tremor."

One day after work, she had a drink with an SP who'd been at the game a while. She was in her early fifties and made $35,000 a year to "pretend."

"Oh, I have *seen* some shit," she said, with a devilish smile. "I wound up fucking a student who did a pelvic on me."

"Oh my God!" said Celeste, not expecting that. "Isn't that dangerous?"

"For who?" she laughed.

"For *both* of you."

"Are you one of those paranoid people? Or are you just Debby Downer." She laughed again. "We were doing a morning of P.I.D.s – Pelvic Inflammatory Disease. Which I actually once had. *Twice.* P.I.D. is *not* a good look. The smell! So I was good at 'presenting.' Not good *enough* though, 'cause the dummy thought it was uterine cancer."

She cackled and finished her drink.

Celeste hadn't yet been asked to "do" a pelvic – that's where the big SP money was – and was curious. "When he… when they do an exam like that, are there other people in the room?"

"In this litigious world? Oh, *hell* yeah. They got *cameras* – they say they're for 'training purposes' but that's bullshit. It's for legal *defense,* should the need come about. Your privates become public! I call it *candida camera* – "

"Is it, like, a gynecologist?" smirked Celeste, trying to mask her prudishness. "Does he go all the way in?"

"Not till that night he didn't," she winked. "But for real – they do a straight-up, gloved exam. It's legit, has to be. That's why they're here. But lots of students and SPs hook up. Oh, I have *seen* some shit. Like one time we had an SP doing chronic myeloid leukemia? In the script, it presented as a spider bite. A makeup person – a real, Hollywood makeup person – made a bite on him, all *red* and inflamed with *pus.* It was nasty."

She paused for dramatic effect. "Two weeks later? The SP was diagnosed."

"What do you mean?"

"Got diagnosed with chronic myeloid leukemia! He didn't live but ten more months."

"What?"

"That's right."

"You are not serious."

"Baby, I *am*."

"That's so crazy!"

"Girl, you are just getting *started*. One time, this chaplain came in. Young hospital chaplain. He was *fine*. Looked just like Matt Damon. I was playing a woman whose husband got hit-and-run by a drunk. I walk in, all distraught – we did the scene right there in the chapel. In the script, I hated God for taking my husband away. The chaplain was supposed to chill me out. Like, restore my faith. But restoring my faith was the bonus burger, the main deal was *calming me the fuck down*. I later found out the chaplain went through the exact same thing IRL – you know, tried to comfort a woman who lost her husband the same way. In a car accident. That *first* time though he didn't do so well. The whole encounter righteously fucked him up. Rocked his *own* faith. Matt Damon said he just about threw in the collar. That's why he enrolled in the course, you know, to 'brush up,' get a better handle on some future, similar situation. So we're just a few minutes into the scene and I'm screaming, 'God is dead!' – I'm yelling, I'm crying, I am *slobbering*. I put that altar boy some through major drama. Oh, I was a handful! And he was *shooken*, shooken to his *core*. If that shit were filmed, I'da won me an Oscar! And you know what? There *should* be awards for what we do – the SP Awards! *Awesome* idea. Gotta bring that up to the supe."

"So, what happened? With the chaplain?"

"You know what happened."

"You're being serious?"

"We locked the door and did it right there, with Jesus watching – the son of God's fuckin wounds *reopened*. I know mine did."

It was too lurid for Celeste, so she changed the subject. "I know you do really well for an SP, but do you make enough to live? I'm don't mean to be too personal. It's just – I guess I'm looking for something more full-time."

"Are you forty yet?"

"Soonish."

"Hard being out there, huh."

"It is," said Celeste. "I have zero savings and I'm kind of starting to get scared."

"Tell you a secret. I do this for two reasons. The first is that it's a valuable service that helps others. I really do believe that. Changed my life that way. You can't know what effect you're going to have on other people. How it's going to *ripple*. What we do as SP's… what you teach those students might save someone's life. It *will* save someone's life, down the line. *Tomorrow*, for all we know! We don't know *now* because we *can't*, that's not for us to determine. That's for God. That's God's will. The second reason I do it is being an SP taught me how to be real, how to own shit that ain't mine. Because it *is* mine, right? It's *all* mine. See, if a disease isn't mine today, it'll be mine tomorrow. See what I'm saying, Celeste? Just like that poor man with chronic myeloid leukemia. It wasn't his, but then – two weeks later – it *was*. Being a Standardized Poodle – that's what I call us, heh! – is like a sacred rehearsal, understand? It's a rehearsal for life and it's a rehearsal for death, feel me? Because we're all going to be in that bed dyin', we're all going to be in that chapel wrestling with God or whatever, we're gonna be in that *waiting* room watching a doctor come down the hall, head hung low, to tell us our baby or boyfriend or grandchild or mama is dead. Everyone we know and love is gonna get cancer or murdered or T-boned by a drunk or go peacefully in their sleep. The lucky ones die in their sleep, like my granddaddy did. That's the circle of life and death's part of that too. Maybe the most *important* part. It's God's way and God's will. SP work has been very – I don't know... super spiritual. For *me*. Truly, it's helped me grow, helped me *evolve*. To be *present*." She looked away and smiled. "And led to the *other* work I do."

She dug in her purse and pulled out a card printed in black-matte:

Imogen Waldorf-Windsor
The O Group

"Are you free on Sunday? I'm having an all-ladies brunch. You'll meet some amazing, powerful women – one, I think, you know. Do you know Maggie Mae? She's an SP..." She looked deep into Celeste's eyes. "You might learn something new – real talk – maybe even about *yourself*. Come to *mi casa* in Hancock Park. You'll laugh your ass off girl, that much I guarantee. 'Cause you know if I'm around, I will *see* to that."

Garry Gabe

Even Though It All Went Wrong

He lay by the pool of the Trousdale house on Carla Ridge, just downwind of the Ruschas.

Dusk.

If he blinked, it was easy to imagine none of this ever happened. No women denounced him; the Paley Center gala was proceeding as planned; Ryan Murphy was licking his wounds after losing the Fat Joan project to the hardest-working *alta cocker* wunderkind in Hollywood.

Alas, this is the way the world ends... not with the bang of a tribute gala but a spurious gangbang and the whimper of a cancelled man.

The Waldorf-Windsor papers sat under the chaise longue, waiting for a single chemical drop of his attention to come alive and sting him into rage, panic, suffering. Even a glance at the document nauseated him. But Marmal was right; it was time to man up. In the morning, his assistant would do an archival spot check of the infamous ScreenTime convention.

Santa Anas fluttered the file and scudded the pool water.

How strange, he thought, was the world – how unpredictable its anguish, glories and madness. He held up his hand to see if it shook from the newborn disorder. This evening it was steady. GG lifted the remote he'd been using as a paperweight to anchor the asseveration of the blackmailer and prospective plaintiff. He clicked on a track from Leonard Cohen's exit album. "You want it darker" – *you got that right, my friend*. He still couldn't believe how lucky he was to have met the man.

Both were fans of the brilliant Mordecai Finley, and regulars at Ohr HaTorah during Shabbat. One night, Garry took a furtive, sidelong look and slowly the veil lifted: the genial, washed-out old gent beside him was the mournful saint whose songs had navigated him through so much heartbreak and general tsuris through the years. When Summer Cobain died, Leonard's songbook saved him. He didn't think he would have had a chance without them.

After the rabbi's exhortations, they shared coffee in the little synagogue café the singer helped to fund. It didn't surprise that Leonard was a *tummler*, a true comic genius, or that he was casually, deeply erudite – the man lived up to his press and then some. He spoke in meticulously crafted sentences that still felt improvisational, as if drolly reading to the blind from a holy instruction manual. An unspoken rule was never to touch upon the personal. But one time, Leonard brought up Joni Mitchell, probably because a recent illness of hers made the news. "Joni thinks a lot about her legacy," he said. "That's something I have never been infected by. Joni's trouble is that she doesn't believe she's famous enough." It sounded bitchy yet wasn't; it sounded true.

Discursive talk invariably circled back to Joshu Sasaki Roshi, the Buddhist teacher who played such a big part in Leonard's life. At the age of 105, former students accused him of sexual misconduct from decades ago. "They're writing terrible things about him," he said, "when they should be honoring him. Still at it, at 105! That's why I don't dare go into the zendo anymore. What it's really about is people looking back on the shipwrecks of their lives and trying to find the *cause*. 'Oh, I remember sesshin, in the 70s, and Roshi asked for the nipple.'" A year later, the teacher's obit in the *Times* blared

TAINTED MASTER. "Fuck em if they can't take a koan," said Garry, pleased with himself. Leonard smiled, responding with a phrase the showrunner thought was wonderfully memorable: "The revenge of the practitioners."

Ever since the *Reporter* exhumed Summer Cobain, he returned to Leonard's music by instinct, trying to make sense of the insensible.

† † †

It was January of 1987.

Garry was forty-two and directing the first season of *Angela*, a hit half-hour starring Angela Lansbury as a sarcastic ghost.

In just ten years, he won 12 Emmys, three Peabody's and a Humanitas Prize.

Back then, he and Gita, his high school sweetheart, lived on six acres in Encino. They had a beautiful five-year-old daughter, Regan.

These days he had his own building but in the late-80s the production company worked out of the former *I Love Lucy* wing at the old Hollywood Center Studios, a few blocks west of Paramount.

He was so busy that his assistants were hiring assistants. Summer Cobain was a dark horse finalist. She had a BFA from CalArts and was a stay-at-home mom. Her husband, a best boy on *Angela*, heard about the headhunting and urged her to apply. When Garry learned she had a little girl, it was a deal breaker – he demanded that his team work long hours. But his executive assistant loved her and kept pushing. "She's *perfect*. She and Conrad live two seconds from the studio with his parents, so daycare won't be a problem. She already told me she'll work till midnight."

† † †

Twenty-three, with jet-black hair.

When she swept into the room, he went speechless, falling back on a phrase from Isherwood that stuck in his head since college days: "eyes the violent color of bluebells."

He could smell her.

He knew he was done.

Garry had been saving himself for adultery the way that his mother saved herself for marriage. He had a history of emotional micro-affairs in the workplace and was convinced they were healthy, even essential, because the harmless cycle of sleaze allowed him to "return" to his wife and fall in love all over again.

None of them led anywhere but now it was graduation day.

He was careful in the first few months. He gave her a raise when his second assistant moved back east. It was good Summer was married, even better that she had a child. The kinship they shared (each with a daughter the same age) excited him because it guaranteed the safekeeping of pending betrayals. The poisonous plant they watered – the kind that blossoms at night – would perforce be jailed in a secret garden, fenced in by mutual contracts and inviolable responsibilities. In that sense, it was malice aforethought. He calibrated the courtship, slackening the line when she shrunk from his overtures, then reeling her in when she grew fearful of his indifference. It never occurred to him that she was afraid of losing her job, not his affections – more importantly, her husband's job, because it was possible Conrad would be fired if she were forced to quit. (Summer didn't know her boss well enough yet to gauge his vindictiveness.) For his part, Garry conveniently believed they were in a dance, the timeless, archetypal dance of romantic duplicity that was a dynamic, imperative part of the human experience, of being a man, of being a woman.

Ironically, the first time happened in daylight.

When he called the office and told her to come to the Ambassador Hotel, she was flustered. He lied and said he was fighting with Gita and they were taking a little break, "something we do periodically," and he didn't feel like coming in to the studio. He was "a bit raw" and would she mind if they worked today from his suite? When she arrived, he apologized for being in a robe and made the scripted excuse that he'd been trapped on a phone call with his wife. But he never changed out of it. (Years later, when he read about Harvey in his terrycloth robe, it sickened.) He was in a state of erotic frenzy, disguised as fractious marital mania. He erred toward expressing an intensity of emotion; lustfulness made that easy. He admitted to having feelings about her from the moment they met that he "didn't know what to do with." His affectedly boyish pronouncements were peppered with glib counterbalances: how he thought they had – *I'm so sorry but please hear me out* – or might have – *I didn't expect to say any of this, if it's offending you, I'll stop* – some kind of "strange destiny" – *Are you sure it's okay to be telling you this? I don't want you to be uncomfortable* – knowing she'd be too blitzed to protest. He made sure to be funny while baring his terrycloth soul. Humor was another skillful stratagem: leavening his stormy, artless, heartfelt declarations with that famous high-end sitcom wit, in order to soften the blows of what he prayed in the end would be taken by her as a mystic, Neil Simon soliloquy, a sort of marriage proposal of its own. In the wild horny cocaine throes of his grandiose rapacious self, GG even said he'd envisioned her co-running his production company – two words that suddenly acquired such timeless, positive valence! Such gravitas: he may as well have said Valhalla. *They would create shows together.* "I'm out of my mind, right?" he wondered aloud, a real charmer. "But I think it's *important* to go out of your mind now and then, right? Don't answer that!" She smiled. *Smiled.* He'd been watching her closely during his pitch, not knowing if Summer's head or ovaries would be the first to explode.

Wasn't going too far the whole point? Wasn't he *ready* to go too far – he must be, because it was happening – and suffer the consequences?

He said he was in love with her and in the moment, mostly meant it.

Again, he searched her features, to identify an opening, a reciprocity – and thought he saw that she'd been moved. It was altogether possible he had touched upon something *she too* already imagined.

When he asked if she'd ever felt any of the things he confessed to, she stammered, "I don't know," and he liked that.

It green-lit further prosecution of his case.

And then – from exasperation, fear, confusion, all of the above (*maybe love!*) – something inside her collapsed.

"Sometimes," she whispered.

He wasn't sure if she meant it or was stalling for time, wanting to just get the hell out of the room. In the end, it didn't matter.

That was when he put his hands on her.

Please, she mewled, but never told him to stop, which emboldened him. She bleated (like a puppy) but never withdrew, which emboldened him. She didn't become hysterical, which emboldened him. She resisted while he undid her dress but didn't push him off, which emboldened him.

"*Garry*," she whispered – and that she said his name emboldened him. "My husband," she murmured, in a cousin of a whisper, but hoarser, heart-in-throatier…

Which emboldened him.

His robe opened and his dick was dumb-waving.

She averted her gaze then looked up again, in nuanced supplication. He rolled her panties down and she covered her eyes with a hand, leaning back like a cat stretching. (Which emboldened him.)

She needed to use the bathroom, she said, and he wasn't sure if that was good or bad – if she going to prepare herself for him or plan an escape. *Out of my hands now*, he told himself bullishly. If she bolted, he'd just have to live with it. They would *both* have to live with it, one way or another; either he would never see her again or she'd show up the next day at the studio and pretend nothing happened. Nothing *had,* not really (he told himself), not yet. She didn't fully shut the bathroom door, which emboldened him. Was it the sloppiness of nerves that made her leave it open? Or some primal fear that if it closed, he would break it down? Still, the effect on Garry was calming – at least he knew that she wasn't going to lock herself in and have a meltdown. Hotel staff and even paramedics might have to be called, then police… it would be messy and awful, with dangerous repercussions to his marriage and career. She turned on the faucet to mask her tinkle, but he heard it anyway and the sound made him insane. *What am I doing, I need to stop. Stop!* When she came out, she looked radiant and afraid. Her shirt was off, but she still wore her bra. Its magenta color was seared into his brainpan. (He went out and bought Gita one just like it.) Out of decorum, he refastened his robe and walked toward her. When he held her, she pup-squeaked some more. He noticed the athletic crimp and ripple of her flat tummy, the muscles spasming in fright, and when he kissed her, he got blasted by hot, nervous, near-malodorous animal breath.

"Please," she said – not "please don't" – which emboldened him.

He walked her to the bedroom and laid her down, whispering, *You'll have everything, we're going to have everything. I love you. Trust me. I love you.*

Then he added the haunting thing, the words that her exhumed, death rattle mouth had thrown back at him for 30 years of nightmares:

"I will never do anything to hurt you."

† † †

Regan drove down from Ojai to stay with him in his time of need.

Garry hadn't encouraged it but what could he do? She was all over the place – a recovered bulimic and cutter, she'd blown through rehabs, gurus and pop-up boutiques featuring her jewelry, her gloves, her hats – the entrepreneurial fits, starts and misfires underwritten by her father. She'd been married three times – once to an old grade school chum, another to an opiate-addicted venture capitalist, the last to her guru's daughter. Her latest thing was being a producer. She was committed to bringing him literary properties. He was all for it; he loved her to death.

"I *hate* this, Daddy. I hate what they're doing to you. Hate it!"

"Welp. Love it or hate it, it is what it is."

"Look at *you*, Mr. Rogers. Look at Mr. *Zen*! Mr. Jolly Zen-Rogers *Vicker*. The student has surpassed his teacher." She was being ironic, because Regan was the one who had introduced him to the joys of Vipassana meditation. "Anyway, I'm just glad you have an amazing attorney."

"Me too – oops. Can I say that or am I banned from using the term?"

"Say the fuck what you *want*. If anyone can beat the shit out of those man-hater grifters, Sam Marmal can."

Garry was going to tell her about the ScreenTime psycho but didn't have the energy. She'd probably be more pissed off than he was. He nearly swapped the onerous Waldorf-Windsor bulletin with the revelation of his Parkinson's diagnosis, then decided he wasn't up for that either.

"When's Mom back?"

"Saturday. But I told her she should probably extend the trip," he said, in a playful nod to the scandale.

"I talked to her about it a few days ago," said Regan, already laughing. "She was in Kyoto. She said she stopped having *conversations* about Me Too, because" – imitating her mother's nasally voice – "'If you go against any tiny part of it, they look at you like you're a Sandy Hook denier!' She is *so* fuckin funny. Don't you love her?"

"Gita definitely has a sense of humor. She thinks I should do a *Handmaid's Tale* for canceled men."

"*That* is fucking brilliant. That's *hilarious*."

"I'm trying to find the humor."

"I know. I know, Dad. But we'll get through this."

She touched his arm.

"I'm already designing my bonnet," he said.

"*None* of this is going to stick. But you need to rally the troops! Call Jane Fonda – call Jane *and* Lily. Get fucking Julia Louis-Dreyfus, get fucking Sarah Jessica, get fucking *Angela* before she drops dead – *is* she dead? Ha! – get em all to do fucking *testimonials*. Have em say what the French women did, that this shit's gone *far enough*. That it's an affront to fucking feminism! They can take an ad out in the failing *New York Times* – "

"Kinda backfired on Tom Brokaw."

"Brokaw got Me Too'd?"

"A hundred and thirteen women defended him in an open letter and it made things much worse."

"All you've done for *years*, Dad, is put yourself out. For everyone but yourself."

"Sweet of you to say."

"It's *not* sweet. It's fucking true."

"Asking folks to – Regan, you don't know what sort of problems that creates. There's so many crazies out there. Who needs that shit? And I don't want to dignify what these – these women are saying. Anyway, it's never enough. It always looks like smoke after fire. You know, 'He's *responding*, so there must be something there.'"

"Then let's get *proactive*. I know some kids who could hack those lying *Reporter* bitches' phones. These kids are *bored*. All they do is ransomware hedge funders and evangelicals. They're for-hire but do anarchy for fun."

"You run with an interesting crowd."

"Better to run than to hide."

"Your Vipassana practice really mellowed you."

"Awesome idea for a film though, right? A gang of gender-queer Black Mamba assassins hunting down mutant Time's Up *fems*. 'Kill Jill'!"

He laughed out loud for the first time in days.

"That'll be easy to set up," said Garry. "I'll get right on it."

"And by the way, I found your next series."

"They're not going to let me *have* a series, Regan."

"I don't want to hear that, okay? Because it's *bullshit*, Dad. Look, you seriously cannot *fold*, you've got to keep on keepin' on. Okay? That's what I love about Woody, he gives zero fucks, I *love* him. Put one foot in front of the other, one day at a time – one streaming fucking amazing award-winning series at a time. Okay? Speaking of which, I brought you a *Vanity Fair* article that hasn't been published yet. I know the writer. You need to read it like *yesterday*. Will you?" He nodded. "You *promise*?"

"Cross my canceled heart."

† † †

He refused to look at the Waldorf-Windsor dossier, a small act that made him feel brazen, as if taking back control. But on awakening at 2:43AM, Garry made the mistake of propping himself up with pillows and tracking the digital metastasis of the *Reporter* allegations. (An activity his therapist strongly discouraged.) What he read was vile enough to send him hurtling in another direction entirely – an Internet search for omniscient gurus.

It was a YouTube harbor in stormy seas. A lama was discussing the "Unfathomable Questions" that the Buddha apparently refused to answer. The singsongy questions went like this: "Is the world eternal, or not? Or both, or neither? Is the self identical with the body, or different? Or not? Or both, or neither?" Garry loved the idea of the Buddha taking the fifth. That was something he and Leonard would have laughed about.

He switched to Pornhub.

He landed on an incest site. A girl was telling her brother how she'd been shamed by her college roommates after drunkenly admitting to having sexual feelings toward her sib. The acting wasn't bad. It seemed improvised but wasn't dumb, and of course ended with them fucking. The sheer believability was a turn-on. He clicked another about a drunk who stumbled into his daughter's room. She kept saying she had to get up early for school. He made her jack him off, but she kept looking away. He put his fingers inside her and said, "If you don't like it, why are you so wet?" He thought, *Wonder if the Buddha'd answer* that *one.* Garry got even more excited when she nervously replied, "I don't know." It was strange to feel what he was feeling because he'd never been remotely turned on by the idea of having sex with Regan. Then he realized the little scene reminded him of that first time with Summer. It sickened him but he kept masturbating. After he came, he got paranoid that someone – some *agency* was already tracking him – like the Black Mamba assassins Regans joked about, or even Moishe Fineman. If he *did* turn his phone or computer over to Sammy's forensic crack team of deep-diving digital heroes, there might be questionable things on the old hard drive that he'd forgotten about...

As if to cleanse himself yet stay on topic, he linked to an 84-year-old Korean poet, accused of groping. His illustrious

body of work was being systematically erased from school text-
books. Even a library bearing his name was being torn down.
Garry went to the poet's shockingly dramatic Wikipedia page.
A gravedigger during the Korean War, he'd gone deaf from
pouring acid in his ear to drown out the noise of carnage. He
eventually became a monk, then activist. Accused of treason,
he was tortured in prison and pardoned from a 20-year sentence in 1980.

His alleged recent crimes were catalogued in a poem
called "Monster," written by an accuser. In response, the old
man released this statement:

> I have already expressed regret for any unintended pain my
> behavior may have caused. However, I flatly deny charges of
> habitual misconduct that some individuals have brought up
> against me.

In the end, wasn't that the final, universal declaration? The
inevitable, enervated war cry of Everyman, made before God,
in answer to all the unfathomable questions? Garry read it
aloud, prayerfully repeating the words until the litany became
a yowl and horrorshriek (Regan was staying in Ojai tonight,
thank God), shaking the rafters and black skies above. He
begged Summer's forgiveness...

He closed all the masochistic tabs and windows – the cuffs
and clamps of a B&D dungeon – and when he was sufficiently
recovered, checked his email. He'd been out of the office all
day and his assistant sent a list of phone calls and messages.
There were nearly a hundred. A dozen journalists were asking for interviews and a flurry of friends, agents, and creative

types expressed outrage over the *Reporter*'s "hatchet job." Most were just playing chess; at this juncture, it didn't cost anything to be supportive. Their preemptive goodwill would pay professional dividends in the event his name was cleared.

At the end – the last call of the day – Gabriella wrote: "Celeste Cobain/says it's personal."

His heart skipped a beat and the room went black.

She's found something. An entry from Summer's diary...

"It's over now," he said.

And felt the relief of the fugitive finally captured.

Celeste

How Can I Help?

She waited until after 8PM, because she only wanted to leave a message of support. Dialing his production office, she felt like one of those clairvoyants on *Law & Order*, reaching out to a detective. An assistant answered, taking her aback. When asked what it was regarding, Celeste said it was personal. She was grateful the woman wasn't rude and asked nothing further.

Part of her was reluctant to impose because the man had a lot going on, to say the least. In the last 72 hours, there'd been a storm of press releases. The announcement of the Paley Center cancellation was a flash of lightning in a rolling thunder of resignations from sundry boards that he sat on as esteemed male mascot-emeritus. Without admitting

guilt, he stepped down gracefully from each, while expressing solidarity with the very movement busying itself with his
crucifixion.

Social media had the usual cannibalistic feast:

Lady Alicia @turfeetootles 3 m
YASS!!!! rumors about that GROPER PIG for YEARS, hiding
behind his money and entitled ADVOCACY mask. Hang
em HIGH!!!!! HAP-HAP-HAPPY days are here again. You
are DONE, bitch. Hope you go to JAIL and they do you
like Whitey Bulger and JEFFREY DAHMER, sock-wrapped
PADLOCKS and iron bars to the FACE till you look like you
TRULY ARE, a bloody bone-through-the skin RAPIST PIECE
OF SHIT
11 replies 42 retweets 157 likes

Jonny Come Lately @donteffwithjonnster 7 m
Due process please but if it's true he needs a major Walk of
Shame. We are all not like this, ladies. There are men out
there who respect women and will ALWAYS give them the
benefit of the doubt. Try not to let rotten apples spoil the barrel
please
11 replies 42 retweets 157 likes

Wuaneeta Wakanda @mairzeedotes 9 m
suck my clit you RAPIST/the REELZ golden state killer DUH,
NO WONDER HE COULD RELATE! that shitty minni-series
was a CRY FOR HEP. strip of all awardz/ABORT from tv
academy JOIN THE BOYCOTT AGAINST NETFLIX THE
ENABLER
7 replies 113 retweets 87 likes

Had there been rumors for years? Celeste couldn't find anything to substantiate that. But lots of people were tweeting their sadness, shock and support as well – it hardly mattered, because that's what the Internet did. In a millisecond, old reality got swapped with a new reality shitshow.

The night before, Celeste awakened from a dream that she was sitting in Garry's office. (Never mind that it was an outdoor, tropical place.) The *feelings* were all there, of empathy mixed with pity. Her dad was in the mix too, the sad, lost thought of him, the wanting to protect. Maybe that's what getting in touch with him is all about. A daddy thing.

She hoped it was something simpler – a human thing.

† † †

She was having her morning coffee when the phone rang.

"Hello?" There was silence. "Hello?"

"Is this – Celeste?"

"Yes."

"Hi Celeste, it's Garry."

"Oh, hello," she said, with nervous solemnity. "Thank you for calling me back."

"How can I help you?"

Either he didn't recall who she was or chose not to acknowledge the old connection. She stuttered, saying she only wanted to tell him that she thought it was all "a load of crap" and to ask if he was okay. She rushed through it because now she was embarrassed.

More silence on the line, and rustling sounds.

She said "Hello?" then heard him talking to what sounded like an assistant. When he got back on, he asked, "Can you come in?"

"When? Do you mean – "
"Today. Can you come after lunch, Celeste?"

It was a free day – no movie extra work this month. She was due in Lawndale for an SP gig, though not until six. (Sometimes there were night classes to accommodate doctors' schedules.) Celeste wondered what to say to him before deciding words weren't important. It was her presence that was meaningful. *But why does he want to see me?* Maybe he just needs a friend, or friendly face – maybe everyone abandoned him. Hollywood was like that. Then she had a gremlin notion:

What if the accusations – or some of them – were true?

He was at his desk when Gabriella showed her in. Garry looked up, smiling, and walked around to greet her as the assistant closed the door. He looked befuddled, and heavier than she remembered.

"Thank you," he said. "For calling. And for coming in."

"How are you?" she asked.

He made a bleak little laughing sound. "I think I'm okay. It's been... *interesting.* It's an education. It's going to be an education."

"It's just so *terrible,*" she said. "When I read what those women said... it sounded so *stilted,* so *rehearsed.* And I just had the feeling – really strong! – that I should call."

"Well, it's very kind, Celeste. Can I get you anything? Water? Coffee?" She shook her head. "How have *you* been?"

"Good!"

"Are you working?" he asked, by rote.

"Yes. I'm actually working in the medical field."

"*Really,*" he said, pretending to be interested. They would circle back to his miseries soon enough, but she knew that a cordial give-and-take was important to him. It was his inclusive nature.

"It's pretty amazing," she said. "It's been an education." He smiled at the inadvertent echo of his own words. "I think I'll eventually go to nursing school."

"That's wonderful. My daughter Regan wanted to do that for a time but didn't have the stick-to-itiveness. *Still* doesn't!" Hearing that, Celeste got another layer of upset – she hated that his daughter had to deal with what was going on. Garry sighed and turned inward. "What's rough, I guess, is the help-lessness of it. I don't remember these women, Celeste. I don't *know* them. But one's hands are tied, in so many ways. I think everyone – the people who know me, my track record – I hate that phrase 'track record'! – they know what I feel about Time's Up and Me Too. Those movements are *long* overdue. I've been *such* a supporter of women, hell, I crafted, my *company* crafted equal pay stipulations – we were the first to do that, to even *think* about it. It's literally called the Vicker Model, did you know that? That's what lawyers refer to – *the Vicker Model.* Jesus, we implemented it way back in the 90s. But I have to stand there and take the blows. It's 'friendly fire.' I get it." He opened his hands and shrugged. "I just don't know how to fight this thing."

"But you *have* to! You have to because it's not right."

She's a good person, he thought, like her mother that way. He felt the ghostly breeze of Summer in the room.

"No one knows who I am," said Celeste. "I'm not famous – I'm not *anyone*. But I just wanted you to know that if there's anything I can do to help… could I be interviewed somewhere? Or go on a podcast and talk about how I'm the daughter of a woman who worked for you and how good you were to her? How good you were to *me*? Getting me all those jobs…" He smiled appreciatively but said that wasn't necessary. He said she had already helped enormously by just coming to see him. That was when she got emotional. "I don't know – I could tell them – with your permission – I could even tell them you paid for her funeral…"

Like a man knifed by a stranger, a smile slowly expanded on his face until it resembled a gash in a piece of fruit rotting in the sun. His shoulders hunched in a soundless, syncopated sob.

She rushed to cradle him, as a mother would a harrowed child.

† † †

At the college, there was a handsome kid in his late twenties that Celeste had her eye on. He'd only been an SP for a few months. He somehow knew Imogen, who helped get him the job. Tonight they were playing a husband and wife with a brain-dead teen. The exercise was meant to teach third- and fourth-year medical residents how to effectively approach parents for consent to harvest their child's organs for transplant.

They saw five students in succession, each sequestered from the other. The script they studied beforehand served as an improv guide. He wound up having most of the dialogue, which was handy because Celeste could get away with quietly falling apart while staring at her man, who happened to be movie star beautiful. And that performance! So tender and believable that the students seemed affected almost as much as Celeste.

After class, they walked together to their cars. She couldn't believe it when she asked if he wanted to go have a coffee.

And couldn't believe it when he said yes.

"So where do you live?"

"In Silver Lake. My sister and I have a place there."

"Nice. You the older or the younger?"

"Older. And you? You live…"

"In Highland Park."

"Oh nice. There's supposed to be amazing vintage shops. What's that famous street there?"

"York."

"York!"

"My daughter and I have a cottage."

He used the word ironically.

"Oh wow."

"She loves it because we're a few blocks from where Billie Eilish lives. Or used to."

"Oh wow." *Stop saying that. You sound so dumb.* "And your daughter's how old?" *You sound like your seventy years old!*

She hadn't been on a date – if you could call having coffee with the SP a date – in four years.

"Trix is fourteen now. Going on a hundred-and-seven."

"Haha. Trix?"

"Short for Trixanna."

"Oh wow, that's really unusual. That's really cool."

"I think her mom regretted it. She used to want to call her Anna but the girl insisted on Trix. Hardheaded."

"And the mother? – oh shit, *I'm* sorry, that was rude. I didn't – "

"It's fine."

"I don't do much hanging out! As you can maybe tell."

"They don't let you out too often, huh. I can totally relate." After a moment, he said, "Her mom actually passed away. I kind of adopted her – hey, no, that's not right. I *did* adopt her. Like, the whole legal deal."

"Oh my God, that is so amazing."

She couldn't believe how stupid she was sounding. Word-for-word, sentence-for-sentence stupid.

"Want to come see the place?" he asked.

"What?"

"The kid's on a sleepover – it's a good time to see the *cottage*. I mean, if you're interested in cottages." He winked and said, "We're just off York, your favorite street."

Adele

Just Soho Stories

In a good week on the road, after gas and motels, Adele cleared about $400. She kept falling behind in rent, which wasn't cool. Celeste didn't nag but it was obvious she was having hard times herself. Adele joked about how they should go on one of those sugar daddy websites to find a guy who was into sister acts. She was working on a monologue about that.

To make ends meet, she got a job at Soho House. Adele was older than most of the servers, but everyone liked her. It was a good way to network. She waited on so many famous people that it was like flipping through one of those celebrity magazines you could still buy at supermarkets. (One day, at separate tables, she waited on Lana Del Rey, Keanu Reeves, and Monica Lewinsky.) On Sunday, they all came for brunch – Ashton and Mila, Nicole and Keith, Chrissy and John Legend,

Sharon and Ozzy with their kids and grandkids. During the week, there were personal heroes too: Seth MacFarlane, Aubrey Plaza, Sarah Silverman. There were rules against gushing over stars, but you could always get away with a fulsome, flirty word or two. A few weeks ago, she waited on Judd Apatow and he'd been open and gracious. After she had a few more encounters under her belt, Adele planned to give him a slip of paper with a smiley-face and a link to her fledgling YouTube channel.

She got her chance when he came in for an early breakfast. Before she went over, Adele loitered at the server's station and allowed herself to fantasize about their looming collaboration. She would go into intense training – like Uma in *Kill Bill*, being taught the Five Point Exploding Laughter Technique by Pai Mei. She knew she would be a quick study; bruised and battered, Adele Cobain would soon harden into a comedy samurai, gaining the master's complete respect.

When a few others joined him, she gathered up some menus. Approaching the table, she gasped: sitting at his side, already laughing about something, was Mustang.

Adele backed off before she was seen.

Being a student of comedy, she recognized Judd's second guest, a thin man with a goatee – Neal Brennan, the legendary co-creator of *Chappelle's Show*. Weirdly, she'd just seen him on *Lights Out*. His appearance on the show inspired her to go down the Neal rabbit hole. She watched a ton of videos, culminating with him doing a long, amazing monologue at the Kennedy Center when Dave got the Mark Twain.

She ran to the bathroom and pissed like a horse. She stood at the sink, splashing her face. She looked in the mirror and thought: *Get it together, cunt. This is your Five Point samurai fucking moment.*

She strode toward the table, reinvigorated. It would worse for Mustang to recognize her first – better to take the bull by the horns.

"Oh my God, Mustang, hi!"

"Adele! Adele Cobain! Hiya!"

The vibe was super chummy – to say that the aging server was relieved was the understatement of all time. It wouldn't have been surprising if she recoiled at the very sight of Adele, triggered by association with those grimy, damaged, loser years of humiliation and thankless touring. And on top of it all, she had licked the rising star's shithole – a memory best kept in the dark place where it lived, and died.

But it was the *sincerity* of her sweetness that surprised.

"This is Adele Cobain," she said to the legends. "Adele is an *amazing* standup. Oh my God, she is dark! We did about a thousand clubs together – didn't we, Addie?" (More like half-a-dozen but Adele didn't mind the hyperbole.) "I learned a lot from this woman. I learned how to be more... fuckin *fearless.*"

"Wow," said Judd, beaming. "That's crazy."

"Fearless is good," said Neal.

"I hope you're still out there," said Mustang. "We need you to be out there tearing it up."

"I think they're tearing *me* up – 'A Star Is Torn.'" It wasn't so clever, but they were on her side, giving Adele the first, easy laugh of her "tight five." "But thank you. And you're amazing. I'm so proud of you."

"Very cool name, *Adele Cobain,*" said Neal. "My two favorite singers."

"I named myself that because after I lose a bunch of weight, I can do what I've wanted to since I was a kid: blow my brains out."

Good one.

Judd and Neal laughed.

Mustang said, "See? I *told* you she was dark."

"I'm actually going to be at the Kollective tonight," said Adele.

It blurted from her unconscious – born of the need to let them know she was still in the game – and she wished she could take it back because now it looked like she was soliciting them to come to her show.

Ugh.

"In K-Town?" said Mustang. "With the karaoke?"

"Yup."

"*Love* the Kollective."

"But enough about me," said Adele, trying to climb out of the hole. "Have y'all decided what you'd like?"

Forty minutes later, Mustang nearly ran her over as she dashed down the narrow corridor to the ladies room.

"I am *so sorry*," said Adele.

"For what?"

"I didn't want it to seem like I was inviting you guys to that shithole tonight."

"That's *crazy*. And I would *so come* if I could."

"Oh no! See? You *do* think I was inviting you!"

Mustang laughed. "You're *funny*, girl. How *are* you?"

"I'm good, I'm great. And I wanted to tell you how *amazing* everything that's happened to you is. You fucking deserve it, Musty."

"I don't know about that!"

"It gives me hope. And the *Marvel* movie – Musty, oh my God!"

"Right? It's *so* fuckin weird. I mean it's *great* but it's fuckin *weird*."

"And the Netflix special – I saw you on *Ellen*. I want to *be* you."

"Oh no you *don't*. If anyone around here wants to be anyone, I want to be *you*."

"Stop."

"It's true, Addie. You *are* fuckin fearless, and I *did* learn from you."

"Come on."

"I am *serious*. And the guys really liked you! Neal said you were *really funny,* and Neal *never* says that."

"I think I'm going to cry."

Mustang hugged her. "Get it *togethuh*, bitch. And oh! Remember that nasty thing we did in Boston?"

"Do I remember the ass-to-mouth? Uhm, well, *duh*."

Mustang guffawed. "I'm putting it in my special. I'm serious! I'm doing a whole thing about comedy clubs and going on the road."

"Ha!"

"*You're gonna be in my special*." Adele gaped at her. "I won't mention your *name* but our whole nasty deal's gonna be *in* it. And by the way: that was the first and last time that ever happened!"

There was something sweetly prudish about the qualifying remark.

"*Please* mention my name – it might get me work!"

"Maybe not the kind of work you want!"

"Tell me more about the special?"

"Well, *as you know,* it's for Netflix."

"That little old network?"

"Hey, I'm slumming."

"Is Judd producing?"

"No – but we've been workshopping something for maybe a film... you know: my checkered past. My Chinese Checkered past."

"Hahaha!"

"I don't actually think anything's going to come of it, but the process has been *beyond. He's amazing.*"

"Well – you're just – I am *so happy* for you."

"But I gotta pee. Bye!" She turned and said, "Still have the same number?"

"Yup. They're retiring it when I die. Like Gianna Bryant's jersey."

Mustang laughed and said, "I'll *call.* We shall hang."

†††

The KTown Kollective had a back room for comedy and a dozen low-rent cubicles for karaoke. Adele gigged there last year with her friend Kevin Lee but hadn't seen him since. Kev was a shitty standup who made a living impersonating Elon Musk at private parties (and occasional sketches on *Kimmel.*) Though she *did* hear some freakish story that he got beat up at a comedy club in Hermosa Beach by a Joe Rogan impersonator.

When she took the stage it was pitch-dark. She saw the scattered shapes of about a dozen people. She was guaranteed $50 for a ten-minute set, on the high side for the Kollective, because the shy manager wanted to ball her. After the show,

Adele half-resolved to tell him she'd throw in a handjob if he gave her a hundy – no joke.

Still glowing from the Soho House reconciliation, Adele couldn't help wondering if her fortunes were changing. Nothing could dampen her spirits (she was loaded too), not even when she had to shout through her set to compete with the raucous "Dance Monkey" karaoke that came pounding from next-door.

She did her usual girly standup fodder: the joys of scurvy online hookups, the joys of anal, the joys of Kickstarter abortion funds. The wretched, ragged ugliness of the labia majora... then stopped in her tracks and said, "Fuck all that. I want to talk about my mother."

Walking the thin comedic line between bathos and horror, Adele forgot where she was. There was so much to explore; and suddenly, she was free. She was born that night. It was like flying in a dream – flying home. It wasn't until a through-the-wall group-sung karaoke of "Every Breath You Take" that she was finally nudged from her trance. She realized she must have gone way over her allotted time.

"All right, I think I've had enough. You've been a horrible audience. Thank you and fuck you and goodnight."

No applause –

Nothing...

Suddenly, a light above went on. Someone in the back must have leaned against the switch. When she focused, she found herself staring at David Spade, who was only a few feet away.

"Addie! Addie! Addie!"

Sitting beside him was Mustang, who stood and approached.

"Oh my God!" said Adele, crouching on the lip of the stage. "Musty, what are you *doing* here?"

"You were fucking *amazing*," said Mustang. "That stuff about your *mother* – was *so sad* and so *amazing*. I never *knew* any of that, I was *crying*."

"Really, really good," said Spade, shaking her moist, clammy hand.

"Thank you so much! I can't believe you came! *Both* of you – "

"She twisted my arm," said Spade. "She said great things about you – in between all the libelous stuff. But I put that aside."

"But aren't you supposed to be taping your show?" said Adele.

"We don't do it *live*," he said, charmed by her rookie naïveté.

"They tape in the afternoon," said Mustang.

"Oh!" Adele gave a quick nod to the dank, depopulated surroundings. "It's so embarrassing! This *place* – "

"In my seventy years of doing standup," Spade dead-panned, "I never knew clubs like this even *existed*. My first gig was actually a six-month Vegas residency." Adele guffawed with nervous energy, touching his arm. "Listen, you want to maybe come watch the show next week? Like, on Wednesday?"

Adele saw Mustang throw him a smirky look.

"I would love to!"

"*David*," said Mustang, admonishing.

Adele had a sinking feeling that she was being pranked.

"Great," said Spade. "Come watch on Wednesday."

Mustang rolled her eyes. "He means watch from the *stage*."

"What?" said Adele, not understanding.

"Addie, he wants you to be on the show!"

"Come do a Tight Five," he said drily. "You're ready for that, right? Cause *I* think you are."

Adele burst into tears.

Garry Gabe

Widowers

That night when he saw Celeste's name at the bottom of the phone log, he was certain she'd uncovered something – a diary? a note? – implicating him in her mother's fate.

> Whomsoever finds this MUST report to the proper authorities
> that Garry Gabe Vicker, my RAPIST, is solely responsible for
> my death. And that my 2nd child, ADELE, belongs to HIM!
>> I can no longer live with the lie.
>> May God and my daughters forgive me.
>>> (*signed*) Summer Cobain

Sleepless, he comforted himself with a certain rationale. If such a note *had* been found, it was unlikely she would have called him directly. The errand would have been left to an attorney at best, to the media at worst. Though maybe not. Maybe the discovery was too fresh – and hearing her mother's voice from the grave had compelled a stark, impulsive rage. Maybe Celeste wanted reparations... he calculated an amount he could live with, to make it all go away: five million dollars. (The Golden Age of sitcoms had been very good to him.) Yet Gabriella said there was nothing memorable about the woman who left word, not in speech or affect. The Cobain girl was such a sweet, submissive soul. When she graduated, he helped get her little acting jobs here and there. But she wasn't a "talent" – in fact, as an actress, she had no talent at all.

The fantasia of the suicide note made him realize he still harbored thoughts that Summer's second child might be his.

When he ended it, Garry gave the obligatory spiel that she could keep her job – though it might be "cleaner" if she didn't. Her severance was generous. They didn't talk for a few months and he struggled not to reach out. One day she reached out and said she was pregnant. He said *how many months* then asked if it was his. She said no but he had his doubts. So he offered money and she laughed in his face. He didn't know if it was a hate call or a love call; what was the truth, what was the lie. Regardless, he had a perverse epiphany and asked *Will you come back to me*. She said that she couldn't. He never spoke to her again. He was on set the day her husband was given It's A Girl! cigars by the crew. He even shook Conrad's hand.

While part of him was excited about being a baby daddy, another part was angry that she cut him off. He retreated to the war room of his office and drew up a timeline of their lovemaking, effectively debunking any claims that he could be Adele's father. Looking back now, everything was blurry; as blurry as the ScreenTime convention. Was a customized timeline to be trusted? He had every reason to overthrow a hypothetical paternity, he was *invested* in denial, because a child by another woman – a married employee at that – would have ransacked his world.

After Summer died, he closed the door on the possibility forever, relieved that she'd never come knocking on his door to demand DNA. He knew through Celeste that the child became a comedian, so the genes might be there. But force of habit – decades-long disavowals – made it easy to throttle the random urge to look up his fantasy daughter online.

† † †

He decamped to the beach house in Carpinteria.

The voices of friends who called to commiserate over the *Reporter* imbroglio were infected by fear and caution. The men were jauntily self-editing, as if aware that their remarks – instantly recorded by the Cloud – would become part of the encyclopedic transcript that would comprise the official oral history of the 21st century's Women's Revolution. Garry's faux-simpatico cohorts thought they could lift his canceled spirits by cavalierly implying they would soon be joining him to burn at the stake. Some tried being tough guys – profane and pugnacious – but admitted they hadn't been altar boys (strange how many used that exact phrase) and were haunted now by the rough beasts of consequence whose slouch would soon become a gallop. All were certain to suffer the attack of the 50-foot woman; whether the accuser from the forgotten past was a colleague, secretary or intern, and whether she wore Tom Ford, Zara, or vintage from Etsy wouldn't matter. Whether she asked for your money, reputation or life would not matter – the piper simply needed to be paid. "We learned it on the schoolyard," said another. "That was all we knew. Caveman shit." As if to remind themselves of the Orwellian Cloud, they threw in requisite bromides like "A course correction's been a long time coming" and "I'm so glad this is happening in the time of my daughters and granddaughters – and sons and grand-sons!" Not wanting to sound too soft, they fired off weak addenda: "A lot innocent men are going to suffer. But war is hell!" or "You'll get through this, bubba. We all will – hope-fully. *Zai gezunt!*"

The response of Garry's women friends was more complex.

None thought he was guilty – not really – because he was so warm, so menschy, impeccable in his behavior. After all, without GG many wouldn't have had a career. Still, the winds of feminist Spiritus Mundi stirred, lifting the curtain to reveal the axiom plainly etched on hearts and wombs: *All men are guilty.* It was complicated because Garry Gabe Vicker was a powerful, charming, seductive, protective man. After his denouncement, some kept in touch so as not to awaken painful memories of messy rapprochements with their own ICU-deathbed-daddies. Some erred on the side of compassion and justice, while others could never admit they were titillated by the idea that Garry the charismatic *ubermensch* was capa-ble of such ribaldry. His instant sexualization was a lifting of the curtain as well… ladies with longtime secret crushes grew insecure, wondering why he'd never made a move, fantasiz-ing about being chased through the famous, naked, *Hollywood Reporter* streets as the rutting stag famously bellowed, "You want my big penis, don't you? You must not resist!" Then there were the vulnerable ones, still hiding their cancers and che-mos and sundry brushes with death, fearing livelihoods would end; ones who just learned their husbands had been cheat-ing forever, but were too frightened to divorce; ones whose jam leaned toward bondage and roleplay. In the end, all were angling to be rewarded for their unwavering loyalty, once the smoke cleared.

It was complicated.

There were side benefits to staying in touch. Communing with GG elevated the women's cliquish status amongst powerful men who weren't as close to the disgraced showrunner. A favorite pastime was asking Inner Circle Ladies for dirt and a little bavardage (aka "updates").

But *all* of the women had heart for this man, this mentor, this drowning Daddy – yet hearts (and minds) were arrhythmic because regardless of what was right and just, they would join their sister soldiers in blowing up the houses built on the ancient foundations of patriarchal abuse. The bloody battles to come – war is hell – transcended the picayune details of any particular case despite its merits, rolling like a tank over the carcass of a horse. They were members of a primal sorority now and knew the Movement was the defining, unifying event of their lives. Perforce, their feelings for Garry remained on the down-low; going public in his support bore dire ramifications. The slings and arrows aimed at them by their own tribe were poison-tipped. Knowledge of heart and womb contained a second axiom, trickier and more clandestine than the first: women were capable of being crueler to their own than men could ever dream.

He put on a Leonard album and sauntered through the living room like a drugged panther, to amuse himself.

He soft-shoed toward the sliding glass door – past the Avery Singer, past the Mungo Thomson, past the Idris Kahn and the beautifully boxed photos of Marilyn Monroe bought at auction last year. Every few months, a trove of half-pornographic, heartbreakingly poignant images of "newly discovered" Norma Jean came up for sale. *What a fuckin racket.*

Outside, he plunked himself on a chaise to enjoy his first cigarette in three years. He carried a printout of the *Vanity Fair* piece that Regan wanted to produce. He threw it on the ground like a dead thing. His Master's Voice – Leonard – was stereophonic, chastising from million-dollar speakers embedded in the pool, the rocks, the tree branches, the stars.

> The last time that I saw him he was trying hard to get
> A woman's education but he's not a woman yet

Garry thought about the last time he saw him. He remembered being overtaken with grief by the valedictorian mood and the same sadness descended when he began to reminisce.

As they got friendlier, they would meet for lunch at Café Sicily, a modest corner mall joint near the singer's mid-Wilshire home. (Like a mirage, it vanished a few months after his death.) In the last few years of his life, Leonard was more desiccated than dapper; accounts of him as a timeless bon vivant were sweetly exaggerated. His grooming began to slide, and the famous suits were genteel-shabby now. He told Garry that when he turned 80, "a catalogue of permission" had presented itself. "I lie in bed in the morning – I still get up very early, a habit from the monastery – and say to myself, 'Why get up?'"

He never told his friend about Summer, something he sorely regretted. Of all people, Leonard would have understood. He'd have *got* it. Sage counsel from the man who wrote *Death of a Ladies Man* would have bestowed a healing. But instead, Garry danced around it, asking the pull-quote question of how low the old man had ever been laid by a woman.

"I was creamed from the beginning!" he shot back. "*Wrecked* – I'm still being wrecked. And there's always wreckage from the one that came before. Just yesterday, I found myself on the Internet looking at houses to buy for... a new *interest*. There's a certain *repetition* one notices. We think we know what they want: to be caressed, to be protected. What they really want is to be obeyed. I couldn't obey – that was my trouble. It was wonderful having Roshi around because he was 20 years older. He was already where I was heading. He told me that I would get lonely and that it was important to provide for a woman but not to marry. When I was very young, I saw a gentleman in Montreal named Mir Bashir. He looked at my palm. He said I would spend my life going from monastery to charnel house – this was long before I had dealings with the monasteries. He was straight out of Raj India and spoke in gorgeous, unbroken paragraphs. Tolstoyan. He said, 'You know *nothing* about women, but you will learn. You know *nothing* about marriage, but you will learn.' Now I spend my time between solitariness and loneliness. I find it amenable; I can navigate that. When I get lonely, I take care of it. I have an assistant. She's Turkish – beautiful. Sometimes I feel like I'm on a date with her; other times, I feel like she's my assistant." That would have been the perfect time for Garry to bare his soul but he punked out. "If you're looking for a woman to be with, to marry, and you see one in a restaurant, there's really only one thing to ask yourself:

"'Is that the one I will agree to obey?'"

Garry sighed and picked up the papers next to the chaise.

Love Child and The King of Parts

When Arnold Neidhoff – the Ohioan auto parts magnate – came to Lalaland to close a deal, he met Portia Coldstream, a gorgeous Goth grifter claiming to be Elon Musk's secret daughter. She wound up dead. Months later, with City of Angel flatfoots hot on his trail, Neidhoff killed his wife and autistic son, then took his own life. Devon Morris delves into the murder that rocked Tinseltown – and Cleveland – and the surreal aftermath of that fatal night.

With each paragraph, his interest grew. Before even finishing, he picked up the phone to call Regan.

"I want to do this," he said.

"Do what?"

"The *Vanity Fair* piece – it's brilliant. It's *exactly* what I want to do next."

"Oh my God, you're serious?"

"Regan, I'm telling you: we are going to do this."

"Oh Daddy, I am so happy!"

"If we can get the boyfriend's life rights, what's his name – "

"Jaxx?"

" – if we get his rights, we don't *need* to buy the fucking article."

"Oh my God, I knew you'd love it! I am *so* excited. I love you!"

"We have to snap this up before Ryan Murphy gets his faggot hands on it."

† † †

It must have been that archaic phrase – *charnel house* – that stirred the pot, because that night, Garry dreamed he was in a grave. When he awakened, he realized the nightmare was a riff on a Zen story Leonard once shared about a man and woman who were deeply in love.

It was about a rich and happily married couple. Their life was a kind of paradise until one day she died after a short, violent illness. The widower was in disbelief, as were his family and friends. He wouldn't allow his wife to be taken from the house and was given a wide, respectful berth. After a few days the body began to smell. The widower agreed that she could be taken away in the morning – but in the middle of the night, he and the body disappeared. His delusion was such that he believed she was still alive, and the world was conspiring against them.

. He carried her to the only place the superstitious townspeople would leave them in peace – the graveyard. In the afternoons, he went to the village and begged for food. He ate whatever was rotten and saved the best for his wife.

When the king heard about it, his heart broke. He offered gold to anyone who could bring the man to his senses. A madwoman stepped forward but wasn't allowed to enter the palace. When the king demanded she be brought to him, the madwoman offered her services for free. She said that she needed the body of a man about her age that had recently died. Thus, it was arranged. She brought the corpse to the cemetery and set up camp not far from the widower and his wife. She made sure to do exactly as he did. She spoke lovingly to the body the king procured and "fed" it scraps that she begged for in the village.

After a few days of watching, the curious widower approached. Before he could speak, she told him that the world had convinced itself of a great lie – that her husband was dead – and was hell-bent on destroying their perfect union. The widower couldn't believe what he was hearing. "That is exactly what happened to me and my wife!" They made a pact to watch over each other's spouses whenever they went begging for food.

When the widower came back from the village one day, the woman said that she heard her husband whispering to his wife. The seeds of jealousy were sown and would soon bear fruit. A few days later, while he went begging, she threw the cadavers down a well. When the widower returned, she ran toward him, yelling, "They've done it! They ran off! They said they finally found their true love!"

At first, the widower was distraught. Then he became enraged. "After all I've done! I loved her! I protected her! I saved her!"

That was when the madwoman straightened up, transforming into a steel sword. "You protected *nothing*!" she said. She glinted in the sun and looked ten times her size; the widower fell to the ground in shock at what he beheld. "You fool! Everything is impermanent! All unions end! All risings leads to a fall! Wake up! Wake up! Wake Up!"

The ghoulish face of Summer was still before him, a face that for so many years he refused to bury, under the deformed aegis of Love.

And just when he thought he was finally able to make peace, the body got reanimated by the clamorous spirits of the times.

Celeste

Heart Palpations

She came to the enchanted cottage on Friday and by Sunday was still there.

Jaxx made "full disclosure" about his herpes and how he didn't get outbreaks anymore because of the Valtrex. When Celeste said that she had it too, he gave her a pill from his stash. *Modern dating,* she thought.

She hadn't fucked like that since college. She got so wet, he had to put down a beach towel. She was beside herself. She ate his ass, something she'd never done before, laughing to herself how she'd become one of her sister's disgusting monologues. The puzzle was: *Why me?* He was so handsome, *dangerously* handsome, and Celeste – well, she always remembered her grandmother's words: "It's better to be almost pretty, Cellie. Men don't marry knockouts."

They were in bed (which they'd only left for fridge raids and bathroom breaks) when Trixanna barged in from her Saturday night sleepover. Celeste yanked the sheet over her head as Jaxx leapt to his feet and said, *"Privacy please"* – then pushed the kid out, slamming the door so that he and his guest could pick up where they left off.

"Daddy?" came the subdued little girl voice from the hall.

"Babe, I said we'll be out in a *while.*"

"You *didn't* say that."

"Well I'm saying it *now.*"

"Let's just stop," whispered Celeste, feeling sleazy.

"It's *okay,*" he whispered back.

"Where's Tabasco?" Trixanna demanded.

"I don't fucking know, babe."

Moments later, she heard the girl coo, "*There* you are, Tabby, *there* you are. *There's* my Tabby."

Her bedroom door thundered shut, sequestering Girl and Cat.

Celeste loved that Jaxx held nothing back, even if it made him look like the shittiest person. He told her that he went to jail for hacking nudes from the phones of celebs, and how he and Trixanna's mom used to steal money from "rich tourists." He proudly showed her a *Vanity Fair* article about their adventures that (if he could be believed) "was going to be huge on Netflix." He cooked dinner while she read the pages.

She never paid much attention to crime stories but a dim awareness of the notorious case trickled in. A woman got thrown off a cliff in the Palisades last year – that much Celeste remembered – but the rest was brand new. She couldn't believe that she was reading about Jaxx and his ex! All that stuff about how they used to do porn together and how they ripped off "rich tourists" by claiming she was the daughter of Elon Musk! The last part of the article was *crazy*: Jaxx tipped the police to the killer, who shot his wife and son then took his own life. Jaxx told the journalist that he felt responsible for the death of those innocents and adopting Trixanna was a way "to square the karmic circle." He insisted it wasn't an act of charity and that he'd come to love the girl, not as a mini-me of Portia, but in the pure way a father would love a daughter.

Something else in the article got her attention.

In the photos, Celeste's resemblance to Portia was uncanny. Put another way (as her grandma might have said), she was an *almost pretty* version of Portia Coldstream. Side by side, Celeste.

thought they'd look like those red carpet photos in magazines of movie stars standing next to their chubby, cheap-copy sisters. She was okay with that. If his ex could pretend to be Elon Musk's lovechild then Celeste was perfectly comfortable doing some pretending too, on Jaxx's behalf. She was *already* being paid to impersonate the sick and the dying; why not play the ghost that haunted Jaxx for free? It was so sexy and *interesting*, so unexpected – and exciting beyond measure because she'd pretty much surrendered to spinsterhood. Celeste hadn't felt fuckable in God knows how long. It'd been three years since she was with a man. Her last hurrah was a serial six-week binge, faces and bodies long since muddled into a doughy golem that told bad jokes, hated to spend money and didn't know how to fuck. Celeste thought she didn't know how to fuck either, until Jaxx proved her wrong.

Now she found herself having a fling with a pretty-boy ex-felon whose final, outrageously imaginative confidence game ended in both tragedy and redemption. She'd be part of that redemption – or bust. She'd dress up like Portia, Zendaya or Wonder Woman, if that's what it took.

But the sexiest thing of *all* was his thieving heart:

Big and brash enough to tame a wild child with love.

As Jaxx served Sunday morning breakfast, Trixanna pretended that Celeste was invisible.

"Is she *ever* going to leave?" she asked.

"Hey hey hey, don't be rude," said Jaxx.

"That's okay," said Celeste, amused. "I'm not offended."

"But when?" she importuned. "*When* is she going to leave?"

"I said, hey now! She's our *guest*."

"We've had a *lot* of 'guests.'" She raised an eyebrow in Celeste's direction. At least it was the beginning of an acknowledgment.

"Hey, Tricky," said Jaxx. "Lemme ask you something – "

"Don't *call* me that!"

"Okay – how bout Trickster? Can I call you Trickster?"

"Do *not* call me Tricky. Do *not* call me Trickster."

"But that's what you are. You're Lodi the Trickster."

"And you're loaded. Loaded the Asshole."

Celeste laughed at the well-worn routine.

"Come on," said Jaxx to the girl. "Didn't you notice that she looks like someone? Who do you think she looks like?"

"Uhm… a very old Kesha? And I mean *really* old."

"Wrong."

"A fat Kourtney Kardashian?"

"Do not be *rude*. Guess again."

"*You* guess again," said Trix, annoyed.

"Portia. She totally looks like Portia – don't you think?"

"Jaxx – " protested Celeste. She felt it crossed a line.

"She does *not*!"

"Jaxx, please don't – "

"But you *do*," he said. "If we made your hair just a *little* darker, and we tatted you up…"

"You're *crazy*," said Trix. Celeste thought maybe it was time to leave. "If she lost about a *thousand pounds* and got a facelift and a million tattoos, she *still* wouldn't look like her."

"I agree," said Celeste. "Now can we please change the subject?"

"Yes!" said Trix, siding with the guest. "Please change the subject!"

"Okay, will do. Will do, Woofer. "

"Don't *call* me that!"

There were a lot of names she didn't want to be called. Tricky and Trickster annoyed her; Woof and Woofer were variations of Wolf, short for Wolverine. It was obvious to Celeste that the tantrum was ritualized because as Trixanna laid down the law, she scampered into Jaxx's arms and fussed with his neck, tangling his hair with absentminded caresses.

"Woof, woof!" he said, inciting a seizure of exasperated delight. While pleading that he stop, the girl burrowed into his chest, as if wanting to meld. "Woof woof! Woof woof! Woof-*Wolvereeeeeeeeeeeen!*"

They strolled around the neighborhood, an instant family. Trixanna wanted to show "the guest" (she refused to use her name) where Billie Eilish used to live. When Trix ran off, the couple kept walking.

"I was supposed to go to brunch at Imogen's today."

"Really?"

"At her house. For some event."

Celeste showed him the card Imogen gave her.

"Ah… 'the O Group,'" he said knowingly. "As in *Oh, shit!*"

"What's it all about?"

"It's her latest deal. I have to say, it's actually kinda brilliant."

"How do you know her?"

"Through her brother Cage, when I got out of jail. When I met her, she wasn't Imogen – she was *Utopia*. When it comes to names, the girl gets creative. She was doing ADA scams back then, civil rights disability shit. Like, if you're a barista? And she comes in with her emotional support dog for a mocha frappuccino? And you give the mutt a 'look' – big mistake! – 'cause the nasty little shit's growling at you and looks like it's about to fucking *attack*? She'll sue the shit out of you and the whole goddam chain for being prejudicial, you know, violating her rights as a *differently abled* fuck or whatever. They *always* settle. Three-thousand here, four-thousand there – it adds up. She had this partner, Maynard – shoulda asked Imogen for a name-change – a junkie attorney with a blind sister. For real blind, not making this shit up. Maynard's whole practice was tracking websites that weren't 'friendly' to the *unsighted* – like, if when you logged on, they didn't have audio. Like, you know, the website took away your rights and your dignity by not having nailed their audio shit. It didn't matter if it was a tiny publisher of children's books or an Alzheimer's hospice or whatever. And *everyone* paid – 'cause nobody wants to go to court. Nobody can afford to! But Utopia hit a little speed bump and went to jail. She was supplementing her little scam with a side gig." He started to laugh. "She was trying to pass herself off as Mariah Carey's sister! *So* fucking lame – "

"You mean, she was doing what you and Portia were doing?"

He shook his head. "She *wishes*. She was rolling tricks!" (Celeste was still confused.) "I mean, there's *kind* of a similarity between her and Ms. Carey, but *newsflash*: Utopia ain't black! Hahahahaha! She tried rolling a plainclothes guy and got busted. Only did six months but was duly chastened. Her *pride* got wounded. What can I say? The woman is vain. Cage said she found religion behind bars and that's why she's gung ho about the whole Standardized Patient deal. Maybe it's a way of making amends. Which ain't a bad thing, but... after a while, she always gets greedy. So she's into this next-level *other* thing."

"Jaxx, *tell* me!" she laughed. "What *is* it!"

"No spoiler alerts!" She swatted him. "You need to go see for yourself. I'm actually kind of surprised she asked you."

"Why?"

He grew circumspect. "Were you – did you have a conversation with her about being a... victim?"

"A victim of what?"

"Never mind. She's just super-careful about who she lets in... and it's fucking *expensive*. Did she – you're not paying her anything, are you?" he asked, with some alarm.

"Not that I know of. But now I'm *really* intrigued."

"Just go! Go next week. And *do not* give her any money... but here's what you need to do first. You gotta clean up having missed the meeting. You need to tell her you had a *family emergency* because she can get pissy – I mean, if she was expecting you and you didn't show. That's part of the con. She'll want you to think you totally fucked up this rare and amazing *privilege* that was being offered. She'll want you to be grateful she's letting you back in. Be prepared to do a little groveling."

"Okay."

"And report back *all*."

"Okay!"

"Good girl."

"Jaxx – can we not... I'd rather Imogen not know we hooked up. Okay? Just, because, whatever."

"I *never* talk to that woman about personal shit, *aight*? She don't even know where I live, 'kay, Jello?" He liked calling her Cello and Lester too. "*Plus* I don't kiss and tell. Speaking of which, let's run home and fuck."

† † †

When she saw Imogen at the college, she did just as Jaxx suggested and got invited for brunch, two weeks out. He was dead-on: frosty at first, she thawed when Celeste lied about having to take her sister to the ER after she got food poisoned at Zankou Chicken.

Today, the students were palpating her abdomen to rule out a ruptured bowel and pneumoperitoneum. The supervisor and a medical resident ducked their heads in. After Celeste gave feedback, the doctor complimented her acting skills.

"Your face was totally flushed – it looked exactly like patients do, with those kind of issues."

She'd been thinking about Jaxx all during the exams, and when the interns touched her stomach, one after the other, she came.

Adele

Tight Five

The night before she appeared on *Lights Out*, Adele had trouble sleeping.

She kept practicing her Tight Five in front of a mirror – she must have done it forty times. Her slot was at the end of the show.

She googled the comedians scheduled for tomorrow: Brendan Schaub, Chris Franjola, and Kira Soltanovich. Must've been a slow week. Spade usually had a heavy hitter on the panel (or half a heavy) but these folks were relative nobodies, real comedy circuit grinders. Brendan had a podcast called "The Fighter and the Kid" (*huh?*). Chris's was "Cover to Cover" (*snore*). Kira had a YouTube channel, "Let's Get Sweat!" (*say what?*). No one had it goin' *on*, which Adele thought was probably a good thing – the C-list troika wouldn't be that tough an act to follow. Anyway, she banned her big sister from coming because "seeing you in the audience would totally fuck me up."

In between mirror rehearsals, Adele googled Sunset Las Palmas Studios, where the show was taped. She was shocked when Celeste told her that Mom and Dad used to work there, back when it had a different name. The place had been around since silent films and now Comedy Central had kind of taken it over. The Cobain family's old apartment was on Lillian Way, just around the corner.

As she pulled onto the lot, Adele noticed a line of tents on the sidewalk across from the soundstages. The city belonged to the homeless now. It was only 10AM – taping didn't begin until 3 – but a few audience members already waited in line. A gravely disabled woman in a wheelchair sucked on a water bottle held by her caregiver; just behind them, an unkempt fellow in a loud shirt was having bursts of hysterical laughter. The wild bunch looked like they wandered over from the canvas condos. The sun beat down for that extra-skitzy *Day of the Locust* vibe.

Everyone on the show went out of their way to make her feel welcome. They blocked and rehearsed until Spade came in to watch her monologue. Adele was surprised not to have a case of nerves – probably, she guessed, because none of it seemed real. Spade had some really good ideas. He knew which jokes to dial back and which to hit harder; he had no problem going super dark, as long as it was still relatable to the audience. He was a consummate pro and made Adele feel like one as well.

Right before the show started, Spade came to her dressing room and said, "Hey: surprise guest." Mustang rushed in and gave her a big hug. Adele almost cried. *Why's she being so nice?* Part of her was waiting for the bucket of pig blood to pour down on her head. "You're gonna be *amazing*," said Mustang. "Just have fun! We'll go out for a drink after."

And it *was* fun – like the best dream she ever had in her life.

Time collapsed and she was aware of everything: Spade watching from the wings with that raffish, wolfish smile ... the woman in the wheelchair, laughing her diapered ass off ... she even thought she could smell the cameras. She talked about her mother's suicide, and her failure as a woman *and* comedian. She was closing with a Harvey joke about confused showbiz rape victims lobbying for conjugal jail visits when a woman in the audience got disruptive. Security escorted her out and they stopped taping. The warm-up guy jumped onstage and said, "*Someone* was off their meds today," then Spade shouted out, "That would be Adele," which got a huge, cathartic laugh. He walked over to her as the crew reset.

"What just happened?" said Adele, with a frozen smile. She was used to hecklers but didn't expect one during her Tight Five.

Spade grinned and said, "I'm gonna put that on my headstone: 'What Just Happened?'"

"Ha!"

"Pay it no mind. Half our audience is on SSI."

"Should I cut the Harvey joke?"

"Naw – the confused showbiz rape victims might protest. Don't change a thing, you're doin great."

When she was introduced again, the crowd, bolstered by the "inside" anecdotal event, went wild.

She killed.

† † †

"You were *so good*," said Mustang. They were down the street at Rao's, having the drink she promised. "Your life is about to fucking change. You don't even *know*."

"Ya think? I mean, does he even get ratings?"

"Doesn't matter – *important people* watch because they want to see who he's into. And Spade has a *huge* audience online. Plus, you'll be all over YouTube."

"Will he ask me back? To be on the panel?"

"Honestly, girl? In a few months you'll be doing the main room at the Store. I *totally* see you in Toronto at JFL – you're the next big thing."

"I'm too old!"

"That's part of why you're so cool! You're like an old blues singer."

"I've got those wrinkled, leathery Muddy Waters genitals."

"You know what I mean."

"I've always wanted to be the menopausal Dave Chappelle."

"You *hurt* and people *love* that. I am so fucking envious. Because no matter what I say onstage, I'm 'cute' – I'm *always* Ali Wong. Or trying to be... but you! You have that dark, tragic thing and it's disarming. It *almost* scares people away but they wind up being *educated* and it's fucking *transcendent*. You haven't even scratched the surface. Keep exploring the Mom and Dad shit. If you can do that, trust me: Judd'll make the movie."

Suddenly overcome, Adele broke down in tears. She admitted how jealous she'd been of Mustang's success, not only in her heart, but – full confession – in occasional toxic onstage rants at whatever slap-happy shithole she found her jokes dying in. Unburdening herself was like therapy; Mustang held her hand as she expelled the poison.

"One thing I don't understand," said Adele, "is why you did this to me – *for* me. Why you advocated with Spade… why you even came to *watch*. Why you're even here *now*, still listening, after what I just told you."

"Life's so fuckin funny, Addie," she said meditatively. "We're the same person, you know that, right? There's this – *was* this… shitty, shitty part of me that *reveled* when my star rose, and yours didn't. It's so sick! So much anger… and anger's just another word for being depressed. I've struggled with that fuckin mood disorder my whole life. Fuckin trauma, about *so* many things… my dad, my mom, the rape and abduction shit when I was in college – which I *never* talk about onstage by the way. So much stuff I couldn't deal with – *still* can't – so I shoved it down. I can't work out my shit onstage like you do. I do ketamine therapy instead!"

"Where do you do *that*? Coachella?"

"It's totally legal in California. I see an amazing practitioner, Dr Pirouette – he's like this *shaman*. A magician. I've learned *such* amazing things, Addie. Like, I need to forgive my mother, a process that's already started and is so amazing and beautiful. That's why I love that you're talking about your own mom. Another thing I learned was how I needed to make amends, to *so* many people. And one of those people is you."

On the way to the parking structure, Adele replayed the surreal highlights of the day. She called Celeste but her sister didn't pick up. *Who else can I tell?* The sad thing was that she couldn't think of anyone else. Suddenly, one of the tent people lurched out, startling her.

"I'd tell you my name is Bud Wiggins but that wouldn't be the truth."

She stepped back, almost losing her balance.

Tall and bearded, with rapscallion energy, there was warmth in his eyes. Realizing he wasn't a threat, Adele smiled. She *loved* shit like this; encounters with street psychos usually worked their way into her act.

"Wiggins is an interesting fellow," he went on, "or should I say *was*. Which is debatable. Meaning, whether he 'is' or 'was.' It's *arguable*. Eminently so." Her smile deepened before this gentle, troubled man who spoke as if they were old friends kibitzing at the Farmer's Market. "Haven't seen him around though, not in a year or two, which don't bode well – not for *him* anyway. If you didn't already know, and why would you, the man was deeply into scratchers and I pray they didn't get the best of him. Oh, those scratchers are worse than the ponies, and I could tell you a thing about *them*. Fact is, I met him right over there" – he pointed northeast – "at Nic's Liquor, on the corner. When Mr. Wiggins *won*, which I must say seemed not *infrequently*, he was kind enough to tithe a small portion of his earnings to *yours truly*. I was his lucky charm in this area. Don't get me wrong, the man's scratcher kingdom stretched far and wide; I was but serf and jester. A generous soul, Bud Wiggins! Godspeed…"

Adele fished a twenty from her purse. She didn't have anything smaller but was okay with the largesse – what goes around comes around.

"Why thank you!" he said. "I wasn't soliciting, I'd hate you to think."

"My pleasure. I had a very good day."

"May we *all* have very good days."

"I'm Adele," she said, shaking his hand.

"Randolph 'Squat' McCleary." Nodding at the studio gate, he said, "Used to work here, you know. My *hood*, as they say – "Fountain and Lillian Way – locus of my once humble, homey, homely abode."

A wave of exhaustion passed over her; it was time to break away. As she did, he tottered forward.

"Adele!" he shouted tearfully. "Such a lovely name! I'll give my regards to Broadway – *and* the Scratcher King, if and when I see him."

Her big sister wept in shock and awe when Adele recounted the wonders that transpired.

"Our fortunes are changing," said Celeste, like a sooth-sayer, holding the hands of the wild child whom she'd prayed and worried over for so many years.

Everyone wanted to hold her hand today.

At the end of the week, as was their custom, Adele debuted a new routine in the living room – a pitch-perfect channeling of the tent-man. When she came to the "homey, homely abode on Fountain and Lillian Way," Celeste blanched.

"That's where we used to live," she said. "What'd you say his weird name was?"

"*Squat*," said Celeste, savoring the queerness of it. "Randolph Squat McCreary, to be exact."

Celeste shook her head. "That's totally the name of the guy from *Angela*."

"Say what?"

"The character who played the husband of the ghost! Of Angela."

"What are you talking about?"

"On the *show* Dad worked on. He was totally friends with that actor."

A quick google search revealed that "Squat" (played by Brion James) died of a heart attack in Malibu, in 1999. He was 54.

Celeste

Guided Mediation

The house was on South Windsor – an anomalous, somewhat ramshackle two-bedroom in staid, old-money Hancock Park – and Celeste was certain Imogen stole the name. She probably told her workshop "enrollees" that the street was named after her family or some such swindler bullshit.

And yet: the flower-filled house, with its baby grand in the solarium, its small and large oils, its rented butler serving tea and plates of Ladurée macarons, created a cocoon of sunlit prosperity and good cheer. Most of the guests were older – gals from their mid- to late 50s – but Celeste instantly recognized them as members of the same damaged coterie of outsiders and also-rans that she'd belonged to since childhood. Life had roughed them up and they were thirsty. It didn't matter that they were either too fat, too skinny, too plain, too done-up, too loud, too wallflowery, because they were invisible, and that was all changing due to their radical alliance with Imogen Waldorf-Windsor. They eyed the fresh young newcomer with suspicion, shrinking back whenever Celeste tried to be friendly. As if she had been remiss, Imogen strode over and brusquely took Celeste's arm, ushering her into the library to sign an NDA.

"You're here on a 'scholarship' and that's something I rarely do. It's a *little bit* selfish, because I've been looking for someone in your bracket – your age. But I wouldn't want the others to know that. About the scholarship."

"Of course! And thank you – "

"I knew from the first time we met that you *belong*. I'm a feeler, Celeste, and I *felt* you. You're signing this not because I don't trust you – but because everyone signs and my attorney insists. There's a lot of people gunning for us and the work we're doing is just too important to be distorted by social media."

Reentering the living room, conversations grew hushed (Imogen was about to hold forth) and Celeste got a jolt of paranoia. She wondered if whatever was going on was legal and if she'd already incriminated herself simply by being here. She wanted to call Jaxx for reassurance but remembered the cellphones had been seized in the foyer, embargoed by the rent-a-butler. Her imagination ran wild. Maybe it was a QAnon sisterhood or some Kombucha-swigging Mary Kay coven whose primary purpose was fleecing the widows of first responders.

"A few weeks ago," said Imogen, "we talked about rape and its definitions. 1 – You were threatened. Because – newsflash! – that is now acknowledged and accepted as a rape variant. 2 – You were forced. 'Forced' applies to situations where you gave consent to everything *but* intercourse. Yes, ladies: he can pee in your mouth or vice versa, but if you did not want the penis in your vagina, that's 'forced,' i.e. *rape*. 3 – You were asleep, unconscious or disabled by drugs, alcohol, whatever. Point being, you could not give consent. 4 – You were underage. If it happened 60 seconds before your 18th birthday – and you can prove it – you were underage. Which means, girls and girls, you were *raped*.

"Last week, I led you through an exercise where you tried to recapitulate those encounters and scenarios, even if the memories weren't initially clear – *because clear they shall become*. Don't rush; it takes time. Did everyone bring their journals?" There was a rustle of smiles, pens, and decorated notebooks. "Today, I want to talk about criminal versus civil. Once you retrieve those memories, and you *will*, you still may have doubts. Like: What if it goes to trial and my perpetrator's found 'not guilty.' *That does not matter* and we'll talk about why. One of our O.G.s (what Imogen called O Groupers) just received a seven-figure civil settlement after a jury dismissed the case out of hand. *A guilty plea is not necessary for you to triumph civilly.* The perpetrator can still be held liable! And the awards can be *much* greater than those in a jury trial. We're talking pain and suffering, psychotherapy, lost wages and future earnings, loss of companionship with past or present partners... *that* list goes on and on." The ladies scribbled furiously. "It's *very* important that you attend our next session. Is that the 18th?" One of the women parroted *Is that the 18th* like a court stenographer reading back a transcript, before confirming that indeed it was. "I know some of you called with conflicts," Imogen went on. "But you've paid a lot of money and skipped sessions are not refundable. *Value yourself*, girls and girls! More importantly, the session you *skip* is likely to be the one that is *vital to your case* – Murphy's Law, right? It's *doubly* important you be here on the 18th because Deeta Reynaud will be joining us. Deeta received what's called a 'secret settlement' and is going to enlighten us on the hows, whys and wherefores. My wonderful attorney Maynard Krebs will also be here to talk about statutes of limitation. He's a master when it comes to what I call 'The Wayback Machine.' *This cannot be missed.* He'll be talking about the Timothy Hutton case, and what the victim did wrong. And no, she was *not* an O.G.! If she'd come to one of my workshops, I *guarantee* it'd have had a different outcome!"

Hoots, laughter and applause.

After the hour-long lecture, Celeste mingled by the pool with the enrollees. They dropped their guards. Each talked how excited they were and how much they admired the host who'd shown them the way toward courage, renewal, and security – the last, said with a glint in the eye, like a code word for untold riches. A buffet was served. Imogen presided over an impromptu alfresco Q&A. Everyone got loose, even bawdy, but then it turned spiritual because after all, they were spinning gold out of get-back.

The symposia ended as it began, with a guided meditation.

The O.G.s sat in lotus position as Imogen walked them through the fog of recovered memory. She asked them to focus on their skin and what it felt like when it was cold or warmed by the sun. She told them to imagine a feather lightly drawn across an arm or a leg; then replace that feather with the tip of a caressing finger. The ladies were instructed to conjure the faces, smells and voices of anyone who rose to the surface, be it child, mother, schoolyard bully, or former boss. In a separate exercise, they explored paralysis – the type associated with panic, sleep disorders and victimization. Slowly, deftly, Imogen brought them to "the sweet spot" of anger. The goal of the 10-week gathering was to "integrate your trauma antagonist," so as not to waver under deposition. She asked them to visualize the predator being "notified" and the wheels of justice beginning to turn. *Imagine what the wheels of justice look like. We've heard that phrase all of our lives, but I want you to see them. See those wheels. Are they rubber? Are they steel? How big are they? Are they the size of wheels on a car? or tall as the ones on a tractor? Or… are they so big, they reach to the sky and you can't see where they end? I want you to see them – so big that they reach to the sky and touch the clouds.*

Celeste was one of the first to leave. Imogen walked her out, asking, "Was there someone you envisioned?"

"I *think* so," said Celeste.

"Sometimes it takes a moment. We suppress so much! That's the irony – we're wired for survival. Too often, 'survival' means 'forgetting.' We need to convince the subconscious it's *okay* to remember. Not just okay, but essential. Because if you don't remember, you cannot be whole."

"I had no idea what this was about," she said, trying to merrily wrap it up. She just wanted to get out of there. "It's… amazing."

"Wouldn't you love not to be a fucking SP anymore? This is our time, Celeste, and it could be – *should* be – yours. Don't let the parade pass you by."

"Thank you again for inviting me. It was very, very generous."

"Start keeping a journal. It's such a useful tool. It's more than that! It's the diving board into the infinity pool of the rest of your life."

"I will," said Celeste earnestly.

By then, she was standing next to her crummy car. Imogen impishly peeked in, as if to say, *You can kiss this piece of shit goodbye.*

"If you do the *work,* you *will* 'find your man.' Keep coming back! You don't want to miss my attorney, Maynard – *or* Deeta, our very special guest. That's on the 18th, so put it in your calendar. Ciao, bella!"

† † †

Back home in Silver Lake.

Mulling…

The strange afternoon left her on a jagged adrenaline high.

Celeste rifled her drawers, thinking she might come across one of the unused journals bought over the years, but there weren't any. *Why am I even bothering?* Imogen's powers of suggestion were impressive.

She went outside to meditate, clearing her head from the afternoon. A reset. She closed her eyes and still heard Imogen's voice.

The infinity pool of the rest of your life –

She felt Jaxx's touch, pushing the sensation away. She didn't want to muddle the exercise with perversity … she remembered struggling with a boy in middle school who ended up putting a finger in her twat … focused on distant sounds of traffic, but Jaxx's cock kept intruding … her breath became deep and grounded … she thought of her mother – whenever Celeste wasn't feeling well, Mom laid a hand on her forehead to see if she was feverish. She couldn't remember the touch of her dad. He was never a demonstrative man. Finally, she felt pleasantly empty. She listened to the amplified sound of insects, then heard faraway music: was that REM? Or … she thought of Adele and the warmth of hopefulness suffused her body.

Toward the end of her quiet time, she was startled to find herself fantasizing about someone else's touch – not a predator, but a victim's.

Garry.

Garry and Celeste

We Too

It was Sunday afternoon and he was at the Malibu place.

Gita was in Carpinteria at the other beach house; in a few days, Regan was supposed to come down from Ojai and introduce him to Jaxx Snowcroft, a key player in the optioned *Vanity Fair* piece.

He was in his favorite ratty deck chair, politely drinking, when he got the text: "need discuss something urgent? best in person." No hello, no preamble – a little strange because they hadn't spoken since that time of commiseration in his office. He'd even forgotten giving Celeste his cellphone number when he extended a helping hand all those years ago. *This cannot be good.* His gut flipped the same way it did on the night he saw her name on Gabriella's callback sheet, and *again* presumed Summer's diary had been found.

Best get it over with.

He texted her the PCH address. *door's unlocked, come out to the deck.*

Whatever she had to share would be diminished – or drowned – by the mighty ocean's riot.

† † †

He couldn't believe what he was hearing: a Me Too plaintiff factory for discarded women! So dark, so genius! Her text said it was "urgent" but none of what she was telling him – as grotesque and fun as it was to hear – sounded pertinent to his own case.

The world had gone mad, but so what?

Egged on by his dumbstruck eyes, Celeste giddily conveyed the details. She felt like she was in one of those old movies where a precocious cub reporter-cum-*ingénue* hands her grizzled editor a clue that exposes a vast conspiracy, rocking the world.

When she passed him Imogen's card, he was thunderstruck.

"*She's* the one – " he said, staring at the name in horror and delight.

"What do you mean?"

"Imogen Waldorf-Windsor! The one who's *extorting* me..." Celeste still didn't know what he was talking about. Garry leapt to his feet, stood her up, and held her shoulders. "Celeste? I think you just saved my life."

"What?"

"I've got to call Sam."

She followed him inside and sat in the banquette. Clutching the receiver, waiting to be put through, he had the prehensile, poised yet manic look of a man who about to deliver earthshattering news. When Sam got on, they animatedly spoke for around five minutes and Celeste was shocked at what she heard. She fought not to interrupt because there was much more she still had to tell him – the Mariah Carey hustle! The emotional support dogs! Imogen's attorney's blind sister scam! Thoughts of Jaxx intruded… when more details were solicited, either by Garry or his attorney, she would leave him out of the picture. After years of watching cop shows, she knew his parole would be revoked if it were discovered that he'd been hanging out with an active felon like Imogen *aka* Utopia. In the same thought-breath, she realized something else: she didn't want Garry to know she had a lover.

He hung up and stared at her, drained.

He'd spent the last few months wondering – if it came to that – if he would have the stones to hang himself like Summer did. Something else Leonard once said bubbled up: *No more room on the gallows.*

But now, he had permission to rejoin the world.

To Celeste, he looked younger, lighter, perilously vulnerable. When she walked over to him, he collapsed in her arms – tableau of nurse and brave, wounded soldier.

"The long national nightmare is over," he intoned. Adding with a crinkled-eyed smile, "Maybe."

The embrace went on too long.

As he pulled away, she drew him closer. He flinched when he became attuned to what his head refused to believe was Celeste's intent.

"It's okay," she whispered. She gushed down there, wondering if Jaxx had turned her into some kind of nympho in record time.

"I can't," he said, nodding his head.

"You can," she said, almost inaudibly. "I'm giving you consent."

† † †

Every three weeks or so he popped a Cialis and let his wife climb on top, fuck-by-numbers that kept the marriage viable but only according to Talmudic law. In the carnal sense, they divorced years ago; he no longer had any idea of Gita's cravings. She traveled so much, alone, and for all he knew had a rich, motley erotic life.

His lust for this new body, supercharged by a lonesome, moribund celibacy, was exponential, because Summer *made* her: Celeste's bones and hair, eyes and flesh, her rogue miscellany of smells. *Made* the scented agglutination of cells, *made* her birth – and its built-in, death – with a hand and womb in all the young woman's hardwired quirks, predilections and aspirations. The laugh *itself* came from Summer, and the water of Celeste's tears... she was behind her thoughts and dreams; behind each choice, each hesitation, each decision.

She even crowned her with that name, whose root was *heavenly*.

The core of him was all right with what happened between them. He trusted Celeste yet was powerless over the heinous fantasies that came to persecute: an article in the *Times* – or *Vanity Fair!* – profiling his arrest for the rape of the daughter of the woman he raped and drove to suicide. *Ryan Murphy could do a series,* he thought, *like the one on Andrew Cunanan.* At least could laugh about it.

Celeste had her own insecurities. She knew it was absurd but felt like she was cheating on Jaxx. She wasn't sure *why* she'd seduced Garry, even though it felt good and right (still did). She hated not knowing her own mind. The O Group infected her with the notion that she might even be a predator; the thought of Garry attending the workshop on South Windsor Boulevard made her giggle. She worried too that she might have a volte-face and ghost him. She would never want to hurt Garry like that.

Yet there they were, sans attorneys, representing them-selves in the court of taboo teen spirit – all trial and error.

† † †

Sam Marmal was over the moon.

Richie "Snoop" Raskin had already made inroads, not just on "Miss Waldorf Salad," but the sketchy life and times of Maynard C. Krebs, Esq., confidence man-at-law, whom the private eye alternately referred to as Manure T. Krebs and Dopey Gillis. For example, he discovered that on top of the $5,000 O Group workshop fee, Imogen and *Manure* split a third of each enrollee's settlement or award.

They had another meeting with the publicist but this time the mood was celebratory instead of funereal. Sammy wel-comed the PR maven as if she were the most important person in the room, which at this stage of the game was probably the truth.

"What we *need*," said the flack, "is a heavy hitter. Because this is almost going to be as much about the journalist who breaks it."

"You mean a Bob Woodward?" said Garry, showing his age. "I don't think this is in Bob's lane. But he's a friend. No harm in asking."

"I think Ronan Farrow is the one."

She grinned like she'd swallowed the canary in a canceled coalmine.

"That's sexy," said the attorney, with a caveat. "But Ronan's had some trouble of his own."

"Oh, he's fine," she said. "We're living in Short Attention Span Theater, in case you haven't noticed."

"It's kinda genius!" said Sam.

"Would he do it?" asked Garry.

The publicist was sanguine. "I was at his book-signing at Rosanna's. Kathy Griffin was screaming, 'We just don't want them to rape us! Is it asking too much?' But Ronan was very cool. Everyone kept wanting him to take sides but what I remember him saying – and he really stuck to his guns – was 'First and foremost, I'm always a journalist.'" The canary left the gullet for her stomach, where digestive juices began to attack. "So why wouldn't he write our piece?"

While the publicist took a call, Sam rubbed his hands together, cartoonishly licking his chops.

"Snoop's trying to determine if any of the *Reporter* complainants knew Waldorf Salad and Dopey Gillis – if *any* of 'em were O Group graduates. Hey *hey*! Ho *ho*! Wouldn't that be nice?"

† † †

Aside from a few cognitive glitches – and a shakier hand than usual – Garry was beginning to feel like himself again. He was adamant about having a woman write the Waldorf-Windsor piece (Regan agreed) and they were lucky to have Daphne Merkin come aboard. The profile and its bombshell revelation were still six weeks out; the showrunner was comfortable to remain a pariah until publication. Slowly, he returned to cautiously raucous email threads with the old showbiz wrecking crew.

Celeste literally brought him back from the dead in more ways than one. She made him careless, too – sometimes he didn't bother showering after trysts. He'd crawl into bed with

Gita, the barely dry juices of his lover tattooed on him like perfumed cobwebs.

He still sat by the pool listening to Leonard. It was his ritual. The windblown whoosh-clack of the leaves made him recall something the singer told him during one of their Café Sicily forays. They'd been talking about a guru that Leonard discovered in Mumbai.

"I didn't tell Roshi about him," he said, with a sly smile. "It was during a period when I came 'down from the mountain' – Mount Baldy. I told him I was having trouble with the ladies, but I was in Bombay. Have you been?"

"Haven't," said Garry.

"If you liked acid, you'll love India! I was very depressed when I went to Bombay to see Ramesh. A small group gathered in his apartment each morning. Fifteen or twenty people – the lost, and newly found. I was among the lost. But the moment I heard him say the Buddha's words – 'Events happen, deeds are done, but there is no individual doer of the deed' – the depression fell away. The guilt and remorse disappeared. *Everything was predetermined.* I stayed for months. Later, I was surprised to learn that Ramesh was part of a secret society, a very mysterious group who kept 'a library of leaves.' It was like something out of Borges. Each leaf had a name written on it – the names of everyone who ever lived. Their destinies are written there as well. Ramesh told me that he visited the library when he was much younger, but they couldn't find his leaf. Then he remembered that his name had been changed; he told them to look for 'Ganesh,' and they found it. I only tell you this because I know you might have an interest in such things."

Garry took it as a compliment. He felt like a compadre, a freemason and soul brother.

"The predictions on the leaves are one hundred percent accurate, *until they're read aloud*. The reader's ego and the listener's desire clouds the prophecy. The predictions are no longer pure."

Celeste

Clearblue Skies

One time after making love, she sportively asked if he had ever lusted for her mom and didn't know what to make of GG's startled response. She chalked it up to some kind of idiosyncratic generational prudishness. He was old, yes, but so vital, brainy and creative in his work – that's what turned her on. He opened her eyes with his fingers so he could look into them when he came. Sometimes she had to suck him a while to get him going. He fucked her slowly, gently, majestically, and she liked it more than Jaxx's pounding. To pound and pound was a young man's way. (Though she had to admit that sometimes a girl liked a pounding.) The old one ate her out like a pro. The old one smelled of Hermès and Tom Ford warlock; the young one, of the musk and metal of a sorcerer's apprentice. Her body was on fire. The sheets were soaked from 4AM wet dreams and in the afternoons she could daycream without even touching herself.

† † †

She stopped being a Standardized Patient because the publication of the investigative story was imminent. It would be obvious that Celeste had been the source of the damning, detailed description of the workshop and she genuinely

feared the woman's wrath. Garry told her not to worry –
"You're completely protected" – assuring her that Imogen
would soon be underwater, with no time or resources for
anything but legal defense. And besides, it was likely she'd
be arrested.

The O Group CEO still texted –

> how wonderful it was to see your
> light begin to shine see you on the
> 18th!!!!!

And

> the o group will show you the way to
> empowerment&independence
> beyond wildest dreams! keep
> journaling and meditating til you
> FIND YOUR MAN. & dont
> WORRY: he will find YOU because
> whoever and wherever he is,
> TRUST me, celeste, somewhere
> inside he is desparate to make
> REPARATIONS&AMENDS
> somewhere inside he knows he
> OWES you that. keep BREATING
> keep MEDITATING keep
> JOURNALING!!!!!!!!!!

† † †

Jaxx invited her to a "celebratory" dinner at a restaurant in Malibu, not far from Garry's beach house. She imagined GG wandering in for a drink and the three having an awkward moment, like a scene from some middling French farce. *My Two Lovers.*

He said that Geoffrey's was "one of the places we took Neidhoff. We're probably gonna use it as a location." She asked what he meant and he told her the reason they were celebrating: the *Vanity Fair* article was being made into a series for Netflix. When he dropped the name of the producer that optioned it, she almost choked on her calamari.

Being a good double agent, Celeste quickly recovered. She clapped her hands and kissed him in delight. If things were different, she would happily have told him the whole cosmic coincidence of her mom having worked for the man back in the day, even how they'd recently gotten back in touch. But it was all too sticky now. And if she told a partial truth (leaving out the intimacy) she couldn't count on his discretion – the next time Jaxx saw "my producer," he might brashly confide to Garry that he was sleeping with a "mutual friend."

That simply wouldn't do.

There was another unknown factor. If Celeste went with the half-lie, his hustler's sixth sense might alert him to the deception. One of things that excited her about Jaxx was his criminality – *yes* he was reformed, *yes* he was a wonderful dad to Trixanna but there were still a lot of unopened doors, each one marked with giant question mark. She couldn't predict what form his jealousy might take. He might laugh it off or even be turned on; he might be embarrassed or offended and feel threatened that she was sharing someone else's bed. Far worse, that it was the bed of the powerhouse now ruling his world... she assumed Jaxx had a hundred other women in his life, but still. Men were funny, violent creatures.

But once he read the exposé, wouldn't everything come out? Wouldn't he be pissed that she hadn't mentioned her connection to Garry, even *after* he told Celeste they were in business together? Wouldn't he think that was conniving? Then wouldn't he drill down until he got the truth out of her? It wasn't like she could hope he wouldn't read it – he was a news junkie. And what would he think about her ratting Imogen out? Wasn't that a fatal violation of the jailhouse code? Jaxx said that he and Imogen weren't close but what if that was all bullshit? What if her arrest seriously fucked with some scam Jaxx and Imogen were cooking up? What if Jaxx *himself* had something to do with the O Group – and by snitching on Imogen, Celeste was sending him back to prison?

By dessert, she decided it was best to taper things off.

She was proud of her reasoning: both affairs weren't really going anywhere, but the one with Jaxx was going nowhere faster.

All week long, she patted herself on the back for having the discipline (so far) to cut her losses. Then she learned she was pregnant.

Adele

The Velvet Underworld

Were we ever not obsessed with serial killers? Right? I mean, Ted Bundy's on kids' lunchboxes. When did all that shit *start*? The Internet's the *real* serial killer now! (Except it ain't *serial*, it's fuckin *genocidal*.) Say the wrong thing and you're tortured by trolls; your dead raped digital body lives for-evuh – like the bodies serials leave in the forest so they creep back for a moonlit skullfuck and a bit of rotting nookie. *Nudge nudge wink wink.* But where oh *where* did the primetime pop obsession begin? With Norman? Was it Norman? Norman Bates? Was *that* when we got horny? Was that the origin story? When serial killers became superheroes?

Celeste couldn't believe who was at her sister's show – Matthew Perry and Jason Bateman; that funny, sexy actress from *The Office*; the odd-faced girl from *Girls* whose name she could never remember… and Robert Pattinson! *Oh my God how perfect is he.* (He reminded her of Jaxx.) She had a prime table and people kept staring, wondering if she was somebody. Celeste overheard them talking in whispers, trying to be discreet as they pointed out more celebs, whose faces she didn't even recognize. Mustang was right: after *Lights Out* – her Tight Five had 7 million views on YouTube – there was such crazy heat around Addie that almost overnight she was playing the Main Room at the Store. When Judd Apatow came over and introduced Whitney Cummings, she said to Celeste, "Don't mind me. I'm just one of the acts opening for your sister.'"

…that deep down *victim* thing women have – you can't really talk about it, *women* can't talk about it – maybe Chappelle can! [laughter, applause] God Bless Dave for being the strongest woman among us. But it's true. We have this helpless, tie-me-up thing… which is even *hotter* now because it's so fuckin anti-Me Too – the hotness of victimhood, being weak and helpless, even *unattractive* but still having this *thing* they all want, this thing they all fuckin *need* – the incels, the normies, the Bundys and BTKs – they all want it *bad*. Pussy! You can be totally *out of shape,* you can have a fucking *gunt,* and they *still* want that puss, any way you can slice it! Literally. They'll lift your fat folds to find that buried treasure. What gal doesn't want to be wanted? Even if you're wanted so bad that you, uhm, *have to die?* Oh fuck it, we gotta go sometime, right? Some of these serial killers don't know what to do with a pussy once they have it. *Ironic,* huh. You finally have that thing you wanted, all to yourself, but there's no instruction manual. So, they keep it in a drawer, thinking, you know, "One day I'll figure that shit out." So they just throw some car deodorizer on it, you know, one of those hula girls. Shpritz it once in a while with a little Windex, Lysol, whatever. They don't know what do with it but they sure as fuck *want* it... they want to be *around* it – you know, like a kid at a campfire. God's campfire. This hole. *All* the holes. They want it so bad that they keep it as a trophy. Throw the bod away but keep the vadge. [*groans, laughter*] Even when the campfire's out, it still manages to keep em warm... fancy that. All the smart, crushed-out podcast girls fantasize about it like kids reading under the sheets with flashlights. They're cool imagining an "encounter" – until push comes to stab. Until push comes to cut off your nipples and eat em in front of you while you're still conscious. [*groans, laughter*] Until then, it's all fun and games! Until then, life is but a dream, a hilarious fuckin Instagram dream. *Roll roll roll your vadge, gently down the stream. Merrily,*

merrily, merrily, merrily – but when did BTK become a *rock star*? That's what *I* want to know. David Fincher did a whole fucking series about him... may I ask *why*? Oh! That show was *so artistic*. BTK hung a little girl from a basement pipe after murdering her whole family – you can see the photo on the Internet. She's in the basement, just hangin' there in her panties. [*more groans*] Oops – sorry! Am I losing you? Am I losing the crowd? Just be patient, the comedy is *coming*, I swear to *God* it is. [*laughter*] So just be patient... Oh the Internet is our friend! I can't tell you how many hours I've spent obsessing on the image of that poor little girl. We make these men, these monsters, into fancy little Fincher franchises, you know, we *class 'em up*, or put em in big shitty Marvel movies, that's how fucked we are! Thanos snaps his fingers and kills hundreds of millions! We put em in a shiny Netflix box and wrap it up in Marvel ribbons. Poor Robert Downey Jr. got killed by Thanos, then killed *again* – by Dr. Dolittle! *Dr. Dolittle* should have gone up against Thanos! Now *there's* a movie I would definitely want to see...

Okay, all this shit goes back to Daddy. I know, I know. Bad, bad Daddy. Doesn't take much to be a bad Dad, right, girls? You know, the first time – and I don't care if he's the best father in the world – that first time he looks at you and realizes you've got tits. You're, like, twelve. And he looks at you like that, maybe only *once*, but it gets seared on your reptile brain. You hate him and love him for looking at you the same way he looks at Mama. [*groans, laughter*] See, I have the *ultimate* Daddy Issue: my father vanished when I was pretty much a newborn. My sister and I went to live with his parents – our grandparents raised us, sissy and me. Nothing worse for a girl than a bad, vanished daddy – or maybe nothing better! 'Cause sometimes it's better to get fucked over by someone who isn't there, than to be fucked over by someone who *is*. Right? Our mom hanged herself when we were little. Nice, right? She was depressed. Way back in prehistoric days, before there was ketamine. My big sis remembers her but *I* don't, though sometimes I sorta think I remember... how she smelled (which is probably impossible, because I was like four months old when she died)... When people find out she hanged herself – when I tell em! – they're like, *Oh my God, Adele! You should write a memoir!* Like I automatically *qualify* for the futile memoir sweepstakes. I just tell em, "Bitch, I do standup." I work this shit out onstage, thank you very much... [*laughter, applause*]

So my mother hanged herself and that's why I can't stop looking at that desolate, brain-killing, heartbreaking police photo of Josephine Otero – I need to say her name, she deserves to have a name – one of God's children, strung up in her basement by BTK. Who I guess was one of God's children too. At one time. And I'm *still* looking at that photo. I'll always keep looking, *willing* her to come alive and cut herself down and... slay the monster. Or not. Willing her to just go and brush her teeth and get ready for school. I couldn't stop looking at pictures of my dad either. I kept willing him to turn his head toward me – in those old Kodaks, he was always looking away from the camera – to turn his head my way and smile and say, *There's my girl*. But now I need to tell you something – I hope my sister doesn't mind – she's here tonight. Where are you, Cel? [*Celeste shyly raises a hand, applause/whoops*] Hi, baby! I love my sis, she took care of me after everyone left, takes care of me still. I'm going to tell you something that I haven't even shared with my imaginary therapist: *we found him.* We found our father, after all these years. [*audience gasps, laughter. They're uncertain if she's being serious*] That's right. True story. Out of the blue. We didn't have to hire someone to look for him, we didn't go on 23 and Me… didn't have to Golden State it, or however they do now, to solve cold cases. God just dropped him down in front of us – of me – right after I taped *Lights Out*. There he was, a homeless guy living on the sidewalk across from the studio. Thank you, Spade! I love you, Spade! But I'm out of time, so I'll tell that story to you on *another occasion.* [*audience groans. Shout-outs of encouragement for her to keep going*] So we just met our father and now we're all getting reacquainted. *Our father, who wasn't in Heaven, hollow and haunted be his name and his eyes.* My sister says I have his eyes… and only now do I realize that all these years there was a huge part of me that fantasized I'd finally find him. And you know who I imagined he'd turn out to be? Not a movie star or some fucking twat billionaire, no – but a Dexter or a Bundy or a BTK. That's where my nerd-girl tie-me-up tie-me-down head, heart and holes went. But nope, sorry! *Sorry.* Just a sad, broken dad trying to find his way back home, find his way back *homeless* to the apartment where we used to live on Fountain and Lillian Way. It was my mother's death that destroyed him. He used to take care of her, but when she left, he couldn't take care of... anything. God wants him home now, so his girls can love him back to life.

[pauses. *The audience is silent*]

I can really relate to the late, great Robert Downey Jr aka Tony Stark in his final battle with Thanos. Thanos looks at him and said, "I am inevitable." I look in the mirror and see all those serial killers saying, *I am inevitable*. Mom and Dad are in the mirror too, saying, *I am inevitable*. Josephine Otero, the little girl in the basement, is saying, *I am inevitable*. I see the faces of Bachelors and Bachelorettes from seasons past, all saying, *I am inevitable*. I see superheroes and supervillains, I see Death and defeat, I see depression and madness, I see the whole monetized Marvel Cinematic Universe destruction derby saying, *I am inevitable*. (And now, dear audience, I'll see *your* beautiful, laughing faces in the mirror. Because you are inevitable.) Thanos speaks to me now. I quote from *Avengers: Infinity War* – "I know what it's like to lose. To feel so desperately that you're right, yet to fail nonetheless. It's frightening and turns the legs to jelly. I ask you to what end? Dread it, run from it, but Destiny arrives all the same. Now, it's here." [*pause*] I listen to *all* the voices. And when that great roar comes through the mirror, shouting *I am inevitable*, I look back at in the glass and stare it down. That's when I answer, with my resting Infinity bitch face and say, "And I... am Adele Cobain."

A woman was softly crying.

Adele composed herself then did something no one – not even her – was suspecting.

She sang.

She sang the Lou Reed song as if it were inevitable.

When you think the night has seen your mind
That inside you're twisted and unkind
Let me stand to show that you are blind
Please put down your hands
'Cause I see you

I'll be your mirror

She looked out at the crowd, a smile plastered on wet-cheeked tears like a once-in-a-century storm, some virgin supernova who just blew the eternity roof off *America's Got Talent*.

She blinked and said

"Thank you and fuck you and good night!"

Garry

Candelabra

After the exposé in the *New York Times*, exoneration came swiftly.

Garry refused all interview requests. Instead, he issued a short statement through his attorney that thanked friends and family before expressing admiration for "the many heroic women who bravely continue to make their voices heard and in so doing, are reshaping our culture – and the world's." Old confidantes and associates who froze him out during the moratorium were back in touch. Some were repentant, blaming their absenteeism on personal troubles; others behaved like nothing happened at all. Garry was uniformly gracious. He wanted to put everything behind him and get on with the business at hand: writing and producing *Lovechild.*

The women of the *Reporter* – dubbed "traumanauts" by an op-ed in the *Washington Post* – rocketed back to the angry red planet whence they came. (One of them *did* turn out to be an O.G. grad.) Imogen Waldorf-Windsor aka Utopia Cunningham Oostvund was jailed on extortion and other charges, including old warrants. A handful of power players began circling the somewhat culturally delicate, borderline-radioactive story, including Patricia Arquette and Adam McKay. Garry got a kick out of the idea of being portrayed by Anthony Hopkins, Jeff Bridges, or some other legendary, glorious old fuck. It was a hoot.

Then the virus shut everything down.

They quarantined up in Carpinteria and he welcomed the cushy reset – it felt like he'd been bonused out. He needed an enforced break, not just from his own life, but everyone else's. The time away from Celeste would allow him to take a step back and see what was real.

With the stress of career death and pending litigation removed, he and Gita ran out of excuses. So, they started in again, nervously exploring their bodies with a shyness that delighted. Making love to her became a catechism of the historical, fleshy calendar of their lives, and he had her in all versions: the fiery, goosepimpled girl who made his heart catch in his throat; six months pregnant with Regan; the one he guiltily came home to after rendezvousing with Summer Cobain. He fucked rainbow and storm – sad Gita, mad Gita, ecstatic Gita; Gita needy and Gita arrogantly independent; Gita who wanted to renew their vows in Bhutan and Gita who wished they had never met. In the midst of those healing sessions, he revisited other lovers, inevitably culminating in a toggle between Summer and Celeste – Mr.

Showrunner sweated and labored atop that three-headed goddess like the dung beetle that he was.

And began to seriously jones for Celeste.

Being apart from her reminded him his last phone talk with Summer. When she called to tell him that she was pregnant, he didn't believe that the baby wasn't his. He remembered saying that if it were, he would provide for the child through a blind, secret trust. He remembered her laughing at that – didn't she? Laugh? He asked her twice if it was his. (Didn't he?) After a long pause, she eerily whispered *blind, secret,* before telling him no, it was her husband's, she was certain. They'd been careful (if careful about nothing else), so he wasn't surprised yet still wanted to go on record as having wanted to do the right thing. He owed her that much. He said how happy he was for her, which was genuine and true, because a newborn would help her move on from the glorious city of cathedrals that he bombed. But *did* she want to move on? Did *he*? At the time, his feelings were too complicated to sort out. He remembered being disgusted with himself for plotting a continuation of their adultery; even if it wasn't his, the baby became an erotic prop, enflaming their treasonous bond. More than a year later, when he learned of her death, he hated himself all over again for feeling validated – *vindicated* – that the relationship must have been as complicated for her as it was for him.

Celeste was her mother reborn, without the drama – Indian Summer, after the fall.

But was it love?

The inanity of the question made him nauseous.

They began to FaceTime.

Garry was in the second-floor study and monitored his wife's whereabouts as they spoke: walking on the beach, reading on the deck. They made plans to see each other "when Corona starts getting tired of itself." Phone sex was better than good, and fun too.

Once, after they both came, he said, "That was important" – it sounded so earnest that they laughed until they choked.

† † †

He was deep into writing the script for *Lovechild*. The material continued to enthrall but he had issues focusing. Sometimes he couldn't find the right words; when he did, they stopped making sense.

He no longer listened to Leonard.

He sat on the beach, reading an old profile of David Milch in *The New Yorker*. He wasn't a friend, but they'd crossed paths over the years and Garry admired him. The essay touched on Alzheimer's and the difficulties Milch experienced while writing the feature film version of his cult show *Deadwood*. The chill of what was coming went up Garry's spine.

A new symptom attacked his sight. He thought they were just floaters until they morphed into the fingery candelabra patterns at the edge of vinegary Polaroids, emulsive designs that ruined the photo yet for some reason long mesmerized. What he saw reminded him of the hourglass eyes of his favorite Miro, "The Beautiful Bird Revealing the Unknown to a Pair of Lovers." How appropriate the title seemed! But *which* pair? Garry and Gita? Garry and Summer? Garry and Celeste? Maybe the beautiful bird was Ali Nell, whose talons carried all lovers away to the Unknown, dead or alive.

At dusk, fresh phantoms and oracles visited.

Portia Coldstream stood on the shore, beckoning, then Summer replaced her and began to walk toward him. He didn't flinch. He hoped she came closer; he wanted to feel her arms around him.

When the hallucination broke, Garry convinced himself that it was just a vivid imagining but he knew they had changed their throats and had the throats of birds, beautiful birds sending flares from the place called *things to come* – part of the divine emulsion inching toward him like lava, invading the tidy margins of the snapshots of his petty, poignant, dispensable life.

† † †

Regan joined them in Carpinteria for quarantine.

She was so excited about *Lovechild* – to have brought her father something worthy, to show her worthiness and be journeying at last toward her authentic, creative self (as a producer) – that she couldn't see the fear in his eyes. She thought he was kidding when he repeated a sentence ten times, word for word. She rushed to him but he was in a blind trance. She got so scared. When she put her arm on his, he snapped out of it and smiled at her. "Daddy," she said quietly. "I'm worried you might be having a stroke." Regan started to call 911 but ran and got her mother instead. They zoomed with his doctor.

Waiting for the paramedics, Garry told them about the Parkinson's.

Celeste

Superfecundfragilistic

Her plan was to get an abortion, but she kept putting it off and by the time she was ready, Covid put a kink in it. She thought they wouldn't let you get one, which turned out not to be true. That was in the red states.

She was lying about so many things now. Most of the time she stayed with Jaxx because lockdown with Adele was a drag. Her sister was being a total paranoid gloves-in-the-house bitch about the virus and wouldn't let Celeste near her anyway. Jaxx thought the whole thing was nuts and so did Trixanna, a mask refusenik on a 24/7 conspiracy theory sugar-high. So, they all hung out, ate junk food, and watched *Plandemic*. Celeste lied to herself as well, her latest fantasy being the baby belonged to Garry and Jaxx *both* – one of those rarities she read about on the Internet where a woman had twins from different biological dads. They called that "superfecundation"; there was polyspermy too, when an egg got fertilized by more than one sperm. Apparently, sperm could live inside a woman for three days and Celeste was certain she fucked the two of them multiple times inside three-day windows. She saw herself as a woodpecker, mating with more than one male to hedge her bet against giving birth to a low-life. (That would be Jaxx.) She'd been wiki-ing her widening ass off. In Greek mythology, the father of one of Leda's twins was Zeus; the father of the other was her husband Tyndareus.

Celeste decided to wait until lockdown was over before ending the relationship. The abortion was scheduled in two weeks. She wondered what it would be like to have a child, something never too high on her list. She'd *still* have to prove the identity of the dad, which would be embarrassing in itself. If it was Jaxx, she couldn't deal with the general weirdness and unpredictability of his life. There was no way to depend on him for any kind of emotional or financial security.

And if it were Garry's... how could she do that to him?

† † †

She was two-and-a-half-months now and Jaxx started to notice, but not in a good way. "Man, you *thick*!" he'd say, gawking at her like some wide-eyed hillbilly. He kept sending her TikToks: a morbidly obese dog would lumber into the frame and a good ol' boy would holler off-camera, "Damn... *damn, boy!* Damn boy, he's *thick!* That's a thickass boy!"

It pissed her off, but the sex was better than ever.

After they made love, he'd start in again. "Watch your diet, that's all. You don't want the Quarantine 65 – that's when you pack on 65 pounds. If you pack on the *poundage*, say goodbye to packin' on the *PDA*, 'cause no one wants to see that shit in public, it's too gross. Personally, I think sixty-five pounds is *manageable*. Anyone can lose that shit. Might take a year or two but it's doable. It's the *Quarantine 200* you need to avoid. Now, *that* is fuckin *thick!*"

"Jaxx, would you just stop?"

He left the room and came back with a joint. He put on some music, got back in bed and lit up. Celeste stared at the ceiling, thinking she should maybe google some local hotels. She didn't even know if they were open anymore. He cleared his throat and she got ready for an apology.

"Hey listen, there's something I want to talk to you about. Now's probably not a good time, but as they *say*, there ain't no good time, so whatever. Honey, my life is getting *com-plee-cated*. There's all *kinds* of shit going on and – uhm – I just don't think it's fair to… like, I need to go back down to *Meh-hee-ko*. I'm workin on a new project. I'm startin a production company, did I tell you that? I need to strike while the iron's fucking *hot*, which because of this *Netflix* deal it *is*. And that shit won't last forever, right? So I'm taking Trix and we're gonna stay in a – some sort of villa owned by Hugh Jackman and his wife. In Puerto Vallarta. They invited us down. The Jackmans are cool, they actually played a pretty big part in getting Trixanna the help she needed. They have a foundation. That piece of shit *Neidhoff* – Mr. N-word – actually gave money to it, to their foundation, it's crazy, and the money – *some* of it – went to Trix. But whatever, like, I can't bring anyone down there, it wouldn't be cool to have a 'guest' and anyway I'm not there to party, I'm down there to work. And it's *serious*. So what I'm saying is, why don't we hook up down the line – gotta do this mogul shit first. I mean, it's probably better, for *you*, to be out there, right? I don't want you to be tied down, waiting for your mogul man to come home."

She was violently angry but suddenly had a plan.

"I'm pregnant."

"You're what?"

"Preg. Nant."

"Whoa! *That's* why you're thick, I should have known that shit!"

"So – you still want to break up?"

"Well, uhm, *shit*." He scratched his chin and got stoked. "Trix always wanted a sib. Do you know what it is?"

"A boy."

She had no idea but knew that's what he wanted to hear.

"Are you serious? That's fucking *amazing*. Hey, you know what? We'll figure it out. I'll talk to Hugh – he's cool. He'll probably say, 'Bring em down!' Deborra-Lee'll *love* it. It's not like there won't be room, the villa's got like 15,000 square feet. Yes!" He clapped his hands. "We'll get you a doula, fuck it, we'll get you *three*. Doula's are probably cheap as fuck down there – "

"I don't know," said Celeste.

"You don't know what."

"I think," she said, as if musing on the color of wallpaper for the nursery. "I think I'll just kill it."

"Ha!" His face scrunched in a wack grimace. "Say what?"

"I'm gonna fucking kill it, Jaxx."

"What are you talking about?"

"How could anyone bring a baby into this world? This horrible world where everyone gains 700 pounds?"

"Come on now, that's just your hormone's talking. That kid's gonna be *king* – "

She got up and dressed while he tried to chill her out.

"Look, I didn't mean that sayonara shit. You took it wrong, anyway. When I said don't come down to Mexico, I meant you'd come *later* – "

"You are so full of shit, Jaxx."

"I was thinking of what'd be best for *you*."

"*Fuck off.*"

"Come on, Lester – "

"Don't fucking call me that!"

" – let's have a *baby*. It'll be *amazing*."

"We're going to have an amazing abortion."

"Don't do that to Trix."

"Oh, she'll be fine. She always lands on her mentally ill feet." It was the worst thing she'd ever said to anyone in her life, worse because Celeste had grown so fond of her. "I didn't mean that and I'm sorry."

He followed her out.

"Come on, Celeste, come down to P.V. with your baby daddy…"

She turned around and resolutely said, "Okay. I'll come."

"Yes!" he fist-pumped.

"But I need to know something first."

"You got it. Anything!"

"I need your *reassurance*…"

"I'm *telling* you – "

"…that you'll raise him like he's your own."

"My own," he laughed. "What does *that* mean?"

"Because you're not the father."

"Oh really?" he said with a smile and flash of venom.

"That's right."

"*Okaaaaaay*. Then whose is it?"

She turned at the door like a vindicated 80s romcom lady, said "Hugh fucking *Jackman's*," then slammed the door behind her.

It took two weeks for his calls and texts to die out, but she never answered one of them.

† † †

Adele's life blew up, as they used to say.

On her triumphant night at the Comedy Store, she insisted they break policy and allow the audience to take phone videos; the results were more than 10 million views on YouTube and Instagram. Her confessional fearlessness struck some kind of lockdown chord and she was gaining 20,000+ followers a day. A *New Yorker* profile ("Who's Afraid of Adele Cobain? Everyone") wrote, "She is that staple of American show business mythology: an underhanded overnight success. Though *Sleight-of-hand* may be more accurate, for behind the profane standup *comédien* is that rara avis: a classico-populist dramatist and Swiftian social satirist of the highest order. Watching her performance at the Comedy Store is like watching the lovechild of Eugene O'Neill and Lenny Bruce." Spade invited her to zoom parties with Sandler, Apatow, Schumer, Chappelle, Bill Murray. She got DM'd by Madonna, Tarantino, AOC. The Stern show's Garry Dell'Abate reached out. She did an at-home *Real Time* with Bill Maher and wound up doing a full week of at-home guest host chores on *Kimmel*.

Money started pouring in.

"I'm going to get us a house in Studio City."

"Really," said Celeste.

"I need to up my zoom game. People need to see me in my shitty old Target bathrobe, chillin' in *Versailles*. Need me a Cardi-B-sized airplane hangar living room. *Fuck* all that humble bookshelf background bullshit."

"Haha."

"I am *serious*. It's in escrow."

"Wha?"

"Did it all online. Took the virtual tour. Fucker's on two *acres*. Has a pool and guesthouse too."

"Oh my God!"

"Oh, you *know* it. And guess who's gonna live there?"

"Well I hope I am."

"Aside from you, bitch. You have your own *wing*. Guess who else?"

"Mustang? Jimmy Kimmel?"

"Daddy."

"What?"

"Our *father*. Who art in guest house. 'Hel-*lo*' be his name."

"What are you *talking* about?"

"We're gonna be a family again! And again and again, apparently."

"Addie, we don't even know where he is…"

"Yes we *do*. My friends at Homeless Healthcare *located* our little runaway. He was taking a shit under a bridge when they threw the net on him."

"*Stop* it, he was *not* – "

"Naw, he's okay. He was just sleepin on a sidewalk some-where, you know, doin his thing. But he's all cleaned up now and living in a motel over on Eighth and Alvarado where they can keep an eye on him."

"And *when* is all this going to happen?"

"*Soon*. You can still move into houses during the Corona. They just soak the place in a giant fucking sanitizer – you have *got* to see the video the realtor sent me, it's friggin *crazy*. We'll get him a young buck caregiver who'll fuck us on the side when he's not chasing Dad down the street."

Celeste began to weep inconsolably.

"Baby!" said Adele, rushing to her. "Honeychile! It's *okay*, it's all *right*. Everything's going to be *more* than all right…" The convulsive tears wouldn't subside. "Sweetheart, what's wrong? What is it?"

Celeste vomited a torrent of words about the two men in her life, ending with the news of her pregnancy. Speechless, a smile slowly spread across Adele's face. She never expected such pyrotechnics from the one who'd been her anchor and voice of reason throughout childhood and adult life. She was beyond excited for her – "for us" – ordering her *not* to have an abortion under *any* circumstances. The command was the antidote to Celeste's confusion and suffering. It was funny how that worked: one moment, she saw herself alone and bereft, getting her forlorn womb Dyson'd at the clinic – the next, she was shopping for baby clothes, plotting the best way to break the news to Garry. Adele urged her to tell him everything. "He can't be upset about you sleeping with someone else, he's fucking married! But he's a good man, right? Let me tell you something – I'm psychic, you *know* that about me – well *let me tell you,* this rich old motherfucker *loves* you. Are you in love with him?"

"I don't know, Addie… I don't fucking know!"

"He may *never* leave his wife, okay? That's just the way shit usually is. 'Modern problems,' right? *Modern dating.* That's what you always say. But he'll take *care* of you, for real. Psychic Addie knows all! He'll take care of you and that kid for *life.*"

"Not if it isn't his. I can't have him take the test, Addie."

"Why not? He'll be totally happy to!" Celeste shook her head and cried some more. "Then fuck him, we'll raise it *our-selves.* Oh my God, Celeste, I am so excited! I love you so much! Don't you see, can't you see? *This is our time.* That's *exactly* what you said after I did *Lights Out,* remember? The world's going to shit but we're fucking *giving birth,* in our own ways… it's God's crazy fucking plan. And you know what else is part of his plan? *Listen* to me, because I'm *psychic.* It's *his* baby, okay? *It's the TV guy's baby.* Celeste, *look* at me. It's *his,* I *know* it is, it is *not* that scumbag's." She smiled. "And if it isn't… you just *tell* him it fucking is." They laughed and laughed. "That way, you don't even have to tell him about Jaxx or jackoff or whatever the fuck his name is. Problem solved!"

The End of the Affair

Cedars was like a ghost town. They even left the gates of the parking lots open. In the early weeks of skittish, depopulated CoronaWorld, the series of tests – the myocardial scintigraphy, the fluorodeoxyglucose PET scan of the brain, the SPECT imaging – took half the time than usual.

When the doctor called on Sunday with the results (Lewy Body Dementia), Garry was alone in Malibu. Regan was back in Ojai for the day, digging around in old journals that she hoped to turn into a memoir. Her new life as a working producer had gotten the creative juices flowing. Gita was on a chartered jet to Seattle, where her 93-year-old father was dying. One of his wife's pet peeves was this business of not allowing folks to be with their loved ones as they succumbed to the virus. "There's two possibilities," she said. "I'll be holding Daddy's hand when he leaves the world – or setting fire to the hospital and everyone in it."

He was glad the girls weren't there. It wouldn't have been fun to hear Regan screech, *"Shit shit no! That's what Robin Williams had!"* as Gita assumed the fetal position on the Roche Bobois bubble couch. He wasn't feeling the drama so much himself. It was shitty news but explained a lot, especially the hallucinations. He was glad to have a little time to himself before the big announcement. The one person he urgently wanted to tell was Celeste.

When he called, she asked what was wrong – she heard it in his voice. His courage flagged and he softened the request.

"It's just been too long. I'm alone for the day – can you come up?"

"Malibu?"

"Yes."

"Are we socially distancing?" she asked, a smile in her voice.

"Full hazmat suits," he answered.

As he waited, Garry tried to write the scene where he told her the diagnosis. Like everything else lately, it was a surreal predicament. He'd been on the elliptical and feeling physically fit. His work on *Lovechild* was going better than ever. He had even started whispering to himself those fatal words: *Gonna beat this thing.* He didn't want Celeste's sympathy. But mostly, he didn't want her backing away from him sexually. Maybe he'd just leave it at Parkinson's sans Lewy body. He couldn't trust himself. He was so emotional lately he'd probably end up just blurting everything out. Gita and Regan were already acting like two hovering mommies; he didn't need his young lover to become a third. He decided to put those thoughts away and see how things played out.

On her way to the beach, Celeste was all butterflies.

She wanted to believe her sister's psychic read – that the baby *was* his – but each time she went down that road, banditos from Jaxx's Mexican villa jumped out of the bush and carjacked the notion. Anyway, she took Garry's invitation as the way of the Universe, forcing her to come clean. She wondered if they should fuck first, to take the edge off, though she had some Covid trepidations about that because the man *was* over 65. Celeste wished it were nighttime because she was self-conscious about her weight. (Sometime in the last week her hips went missing.) She was hormonal and kept vacillating between telling him nothing, telling him everything, or a broken linkage of truths and half-truths. *Say it's his. Say it's someone else's. Don't say anything. Have it anyway. Say nothing but get the abortion....* The *real* truth was that Celeste was starved for him, starved for his touch. But what did any of it mean? She wasn't even sure *his* touch was what she hungered for – maybe anyone's would do. Because Jaxx was no longer on the menu, maybe her feelings for Garry had grown stronger than they actually were. Adele said he would be accepting – of the baby itself, whether or not it was his – even accepting of Jaxx as the potential father. But what if her sister was wrong? *I've been fucking the lowlife whose life rights he bought! The person I met through his tormentor, Imogen!* It was a nest of Russian dolls. It all gave her a terrible headache on top of the morning sickness.

His hands shook uncontrollably after sex.

"You still got it, kid," he joked. "You make a man crazy."

He explained that it was innocuous, something his doctor called an "intentional tremor." He got creative, adding that the pills occasionally had an "antagonistic effect" that temporarily made the tremors worse. He didn't say anything about her weight (she knew he wouldn't, he was a gent) but Celeste got that out of the way by telling him she was on a new antidepressant that caused the gain. Concerned, he asked about her mood. She laughed and said the world was so effed up right now that people who *weren't* depressed were the sick ones.

She wasn't sure what was different about him. For a PTSD minute, she thought he was going to give her the Jaxxian heave-ho, but that wasn't it. It was deeper – something melancholy and opaque. He prattled on about the avalanche of work since getting out of Me Too jail, the artistic challenges of the *Lovechild* adaption, all that. She pretended that everything he was saying made sense.

He kept checking his phone. He said that he was waiting to hear from Gita about whether her father had died. When he texted his daughter, Celeste knew he was surreptitiously checking to see if Regan was on her way home. When he tried to call, she didn't pick up. Celeste didn't want to be the source of more stress; best to leave on a high note. Garry said *please stay, we have a few more hours* but she said *I really should go*, knowing he felt that way too. "We'll have plenty of time to hang out," she said, "after they find the vaccine." He sweetly insisted they go for a walk on the beach before she left. *Why not? The ocean air'll do us both good.* He suggested they put their masks on "because my neighbors are a little fussy." If Regan came home unexpectedly, being caught taking an innocent beach walk was better than the alternative. Later, he could say that he was simply advising her on a pressing personal problem. His daughter had already met Celeste at a smallish dinner party that he'd thrown to celebrate the arrest of Imogen and the dismissal of the *Reporter* lawsuits. Celeste had even been given a hero's toast.

It was red tide and she almost stepped on a purple starfish.

"Do you need anything, Celeste?"

She knew he meant money. For the moment, her sister was flush, but Celeste didn't trust the world – or the social media it rode in on. Just when you were sitting around the bonfire having a grand old sing-along, a whole crew was busy hammering down a stake in front of your eyes. The one you were going to burn on.

"No, I'm fine, Garry. But *thank you*. Thank you."

"Listen… why don't you come work for me. Come work *with* me."

"Sweetie, are you for real?"

"I mean it. Would you at least think about it?"

"I don't think I'd be able to do both."

"Both?"

Celeste realized he thought she was saying that he couldn't be her boss and her lover at the same time. She cleared that up right away, with no idea where the words were coming from.

"I want to go to school. The work that I did as a Standardized Patient actually kind of inspired me to go to nursing school. My mom wanted to be a nurse too. She regretted that she hadn't."

"Summer never mentioned that to me." He was deeply moved, which moved her as well. His eyes brightened. "I'll pay for it! I'll pay for your schooling." When she waved him off, he said, "You *have* to let me, Celeste – this is something you have to let me do." He would not be refused. "I'll pay for five years of schooling and rent."

"Dumdum, it doesn't take five years!" she said, abashed.

"Five thousand a month or whatever it takes for you to be 100% focused on your studies. This is important work, *essential* work. It would be an honor for me to help in any way that I can. Case closed."

† † †

Adele was right, in a roundabout way – the money he offered felt like an unconditional promise to take care of her and the baby, no matter what.

She had a feeling it would be a while until they saw each other, so there was time to sort things out. Maybe she'd tell him a few months after quarantine lifted, including the uncomfortable business about Jaxx; it felt like the right thing to do before he wrote that first check. It wouldn't be like him to renege, whatever his thoughts about the child's provenance were. Regardless, she would have the child and the sisters would raise it. If he asked for DNA, she would of course provide.

Army tanks were at the foot of the California Incline, closing it off.

They were looting and burning stores on the Promenade.

She saw little fires burning by the pier.

She pulled over to let ten police cars speed by.

Back on PCH, she thought

why is my seat wet? can your water break so early?

She looked at her hand, dripping with blood.

She fainted and crashed into someone's garage.

It took 45 minutes for the paramedics to come and she was almost gone. But they got her to St. John's just in time to save the mother's life.

And Their King It Is Who Tolls

Cocky Trixanna Coldstream, in Mexico, with a swollen head because she'd predicted everything that would happen.

...that after Corona, the riots would come.

She knew that its next mutation would unleash the plague of the Legacy Virus – that friendly devil Dr. Fauci, working hand in glove with Transigen and the Reavers, would see to it. Legacy-19 was already laying waste to her community.

Younger mutants like Trix and Greta were safe; older ones with underlying conditions were most vulnerable.

Only Wolverine could make the right antibodies.

But the Reavers never saw the enemy that had come to vanquish them: the Black ones, whose skin looked a little like hers but mostly like Old Boy's. The Black ones knew the Reavers killed her father in Pelican Bay, kneeling on the adamantine bones of his neck with their Dargonite and Vibranium legs. The Reavers never saw the Black ones, who, with *violent Love*, had come to make Wolverine rise again. They would give George Floyd the Legacy-19 antibodies so at last he'd break free of the earthen ground he was banished to, and join his mama before setting out for final battle.

In the same way, Trix would be reunited with her own mother as well, whom she missed so much. She still called out "Mama! Mama!" in her sleep, to the version that called itself Portia Coldstream.

Each night she whispered a tender prayer, "*Mutatis Mutandis* – change only that which needs to be changed."

But like all the Black ones, Trixanna knew the "only that" part meant "everything," that soon she would be joining their Holy Crusade.

† † †

Regan was terrified that the unrest (that's what she called it) was on its way to Malibu.

Gita said, "Oh, we went through that in '92, and it never happened."

"This is *different*," shouted Regan. "It's different!"

"Maybe it is, darling. But we're a bit of a drive and there aren't any shops up here. I think they're more interested in the malls."

"They're marching toward Rodeo Drive!"

"Is that like the Freedom March? Let my people loot. Would you feel better if we put a nice big BLM banner across the front of the house?"

"Fuck you, Mother."

Regan's fears were exacerbated by the diagnosis. Since learning her father's fate, she holed up in the guestroom watching the Robin Williams documentary, imagining Dad would soon follow in his hanged footsteps.

† † †

The showrunner sat on the deck, looking out.

Life was a streaming series now. Like a boy king born of incest, its mad, violent content ruled. Yet the chaotic cultural moment wouldn't last; in the natural order of things, all shows got defunded. Everything would be canceled (except Lewy Body); the great cathedral bells of BLM tolled, drowning out the virus (for now) and flattening the puny bedside ringers of Time's Up: all the harried gropers, demoted from the national stage, became instant, rapey museum pieces, flash-frozen in their ridiculous bathrobes and grope-under-the-table poses, showcased in quaint, turn-of-the-century cancellation diora-mas. A free-for-all: platoons of canceled men and women were mowed down en masse like amphibious soldiers taking a beachhead. The cancelers chased the canceled down Internet-torched streets, chased themselves by righteous, next-gen

Cancelots. Statutes of limitation were revoked; legions were canceled from birth.

It tolled until it cracked yet rang on.

Liberty Bells die hard...

The revenge of the practitioners.

But Leonard was wrong – room for everyone on the gallows.

Garry smiled and thought, *Let them come.*

His daughter's snarky No Lives Matter t-shirt had it right.

Couldn't anyone see?

what could be more magnificent

THREE
YEARS
LATER

He had done for her all that a man could,
And, some might say, more than a man should.
Then was ever a flame so recklessly blown out
Or a last goodbye so negligent as this?
'I will write to you,' she muttered briefly,
Tilting her cheek for a polite kiss;
Then walked away, nor ever turned about...
Long letters written and mailed in her own head –
There are no mails in a city of the dead.

– *Robert Graves*

PROUST QUESTIONNAIRE
DECEMBER 2024

Adele Cobain Answers the Proust Questionnaire

The Oscar winner, bestselling memoirist, social activist, philanthropist, and "aged-out Comedy Queen" who made us laugh during her legendary Covid-19 zoomologues – then made us cry with her incendiary 2020 Netflix special, *Girls Just Want to Defund* – lives out the dream of starring in her first Marvel film, debuting next month. Here, the star reflects on Toto, Moms, and how she always sees the Cheetos bag half-full.

What is your greatest fear? That I'm fearless. "We have nothing to fear but the lack of fear itself." FDR's little brother, Seymour Roosevelt, said that. He died of fright.

Which historical figure do you most identify with? Seymour Roosevelt.

What is your favorite journey? From bathroom to bed after a fab dump.

On what occasion do you lie? Whenever someone says, "You got the vaccine though, right?"

What do you consider your greatest achievement? The day I had a Toto installed. I'm talking about an automaton of the band Toto – it plays "Africa" *and* "Rosanna."

What is your most treasured possession? A poem my father wrote. He was living in my guesthouse and Celeste and I found it after he disappeared. It was called "Like There's No Tomorrow" and I'm gonna name my new Netflix special after it.

What or who is the greatest love of your life? My baby Dinitra – she just turned three. (She's *so* fuckin funny. I call her Moms, after Moms Mabley.) She's the daughter of Dellarious Martin, who was killed by the police in Tulsa. Her grandma lives with us out to Encino. She's raising, along with my sister Celeste.

What do you regard as the lowest depth of misery? "We're out of Flamin' Hot Cheetos."

Who are your heroes in real life? Last responders.

How would you like to die? At the beginning of a questionnaire…

* * *

The New York Times

Garry Gabe Vicker, Writer and Producer of 'Angela,' 'Golden State,' Dies at 69

By Clement Richel
Aug. 18, 2024

Gary Gabe Vicker, who wrote spec scripts by night while working as a day trader in Beverly Hills – sending them to Norman Lear, who was sufficiently impressed to hire him as a writer for such shows as "Maude" and "Sanford and Son" – and who went on to create and produce hit television shows in his own right, died on Wednesday at his home in Trousdale, California. He was 69.

His death was confirmed by longtime family friend and attorney, Sam Marmal. The cause was complications of Lewy Body Dementia, diagnosed in 2020 after his Parkinson's.

Mr. Vicker, a director, producer, writer and multiple Emmy Award winner – mostly of sitcoms – had something of a late-career renaissance with his limited series "Golden State," about the 1970s California serial killer who was finally captured through the use of a personal genomics website. He was working on another series, "Lovechild," but the production was suspended during Hollywood's Covid shutdown and never resumed, due to Mr. Vicker's health issues. Ryan Murphy will now adapt and expand Mr. Vicker's script for a Netflix series.

In 2018, a number of sexual abuse allegations emerged to cast his character and legacy in a harsh light. "The sting was all the worse," said family friend and onetime intern Judd Apatow, "because Garry was a beacon for women's rights – not just a pioneer in the arena of equal pay but an important figure in the fight against Hollywood's endemic abuse. His voice in that ongoing conversation will sorely be missed."

Mr. Vicker is survived by his wife Gita and their daughter Regan, of Ojai, who went on to form a partnership with her father called Gita Filmworks. "He wanted to name it Tower of Song Productions, from one of his favorite Leonard Cohen songs," she wrote in an essay for The Daily Beast. "But I told him it didn't exactly roll trippingly off the tongue. He thought I came up with Gita Filmworks because it's my mom's name; it's actually named after the *Gita* – the

Bhagavad Gita, which means 'song of God,' a book I introduced Dad to a few years back, and that he very much came to love." Mr. Vicker met Leonard Cohen at a Los Angeles synagogue and formed a "strong acquaintanceship" in the last ten years of the singer-songwriter's life. *Let's Take Sicily: Conversations with Leonard Cohen* will be published next month with a foreword by Mr. Cohen's son Adam.

Garry Gabe Viconicz was born in Los Angeles, at the City of Angels Hospital, on June 11, 1954, to Maurice Viconicz, who owned a grocery store in Mt. Washington, and the former Vickie Roseman...

* * *

Six months before Garry died, Sam Marmal called to tell her the monthly checks would need to stop. ("And congratulations," he added, "on getting your license. Well done.") Celeste was actually relieved. She hadn't spoken to him at all and the money didn't feel good anymore.

"He was so glad to have helped with your studies."

"He hasn't returned my calls." She said it without attitude. She was fairly certain the attorney knew what was up but didn't want him to think she felt spurned or was the type to make waves. "How's he doing?"

"Not so well," said Marmal. "Which is to be expected."

"Oh! What's wrong?"

She could see him blanch on the other side of the phone.

"I made the mistake of presuming you knew." He told her about the Lewy Body "in absolute confidence" because it was Garry's wish to keep his condition private.

After they hung up, she didn't get out of bed for three days.

At the end of her self-quarantine, the *other* one called, like it was nbd. She and Jaxx hadn't talked since a few years ago, when Celeste stormed out of his house. He didn't ask about the baby; maybe he'd been stalking her and already knew she was childless. Or maybe he thought she was just trying to fuck with him for trying to break things off.

"The Netflix show's in development hell – fuckin *weird*. First Vicker wouldn't return my calls, now Ryan *Murphy's* shining me. I'm gonna sue." She could finally see him for what he was: a clown. "I'm one of the top people at Zoom," he said, telling her that he helped fix their software "so the hackers couldn't porn bomb 'em. They're giving me a shit ton of money." She could never believe a word he was saying. But when she asked about Trixanna, Celeste knew that he was telling the truth.

"I don't know where she is," he said with sadness. "She's off her meds and living on the streets." Suddenly, he grew animated. "I'll find her though, in time for her birthday – we'll have a party and I'd love you to come. She really *liked* you, she'd love to see you. The Wolver's gonna be 17 next month, can you believe? No *way* I won't find her." His voice cracked. "There is just no way."

She preferred to work not in hospitals but in homes. When her last patient died, she did something Celeste promised herself she would never do.

She called Garry's cell.

"Hello?" said the woman who answered.

Celeste wanted to hang up but instead said, "Hi!"

"Who's this?"

"Celeste," she said cheerfully. "Celeste Cobain. I'm an old friend of Garry's."

"Well *hi*, Celeste. It's Regan."

"Hi Regan!"

She was relieved that it wasn't Gita – and wondered if his daughter knew of the *arrangement* as well.

"Long time. How've you been?"

"I'm well!" said Celeste.

"Keepin' it together?"

"Not *really*. But I guess it sometimes *looks* like I am. Kinda sorta."

"Ha. Been there, done *that*. Are you calling about Imogen Waldorf-Whatshername?"

"No. I was – "

"She's supposed to be getting out next month."

"Yuck. That's awful."

"That's why I thought you were calling."

"No... I was just calling to say hi."

Regan's voice slowed down, the way a recording would. "Well *that's* nice. But Daddy's indisposed just now."

"That's okay! Sorry to have disturbed."

"I'll give him the message. It will make him happy."

"So nice to talk to you, Regan!"

Strangely, Regan wasn't in a hurry to get off. "I think Daddy *liked* you," she said scampishly. "He had his *eye* on you." When Celeste lightly protested, Regan said, "Oh I *know*. Daughters *know* these things. He told me you wanted to be a *nurse*." The last, said with a wink.

"And now, I am," said Celeste, at a general loss.

"I always knew when you called. We'd be working on scripts and he'd get this look and say, 'Let's take five.' Ha!"

"That's so sweet," Celeste deadpanned.

"'Sweet' probably isn't the word Daddy would use! – but whatever y'all had going on was cool with me."

"There wasn't anything…"

"Delete, delete! Sorry – don't mind me, I've got a mouth. So, the nursing thing worked out?"

"Yes, it did."

"What are you doing later?"

"What am I – "

"Can you come by? There's something I want to discuss."

"Oh – Regan, I really don't think I…"

"Come on – I'm not going to blackmail you. Come see me. Come and see *dad,* it'll be fun. Three o'clock. 1841 Carla Ridge."

He had 24-hour care now.

"The night nurse said she was quitting and *two minutes later* you called. How's *that* for fuckin karma? You and Daddy must have been connected in some other life. Maybe you were his consort – *oops, no* – that would be *this* life. In *some other* life, you were… Gita! Haha!"

Celeste didn't mind the ribbing. Regan reminded her of Adele. She had the same brusque, fierce, uncensored way, and was funny as hell.

Aside from the RNs, there were "burlies" whose main function was lifting Garry from bed to toilet – he refused to use a bedpan – or bed to wheelchair. (They brought his food too.) Poolside was still his favorite place to be. That's where he was when Regan reintroduced them.

"Daddy, look who's here! Celeste!" His face lit up as he stared. "She's a nurse now, thanks to *you,* and she's gonna help take *care* of you. Aren't you happy to see her, Daddy? Aren't you happy to see Celeste? Yes you are! Just don't kiss her – no kissing allowed."

It was jarring to see his scrawny half-nakedness, slack, undignified mouth and warm, glazed-over eyes. But as Celeste spent more time with him, there were plenty of moments he seemed a hundred percent there – which was more than could be said of globetrotting Gita, who FaceTimed from the Maldives, Reykjavik, Goa. The burlies would prop him up until the connection invariably failed. Every three weeks or so his wife alit for the weekend before vanishing.

They went on little field trips, at Regan's insistence. The burlies loaded him into the Tesla and off they'd go to the Point at the Bluffs, in the Palisades. The view of the Pacific was like a spectacular iPhone pano.

Beyond the low fence lay a homemade shrine to honor the cosmos, with flowers, rocks and a framed picture of a guru.

On the evening he died, the showrunner was treated to a chimeric firework of visitations.

Garry's mother came to ruefully say, "How I wish you had been a sculptor of stone or wood," and her face was like a burnt carving itself. Gita visited too, FaceTiming from that place where he would soon be; even then, amid the apocalyptic swirl of dust and dying cells, her husband knew he would never reach her. His darling daughter arrived, causing a shower of muscle spasms (alarming to Celeste as she sat in bedside vigil) – an electric discharge in response to Regan having shown herself as a cube-like compressed being instantly and poignantly identifiable by all of her unmistakable body smells and chronological phases: from the caroling, chirps and bellows of infancy to the cries and whispers of childhood to the yawps and imperious commands of adolescence to the languorous laughter and sensuous outrage of womanhood. Even his ruined friend Bud Wiggins arrived, his desperado, his *desaparacido*, to plaintively ask what happened to their Emmys. Bud said he'd finally finished his "mommy memoir" but was still waiting for Garry's *cheque* – that's how the word appeared in Garry's firework, *cheque,* where is my *cheque* – and the showrunner explained he had done his best but Ryan Murphy beat them to it, he finally had to admit to one and all that Ryan was the best man for the job. Celeste leaned over to pat his forehead with a damp rag, the Harvest moon of her face blotting out the magic lantern cavalcade of flickering friends, Roman candles and undiscovered country-men. He wondered *is it really her?* and laughed, because even his spectral self knew there were no wonderings anymore, only wanderings...

He took her hand, which felt so real, before another sei-zure came – to Celeste, it looked like the one that came earlier but this *glissando* was different, like a great chord, the secret chord, the minor lift of eternal bodyheart romance with his Summer – she was here!

Or there:

At the mountainous base camp.

She reached out with both hands as if to strangle him and

he thought

please let it end like this

– standing beside Leonard in front of the pillared Library of Leaves, how honored they were to be admitted together, instead of one by one! Garry gave his name and a mysterium of tasseographers vainly searched for his special leaf. When he remembered that "Vicker" had been changed from Viconicz and the blade was quickly found.

He began his rough, glorious ascent.

* * *

Gita returned from Paris for the funeral.

Regan was in charge and wanted it to be a small affair. Many of those who attended had stayed close to Garry during the scandal; many had not. Desultory mourners stood in line to shovel dirt onto the casket. One of them whispered to Regan, "I wasn't there for your father *then*; I'm certainly not going to throw dirt onto his grave *now.*"

Adele was shooting a new Marvel and had been noncommittal – such a nice surprise to see her in back of the chapel. It was important to show respect for the man who'd been so good to her sister and may even have fathered the child that she lost. Adele knew their mother's funeral costs had been paid for by the deceased but that act of kindness wasn't a factor in her coming. There *was* curiosity because Summer was buried at the same cemetery. Adele had never visited the grave.

After the interment, she drifted to the other side of the park. Celeste found her standing in front of the drawer where their mother's ashes resided. Summer's parents were buried in the Midwest; their father's parents, who raised them, were at Forest Lawn in Glendale.

They stood a while, looking at the plaque.

Summer Cobain

1964 – 1989

Mother, Wife, Friend

'I will write to you'

"'I will write to you,'" said Adele. "Wonder what that's all about." Celeste shrugged her shoulders. "Weird that there isn't a place for *us.* Maybe Mr. Vicker ran out of money."

"I doubt it."

"No place for Dad either."

"Grandma once told me that he almost didn't make it to the funeral. She said she thought he actually didn't believe Mom was dead."

Adele turned around, taking in the trees and lush grounds.

"I can't believe how *amazing* this place is! Do you *know* who I stepped on, on the way over? Fucking Rodney *Dangerfield*. Fucking Stan *Freberg* and Don *Knotts*. Fucking Tim Conway! I am *totally* going to be buried here, Celeste – like, kill me now!"

She marched to the mortuary office, with Celeste at her heels.

The woman said there wasn't anything available that was nearby their mother's grave. Adele asked "if Mom could be relocated." When the woman said yes, she impetuously dropped a fortune on a gated sepulcher, saying, "I want it white marble and super-minimalist – like the playroom Kanye designed for his kids." The woman asked if their father would be buried there. "At the moment," said Adele, "he's M.I.A., so I kinda think not. He may have *different plans*. At the *moment,* his aesthetic might be leaning more toward the unclaimed-body crematorium in Boyle Heights." The woman didn't have a big sense of humor nor was she aware of Adele's fame and public persona. "We'll be sure to call you if he turns up. Who knows? If I go before Dad, he might read about it in *Variety* and come visit. In which case, throw a net on him and toss him in the Kanye playroom. I'll give him a very *warmed-over* welcome."

* * *

All of the answers came to Celeste in a dream.

The dream said,
Garry is Adele's father.

The revelation dissolved in the morning and only this remained:

She was in an alpine meadow, meandering through flat, wet stones. A young girl walked past and stared at the graves beneath her feet. Celeste was stunned – the girl was herself. She approached the double, who finally looked up, staring back in horror. "It's you!" said Celeste, through joyous tears. "I've looked for so long! And now I've found you."

The double trembled yet stood her ground.

Celeste reached out.

When their fingers touched, she awakened.